27/1⁵

$ 2.00

A Delightful Dizziness . . .

"My brother rode his first joust against Sir Lancelot," Elaine said. "It was his last. As I waited by the surgeon's tent, all the talk was that Sir Lancelot would as lief have stayed at home as waste his skill on such raw country lads—"

"That was your brother?" the knight interrupted. "I—I remember hearing of it."

"It was a bad fall," Elaine went on. "His leg was shattered. He very nearly lost it." What was the matter with her today? She had thought herself long past weeping, yet the knight was looking at her with astonished pity. "I'm sorry. What were we talking about? Oh, it was Sir Lancelot. A subject we generally avoid."

"I'm not surprised."

They reached the edge of the forest.

"Wait," he said. " 'Tis a pretty day for a ride, and I'm sure you know all the best paths. That is, if you would like to . . ."

When he smiled, that strange dizziness came over her again. What could a man like this possibly see in her? She was nearly one and twenty, and she did not delude herself about the damage done by years of starvation. Yet he looked as though he genuinely hoped she would accept. All at once her heart lifted, and it seemed anything was possible, even that she might have caught the interest of a young and wealthy knight.

"I would like to," she said. "Come, we can water our horses by the river."

Coming in the Knights

Ge
Ga

D0456584

Knights of the Round Table

LANCELOT

· · ·

Gwen Rowley

J

JOVE BOOKS, NEW YORK

THE BERKLEY PUBLISHING GROUP
Published by the Penguin Group
Penguin Group (USA) Inc.
375 Hudson Street, New York, New York 10014, USA
Penguin Group (Canada), 90 Eglinton Avenue East, Suite 700, Toronto, Ontario M4P 2Y3, Canada
(a division of Pearson Penguin Canada Inc.)
Penguin Books Ltd., 80 Strand, London WC2R 0RL, England
Penguin Group Ireland, 25 St. Stephen's Green, Dublin 2, Ireland (a division of Penguin Books Ltd.)
Penguin Group (Australia), 250 Camberwell Road, Camberwell, Victoria 3124, Australia
(a division of Pearson Australia Group Pty. Ltd.)
Penguin Books India Pvt. Ltd., 11 Community Centre, Panchsheel Park, New Delhi—110 017, India
Penguin Group (NZ), Cnr. Airborne and Rosedale Roads, Albany, Auckland 1310, New Zealand
(a division of Pearson New Zealand Ltd.)
Penguin Books (South Africa) (Pty.) Ltd., 24 Sturdee Avenue, Rosebank, Johannesburg 2196,
South Africa

Penguin Books Ltd., Registered Offices: 80 Strand, London WC2R 0RL, England

This is a work of fiction. Names, characters, places, and incidents either are the product of the author's
imagination or are used fictitiously, and any resemblance to actual persons, living or dead, business
establishments, events, or locales is entirely coincidental. The publisher does not have any control over
and does not assume any responsibility for author or third-party websites or their content.

KNIGHTS OF THE ROUND TABLE: LANCELOT

A Jove Book / Published by arrangement with the author

PRINTING HISTORY
Jove mass-market edition / September 2006

Copyright © 2006 by The Berkley Publishing Group.
Cover design by George Long.
Cover illustration by Jaime De Jesus.
Text design by Stacy Irwin.

All rights reserved.
No part of this book may be reproduced, scanned, or distributed in any printed or electronic form without permission. Please do not participate in or encourage piracy of copyrighted materials in violation
of the author's rights. Purchase only authorized editions.
For information, address: The Berkley Publishing Group,
a division of Penguin Group (USA) Inc.,
375 Hudson Street, New York, New York 10014.

ISBN: 0-515-14199-2

JOVE®
Jove Books are published by The Berkley Publishing Group,
a division of Penguin Group (USA) Inc.,
375 Hudson Street, New York, New York 10014.
JOVE is a registered trademark of Penguin Group (USA) Inc.
The "J" design is a trademark belonging to Penguin Group (USA) Inc.

PRINTED IN THE UNITED STATES OF AMERICA

10 9 8 7 6 5 4 3 2 1

If you purchased this book without a cover, you should be aware that this book is stolen property. It was
reported as "unsold and destroyed" to the publisher, and neither the author nor the publisher has
received any payment for this "stripped book."

For Michael

A bow-shot from her bower-eaves,
He rode between the barley-sheaves,
The sun came dazzling thro' the leaves,
And flamed upon the brazen greaves
Of bold Sir Lancelot.

ALFRED LORD TENNYSON,
"The Lady of Shallot"

Chapter 1

• • •

ONCE Elaine noticed how like a bull her uncle was, she wondered that she had not marked the resemblance before. The thickly muscled neck, the flaring nostrils and close-set eyes—it was uncanny. Put a ring in his nose, and you could lead the man to market.

"A damned plague, that's what they are!" he bellowed, pounding a meaty fist upon the trestle table. "Worse than the bloody Saxons, those Corbenic serfs, and I'll stand for it no longer!"

"It was a hard winter," Elaine said, holding onto her temper with an effort. She faced her uncle down the length of the trestle, covered with a crimson cloth and crowded with platters of bread and pots of honey, along with two enormous pork and mutton pies made from the remains of last night's feast. The guests between them had been subdued this morning, but now they were wide-awake and rigid with embarrassment.

"A hard *winter*?" Ulfric roared, his face purpling with

rage. "Every winter's hard, but that's no excuse for poaching!"

"Of course it isn't," Elaine answered through clenched teeth, "but you know our harvest was poor, and—"

"The same old story." Ulfric snorted. "But it won't do, my girl, not anymore. I've turned a blind eye in the past, but if you think I'll just stand by while your villeins invade *my* demesne and make off with *my* game—"

Elaine set her cup down very carefully. "It was one man," she said, "and one deer. Hardly an invasion."

"One that I know of! But this is not the first time I've caught those thieving ruffians skulking on my lands, and God knows I have enough to do without defending my borders against yon scurvy pack of rogues! Your father is useless, and as for Torre—by God, when I think of all I've done for that boy, all wasted now—"

Elaine leapt to her feet. "Keep your tongue off my brother! And my father, too! If you want recompense for the damned hind—"

"Oh, I'll have what's due to me. I've—"

"Ulfric," Aunt Millicent said. "That is quite enough."

Ulfric glanced at his lady and deflated like a pricked bladder. Elaine looked to her aunt, as well. *Hypocrite,* she thought with impotent fury; it was Millicent who had raised the subject of the poacher in the first place, waving it like a red flannel before her husband's nose.

"I've complained to the king, that's what I've done," Ulfric muttered sulkily. "And not for the first time, either."

"Elaine," Alienor said swiftly, looking anxiously from her father to Elaine, silently pleading with her cousin to hold her tongue. Elaine was very fond of Alienor, who looked pale and wan this morning, not the blushing bride at all. The groom stared at his father-in-law with well-bred distaste, as though he was already having second thoughts about his marriage, not even four and twenty hours old.

Elaine resumed her seat without a word and forced herself to smile at Alienor, who managed a crooked smile in return. Still, the awkwardness lingered, casting a pall over the remainder of the meal.

The moment she could do so without drawing further attention to herself, Elaine stood. "I must begone," she said, speaking not to her aunt or uncle, but to Alienor, who came forward to embrace her.

"Thank you—for everything," Alienor said, slipping something into her hand. Elaine looked down at the gold chain and shook her head.

"I cannot take this."

"You can. You shall. I don't know what I would have done without you these past weeks. I'm so sorry about Father—"

"Think nothing of it," Elaine said with a charity she was far from feeling as they walked together toward the door. "Belike he has a sore head this morning."

"Aye, I'm sure he does. But if you ask me," Alienor murmured, glancing over to her stepmother, " 'twas Millicent who started it."

"Well, you're free of her now," Elaine said. "I hope you will be happy."

They both turned to look at Alienor's husband, Lord Cerdic, who stood between his parents. A slender young man with a wealth of golden curls, Cerdic was keenly aware of his beauty. At the moment he was entirely absorbed in adjusting the curling feather in his cap.

"Thank you," Alienor said, "I'm sure I will be." Their eyes met, and in the same moment they looked away. There was no more to be said; the deed was done, and Alienor had no choice but make the best of it. "Please remember me to—to your family," she added, her voice breaking as she caught Elaine in a fierce embrace before hurrying away.

Elaine's farewells to her aunt and uncle were far less cordial.

"I am sorry you have been inconvenienced by any of Corbenic's people," Elaine said coolly, drawing on her gloves. "I assure you it will not happen again. You can send the man home with me, and he will be suitably punished."

"Oh, he has already been punished," Ulfric replied.

Elaine stiffened. "Indeed?"

"I hanged him three days ago."

"You hanged one of my father's men?" Elaine demanded, so shocked by this breach of courtesy that she could scarce believe she'd heard aright.

Ulfric's teeth showed in something that was meant to be a smile. "I did consult him first, of course—at least I tried. I wrote to him twice, but he did not deign to answer. You can tell him from me that he'll be needing a new fletcher."

"Fletcher? You mean—are you telling me you hanged Bran Fletcher?" Elaine gripped her hands together hard, lest she give in to the impulse to slap the smile from her uncle's face.

"I hanged a thief." Ulfric's small eyes narrowed. "I know what a busy man your father is. It was my pleasure to do him this small service."

Before Elaine could think of a suitable reply, her aunt leaned forward in a wave of heavy scent to kiss the air beside her cheek. "Farewell, my dear. Godspeed on your journey. *Do* give my love to your father and your brothers."

Elaine left without another word. Bran Fletcher was but a face to her; she doubted she had ever spoken to the man. Yet still she felt bereft, and angry, too, both at Ulfric and herself, that anyone belonging to Corbenic should have met with such a fate.

There is nothing to be done about it now, she told herself as she mounted and rode out of the courtyard. And at least she had the chain. It should fetch enough to buy a new ram—theirs was on his last legs—and with luck an ewe or two, as well, to supplement their dwindling flock.

She was halfway home before she remembered something else Ulfric had said, that he had complained of her father to the king. Not for the first time, either. And Ulfric, unlike Father, had the means to send a dozen knights and fifty men-at-arms to Camelot whenever the king had need of them.

It meant nothing, she told herself. King Arthur was far too busy to concern himself with the quarrels of two country nobles.

But still she clapped heels to her mare, urging the ancient beast into a reluctant, jogging trot, fearing she had been far too long from home.

Chapter 2

· · ·

L ATER, when Lancelot had regained some measure of control, he realized that the silence could not have lasted longer than a minute. At the time it seemed an age crawled by after Guinevere stopped talking and the three of them stood, frozen like figures in some vile tapestry, waiting for Arthur to reply.

The worst of it—if one element of the horror could be seized upon and called the worst—was that it had been such a *stupid* lie, tossed off by the queen as though she were remarking on the weather. Looking at Arthur's face, Lancelot knew the king felt exactly as he did himself, as though he had been dealt a solid blow between the eyes. What possible response could one make when confronted with such a blatant disregard for anything resembling the truth?

Whatever it might be, Lancelot could not be the one to make it. That was Arthur's duty—and his right. Mild as he seemed, Arthur was very much a man, and any man, so grievously provoked, was capable of violence. Lancelot waited, not daring to draw breath, for the royal fury to erupt.

And then, at last, King Arthur spoke.

"That's that, then, isn't it?" he said, turning to gaze out the window. "If you are in pain, Lance, you must stay behind."

Lancelot's mortification, which he had thought complete, increased a hundredfold. He had never been better; he had said as much when he and Arthur dined together just last night. He drew a long breath and looked past the king's broad shoulders out the window, where the garden wavered behind thick panes of glass.

"Sire," he said carefully, "truly there is no need. 'Tis a trifling thing—"

"No!" Guinevere shot Lancelot a pleading look behind her husband's back. "You mustn't risk yourself."

A shift in focus showed him Arthur's face reflected in the glass—just as he and Guinevere were reflected for the king to see. Lancelot's hands clenched into fists.

"My lord," he began, with no clear idea of what he could say next. To go on insisting he was well was tantamount to calling Guinevere a liar, which would be not only redundant at this point, but unthinkable, for he was bound by oath to serve her. Yet even the most tacit acceptance of her lie was a betrayal of his oath to Arthur. Before he could resolve this conundrum, the king spoke over him.

"Guinevere is right." Arthur turned and added with a smile that did not reach his eyes, " 'Twould be folly to hazard my best warrior for the sake of a day's entertainment."

"Just so, sire," Guinevere agreed.

Lancelot stared from the queen to the king, uncomprehending. False, it was all false, the words they spoke, the smiles they exchanged. After his solitary years in Avalon, Lancelot was often confused by the subtleties of human relationships, but he knew the dark emotions swirling between the king and queen spelled danger to them all. His head began to ache as he searched vainly for the words to make things right.

"Sire, I—"

"Stay," the king ordered curtly.

"Stay," echoed the queen.

Two people living had the right to command Sir Lancelot du Lac, First Knight of Arthur's realm and the Queen's Champion. When they spoke as one, he had no choice but to obey.

"I am, of course, your servant," he said unwillingly.

Arthur did not acknowledge his acquiescence or even seem to notice it. "Farewell, Guinevere," the king said, his gaze still riveted upon his wife. The queen raised her face to accept her husband's kiss, and Arthur brushed his lips across her cheek in a perfunctory farewell. "And to you, Sir Lancelot," he added coolly. "I hope to find you both in better health when I return."

The king's eyes burned into Lancelot's for one fleeting moment before Arthur turned and walked away.

Wait, Lancelot wanted to cry out, *stop*—but he could not force himself to make a sound. Like a man enspelled to silence, he watched the king vanish into the corridor. Only the slam of the door snapped the enchantment.

"Guinevere—"

"Wait."

The queen moved as silently as a cat, the furred hem of her sapphire chamber robe trailing behind her. She opened the door a crack, peered out, then eased it shut again. Turning, she leaned her back against the wood and met Lancelot's gaze. Her face was pale as whey, save for the dark patches like bruises beneath her eyes. Unlike Lancelot, she had been genuinely ill, but whatever pity he had felt for her was swept away by the rising tide of anger that shook him where he stood.

"You know you will forgive me in time," she said, "so why not save us the bother of a quarrel and do it now? Sit down—I'll have something sent up from the kitchens and we can—"

"You fool!" The sound of his own voice was strange to him, harsh and trembling with rage. "Do you have any idea what you've done?"

Guinevere paced to the window and threw the casement open, breathing deeply of the cool, fresh air before replying. "Very well, Lance, have your little temper if you must. But you're being quite ridiculous, you know. You've often told me you dislike jousting, and Arthur was quite willing for you to stay, so—"

He crossed the distance between them in three paces and seized her by the shoulders, so abruptly that she cried out in surprise. "Do you not know what is being said? Dinadan and Agravaine—"

Beneath his palms, her slight shoulders moved in a shrug. "The two of them are like old women, forever gossiping in corners. Nobody credits anything they say."

Guinevere was no coward. She met his gaze straight on; only the pulse beating rapidly at the base of her throat betrayed her fear. And she was right to be afraid. This was no "little temper," but the sort of blinding rage Lancelot had experienced only on a battlefield.

"Arthur believes this," he said, his fingers digging into her flesh. "How do you think it looks for him to walk into your chamber and find us here alone? And when you came out with your lie—my God, his face! Did you not see it for yourself? Are you blind? Witless?"

Two spots of brilliant color stained her ashen cheeks. "Unhand me at once! How dare you speak to me like this!"

"I dare because I must! I should have done it long before, but I assumed you knew."

Her pale lips twisted in a mocking smile. "Knew *what*? That fools whisper idle tales about their betters? So what if they do?"

"Think you Arthur has not heard these whispers?" Lancelot shook her hard, his voice rising to a shout. "He has, I know he has, I've seen the way he watches us!"

"You are wrong—mistaken—"

"I am not. I know him, none better—he is no fool, he suspected long before today."

"But even so, he would not believe—"

"He does not *want* to. But now, now that you have openly connived to keep me by your side when he is gone away—what else *can* he think?"

At last he'd reached her. The queen's eyes, so oft compared to woodland violets, widened in terrified comprehension. "Then you must go, right now, this moment," she cried, pressing her soft palms against his chest.

"How can I? My old wound is troubling me," he said in savage mimickry. "I can barely walk. The king himself ordered me to stay behind. And if you think this won't cause more talk—"

"Wait." Guinevere jerked free and put her hands to her temples, pushing aside the thick waves of raven hair that curled loosely past her hips. "Just wait, let me think." After a moment, her head snapped up. "Do you remember that evening last month when the three of us dined here?"

"*What?*"

"We had the brace of partridge—Arthur took them with his falcon—"

"Are you raving?"

"Listen! Arthur said it was hardly fair for you to joust these days, do you remember? He said your opponents are so frightened by your reputation that they are incapable of giving you a proper match."

"Yes, but—"

"You *will* ride in the tournament, Lance, but in disguise. Then you can tell Arthur it was a test—a test of honor— that you wanted to see if you could win without anyone knowing who you are. He will like that, he'll think it a good jest."

Lancelot stared at her, half admiring and wholly appalled at this new proof of her nimble mind.

"Another lie—"

"Oh, no, but it isn't! Arthur *did* say that, I heard him, and you *were* a bit insulted, were you not?"

How well she knew them both. Arthur would believe it, not only because it was the sort of trick he himself would play, but because he wanted—was quite desperate—to accept any alternative to the rumors spreading like poison through the court.

"This is wrong," Lancelot said. "Please, Guinevere, I beg you, let me tell him—"

"No! Do not start all that again! You will tell him naught save what I have said. You *promised*—and I need—"

"I! I! Is that all you ever think about? What of Arthur? What of me? Are you too stupid to understand what you are doing to us both? Or are you too selfish to care?"

Tears welled in her eyes. "How can you say such things to me?"

Lancelot slumped down on the window seat and leaned his throbbing brow against the glass. "Oh, God," he whispered, "what am I to do?"

"I have already told you! If you would only *listen*—"

Wearily, he rose to his feet, rubbing the aching space between his eyes. "I cannot," he said, despairing, "the king has ordered me to stay."

Her brows rushed together in a frown. "And *I* say that you shall go."

He knew that look. Quickly he started toward her, one hand extended. "It is impossible. Surely you understand that I cannot disobey a direct order from my lord. We'll find another way—"

It was too late. All at once the queen of Britain stood before him, gesturing with imperious dignity toward the door. "Don your armor, hide your face, and do not speak your name until the tournament is done."

"Don't," he whispered, "Guinevere, please—"

"Now!" she cried, stamping one slippered foot. "I command it!"

Lancelot had often been impatient with the queen, sometimes angry, but never until this moment had he hated her.

"So be it, my lady," he ground between clenched teeth. "I will go. And I will do your bidding once again, as I have sworn. But this is the last time. I am finished with your lies—and with you."

He spun on his heel and reached for the latch.

"Lance, wait, I didn't mean—please don't go like this," she cried behind him. "Please!" She stumbled on the long hem of her gown and caught his arm. Her eyes were brilliant as she stared beseechingly into his face. "It was a mistake, I wasn't thinking—I've been so wretched, I only wanted you to stay with me. I'm sorry, *sorry*—"

"You are always sorry," Lancelot said coldly, "yet you never change. Good day, my lady."

He shook off her hand and went out. Halfway down the corridor he hesitated, listening to the muffled sobs coming from behind the door. "Damn you," he said beneath his breath. He could imagine her there, crouched among the rushes with the tears streaming down her pale cheeks, muddled and miserable and utterly alone.

Then he remembered the cold fury in the king's eyes before Arthur walked out without so much as giving him a chance to speak.

"*Damn* you," Lancelot said again, no longer certain which of them he meant, or whether he was speaking to himself. Turning, he ran swiftly down the stairway without once looking back.

Chapter 3

• • •

ELAINE pulled her mare up on the forest's edge, savoring her first glimpse of Corbenic's tower in the distance. Home. The sight never failed to lift her heart. Her smile faded as her gaze traveled downward to the north field, acre upon acre of good brown earth, stretching between the forest and the manor. Something was amiss. For a moment she could not imagine what it was, and then understanding hit her like a blow.

The field was empty. No plough, no straining oxen, no peasants toiling beneath the pale blue sky. Not a child picking stones, not a scarecrow—not even a crow to scare, as obviously no seed had yet been planted. Indeed, 'twas clear that no one had so much as touched this field since she had ridden past it near a month ago.

Over the past weeks, Elaine had watched carefully the ordering of her uncle's demesne, hoping to learn the secret of his prosperity. Every morning she was up to see the villeins go off to the fields, shouldering their tools, and her afternoon walk invariably led her past the neat expanse of furrows, lengthening with every day. She had passed many a weary morning in Alienor's bower imagining the same work going forward at Corbenic.

What a fool she'd been.

Dismissing her uncle's serving man with a curt word, she turned her mare from the path and cut across the field, mud flying from beneath the horse's hooves.

She should never have left home. Now the sowing would be late again, and they would have to race against time to harvest whatever poor crop could reach maturity. You would think that after last winter they would have learned. The sheer folly of it, the waste of time when every day was precious—why, why was everything at Corbenic such a hopeless muddle? Was it so much to ask that people simply do as they were told?

The anger that had simmered in Elaine's breast this past month flared into rage as she pounded across the barren field and burst into the courtyard, scattering a flock of chickens—Holy Mother, had no one mended the hen coop *yet*?—pecking among the refuse heaped outside the stable door.

Dung, she noted with cold fury. Dung that should have been carried to the fields long since. Someone had obviously begun the job and just as obviously abandoned it, leaving the barrow upended on the cobbles and the broom beside it, its bristles trampled in the mud. Apart from the chickens and the swarms of flies, the courtyard was deserted.

Elaine could remember how it had looked before the Saxons came: the gleaming cobbles, fresh-scrubbed twice a week, the whitewashed stable where a dozen blooded horses champed their oats, the mews and the kennels, each with its own attendants. And the sounds! Sometimes Elaine thought she missed them most of all. The dairymaids in sacking aprons singing as they churned; the high, excited voices of the squires in the practice yard; the laughter of the pages scurrying about, brave in blue and crimson; and far off in the distance, barely noticed, the voices of the villeins in the fields.

Above all, she missed her mother's voice. "No, you mayn't have a hawk, Elaine, but if you are a good lass, next year we shall see. Chin up, sweeting, that's the way, and shoulders back. You will do your husband little honor if you slouch."

The bright image faded into grim reality. *What would Mother say to this?* Elaine wondered, her gaze moving over the filthy, silent courtyard that could have passed for some peasant's hovel. If things went on this way much longer, it might as well be. The once-proud family was already sinking. Soon they would be little more than peasants. In another generation, the difference would vanish altogether.

"Groom!" Elaine cried, fear sharpening her voice. "Groom! To me—at once!"

But it was no groom that staggered from the stable, his shirt hanging loose as he struggled to tie up his breeches. The unshaven young man did not lift a finger to assist her. He merely braced himself against the stable door and squinted up at her through bloodshot eyes.

And what, what would Mother think if she could see her eldest son right now? Torre scratched idly at the auburn curls showing through his torn shirt and yawned. "Elaine. You're back."

"Well spotted, Torre. How clever of you to notice."

"I could hardly help it. You were screeching like a banshee."

A giggle drifted from within the stable. Elaine narrowed her eyes at her brother. "Help me down."

"Help yourself. I'm busy."

"Torre." Elaine did not sink to the vulgarity of shouting, but still, he halted and turned back.

"All right, all *right*." He limped heavily across the courtyard and extended his laced hands.

The moment her feet touched the ground, Elaine strode to the stable and threw open the door. Two horses raised their heads, looking at her curiously. The nearest stall was empty save for a mound of straw, upon which reclined a girl, naked to the waist. She regarded Elaine boldly through the matted hair falling over her eyes.

"Get up!" Elaine cried. "Dress yourself and go tell Lord Pelleas that his daughter has returned. And find a groom to stable my mare before you get back to the kitchens."

The girl's eyes moved over Elaine's shoulder. Finding no help there, she muttered, "Aye, mistress," and pulled her kirtle up.

Elaine whirled and stalked over to her brother. "The planting hasn't even begun, and this place—" She waved a hand wildly about the courtyard. "What in God's name have you been *doing*?"

"I should think," he drawled, wiping his hands upon his filthy shirt, "that would be fairly obvious."

Unfortunately, it was, even before he lifted the wineskin to his lips. Straw stuck out of his wild auburn curls, and a two-day growth of beard stubbled his jaw. The once-fine angles of his face were blurred, his brilliant blue eyes streaked with red and sunk deep above pouched flesh. Looking at the ruins of her brother, Elaine did not know if she wanted more to weep or rage at him.

"Well?" he said, slouching to take the weight from his bad leg. "How were the nuptials?"

Elaine sighed, her anger melting into confused pity and resentment when he smiled down at her. "Wretched. I should have stayed at home."

"I told you—"

"I know you did. You were right."

"And you were wrong? *You?* Quick, someone fetch a scribe, such a moment cannot be lost to history!"

She smiled, pretending not to notice the bitterness that robbed his words of humor. "Uncle Ulfric was insufferable," she said, "and Aunt Millicent worse. Geoffrey sends you greetings. He said he'll ride over with his hawk soon."

Torre's lips twisted in the cynical grin that she had come to dread. "Right. And Alienor?" he added, his face averted as he bent to gather the mare's reins. "Did she send me greetings, too?" Without waiting for an answer, he went on in a voice that sounded almost unconcerned, "What about that fellow she married? What's he like?"

"Young. A bit vain. But then—" She'd been about to say that Lord Cerdic had plenty to be vain about, being not only young and comely, but rich into the bargain, but something in her brother's face halted her. "Oh, Torre," she said, "you're not still brooding about Alienor, are you?"

"Brooding?" His eyes were hooded as he raised the wineskin once again.

"I know you were disappointed, but there are other heiresses. Not so rich as Alienor, perhaps, but—"

"Is that what you think it was? Her gold? God, what a fool you are sometimes." Before Elaine could respond, he sighed and touched her shoulder. "That was wrong of me. I'm sorry."

"I don't want you to be sorry. I want you to *do* something."

"What? Go out to seek my fortune? Oh, no, I tried that, didn't I? Mayhap I should till the fields myself! Or no," he said savagely, glaring down at his leg, "I'd be no use there, either." All at once, his anger seemed to die. He sighed and ran a hand through his tangled curls. "Sometimes I think our family has been cursed. No, don't smile, I'm serious.

When you look at all that's happened—the Saxons coming, Mother's death, Father and his—"

Elaine held up a hand, stilling him before he could say the word they never spoke. He sighed again. "Father's *illness*," he went on, using the accepted phrase, "and then me. Don't tell me you've never wondered if all of this is more than luck."

Of course Elaine had wondered. The same question had occurred to her many times during the past winter, in the dark of night when sleep refused to come. But if she had refused to credit the thought then, she was not about to now.

"There is naught amiss with us that a bit of hard work and common sense won't cure," she said stoutly.

"Think you so, Elly? Truly?"

"Blaming a series of perfectly natural misfortunes on magic is the refuge of the weak and cowardly."

Torre gave her a wry grin. "If your tongue gets any sharper, 'twill be a very gelding hook. But you are wrong, you know. Magic does exist, and to deny it won't make it go away."

"Stuff and—" Elaine began.

"Elly!"

They both whirled as their younger brother crossed the courtyard at a run. Their father followed more slowly, his head bent over something in his hands, no doubt some scroll or parchment. Lord Pelleas's patched robe hung loosely about his sparse frame, and his hose had been darned so many times with different threads that their original color was impossible to guess. White locks floated in sparse wisps about his long, narrow face as he looked up; he brushed at them impatiently with his free hand and smiled with a piercing sweetness. Elaine noticed that he had an ink blot on his nose.

"Elly!" Lavaine called again, his face aglow beneath his

cap of blazingly red curls. He caught her in a hard embrace and smiled down at her. When had he grown so tall?

"Elaine! I think I've got it!" Lord Pelleas cried, brandishing a sheaf of parchments. "Damnedest thing—right under my nose the whole time, and I didn't see it until last night, when—"

"Did you catch a noble suitor?" Lavaine interrupted.

Elaine sighed. "No, I did not."

"Fools," Lavaine said loyally, "but never mind, I'm sure you will in time. Listen, can you—"

"What does this look like to you?" Pelleas demanded, pointing out a word. "Because I think—by God, I really think I'm on to it at last. See here—"

"Elaine!" Lavaine tugged at her elbow. "My jupon is torn. Can you mend it for me?"

"Just a moment, Lavaine. Father, I must speak with you at once. Uncle Ulfric said—"

She broke off as Sir John, the steward, made his way across the courtyard, leaning heavily upon his stick. "Sir John," she called, "attend me if you would. Do you remember that we spoke of planting the north field before I left? Yet it seems to me that naught has been accomplished."

"True, lady," Sir John said, "I did try—but, alas, since Martin Reeve has left us—"

"God rest him," Elaine said, signing herself with the cross, "but he has been dead these six weeks past. Surely it cannot be so great a matter to find another reeve!"

"No, my lady," Sir John said, "in the usual course of events—indeed, I did speak to the villeins, and Lord Pelleas has promised to consider the list of candidates I presented him."

Sir John smiled so proudly that Elaine did not have the heart to point out that this same promise had been made many times before. Indeed, on the eve of her departure,

Father had solemnly assured her he would attend to the matter just as soon as he could find the time. Which, apparently, he had not managed to do in the month she had been gone.

"Will there be anything more, my lady?"

Elaine glanced at Torre, who held up his hands as if to say, *not me!* Not her father, either, who could scarce be bothered to eat a meal, let alone worry how it managed to arrive at table. And surely not Lavaine, still half a child with his head stuffed full of dreams of noble feats of arms.

"Send to Britt and bid him hitch up the oxen," she ordered crisply. "Have every able-bodied man and woman leave whatever they are doing and go immediately to the north field. Lord Pelleas and I shall join them in one hour."

"Aye, my lady," Sir John said, "I will see to it."

"Thank you. Now, Father, please listen. Uncle Ulfric said—"

"But my jupon!" Lavaine cried.

"In good time," she said impatiently.

"I need it now!"

"Lavaine's got it in his head to ride off to a tournament tomorrow," Torre put in.

"Tomorrow?" *Not yet,* she thought, *it is too soon.* Though she knew it wasn't really. Lavaine had been knighted just before she'd left for Alston. But he was so young still—just eighteen this year, and even mock battles could be dangerous. One only had to look at Torre to see that.

"What tournament is this?" she asked.

"The king's Pentecostal festival," Lavaine began. "Knights have come from all parts of the world to compete—"

"And everyone knows Sir Lancelot will win," Torre snapped, shooting his brother a scowl that Lavaine had done nothing to deserve. Not that Lavaine was cast down in the least. He was far too used to Torre's surly moods to pay them any mind.

"The prize is an enormous diamond!" Lavaine went on eagerly.

"A diamond?" Elaine stopped short. "How strange."

"Not really," Lavaine said, "the king always offers something magnificent at Pentecost."

"And I suppose you think you have a chance to win it!" Torre demanded with a scornful laugh.

"I can try, can't I? Just because *you* can't compete doesn't mean that no one else should!"

"A diamond?" Elaine repeated slowly, and her brothers broke off to stare at her.

"You seem strangely interested in this diamond," Torre said. "Why? Have you acquired a taste for vulgar jewels?"

"Given half a chance, I daresay I could. But I dreamed last night—oh, it was nothing—"

"Tell me," her father ordered, looking up from his parchments, "and perhaps we can divine its meaning."

Dreams! It was always dreams with him! They were as meat and drink to Corbenic's lord, more real than the filthy courtyard all around him and more pressing than his idle serfs. But he was looking at her so expectantly, his bright blue eyes as guileless as a child's, that she lacked the heart to chide him.

Poor Father. It wasn't his fault he could no longer distinguish fact from fancy. Elaine had a sudden, piercing memory of him sitting in the hall on court day, settling each dispute between villagers and manor folk with a few decisive words. And then, later, he and Mother would preside over the feast, while Elaine and Torre danced with the village children in the courtyard.

It was seldom that Elaine remembered any of her

dreams, so she held this one out to him, an offering to make amends for her impatience.

"Very well," she said as they walked together toward the hall, "this was my dream . . ."

Chapter 4

• • •

L ANCELOT was sweating in full armor as he rode toward the tourney field. He longed to strip down to his tunic, but he was too well-known to pass unnoticed through the crowds upon the road. On the deserted stretches, he had removed his helm, but even after all these years the harsh sunlight, so unlike the muted glow of Avalon, troubled his eyes. So he kept that on, as well, with the visor tipped up to allow a tiny thread of air to cool his streaming brow.

At last he drew up his charger on the crest of a hill and surveyed the field below, a broad swathe of meadow surrounded by dense forest, split neatly by a silver ribbon of water. One side of the River Usk was a patchwork of bright color; dozens of pavilions had already been erected, and dozens more were going up. The other held the tilting ground, cleared and fenced, surrounded on three sides by wooden stands. Tiny figures scurried about, and the scent of woodsmoke from many small fires drifted lazily upward on a warm spring breeze.

The Pentecostal tournament had become a yearly tradition in the years of Arthur's reign. What had started as a solemn ritual during which the king dispensed justice to his subjects, and his companions renewed their vows had become, over time, an event of great magnificence.

Last year the castle had been filled and the surrounding fields crowded with what seemed to be every knight in Britain, along with their servants, squires, and families. There were others, too—knights who had traveled from all corners of the world to compete in the tournament, eager to test their mettle against the Knights of the Round Table—and to win the generous prizes Arthur offered.

With so many competitors, the tournament dragged on for days. Even when it was finally over, no one seemed in any hurry to depart. Quarrels had sprung up between the knights, resulting in private challenges that kept the marshal busy. There had been fights between their squires, too, and their servants, until the castle guards were exhausted with the effort of keeping order.

Yet to hear Guinevere tell it, the real war had been waged within the castle. The ladies fought sweet and deadly battles over precedence in claiming this chamber over that, or a seat at table, or, in one memorable instance, who had the right to bow first to the queen. The last had turned into a furious argument in which a stately dowager completely lost her head and accused her rival of resorting to witchcraft to steal Uther Pendragon's notice from herself some forty years ago, upon which the second lady used her walking stick to deal the dowager a stunning blow.

"Oh, it's easy for you to laugh," Guinevere had said sourly to the king and Lancelot when they dined together in the gardens, "*you* didn't have to pull the two apart."

After the last guest finally departed, Sir Kay took to his bed for a week, and the court was reduced to dining on cheese and increasingly stale bread. It was then Arthur declared that this year's tournament would not be the traditional combat fought at Camelot but a melee lasting only a single day and held far enough from court to discourage any visitors. To soften the blow, he was offering a prize of such magnificence that any knight put off by the inconvenience soon changed his mind. Judging from the crowd below, their families had all decided make the best of changed conditions.

Lancelot searched the pavilions, finally locating his cousin Bors's standard floating in the breeze. Bors would keep his secret, little as he might like it. But Lancelot would have to be careful not to draw attention to himself if he hoped to fight unknown. His armor was plain enough; if he kept his visor down, he should pass unnoticed. He took a quick look at his saddle to assure himself there was nothing that could be recognized, and he groaned aloud as his eyes fell upon his shield, covered now in canvas but bearing his own, instantly recognizable device.

He wheeled his charger about, cursing himself for not considering the need for a blank shield, the haste with which he'd pulled his own from the peg, and most of all, Guinevere for putting him in this position in the first place.

But he didn't want to think of Guinevere. That would only make him angry, which could lead to more mistakes. He would have to ride to Camelot and back again, which meant his charger would be weary before the tournament began. A weary mount was easily injured, and Lancelot was fond of this one. To lose him would mean months of inconvenience while he found and trained another to his ways.

His mood was not improved by the sight of a group of horses approaching down the road. With an irritated sigh, he flipped down his visor, though even so, he felt ridiculously conspicuous. But they had no reason to stop for a stranger;

he should be safe enough—and then he noticed the banner held proudly in the squire's hands. His gaze moved past the squire and fastened on a lady, her bright blue hood thrown back to reveal auburn hair glinting in the sunlight.

Queen Morgause of Orkney.

Lancelot told himself he had no reason to fear Gawain's mother—and yet he did. Morgause's sharp eyes saw far too much, and she had once said that magic was her . . . How had she put it? Oh, yes, her *passion*. He remembered now how she had purred the word, and every instinct screamed a warning he did not stop to question. He pulled his horse off the path and plunged into the forest.

An hour later, he was hopelessly lost. The track he had thought would be a shortcut to Camelot had dwindled into a tiny path and finally vanished in a swamp. Rather than turn back the way he'd come, he'd found another path leading roughly west, and when that veered off to the north, he'd tried another that doubled back upon itself so many times that he was now utterly confused.

But at least he was off the road and far from prying eyes.

This latest path seemed to offer some hope; it had clearly been well traveled in the not-too-distant past. It must lead somewhere, and with any luck, to a place where he could buy or borrow a blank shield. It was blessedly dim beneath the trees, the air pungent with the scents of swamp and loam, and birds chattered busily overhead. Lancelot fell into a half doze as he rode along. "Oh, the broom, the bonny, bonny broom," he chanted softly in rhythm to his charger's plodding steps.

As a rule, he had no ear for music, but there had once been a harper in the Lady's hall in Avalon who played so marvelously that even Lancelot had been enchanted. Thomas, the minstrel's name had been, sometimes called the Rhymer, and the Lady had said he'd come from far, far

away, which seemed odd because Thomas spoke the tongue
of Britian with an accent very like Gawain's.

Lancelot's thoughts drifted to Gawain, and a scornful
smile curved his lips. The noble Sir Gawain—what a hypocrite he was! He was always so very courteous to
Lancelot, at such pains to disguise his resentment and dislike. Not that Lancelot was deceived. Nor did he care a
whit. Let Gawain detest him. Why should he care? He remembered suddenly that he had dreamed of Gawain the
night before, a vivid dream of their one meeting in the lists
on the day Lancelot relieved Gawain of the title of First
Knight of Britain. Gawain had fought well that day, but of
course he never stood a chance. It was Lancelot's destiny
to gain that title, the great destiny bestowed upon him by
the Lady of the Lake.

Lancelot only wished the Lady had mentioned how it
would befall that he would win the title. But the Lady kept
her own counsel, he reflected drowsily; she never answered any question straightly. About the mysterious ori-
gins of her harper, she would only say that miles were not
the only measure of distance, which Lancelot still did not
understand.

There had been one song he sang that Lancelot liked
best of all, about a lass climbing a hill on her way to market fair and the lad who wagered that she'd not come down
again a maiden. As a boy, Lancelot had often sung it in his
empty courtyard where there was no one else to hear. Now,
though, he could not seem to catch the tune, and the words
he had once known so well slipped from his mind before
he could quite grasp them.

It was happening again. Lately he'd had the oddest feeling that his past was disappearing, the memories blending
together like a painted panel left out in the rain. That minstrel's song—what had been his name? For a moment

his mind was quite blank, then he remembered. Thomas. Thomas, who they called the . . . the Singer? The Harper? No, something else . . . but it was gone.

Had there ever really been a harper? he wondered with a sudden stab of fear. *Or had that been a dream?* He didn't know. He could not be certain which of his memories of Avalon were real and which he had imagined.

He thrust the disquieting impression away. The past was not important. It was the present that mattered.

But Lancelot found he did not want to think about the present, either, or how he had come to be lost in this dark forest. Arthur's face—but no, he would not think of that. Better—safer—to think about the future, a future so distant that today's disturbance in the queen's chamber would be quite forgotten.

'Twas folly to doubt that it would be forgotten. He was Lancelot du Lac, beloved foster son of the Lady of the Lake, and through her grace he served King Arthur as no other knight could ever do. Arthur knew his loyalty. How could he not? Had Lancelot not proven himself a hundred times already? His fame had spread throughout Britain and beyond, just as the Lady had foretold. Whenever he rode out, people lined the streets to cheer him, and the minstrels competed to make songs of his adventures. Perhaps by now they were even sung in Avalon itself by that harper of the Lady's . . . What had been his name? Lancelot searched his mind, but the memory was gone.

No matter, he told himself, trying to ignore the cold pricking of his spine. *Belike I imagined the whole thing.* Yet a part of him was certain that he hadn't—that there *had* been a harper in the Lady's hall—though now, when he tried to picture him, there was only a blank space where he had sat, and only silence when he sought for the song about . . . what *had* it been about? A market? Or had it been a broom?

If only there was someone he could ask, someone he could tell of his days in Avalon and the glorious destiny that was his, someone who could help him understand all the questions that seemed to have no answers, long though he had pondered them in the dark watches of the night. Even Arthur, who knew him best of all, did not really know him. And it was best that way.

There is only one question that need concern you now, he told himself sternly, *and that is how to get out of this wretched forest.* A moment later he had the answer, when he glimpsed a stone tower rising above the treetops. With a sigh of relief, he turned his charger's head toward the tower and kicked the beast into a canter.

Chapter 5
· · ·

THEY had nearly reached the hall when Elaine realized they were not alone. A knight stood before the
mounting block, holding his horse's reins. She halted,
thinking at first that Cousin Geoffrey had remembered his
promise, until she realized that this was no knight she'd
ever seen before. Even Geoffrey did not have armor half so
fine, and his charger, the envy of five manors, was like a
cart horse compared to this blooded beast.

The knight's helm, adorned with a blue plume, turned in
their direction. Though the visor was up, the face beneath
remained in shadow.

Her father stepped forward. "Good day to you, Sir
Knight, and welcome to Corbenic." He gestured proudly
across the shabby courtyard to the crumbling tower. "I am
Pelleas, lord of this demesne. Whence comest thou, my
guest, and by what name?"

Elaine held her breath, dreading the strange knight's
mockery, yet when he spoke, there was no laughter in his

voice. "I am a knight of Arthur's hall," he answered with grave courtesy, "and tomorrow I joust as one unknown to win King Arthur's diamond. Hereafter you shall know me, but.I pray you ask me not today."

At his last words, Elaine's smile died upon her lips. It was unheard of for any stranger to refuse to name himself. Why, he could be any sort of outlaw—Bruce sans Pitie, who had abducted dozens of maidens to his stronghold, or the infamous Sir Turquine—he could be anyone at all! Elaine and Torre exchanged a look, but before either of them could speak, their father forestalled them,

"As you will," Pelleas replied easily. "I hope that for tonight, you will remain with us."

"Thank you," the knight said with a little bow. "And if I might ask another favor . . ."

"Please do."

"By mischance, I came out with my shield. I pray you to lend me one, blank if such you have, or at least with some device not mine."

Elaine glanced at the shield in question, strapped to his saddle in its canvas cover. What device did it bear, that its owner was ashamed to show? She threw her father a warning glance, but he was smiling at the stranger as though his extraordinary request was no great matter.

"Oh, that we can give you easily. My elder son, Torre, was hurt in his first tilt. His shield is blank enough."

Elaine sensed Torre's shocked anger at this casual bestowal of his equipment upon a nameless stranger, but there was nothing to be done about it now. "Why not?" he said, "you may as well have it; 'tis no use to me."

"Fie, Sir Churl!" Pelleas chided, laughing. "What sort of courtesy is that? I beg you to forgive him, sir."

The blue plume dipped as the knight inclined his head. "I am grateful for the loan, Sir Torre."

Torre nodded briefly, still unsmiling.

"Now, my younger son, Lavaine," Pelleas continued, "who is but lately knighted, he would ride with you to yonder joust. Why, he is so full of lustihood that he will win yon diamond in an hour, then bring it home to set it in this damsel's hand! Is that not what you were telling us, Lavaine?"

"No, Father," Lavaine protested, "do not mock me before this noble knight! I was only joking, sir," he said earnestly to the stranger, "I but played on Torre—"

"Enough," Torre ordered sharply, but Lavaine hurried on.

"He was so sullen, vexed he could not go—"

"Did I not say, *enough*?" Torre growled, and aimed a blow at his young brother's head. Lavaine skipped nimbly away.

"And so I jested with him—for you see, Sir Knight, my sister dreamed that someone put this diamond in her hand, but it was too slippery to hold—"

"Lavaine!" Elaine cried, but he ignored her, too.

"And she dropped it in some pool or stream—belike the castle well—and so I said that *if* I went, and *if* I fought and won it—but it was all a jest, a joke between ourselves—that she must keep it safelier. It was all in fun. But Father," he cried, "do give me leave to ride to Arthur's tourney with this noble knight! I shan't win, but I will do my best to win. I know I am young, but I would do my best."

"He won't want to be bothered with you," Torre began.

"On the contrary," the stranger cut in smoothly, "I would welcome a friend and guide. And you shall win this diamond if you can—for I hear it is a fair large diamond—and yield it to this maiden, if you will."

Whoever he might be, his manners could not be faulted. He had a lovely voice, as well, deep and musical and tinged with the faintest suggestion of an accent she thought might be Gaulish. Surely no man who spoke so prettily could be evil.

Torre was not so easily won over. "A fair large diamond is for queens, not simple maids," he said, both his tone and his expression conveying an unmistakable warning.

"If what is fair belongs only to the fair, what matter if she be queen or not?" the knight retorted coolly. "This maid could wear as fair a jewel as is on earth and never violate the bond of like to like."

Ha! Elaine thought, shooting a triumphant glance toward her brother. *He's put you in* your *place!* She nearly laughed aloud—until the knight removed his helm.

Coal-black hair was plastered to his high brow and heat-flushed cheeks in little whorls. His features were perfectly symmetrical: large, dark eyes and high, chiseled cheekbones, full, ruddy lips above a jaw at once delicate and strong. *No man should be so beautiful,* Elaine thought, the breath catching in her throat. No man *was.* On that she would have sworn an oath. Yet here he stood before her, like some mythical creature who had wandered out of legend into their humdrum little world.

Her last suspicion vanished. Impossible to believe a man so young and fair—for he could not be more than three or four and twenty—and so well-spoken could be anything other than he claimed to be.

"A pretty speech, Sir Knight," Torre said, and by the amusement in his voice she knew he had reached the same conclusion, "but wasted, I fear, upon my sister. Just as that fair diamond would be wasted upon her. Knowing you, Elaine, you *would* drop it—likely in some drainage ditch— and never even notice."

There was laughter at that, and Elaine glanced to the knight, meaning to make some light answer. But when their eyes met, a curious stillness fell over the courtyard, and she forgot the words she meant to speak. In the timeless space between one heartbeat and the next, the world as she had known it shifted, then realigned into a pattern that included this young knight, not a stranger any longer but an essential part of her existence. *Yes,* she cried silently, *yes, at last— where have you been?*

She blinked, and the impression vanished. The world was as it had been, though perhaps a bit more dreary, for the knight was a stranger once again.

"Kind words are never wasted, Torre," she said, and if she was a little breathless, she doubted anyone would notice. "Lavaine, our guest has no squire to attend him; be so kind as help him from his armor and see to the stabling of his horse."

"Yes, of course," Lavaine said, "this way, sir."

The knight smiled at her and bowed slightly before following Lavaine toward the stables.

"Elaine!"

She jumped as a hand touched her shoulder.

Torre shook his head, half laughing. "That's the third time I called you."

"Is it? I was just thinking . . ." What? She hardly knew, save that it was nothing she wanted to share with her brother.

"We don't know who he is or anything about him. Tomorrow he will be gone."

"Yes. Of course." Elaine gave herself a little shake. "Where did Father go?"

Torre shrugged. "Back to his studies. Or to the hall— he's been talking about a hidden stairway."

Elaine groaned and slipped the chain from round her neck. "Here, Torre, take this to the village. Alric of Bedford has a ram for sale. If you can wangle a few ewes out of him, as well, so much the better."

Torre let the links slide through his fingers. "Nice. Where did you get it?"

"I nicked if off Aunt Millicent." Elaine laughed at his expression. "It was a gift, you dolt."

She thought she'd handled that rather neatly. Given what she'd learned of her brother earlier, she suspected he might not be so willing to sell the chain if he knew whose gift it was.

She shook her head, sighing. Love was all well and good, but if next winter was anything like the last, any man of sense would rather have the sheep.

Chapter 6

• • •

ELAINE found her father lingering in the passageway leading to his chamber, standing stock-still and staring into space.

"Father," she said, "a moment, if you will. Uncle Ulfric is full wroth with us."

"Ulfric?" Pelleas blinked as though coming out of a deep sleep. "That is ill news. Have I offended him in some wise?"

"He says our serfs have been poaching on his estate. I did tell you last winter that they were taking deer from the forest, and—"

"Did you? Well, a hind or two is no great matter, and 'twas a cruel, hard winter. Still, if they've strayed onto Ulfric's lands, I'd best have a word with the reeve."

"Martin Reeve is dead," Elaine said. "Don't you remember?"

"Ah, yes, so he is. God rest him." Pelleas signed himself with the cross. "Yes, that's right, I'd meant to . . . but it is so difficult, you know, to find the *time* . . ."

"Never mind that now, Father. The point is that Uncle Ulfric hanged Bran Fletcher."

"Bran Fletcher? Hanged?" Pelleas drew himself up, his eyes flashing. "Ulfric laid hands upon my fletcher without consulting me?"

"He says he did consult you," Elaine admitted. "He says he sent you two messages, but they were not answered."

"Ah." Pelleas's shoulders fell. "Yes, well, perhaps he did. With you gone, Elaine, I'm afraid I got rather in a muddle. I was hoping you'd straighten it all out . . ." He gazed down at the stone beneath his feet. "Bran Fletcher. I knew his father—aye, and his grandsire, too. Ulfric should not have hanged the man. He could have come to me himself, not sent some message that he knew I hadn't time to read."

"You are right. And now he has—"

"I know we never got on, Ulfric and I, but still, 'twas ill done to treat a kinsman so. You'd think that for your mother's sake, he would have come to me himself. He loved her well, you know, but she chose me. He had to make do with Millicent, instead."

He laughed, and the pride in his face was as fresh as though he'd won his lady only yesterday. "Ulfric was at the wedding feast," he went on, "and your mother made us join hands and swear friendship. But I don't suppose he ever quite forgave me. Millicent is nothing like your mother, God assoil her sweet soul . . ." His smile faded, and tears filled his eyes. "What must I do, Elaine? Shall I challenge him?"

Elaine's throat tightened. "No, Father," she said gently, "I'm sure he meant not to offend you. Belike when you did not reply, he only did what he believed you wanted."

"I would not have wanted the man hanged. Not Bran Fletcher."

"I know." Elaine wiped his cheeks with her sleeve. "'Tis

a shame, but such things happen. We'll have Masses said
for him."

Pelleas smiled tremulously. "Aye, let's do that."

"With your leave, Father, I will appoint a reeve today,
and then we'll have no more of this poaching."

Pelleas laid a hand upon her shoulder. "As you will,
Elaine. You must do as you think best. 'Tis a pity Torre does
not take an interest . . . Poor Torre, he was such a likely
lad . . . Do you remember when he won the squire's tournament at Alston Manor? Even Ulfric said that he seemed destined for great things."

"Aye, Father, I remember."

"He was a goodly knight, was he not, the man who
overthrew our Torre?"

"The best," Elaine assured him.

"Sir Lancelot . . . His father was King Ban of Benwick,"
Pelleas said suddenly. "Do y'know, I was thinking of Ban
just now, though it has been years since I remembered him.
He was but a passing knight himself, though nicely spoken.
We spent some months together when we were young. His
wits were astray," he added confidentially, tapping his
brow. "Not then, but later in life I heard he went quite mad.
A terrible thing it was. Benwick taken, the castle burning,
Ban falling dead upon the ground—and the infant stolen
away by some witch who claimed to live in a . . . what was
it, now? A lake? Aye, du Lac, he calls himself, Lancelot of
the Lake. Should be Lancelot of Benwick, of course, but
he's just du Lac. Poor lad," he said, shaking his head sadly.
" 'Tis a great pity, Elaine, when a king loses his wits."

"Aye, Father," Elaine murmured. "A great pity indeed."

Chapter 7

. . .

BY the time Lancelot was free of his armor, he knew
that Lavaine had been knighted less than a month
ago, that his armor was nowhere near as fine as Lancelot's,
that his brindle bitch had whelped the week before, and he
hoped to sell the pups at market fair. That is, if he was still
at Corbenic, though what he really hoped was that King
Arthur might notice him at the tournament and offer him a
place at Camelot.

"I'll introduce you," Lancelot offered, dragging his tunic
over his head. When he emerged he found Lavaine staring
at him, eyes round and mouth agape. *Was I ever that young?*
Lancelot wondered, and knew he must have been, though it
seemed so long ago that he could not remember how it felt.

He listened to Lavaine's thanks with half an ear as he
untied the points of his hose and stripped off his sweat-
stained shirt. "Do you think I could have a wash?" he asked
mildly, the moment he could slide a word in edgewise.

"Water!" Lavaine clapped a hand to his brow. "I forgot! Wait, don't move, I'll fetch it now!"

When he was gone, Lancelot sank down on a stool and removed his boots and hose. Beyond the open window, sunlight lay upon the cobbled courtyard where a flock of chickens clucked contentedly while the rooster preened atop an upended barrow, eyeing his paramours with lordly satisfaction. Lancelot leaned his head against the wall and closed his eyes, enjoying the sensation of cool air on his skin, the cooing of the birds, and the rhythmic champing of the horses in the stable.

He was lucky to have happened on this place and the kindly family dwelling here. His spirits lifted, and all at once he was sorry for his anger earlier. What Guinevere had done was wrong, of course, very wrong indeed, but surely there had been no need to shout at her. He rubbed the space between his eyes as though he could erase the memory of her tears.

Well, he would make it up to her. How exactly he would do it he did not know—and then he had it. Guinevere loved jewels. He would give her the diamond. Better yet, he would give *Arthur* the diamond, who would of course present it to his queen, who would understand it was a gift from both of them.

That Lancelot would win the diamond was something he did not stop to question. Only once had he ever entertained the slightest doubt of victory, and that for but a fleeting moment during his match with Sir Gawain. But of course Lancelot prevailed. Just as he always did. Just as he would tomorrow.

When he rode to the pavilion and removed his helm, Arthur would burst into laughter. If it sprang as much from relief as genuine amusement . . . well, that would just be one more thing they did not speak of. Later, at the feast, Lancelot would grumble about the trouble he'd been put to in order to defend his reputation, and Arthur would apologize for having cast doubt upon Lancelot's abilities in the first place. Then Lancelot would tell him how he and Guinevere had planned the jest, and how he had foolishly ridden out with his own shield.

He would make a tale of it, exaggerating his fear at being lost in the forest and his relief at having found this place, being sure to mention the beauty of the daughter of the house. That, at least, would be nothing but the truth, for she was a very pretty damsel, with her slender neck, pale gold hair, and blue, blue eyes. Extraordinary eyes—when he'd looked into them before, he'd had the oddest feeling, as though they had already met, though he could not remember where or when. He made a mental note to learn her name so he might present it to his king, who took a lively interest in all his subjects.

"Your water, sir."

Lancelot opened his eyes to find Lavaine before him, his face vivid with excitement.

"Thank you, Lavaine," Lancelot said. He poured half the pitcher over his head, rinsing the sweat and dust from his hair, and dipped a linen strip to wash his body.

It was a perfect plan. There was no possible excuse for his strange uneasiness, as though he had missed some vital flaw. Today would pass quickly enough. He would wash and dress and eat, make himself agreeable to his eccentric host until he could excuse himself and go to bed. Tomorrow he would leave early; with Lavaine along he should reach the tourney field in good time . . . and still something was amiss; he was more convinced of it than ever, though he could not imagine what that thing might be.

"Tell me," he said to Lavaine, who stood watching him

expectantly, "have you had much experience in jousting?"

Lavaine chatted on until Lancelot was dressed and combed and standing by his bag, folding and refolding the tunic he had taken off, his mind worrying at his plan as he tried to identify the flaw he was now certain he had missed.

". . . but if you are too tired, I understand."

"Too tired?" Lancelot tried to remember what the boy had been going on about, but it was all a blank. "No, I shouldn't think so."

"Oh, thank you, sir! I'll have them saddle your horse—it won't take a moment—and I'll get my lance."

As it seemed unlikely he'd been challenged, Lancelot assumed he had just agreed to put this young knight through his paces. *Why not?* he thought, tossing the crumpled tunic into his bag. This boy did not know him, but tomorrow he and his family would learn that the stranger they had taken in was no other than Sir Lancelot du Lac, the sort of story that would be handed down for generations. It was like one of the old tales—the hero disguised seeking shelter with some humble family whose generosity would be rewarded a hundredfold.

As it would be. Lancelot would send them something after, a gift astounding in its magnificence. It seemed very important that he do so, though he wasn't sure why he should care so much how some obscure country family might remember him. Countless tales were told of him already, and there would be many more . . .

He whirled, staring at the empty room. Strange. For a moment he'd been sure someone stood behind him. He'd had the oddest feeling, as though an icy finger had been laid, very gently, on his neck.

Chapter 8

. . .

THE sun stood straight overhead as Elaine looped her mare's reins over a low-hanging branch at the edge of the north field. A group of villagers, fewer than she'd hoped for, stood together in a knot, the grays and browns of their ragged clothing almost indistinguishable against the muddy earth.

Fresh from her uncle's manor, Elaine was struck anew by their air of poverty. It was an old jest that lasses looked their best at winter's end, when short rations restored the curves of cheek and waist and breast. But these people had gone far beyond a little hunger, and none of them looked as though they remembered how to jest. Gaunt and hollow-cheeked, they regarded her impassively. Even the children crouched unmoving, all stick-thin arms and legs and enormous, empty eyes.

A tall, light-haired man stepped forward and cleared his throat. Elaine addressed herself to him.

"What's ado?" she asked. "Where are the others? Half

the day has already been wasted, and I wanted to speak to them about the new reeve."

"Oh, thass all settled," the man replied, "I'll be taking over for Martin."

"And who are you?" Elaine asked.

"Will. Will *Reeve*. The matter was decided yestere'en."

Decided, was it? Without so much as consulting her father or Sir John? True, the reeve was traditionally chosen by the villeins, and though the lord had the final say in the matter, his approval was usually a mere courtesy. But in most cases, the villeins knew quite well what their lord expected in a reeve, and were careful to choose a man who would be acceptable. As this man might be, she reminded herself. There was no good in alienating him just because she did not like his manners.

"I shall speak to Lord Pelleas about this," she said firmly but not, she thought, unpleasantly. "In the meantime, let us see what you can do about getting this field planted."

Will Reeve did not return her smile. "Now, lady, there's no need for you to muck up your shoes out here. I'll see to the planting in good time."

"When will that be?" Elaine asked, glancing at a group of latecomers wending their way toward them across the field.

"In good time," he repeated with infuriating stolidness. "Thass naught for you to be vexed about."

"Yet I am becoming vexed, for I have said I want it done today. Is there some problem, Master Will?"

"Aye, lady, there is. 'Tis my decision when to plough and when to plant, and I say wait. If Lord Pelleas has aught to complain about, let him send for me himself."

Elaine was speechless at this effrontery, but only for a moment. "I have my father's full authority in this matter, so you can consider any order from me as issuing from him. Now, let us be clear, Master Will. Tomorrow at sunset, you will present yourself in the hall with a report on the progress of this field. I expect no less than two acres under plough."

He slouched back on his heels, thumbs hooked into his belt. "Can't be done."

"Can't—? I beg your pardon, for a moment I thought you said it can't be done. But of course I was mistaken."

"Nay, you heard me right enough. Now look here," he went on, "we've other things to see to before we get to this."

"Other things?"

"Thass right."

"And what might these things be?" When he did not answer, she felt an angry flush rise to her cheeks. "Explain yourself."

"We'll get to this field once we've finished with our own. Bran Fletcher wasn't the only one went hungry this past winter."

An angry murmur rose from the crowd behind him, which had grown to twice its original number.

"It was a hard winter," Elaine said, just as she had said this morning. She wondered why she had to keep reminding people of this simple fact, and why no one seemed to hear her when she did. Will Reeve was no more impressed than Uncle Ulfric had been.

"For some," he said, "'specially when the grain store ran out and *we* had naught to fall back on."

Nor did we, Elaine thought, remembering the days when Torre and Lavaine had returned empty-handed from the hunt and they had supped upon thin gruel and boiled turnips; the nights when she had lain awake, shivering in the darkness while her belly pinched and gnawed with hunger, worrying that tomorrow they would not eat at all.

"Bran Fletcher took to poaching," the reeve said in his

flat, uninflected voice, "and now he's hanged for it. Well, lady, Bran Fletcher's family was a-starving. Nor were they the only ones. This year we look to our own plots first."

"But that is folly!" Elaine cried. "Corbenic can produce enough to feed us all, but only if we work together!"

"Oh, are you going to pick stones with us, lady?" a woman shouted from the crowd, and amid the laughter, another voice took up the cry. "Will your brothers help with the plowing?"

"Nay, not Sir Torre! He's too busy swilling wine to come down to the fields!"

"Aye, and too drunk to plow a straight furrow if he did!"

"That's all you know!" a woman's voice cried shrilly, "drunk or sober, Sir Torre can plow a deeper furrow than any man amongst ye!" The woman, a slattern with a filthy coif, thrust out her hips amid a roar of laughter.

Elaine's face flamed with anger and mortification. She hadn't realized Torre's habits were so widely known, and had certainly not expected to learn of it like this.

Will Reeve rounded on the crowd, scowling. "Hold yer tongues, fools! Lady, pay those ruffians no mind. We'll get to the plowing, don't you fear, only—"

"Be damned to the plowing," a rough voice shouted, "and be damned to you, Will Reeve! Where were they when Bran Fletcher's childer were a-crying with hunger? Sitting up in the hall, that's where they were, feasting while we starved."

"We were all hungry—" Elaine began.

"Bran Fletcher never harmed no one, he only wanted to feed his bairns!" a woman cried.

"And now he's dead—"

"Hanged for a thief!"

"Go back to the keep!" a deep voice shouted. "Help your mad father dig up another passageway!"

"Enough!" the reeve roared. "Get to your homes, go on—move, I say! Lady, you'd best go, as well," he added, shooting her a frightened look. "I'll deal with this rabble."

"I am not going anywhere," Elaine said clearly. "Listen to me, all of you—"

She stumbled as something struck her leg. Looking down, she saw mud spattering her skirt. The next clod fell to her side, missing her by inches, and a roar that was no longer laughing echoed across the empty fields.

"Give us bread!"

"We're hungry, our children are hungry!"

"We'll not starve so you can eat!"

With a sickening shock, Elaine realized that the situation had slipped out of her control. These people were not just a handful of hungry peasants, they had somehow transformed into a mob. *I could die,* she thought, and though the idea seemed unreal, she knew that it was true. Such things happened—not often, but they were not unknown. A pack of desperate peasants—and the villeins of Corbenic were nothing if not desperate—would be seized by a fever of madness, rise up and slay their overlords.

These thoughts flashed through her mind in the time it took to measure the distance to her horse and realize she would never make it. So she did the only thing she could. She turned to face them, shoulders braced, her heart leaping to her throat when she saw how close they were.

And then they were falling back, stumbling over one another, cursing in their haste. Elaine turned and found herself staring at the mighty haunches of a milk-white warhorse. Her gaze traveled upward, passing over a polished boot, pausing on the jeweled pommel of the broadsword strapped to the gleaming saddle, until at last she reached the face of the knight who had arrived at Corbenic just this morning. He wore a crimson cloak, very bright and fine, and the rings on his fingers flashed in the sunlight when he raised his hand.

"Lady Elaine," he said, his voice cutting through the silence. "Are you in need of assistance?"

Smoothly, almost casually, he lowered his hand until it rested upon the pommel of his sword.

Elaine looked at the villeins, marveling at the change a few seconds had wrought. What had been an angry mob had dwindled once again to a small group of very frightened peasants. At their head was Will, who had named himself reeve without the permission of his overlord. Now he stood, strangely shrunken, humbled in the presence of a knight.

For a moment she was tempted to answer yes and bring the lot of them to justice. And yet . . . they belonged to Corbenic. They might not be much, but they were all she had, and to whip or brand them would hardly increase either their willingness to work or their ability to do so.

Her eyes moved over the group, fastening on the few who were brave enough to hold their heads up, silently forcing them to acknowledge that their fates rested in her hands. Last of all, she looked at Will, and not until he had bent his head did she look up at the knight.

"No," she said. "I thank you, but there is no need to concern yourself. I was just having a discussion with our new reeve—" Will's head raised with a snap "—about how quickly this field could be planted." Her legs were oddly jerky as she turned and took a few steps toward her palfrey. "So we are agreed that you will begin at once, Master Reeve," she said over her shoulder, "and tomorrow we shall expect you in the hall for supper to report upon your progress."

"Aye, m'lady," Will said. "Tomorrow it is."

Elaine reached her palfrey and stood looking at it, praying that her shaking legs would serve to mount. She was aware of the knight moving toward her, but before he reached her side, one of the men slipped from the edge of the crowd and knelt in the mud, offering his knee as a step.

She took it, remembering to thank the man when she was safely on her horse. "Master Reeve, one more thing," she called. "Bid the shepherd choose one of his flock for slaughter and have Cook prepare a stew. Tell her it is by my order." Her gaze swept the field once more. "Whoever works shall eat."

She turned toward the forest and cantered into the shelter of the trees. Only then was she aware that she was breathing in quick, gasping sobs.

"Lady Elaine—"

She dashed a sleeve across her eyes and forced herself to smile, slowing so the knight could pull up beside her. He had saved her, and she should be grateful, but the truth was she wished he'd go away. He was too handsome, too well-bred, too much for her to deal with at the moment. "You gave me quite a start back there," she said brightly. "Wherever did you come from?"

"I was in the practice yard with your brother Lavaine—"

"Dressed like *that*?"

The question popped out before she stopped to think. But he had thrown back his cloak, and she saw that he was clad in silk—pfellel silk, in fact, gossamer fine and so fabulously expensive that even Aunt Millicent could afford no more than a single scarf. The knight's tunic was very simply cut, the thin fabric clinging to the hard breadth of his chest. His arms were corded with muscle, bare save for a silver band above his elbow. The gleaming metal was wrought in an intricate design of oak leaves, as was the silver embroidery about his high collar, the pattern repeated yet again in the silver belt slung low about his hips. She had thought him handsome before, but now she realized that such a common word fell far short of the mark.

He glanced down at himself with a faint air of surprise, as though he had no idea what had prompted her question, then shrugged his broad shoulders as though what he wore was of no consequence at all.

What was such a man as this doing at Corbenic? Could he possibly be real? No, there was some hidden flaw, there must be. Yes, he was handsome, obviously rich, brave and courteous, and possessed of an impeccable sense of timing. But any man who would ride into a practice yard with the entire worth of Corbenic upon his person could hardly be called sensible.

"What was going on before, out there in the field?"

She repressed a shudder. "It was a bit awkward—our reeve is new, and not quite settled in, but I think we understand each other now."

He shot her a look so keen that she was forced to revise her estimation of his intelligence. "I think it was more than a bit awkward. Lady Elaine, why were you all alone? Surely that was a duty your steward should have undertaken."

"Yes, of course, but he has not been well." Before he could reply, she went on quickly, "Whatever brought you out there in the first place?"

"Your father asked your brother Lavaine to find you. I offered to undertake the task myself. And I am very glad I did."

So was she. Lavaine would never have handled the situation with such aplomb. He would have been terrified and so ashamed of his fear that anger would have been his only recourse. What would have happened next was something she could not bear to think upon.

She tried to summon a smile for the knight, but her lips trembled so that she knew the effort was a failure. "Thank you," she said, and to her horror, felt her eyes fill. Bad enough that she had acted as thoughtlessly as any damsel in a third-rate ballad, the ones she had always taken such pleasure in despising. To dissolve in tears before her rescuer would be the final humiliation.

"It was nothing," he answered, looking a bit alarmed at the threat of some awkward display of emotion. "Shall we go back to the hall? I know I would like a cup of wine, and I would be honored if you would share it with me."

Such a pretty little speech, she thought, so courteous and kind. "I know!" she said, smiling. "You must be Sir Gawain!"

He started, looking as surprised as if she'd struck him. "I am not."

"I didn't really think you were," she said quickly, "it's an expression. You know—as courteous as Sir Gawain."

"I see."

Whatever he saw, it did not seem to please him overmuch. For a moment she wondered if she'd stumbled upon the truth, but in the next breath dismissed the notion as absurd. Sir Gawain was said to be quite tall, with hair as fair as falling rain, while this knight was dark and not above the middle height.

"We're very partial to Sir Gawain in these parts," she went on, speaking rapidly to cover her confusion, "and consider him the best of King Arthur's knights."

She had surprised him yet again. He actually stopped his horse and turned to her. "The best?"

"Well, leaving Sir Lancelot aside, but *him* we don't regard."

The black brows rose another fraction of an inch. "You don't? Why ever not?"

"My brother Torre rode his first joust against Sir Lancelot. It was his last. Oh, I know such accidents befall a knight with no blame on either side. But later, as I waited by the surgeon's tent, all the talk was of a remark Sir Lancelot had made, that he would as lief have stayed at home as waste his skill on such raw country lads."

The knight frowned, his dark eyes hooded as he stared down at the reins in his hands. "That was very wrong of him."

"Yes, it was terribly unkind. And most unjust. What happened was no fault of Torre's, I assure you. Some fool left the gate ajar; a child ran onto the tourney field waving a kite, and his mount startled—"

"That was your brother?" the knight interrupted. "I—I remember hearing of it."

"It was a bad fall," Elaine went on. "His leg was shattered. He very nearly lost it—and would have done, if my woman Brisen had not stayed the surgeon's hand."

"It is his shield I am to carry," the knight said, the words not quite a question.

"Yes. He is quite lame. It was such a disappointment—to all of us, of course, but especially to him. He was so promising, you see, he'd won all the local squire's tournaments easily. And he was betrothed—well, promised—but after, her parents said—and now he's so dreadfully unhappy."

What was the matter with her today? She had thought herself long past weeping over Torre, yet the knight was looking at her with such astonished pity that fresh tears stung her eyes. "I'm sorry. I can't imagine why I'm telling you all this. What were we talking about?"

"I don't remember."

She laughed shakily. "Oh, it was Sir Lancelot. A subject we generally avoid."

"I'm not surprised."

They reached the edge of the forest, and the knight pulled up his charger, looking toward Corbenic with something almost like dread upon his face.

"I—I grow weary of halls and company," he said, "and

this is such a pleasant wood. If you don't mind, I would rather stay out here for a time."

Well, she could hardly blame him for that. Such dismal company as hers would put any man to flight.

"I don't mind in the least. There is the tower, you can hardly miss it from any part of the wood—and we dine at sunset. I'll have your chamber readied."

"Wait," he said. "Would you—'tis a pretty day for a ride, and I'm sure you know all the best paths. That is, if you would like to . . ."

When he smiled, that strange dizziness came over her again. Was it possible . . . no, it couldn't be. What could a man like this possibly see in her? She was nearly one and twenty, after all, far past her first youth, and if a month of regular meals had put a bit of flesh upon her bones, she did not delude herself that it had erased the damage done by years of near starvation. Yet he was looking at her as though he genuinely hoped she would accept. All at once her heart lifted, and it seemed anything was possible, anything at all, even that she might have caught the interest of a young and wealthy knight, and having caught it, could keep it for her own.

"I would like to," she said. "Come, we can water our horses by the river."

Chapter 9

• • •

BENEATH the overhanging branches of the oaks, the river flowed through light and shadow, rippling in little eddies over glistening stones. When they reached the boathouse, Elaine halted and dismounted.

"Here," she said, "this is a good place."

They led the horses to the water and tethered them to a branch. The knight spread his cloak on a patch of soft earth while Elaine went to stand before the boathouse, a small thatched building with a few crocuses blooming beside the door. Elaine smiled a little to see them there, remembering Torre scoffing that they would never grow.

"No one is at home?" the knight asked behind her.

"It is deserted now," she said, "since the Saxons left."

"The Saxons?"

"They came when I was ten," Elaine said, her eyes moving past the boathouse to a patch of mounded stone beyond. "We had no time to muster a defense, scarce time enough to flee from bonds or death. So we came here." She gestured toward the door. "And here we dwelt for seven years."

"Had you no kin to go to? No friends to take you in?"

"My father was injured," she said. "A Saxon sword cleft his helm in twain. They left him for dead, but Torre—he was eleven then—stole out by night and bore him hither. Father was insensible for many days, and when he woke, he was—he was not himself. And then my mother—" She swallowed hard. "She miscarried. She and the babe both died."

"I'm sorry," the knight said. He moved to stand beside her, and their fingers brushed. "I lost my mother, too. I was—fostered—from home when I was just a babe, and she died while I was gone. I cannot remember what she looked like, or her voice, or anything about her."

He looked so sad that Elaine was tempted to take his hand but did not quite dare to do it. "Can your father not tell you?"

The knight shook his head. "He died soon after I was born. But come, sit down. You were telling me why you did not go to your kinfolk or friends."

"Father was slow to recover," Elaine said, sitting down upon his cloak and drawing her legs beneath her. "My mother's death—when he understood—he could not bring himself to leave her. We always meant to go one day, when Father was . . . stronger. But somehow the time was never right."

"I see," the knight said so sympathetically that she had to take a long breath before she could go on, making her voice deliberately cheerful.

"And then we were saved. Three years ago, King Arthur drove the Saxons out and restored us to our home. But it was not what it had been. The Saxon chieftan used Corbenic to house his warriors, and all they knew of managing villeins was how to beat them. Many ran off; those who remained kept out of sight, tending their own plots while the common lands lay fallow."

"Then I would think they would be grateful that their lord has returned," the knight said.

"We lost all but the land, and these three years have been . . . difficult," she said with an inward smile at this understatement. "The forest has encroached upon the fields, and we lack the labor for the clearing. Each year we lose a little more, leaving less land to plant—and giving the villeins all the more excuse to tend to their own plots. It is what my father calls a downward spiral."

"What remedy does your father suggest?" the knight asked, leaning back upon one elbow.

"To find the Holy Grail, of course. Then all will be well." She smiled at his confusion. "The Holy Grail—the Sangreal—is the cup Our Lord used at the last supper. Legend has it that his foster father, Joseph of Arimathea, bore it hither after the crucifixion. My father had a vision of the Grail when the Saxons struck him down. He believes it is somewhere in Corbenic and cares for nothing but to see it with his living eyes. He is a very learned man," she added, plucking at the new grass, "and a very good one."

"I'm sure he is."

A rather awkward silence fell, and Elaine cast about for some way to change the subject. "I'm sorry I have nothing to offer you—or, wait, I might at that."

She jumped up and went into the boathouse. The light from the open door lay in a rectangle upon the earthen floor, leaving the rest of the chamber in shadow. As her eyes adjusted, she made out four pallets, still neatly tucked against the walls. The single table was clothed in a thin film of dust.

"You lived here for seven years?" the knight said behind her.

Elaine could scarce believe it herself. "A bit cramped, but the roof was sound, and it was pleasant to have the river so close." Torre still came here often, when some savage mood drove him from their hall, and knowing him, he did not come empty-handed. Opening the cupboard door, she said, "I thought so."

She drew out a jug, nearly full, and two cups, and bore them back outside. "Come, I've been running on too long. Tell me something of yourself."

"There is nothing much to tell," he said, smiling as he resumed his seat.

"You said that you were fostered young. Were your foster parents kindly folk?"

"I do not remember much about them," he said with such finality that she knew the subject to be closed.

"Then tell me about Camelot!" she suggested.

"What would you like to know?" he asked politely but with a marked lack of enthusiasm.

"Anything will do."

He looked up at the branches overhead, then at the river. At last he looked at her and shrugged. "I don't know what to say. Most of the tales I could tell you are already known."

Elaine made one more attempt. "What of your own adventures?"

"They're not worth speaking of." As though realizing that his answer was just short of rudeness, he smiled at her so brilliantly that she forgave him on the spot.

"Here," she said, pouring wine into his cup. "My mother's dowry, or what's left of it. Her family traded in Provence, so they sent her off with tuns of wine. Luckily, the Saxons did not think to look for the cellars."

He swirled the wine in the cup, sniffed it, and took an experimental sip. "I've never tasted better."

"You *are* extremely courteous," Elaine said, laughing. "Are you sure you aren't Sir Gawain?"

" 'Tis true I ride disguised, but even Sir Gawain would be hard put to shrink half a foot and alter the color of his hair."

She glanced at him, surprised at his tone. "Surely it is a compliment to be compared to such a knight?"

"Of course," he said with an ironic smile. "Who would not want to be Gawain? So brave and noble, so courteous and—" He broke off, yawning. "Forgive me. Just the thought of all that perfection is exhausting."

"Oh, fie, sir," she chided, smiling, "perfection is too strong a word, though Sir Gawain is a noble knight."

"So he is. A very noble knight," he agreed soberly, though his eyes glinted with a wicked merriment. "Indeed, there have been times, sitting in the hall while he revels us with some improving tale, when I have been so overcome by Sir Gawain's . . . nobility that I feared I might fall face-first into my ale and drown."

Elaine laughed, then was instantly ashamed. "This will not do sir," she said with a severity that was only part in jest, "no, it will not do at all."

"Tell me, lady, by what stroke of fortune did Sir Gawain win a champion so fair?"

"Sir Gawain was with the king when they took Corbenic back. Indeed, 'twas he who slew the Saxon chieftan, hand-to-hand in single combat, and many a grievous wound he took for the sake of folk he did not even know."

She smiled at the memory of the one time she'd seen Sir Gawain, a mere flash of sunlight glinting off a helm as he rode back to Camelot. "No matter what they say at court, Sir Gawain will always be First Knight to me, even if that Sir Lancelot did knock him off his horse."

"Alas for poor Sir Lancelot that he was not here that

day!" the knight said with a rueful twist of his lips. "Then you might have known that he is no such monster as you think. 'Tis true he oft speaks rashly, but after, he is always sorry. And I do not think—indeed, I am quite certain—that had he realized how gravely your brother had been injured, he would never have spoken as he did."

"He should have known," Elaine said flatly, "and if he'd had the courtesy to send a servant round, he would have. Sir Gawain—"

"Would have sent his squire," the stranger finished for her. "You are right, such has always been his custom. And now 'tis Sir Lancelot's, as well—or so they say."

"At least he has the sense to profit from Sir Gawain's example."

The knight began to speak, then checked himself and looked across the river, his expression dark. *Fool,* Elaine raged at herself, cursing her blunt tongue. *Aunt Millicent is right; you are too forward in your speech.*

Yet a part of her was not sorry she had spoken as she did. Why should she *not* say what she thought, even if this grand young knight did not agree? She had not liked the way he spoke of Sir Gawain, even if his words had seemed to be in jest. But then, she thought, melancholy washing over her, belike this is how they went on in Camelot. For all she knew, he'd said the same to Sir Gawain himself, and it was only she who did not see the joke.

I have grown grim and dull, she thought, *I, who was once so merry that nothing could damp my spirits long.* And with a little shock she realized that there was no going back. She'd always thought she could, but now she knew it was impossible. There was too great a gulf between the girl she'd been and the woman she was now.

She studied the knight's profile, as clear and fine as if it had been carved upon a Roman coin, and sorrow overwhelmed her. *If only you had come sooner,* she thought . . . *but now it is too late.*

"Shall we go back?" she asked, preparing to get to her feet.

She expected him to agree instantly, but he surprised her.

"Must we go quite yet?" he said. "Can we not stay a little longer?"

His anger—if indeed he had ever truly been angry—had died. His eyes were soft as sable, shining beneath winged brows, wistful and a little sad. Lost in his dark gaze, it took a moment for his words to reach her, and then she had to bite back the eager agreement springing to her lips. By the time she realized that a simple yes was what she wanted, the silence had spun out too long. Her face flamed; she dropped her gaze and nodded, feeling an utter fool.

Chapter 10

· · ·

LANCELOT quickly sipped his wine, hoping that his face did not betray his mortification. He should have leapt at the chance to return to Corbenic, excused himself, and taken to his bed. He had no business lingering here beside the river with a maiden who obviously wished herself away. 'Twas clear she agreed to stay only because she could find no courteous words with which to refuse him.

It was rather comical when he came to think of it, for he had long bemoaned the fact that he could go nowhere without attracting a score of feminine admirers. Indeed, he'd often felt a hare amid a pack of hounds when he walked into the hall and all heads turned in his direction. Everywhere it was the same, ladies pelting him with scarves and sleeves and flowers when he rode into the lists, with rings and brooches and perfumed parchments in the hall. Unmarried ladies—total strangers—offered him their hands; the married ones were far more generous in the parts they suggested he make free with.

Every lady but this raw country damsel. The most amusing thing of all was that if she knew whom she had spurned, she would despise him all the more.

But not nearly so much as in that moment he despised himself.

Now when he imagined the tales they would tell of his visit, a fine sheen of sweat broke out upon his brow. He was not the unknown hero, after all. He was the villain creeping in disguised to take advantage of a family who had accepted him in all innocence into their home. Had they but known his name, his welcome would have been quite different. Certes, Sir Torre would have refused him his shield, and Lady Elaine would not be sitting with him now. Once they knew his identity, what would they say? What would they think of his duplicity?

But he had meant no harm; he'd only wanted to borrow a blank shield. He'd never intended to deceive this lady or her family. It was just that he was lost, for he had galloped out of Camelot in a black temper, too—

(*frightened*)

—angry to remember the need for a blank shield, and had lost himself in the forest. Such a thing could befall any knight. It wasn't his fault . . . was it? No, the fault was Guinevere's. *She* was the one who had lied. Yet Guinevere had only lied because—

Because yet another lie had driven her to it. How had he become enmeshed in so many different lies that there seemed no honorable way forward?

The one thing he knew for certain was that he had no business inflicting his company upon this reluctant lady, no matter how little he cared to be alone. He turned to suggest that they return to the manor just as she turned to him. He hadn't realized how closely they were sitting, so near that he could see every lash framing her vividly blue eyes.

All at once her scent surrounded him, not one he could name, but something new to him, as subtle and mysterious as a woodland glade at dusk, and he could not look away.

She was so beautiful. Not just her lovely face or her wealth of primrose hair or her slender neck, fragile as a flower's stem. She, herself, was beautiful in a way that moved him as no woman had ever done before. He had known it from the moment she turned to face that mob, her slight shoulders braced, in as fine an act of hopeless gallantry as ever he had seen upon a battlefield. And she had courage of a different kind as well. This lady would never pretend to be other than she was; she said precisely what she thought, and be damned to anyone who disagreed. Some might call that foolish, but Lancelot knew such uncompromising honesty came only at a price far higher than he had ever dared to pay.

'Twas no wonder a woman of such rare courage had no time for *him*.

At last she turned away, a faint flush on her cheeks. "I really think we should—" she began.

"When I was younger," Lancelot heard his own voice say, "I thought I would be the greatest knight who'd ever lived."

Elaine, who had braced her hands to lift herself, halted. She was still poised for flight, he could see it in the tautness of her muscles, but she allowed him to go on.

"I was very proud," he said, his eyes fixed on the sunlight glinting on the water. "I had some talent—like your brother—but unlike him, I never had to think about anyone but myself. I was . . . encouraged to believe I was destined for great things. When I first arrived at Camelot, I was insufferable."

He chanced at quick look and found her smiling. "I'm sure you weren't as bad as that."

"Oh, I was. If you asked—" He caught himself up sharply. "Anyone who knows me would say the same. The other squires detested me, but I didn't care. I thought them so far beneath me, you see, so vastly inferior that their opinions meant less than nothing."

"Had you no friends?" she asked, her voice warm with a sympathy that touched him, though he knew it undeserved. "None at all?"

"One or two," Lancelot said, remembering his cousins Bors and Lionel with a pang, "who would have been my friends. But I'm afraid I did not much regard them, either. Truly, lady, I was detestable."

She laughed at that. "You seem much improved."

"Do I?" He winced at the eagerness in his voice. "I hope I am, a little. But any improvement is due entirely to the king. He did not think much of me at first—nor can I blame him, since the only time he was forced to notice me was when I was to be punished for fighting. Which happened rather often, I'm afraid."

"And did you win?"

"Always. Which did nothing to endear me to the others. But one day—I'd gotten into the devil of a scrape—King Arthur sat me down and talked to me. He was—is—a very kind man, though he can be stern. He was that day," he said with a reminiscent smile. "No one had ever spoken to me like that in all my life."

"Were you very angry?" Elaine asked. She drew her knees up and clasped her arms around her shins. Pale golden hair spilled over one shoulder, and her astonishingly blue eyes were fixed expectantly on his face, as though she were genuinely interested in what he had to say.

"No, I was not angry," he said, then grinned. "Well, perhaps a little, just at first. King Arthur is—I could say he is a good man, and that would be true, but many men are called good when they possess but a single virtue among a hundred flaws. Arthur is . . . wholly good."

"No man is that," Elaine protested, "unless he is a saint."

"I've always imagined that saints are dreary folk, but the king is very human. He has his faults—as he would be the first to tell you—"

"What are they?" Elaine interrupted. "I've never heard of any."

Lancelot thought a moment, then laughed. "Do you know, I haven't, either. Nor have I seen them for myself. Guin—the queen might scold him for not keeping such state as she deems fitting, but I hardly reckon that a fault. No, if he has one at all, it is that he is too ready to believe that others are as good as he is himself. It isn't that he's perfect, but King Arthur always *tries* to do the right thing, no matter how difficult that thing may be or how impossible it seems."

Elaine rested her chin on her knees. "It doesn't seem like much, does it, to always try to do the right thing? But when I think of it, there are times I've done—not the wrong thing, no one chooses to do that—but what is easy or convenient."

"Yes," he said. "For myself, I have done many things that I would change now if I could."

"I can see why you admire him so," Elaine said thoughtfully. "So after he had scolded you, what did he do?"

"He sent me off in search of an adventure."

"And you became a knight."

"I did. But—but it was not what I thought it would be."

"I understand," she said, and though he knew she did not really, he was still comforted. "I always thought—"

"What?"

"That I, too, was destined for great things." She gestured

toward the flowing river at their feet. "I would sit just here and plan my future."

"What was it?"

"I had been betrothed to Lord—well, it doesn't matter now, but he was a man of some consequence. I imagined I would rule graciously over my people—wearing very fine clothing while I did it, of course, and many splendid jewels. I would be famed not only for my great beauty but for my countless acts of charity. Sainthood would, of course, have followed, but only after I'd lived to a great age and borne at least a dozen children."

Lancelot whistled softly. "Sainthood? Even I never aspired so high as that. But tell me, what happened to Lord Whosis?"

"He did not wait. Alas, when my family vanished, he basely wed another."

"Churl. Shall I run him through?"

"Would you?" She seemed to consider the matter, her head tipped to one side. "'Tis very kind, but you needn't bother. I fancy he is gray and stout these days, no match at all for a knight of your undoubted caliber."

"But lady," he said, "what I cannot understand—forgive me if this is an impertinence—is why you have not wed since."

"Can you really not?" Now her smile was mocking, though whether of herself or him he could not say. "Oh, come, sir, you know how it is."

Deepening her voice, she went on in a drawl—astonishingly accurate—affected by some of the younger knights at court. "Who is her father? Good. Her mother? That will do. What is her dowry?" Her lips twisted into a supercilious smirk, and one hand described a languid, flicking motion. "Quite. And will you introduce me to that other maiden now, the one with the squint and the three manors?"

Lancelot, who had been sipping his wine, choked on his laughter. She obligingly pounded on his back, and when he was recovered, said, "I think I must be somewhat tipsy, sir, to talk to you like this."

"No, not at all. I have heard that sort of thing before—'tis only that I didn't think the ladies were aware of it."

"Of course we are. Or do you subscribe to the common wisdom that females have no sense?"

"At court," he said, "it is generally accepted that a lady's intelligence stands in direct proportion to her beauty. The plainest are reckoned to be clever, the fairest somewhat . . . less so."

"God giving with one hand and taking with the other, as it were."

"As it were," he agreed. "Now, by such a measure, you, my lady," he reached out and touched her cheek, "should by rights be little better than an imbecile."

She laughed, and the soft skin beneath his fingers took on a rosy hue. "Am I meant to be flattered or insulted?"

"Mayhap the common wisdom is not altogether wrong," he answered gravely. "Take all the time you need to work it out."

His hand drifted down to the soft hair hanging over her shoulder. He wound it around his hand and tugged her forward to look into her eyes. She went very still—the stillness of a hind that scents the hunter, of a dove beneath the shadow of the hawk. Yet she did not draw away.

And Lancelot knew why. He knew precisely what he'd done. He had bought her trust with the coin of his own honesty, and she had repaid him with her friendship. It was precious to him, not only because there were few he had ever named a friend, but because he sensed it was not a gift she offered lightly. Let it rest here, and he had the hope of retaining that even when she learned his name. Go on taking advantage of her ignorance, and he was the basest churl who'd ever lived.

"Lady," he said, hating himself yet powerless to stop, "to such as you, a dowry would be entirely superfluous."

His gaze drifted downward to her full pink lips, softly parted in surprise, and before he could stop to think of the terrible mistake he was about to make, he kissed her.

Chapter 11

. . .

ELAINE had been kissed before. Once. At her cousin Alienor's wedding feast—could it have only been last evening?—a knight had trapped her in a corner, grabbed her breast, and attempted to thrust his tongue down her throat. She had been at first revolted, then furiously angry as she jerked away and dealt him a stunning blow across the face. The experience was not one she had looked forward to repeating.

But this kiss was nothing like the first.

It was so hesitant, so soft—the merest brush of lips against her own—yet, strangely, she felt it through her entire body, a sweet fire that seemed to melt her very bones.

Her only complaint was that it was over too quickly, leaving her bereft. But only for a moment. The next time they kissed, her hand cupped the tender nape of his neck, and when he responded in kind, a delicious shiver rippled down her spine. She gasped softly in surprised delight, her lips parting beneath his, and he went very still for a moment before he tilted his head, deepening the kiss, his mouth firm and supple on her own.

Greatly daring, she traced the contour of his lower lip with the tip of her tongue, and he made a sound—something between a sigh and a moan—and caught her in his arms, throwing her off balance so they fell together, laughing, onto his cloak. Lifting himself on one elbow, he gazed down at her, and she saw her own astonished happiness reflected in his eyes. "You are so beautiful," he said, his voice filled with wonderment, and smiling, he bent to her again.

This, this is what I have been waiting for all my life, she thought, dizzy with his kiss. Every hurt she had suffered, each failure and disillusionment were magically redeemed into steps upon the path that led her to this moment, this perfect moment that she hoped would never end.

When he drew away, it was only to bury his face against her neck, his lips moving against her skin. She sighed and ran her hands down his back, feeling each separate muscle beneath her fingertips, breathing in his scent—something spicy and exotic—longing for this precious time to go on and on, yet knowing it could not. Not like this.

They had come to a parting in the road. She could almost see it, two ancient wooden signposts pointing in opposite directions, the writing faded yet very clear. One was marked Dishonor, the other, Respectability. She wound her fingers through his springing curls and tugged him up so she could look into his eyes.

He placed one callused fingertip against her mouth as though to still the question hovering upon her lips, and yet it must be asked.

"Who are you?"

Even before he spoke, she read the answer in his eyes. "I cannot tell you."

She pulled free of his embrace and sat up, smoothing her tumbled hair. Surely that tearing pain in her breast could not be her heart breaking. That was only an expression, after all.

He sat up, as well. "I would tell you if I could, but I *can* not."

"Why?"

"A vow."

"Oh, a *vow*. Well, then, I mustn't meddle. I'd hate to see you damned forever just for *my* sake."

"Elaine—" He caught her hand in his. "The name you seek would tell you nothing—less than nothing—of the man I really am. But perhaps another—"

"A false name?" She shook her head and attempted to withdraw her hand. "Thank you, but you needn't bother."

"Not false," he said quickly, tightening his fingers. "'Tis mine—at least it was. I bore it long ago, so long that I have no memory of ever having heard it spoken. It would please me very much to hear you say it."

"What is it?" Elaine asked.

"Galahad."

It seemed a hush fell over the glade in which they sat, silencing the chatter of the birds and the rushing of the river. Sunlight fell through the budded branches overhead, striking sparks off the rings upon the long brown fingers, still clasped tightly around hers.

"Galahad," she repeated softly. A shiver passed quickly down her spine, as though she had unwittingly uttered some forgotten word of power.

"Yes." He raised her hand to his mouth, brushing his lips across her palm, then laughed aloud. "*Yes.*"

And somehow, in a way she could never possibly explain, all was made right. When he bent to her, she swayed to meet him, her arms rising to clasp him round the neck. All the questions she might have asked, the ones tugging at the edges of her mind, simply ceased to matter when his mouth found hers and they sank together to the ground.

Chapter 12

. . .

THEY reached Corbenic as the sun was sinking behind the trees and walked hand in hand to the entrance of the tower.

"Elaine."

Galahad turned to her, the last rays of the setting sun shining full upon his face. Confronted with such unearthly beauty, she could only stare in wonder. Even after all that they had shared she could scarce believe that such a man was looking at her with such longing in his luminous dark eyes.

"Would you—that is, may I—" he broke off, laughing.

"What?" she breathed.

"May I wear your favor? Tomorrow, when I joust?"

Elaine's disappointment was gone almost before she was aware of it, swept away in an uprush of astonished joy. Long ago, before age and common sense had put an end to such foolishness, she had imagined some knight would ask her this very question. It had once been her favorite fantasy, one she had spent—wasted, she would have said just yesterday—many an hour picturing in lingering detail.

To wear a lady's favor said something very different than the dry business of alliances. It was a public declaration of affection, often the only one available to men and women bound in duty to another. But where no such bond existed, when the man and woman were free, it could mean . . . could mean . . .

"Yes," she whispered, "yes, if you like."

He smiled brilliantly. "Thank you." He raised their joined hands, turning hers to lay a soft kiss against her palm, his eyes closing briefly. She had time to notice the warmth of his lips, the crisp, curling hair springing from his brow, the length of his dark lashes against his cheeks. Then his gaze lifted to hers, and he kissed her mouth.

"Well, well," a cool voice said behind her, "so here you are at last. Where have you been?"

Elaine turned to find her brother Torre leaning in the doorway, arms folded across his chest. He had shaved, she noticed, and combed his hair, and wore his best tunic.

"I took G—our guest to see the river," she answered, willing herself not to blush.

"I see." Torre glanced pointedly at the sun, hovering just over the horizon. "A curious sight, to be sure. Come, sir, I will show you to your chamber. You just have time to wash before we eat."

"Thank you," Galahad said. "Lady Elaine, until later."

He cast her one last smile, bowed, and followed Torre across the courtyard into the low building housing the hall and several chambers. Elaine tripped up the stairway of the tower to her own chamber and threw open the lid of the trunk at the foot of her bed. Her hand moved unerringly beneath the neatly folded clothing and fastened on a garment tucked into a corner. She drew it out and carried it to the window, smiling as she smoothed it between her hands.

She had made this sleeve during the first year they returned to Corbenic, in the days when it seemed that anything was possible. She had worked upon it in secret, stealing an hour before dawn, another before sunset, sitting at her little loom before her window and dreaming of the day her token would flutter bravely from some knight's helm. When it was done, she laid it carefully away.

Now, three years later, the crimson dye seemed gaudy; the embroidery, so painstakingly applied, straggled in an intricate pattern far beyond her skill. But she would use no other. There was something almost magical about seeing her childish dreams come true.

She whirled, dropping it upon the windowsill when her door opened and her woman, Brisen, came in, bright black eyes alight with curiosity. "Your father has been asking for you all afternoon," she said without preamble, "and Sir Torre was about to set off himself. You'd best let him know that you've returned."

"I saw him when I came in." Elaine drifted over to her bed and fell down upon it, gazing dreamily at the tattered canopy.

"Good," Brisen said, placing a cup of ale upon the bedside table. "From the look on Sir Torre's face before, I feared there would be murder done. Not that I was worried. Your guest proved himself a gentle knight before, out there in the fields."

Elaine didn't bother asking how Brisen knew what had happened earlier. Brisen knew everything that went on at Corbenic. Sometimes she seemed to know things before they happened, but that, of course, was due to Brisen's network of informers, coupled with the maid's sharp wits.

" 'Twas a foolish thing you did," Brisen grumbled, slapping a comb down on the table beside the ale, "going out there all alone, what with Bran Fletcher's remains still hanging in the wood and the people so upset. Whatever were you thinking?"

"Don't you scold me, too," Elaine said, picking up the comb and working the tangles from her hair.

Brisen smiled, setting two deep dimples dancing beside her full red lips. "You've been scolded once already? By yon bonny knight?"

"Yes."

"Good." Brisen sat down on the edge of the bed and took the comb from Elaine. "Who is he?"

"What, you don't know?" Elaine laughed. "Don't tell me you didn't conjure his name from the thin air?"

"The Sight doesn't come to me for the asking, lady, I've told you that before."

Elaine had little patience for prophecy; only from Brisen would she tolerate such nonsense. But Brisen was not only an excellent serving maid, she was a healer of inordinate skill—one might almost say uncanny. Indeed, there were many who had said as much, but they did not say it twice where Elaine could hear.

They had met in the surgeon's tent at Camelot, among the reek of blood and groaning of the wounded, for every tournament brought some injury or other. Elaine had forced her way in over the objections of the guard and stood staring at her brother, one hand pressed to her mouth to keep from vomiting. Torre lay insensible with his shattered leg bared. It was the sight of the torn flesh and protruding bone that was responsible for Elaine's nausea, that and the surgeon standing over him, a saw in one blood-flecked hand while with the other he gestured toward a spot above Torre's knee.

"Just here," he was saying, "and it must be done at once. So if you would step outside, lady . . ."

Elaine turned to Sir John, their steward, who had accompanied her to Camelot, for Lavaine and Lord Pelleas had both been stricken with a summer fever that kept them still abed. Sir John nodded, tears winding down his withered cheeks. "Come, lady," he said, his voice choked, and took Elaine firmly above the elbow.

"But—" Elaine began, "but—"

It was all happening too fast. How could this day, so eagerly anticipated, turn so quickly into a nightmare?

A small woman in a dark gown and white coif passed by, an ewer in her hands and strips of clean linen folded over her arm. She glanced down at Torre's unconscious form and halted.

"I must do it now," the surgeon said.

"Oh," Elaine said weakly. "But are you sure . . ."

"Quite. There is no help for it."

The woman, who Elaine took for a sister at some nearby convent, lifted her bright, dark eyes from Torre's face and fixed them upon the surgeon. "You are wrong," she said. "That leg can be saved."

The surgeon made an impatient gesture. "I did not ask you, Mistress Brisen."

"No, but you should have done." The dark-robed nun turned to Elaine. "There is no need for this."

"There is every need," the surgeon snapped. "Lady Morgana will be looking for you; best go to her at once."

"She can wait. Sir Yvaine is in no danger—unlike this poor knight."

"Lady," the surgeon said to Elaine. "This . . . woman knows nothing. Every moment we delay increases the danger to your brother."

"Damn your lying tongue to hell, you ignorant butcher," Brisen cried, and Elaine realized she was not a nun. "Lady, how far is your home?"

"Half a day's ride," Elaine said.

The surgeon snorted. "He would never survive the journey."

"He will," Brisen said, "and he will walk again."

Elaine looked from the surgeon to the small, black-eyed woman, who spoke with such bold confidence though she seemed only a few years older than herself.

"Who are you?"

"Mistress Brisen," the surgeon said with distaste, "is one of the Duchess of Cornwall's women. She fancies herself a healer."

"I *am* a healer," Brisen said.

"And you think—you are sure—" Elaine faltered.

"No, I am not sure. His life is in the Lady's hands. But there is a chance—a very good chance—he can survive this." She laid a hand on Torre's brow. "He is strong and young. The leg is bad—it will never be the same—but still, I believe it can be saved."

"You will come?" Elaine asked.

"I will." Brisen set down the ewer and linen strips. "You," she said to Sir John, "have someone fetch a cart. Hurry, now, we haven't time to lose."

"But—" Sir John began.

"You will kill him," the surgeon said.

Elaine took the smaller woman by the shoulders. "Why?" she asked. "Why would you do this? You do not even know us."

"I must," Brisen said simply. "I cannot say why, only that it is so. I have trained for many years, lady—even *he* will tell you that—" She jerked her head toward the surgeon. "And I swear that I will do my best for your brother."

Elaine hesitated. It would be madness to take the word of a stranger over that of a surgeon appointed by the king himself. She could not live with herself if she brought about Torre's death. Her decision made, she opened her mouth—and at that moment, Brisen leaned to smooth the hair back from Torre's brow. The expression on her face and the tenderness of the gesture said more than all the words that had been spoken.

"Fetch the cart," Elaine said to Sir John. "We're taking Torre home."

"I cannot allow it," the surgeon said.

"Get out of my way," Brisen ordered in a low and deadly voice. "I will bind this up before we leave."

"You have killed him," the surgeon said to Elaine and threw the saw back into his trunk. "Even if he should survive, he will never walk again."

Eight months later, Torre ventured his first halting steps.

That had been more than a year ago, and for a time Elaine lived in fear that Brisen would return to Lady Morgana's service. But she remained, slipping easily into the role of serving woman to Elaine, and healer to the manor folk of Corbenic. And if she insisted on her prophecies from time to time, so be it.

"Who is the knight?" Brisen said now, her comb catching on a snarl.

"Ouch! Torture will not help—I cannot tell you what I do not know myself."

"He did not say?"

"He vowed not to tell anyone until after tomorrow's tournament."

Brisen drew the comb slowly through Elaine's hair. "There are several knights of Gaul at King Arthur's court. Sir Bors—but they say he is as pious as a monk." Brisen peered into Elaine's face and smiled, her dimples dancing. "Clearly not Sir Bors. Sir Lionel, Sir Ector De Maris, and then, of course . . ."

"Who?"

"Sir Lancelot."

Elaine laughed. "But we know it isn't him."

"Do we?"

"You must have seen him," Elaine said, "when you were at court."

"No, I came with Lady Morgana the morning I first met you. I never saw Sir Lancelot."

"But what would Sir Lancelot be doing here on the eve of the king's tournament?"

"What indeed," Brisen murmured. "Turn to me, if you would." She arranged Elaine's hair so it lay over her shoulders, rippling over the swell of her breasts to fall in a golden puddle in her lap. "Lovely," she said, sighing. "We'll leave it loose tonight. If you want to wear the green, you can have ribbons, as well."

"What? Oh, the green is stained," Elaine said absently.

"Then it will have to be the blue—and the fillet, I think, with two small plaits by the temple. Come over to the stool, please."

Elaine obeyed and sat looking out the narrow window toward the northern field, where the tiny figures of the villeins and oxen showed blackly against the setting sun. There must be hundreds of manors in Britain right now where the same scene was unfolding, yet to her, it seemed a miracle. And she knew exactly who had wrought it.

One lift of his hand, a few words, and Galahad restored order to her world. That same hand had stroked her cheek—she still felt the touch of it, burned like a brand upon her skin. He had said that she was beautiful, and just by saying it, had made it so.

"He cannot be Sir Lancelot."

She did not realize that she had spoken aloud until Brisen answered.

"He is the right age. And they say Sir Lancelot is dark

and wondrous handsome. Did he tell you aught of his kinfolk? His parents?"

"Only that he did not remember them," Elaine said, then
realized that if he were indeed Sir Lancelot, he would not.
For King Ban had collapsed—soon after his son was born,
in fact. His lady had laid the infant beside the lake to go to
her stricken lord. By the time Ban was dead, the babe had
vanished, carried off by the Lady of the Lake. Queen He-
len had never seen her son again.

"What of King Arthur?" Brisen asked. "Did he speak of
him at all . . . or of the queen?"

Elaine was having trouble breathing. "A little. Once
he—he called the king familiar. And another time—" She
leaned forward to take her ale from the table, but her hand
was shaking so that she set it down again, not daring to
bring it to her lips. "Another time," she said, staring at the
puddle on the table, "he started to say 'Guinevere,' then
changed it to 'the queen.' "

"Ah. Well, if he is Sir Lancelot, there would be nothing
strange in that. They say he is *quite* familiar with the
queen."

"Idle rumors," Elaine snapped.

"This rumor is persistent, lady."

"That doesn't make it true."

"No, it doesn't. But if Sir Lancelot is out wandering the
forest in search of a blank shield, then something very
strange is going on at Camelot."

Elaine turned to her serving woman. "You think it is him."

Brisen nodded slowly. "I do."

"But—but it makes no sense."

"It doesn't seem to, does it? And I'll tell you this, lady:
Whatever they may say of Sir Lancelot and Guinevere,
I've never heard his name linked with any other woman's.
Not that they haven't tried."

She leaned her hip against the table's edge and laughed. "Did you ever hear the story about him and the four queens? They found him sleeping by a hedgerow and said he must choose one of them as his paramour. When he refused, they put an enchantment on him and locked him in a dungeon until he changed his mind."

Elaine dimly remembered hearing something of the sort, though she had not listened very closely to the tale. "How utterly ridiculous," she said. After a moment's silence she added, "Which one did he take?"

"None of them. A serving wench helped him to escape in exchange for a kiss."

"Of course." Elaine sniffed. "You don't really believe such nonsense, do you?"

"'Tis true, lady," Brisen said seriously. "Queen Morgause of Orkney told Lady Morgana all about it. 'Twas late one night when the wine was flowing—"

"Tipsy gossip," Elaine said dismissively.

"Mayhap it was, but—" Brisen laughed, then put a hand to her mouth and glanced guiltily over her shoulder, adding in a lower voice, "Morgause was one of them. The four queens. She was still furious about it, too. And she isn't the only woman Sir Lancelot has spurned. Scores of heiresses and princesses have tried to win him, but he'll have none of them. Deadlier than the plague *he* is, what with all those maidens pining themselves into the grave for love of him."

"'Tis hardly fair to blame him for that," Elaine protested weakly as Brisen began the second braid. "If he did not love them—those heiresses and princesses . . ."

"True enough. But they say he is in love with a woman he cannot have, the wife of the man he admires above all others." Brisen's hands stilled. "If that is so, lady, what better way to throw the gossips off his trail than to feign devotion to another lady—even if she is the daughter of a poor country lord?"

"I don't believe it," Elaine said at once. "He isn't like that."

"What *is* he like?"

"He is . . ." *Wonderful. Perfect. Every dream I've ever had come true.* "He told me he had made mistakes—done things he regretted—but he is different now."

"Oh, is he?" Brisen grasped her chin. "He kissed you." She turned Elaine's head aside and touched a spot upon her neck. "And more, besides. How much more?"

Elaine jerked away. "I am still a maid, if that is what you're asking."

"It is." Brisen's eyes softened. "You must *think*. I know it isn't easy, not when you're feeling all you do, but please, lady, please be careful. If he will not even give you his name, how can you trust him?"

Elaine stared blindly through the window, thinking how this must look to Brisen. She thought Elaine an innocent, easily seduced by a knight of Arthur's court—the same knight who had wrought such damage to them all. But Brisen did not understand how it had been. She started to explain, then realized she had no idea what to say. That the knight had refused her his proper name, but it didn't matter since he was not that man at all? That Galahad was real, and Sir Lancelot—or whoever he might be—was not? It sounded nonsensical, yet at the time she had been so certain it was true.

Even now, a part of her accepted this strange certainty without question, but another part—the part that spoke in Aunt Millicent's voice—derided her as a credulous fool. *He wounded your brother nearly to the death,* it said, *and mocked him after. He says he's sorry now, but what good are words? If he really cared for you, he would tell you who*

*he is. If he felt what you do for him, he would not have
asked for your sleeve, but for your hand.*

"Oh, lady," Brisen said gently, "I'm not saying this to
hurt you. And I could be mistaken. Mayhap he is some
other knight. Or it may be as you say, that Sir Lancelot has
changed and that there is nothing between him and the
queen save idle gossip. It could well be that none of those
other ladies suited him as you do."

Elaine laughed through the tears stinging her eyes. Sir
Lancelot du Lac, prince of Benwick, First Knight of Camelot
and the Queen's Champion—caught by her charms? It was a
ridiculous thought, and yet . . . yet . . ."

"There *was* something between us—at least, there
seemed to be . . ."

"I'm not saying there wasn't. I just don't want you to be
caught in the middle of some squalid intrigue. And there is
this—" She put her hand on Elaine's shoulder. "Everyone
knows Sir Lancelot never wears a lady's favor in the lists.
Yet he asked for yours."

And how could Brisen have known that? Elaine could
not remember having mentioned it. But there was her
sleeve, still lying on the windowsill. It did not take the
Sight to reason how it had come to be there.

"You think it is part of his disguise."

"If that is the case, 'twas ill done not to tell you so
straight out. And there is this: when his identity is known,
such a break with custom will be noticed. I know how
those people think; the entire court will talk of nothing
else. Any other gossip will be forgotten . . . for a time."

Elaine could hardly bring herself to speak. "Then—if
you are right—it was a rather clever thing to do."

"Clever, but not kind. Or honorable. Your reputation—"

Elaine laughed, dragging a sleeve across her eyes. "Oh,
Brisen, what reputation? No one at Camelot knows me, no

more than I know them! Why should I give a fig for what a pack of strangers say?"

"You shouldn't," Brisen said at once. "But I fear Sir Torre will see it differently."

"He won't even notice," Elaine said, "and if he did, he would not care."

"He notices more than you might think. And he cares a great deal more than he lets on."

So do you, Elaine thought. Fond as she was of Brisen, she suspected it was more than the friendship between mistress and servant that kept the healer at Corbenic, when at any time Brisen could have returned to the luxury of Lady Morgana's household. It was a pity that once Torre left his bed, he had apparently forgotten Brisen's existence.

"What should I do?" Elaine asked her now.

"Change your gown, wash your face, and go down to supper. After that . . ." Brisen shrugged. "Wait and see."

Chapter 13

• • •

LANCELOT remembered well the day of Torre's knighting. The morning had started badly when the king once again refused him permission to leave court and go adventuring. Instead, Arthur sent him to the lists, thinking to appease him, but this only made matters worse. Lancelot, who once reveled in the excitement of the lists, had at some point—during his match with Sir Gawain, to be precise—developed an intense aversion to the pastime.

This was something he could never bring himself to tell the king, for he dreaded the inevitable explanations. *One day,* he had vowed a hundred times, *one day I will speak to the king of this.* Yet that day never seemed to come. On that morning, his courage failed him once again, and he went off, obedient as ever, to dash the dreams of any knight bold enough to issue him a challenge.

As always, there were many.

Lancelot understood. To a point, he sympathized. To unhorse du Lac was to achieve glory in a single stroke, a prospect too tempting to resist. They all knew victory was unlikely—impossible, they said, though of course the poor fools did not *quite* believe it. Torre had been the last that day, and by then Lancelot had been weary of the whole depressing business. That the boy went down so easily did nothing to improve his mood. He rode off, disgusted, not bothering to so much as glance at his fallen opponent. He did not remember making the comment that had so offended Elaine, but it was precisely what he had been thinking.

If only he'd told Arthur the truth that day, how different everything would be. Now, watching Torre limp down the passageway before him, Lancelot could not recall what excuse he'd used to justify his silence. It didn't matter. 'Twas pride alone that had sent him out there to destroy this young knight's dreams, the same pride that led him to deceive his king about the true nature of his First Knight.

Torre threw open the door of a small chamber and gestured Lancelot to enter. He followed and shut the door behind them.

"I think you came here looking for something more than a shield," Torre said abruptly. "And as my father won't think to ask what it might be, that duty falls to me."

"Sir Torre," Lancelot said with his most charming smile, "I assure you I had no designs in coming here. I was lost, and very fortunate to find you. Thank you again—"

"You are welcome to my shield; as I said, I have no use for it. But I wonder . . . why *do* you ride disguised, Sir Knight?"

"For my own reasons," Lancelot answered, "and if you will forgive me for saying so, it would be ill done for a fellow knight to inquire any further."

"Touché." Torre limped over to the table and filled two

cups from the flagon by the bed. "A Gaulish term, but I don't have to tell *you* that."

Torre was auburn-haired, thin to gauntness, and wore a cynical expression that made him appear far older than his years. When he handed Lancelot the cup, their eyes met, and Lancelot realized that Torre had no need to hear his name. He had already guessed it.

"So long as your reasons touch only yourself and your own honor, you are quite right," Torre went on, swirling the liquid in his own cup. "But when you involve others in your deception—"

"*Deception* is a strong word," Lancelot retorted evenly. "It is not uncommon for a knight to ride unknown into a tournament."

"But we are not in the lists now, are we? We are in *my* home, where you were stealing kisses from *my* sister not an hour past."

Poor lad, Lancelot thought, even as he gripped his cup until his knuckles whitened. *He has every cause to dislike me.* "I did not *steal* anything from Lady Elaine," he replied, careful to keep the anger from his voice. "Though I admit I gladly accepted a kiss."

Torre snorted. "You'd be hard put to deny it. But my sister is no court drab to squander her kisses upon a chance-come stranger. It is *ill done* for a knight to take advantage of a maiden's innocence."

Insolent young pup. How dare he mimic Lancelot's own words to his face? "Sir Torre," Lancelot said, grasping at the fraying edges of his temper, "I assure you I have nothing but the deepest respect for Lady Elaine."

Torre eyed him narrowly, seeming not at all comforted by this reassurance. "You say you are a knight of Camelot. Tonight all the king's companions will be with him on the

eve of his great tournament—all save one, who, for reasons
he will not give, wanders nameless in the forest. Tell me, if
you had a sister, would you trust such a man with her good
name?"

"Perhaps I, too, would have my doubts," Lancelot said,
"though I hope I would have the courtesy to learn the facts
before passing judgment."

"The fact is that you and Elly were alone for the best
part of the afternoon. The fact is that you were kissing her
just now. These are the only facts that interest me, and I
warn you, sir, think twice before attempting such a breach
of hospitality again."

Or what? Lancelot thought. *Will you challenge me?*
From the way Torre's eyes flashed, he realized the same
thought was in the young man's mind. *My God, he'd really
do it,* Lancelot thought; lamed as he is, knowing who I am,
he'd still offer me a challenge. Would I have such courage
in his place?

But that was not a question he wished to pursue at this
particular moment. "While your concern does you credit,
'tis a bit misplaced," he said. "If you really care for your
sister, then take the management of your estate from her
hands. She is all too young for such a burden, and too
proud to ask for help. Yet she needs it."

Torre's fair skin flushed. "I fail to see what concern this
is of yours."

Very much my concern, Lancelot thought, *as it is I who
brought you all to this sorry pass.* But even if he were free
to explain and make amends, he doubted this beaten, bitter
young man would accept either his help or his apology.

"None," he said heavily. "Forgive me."

Torre nodded briefly. "We shall eat in a quarter of an
hour." He tossed back his wine and made his halting way
across the floor, pausing at the doorway to look back.

"We are somewhat secluded, but not ignorant of the doings in Camelot. My sister is too fine for the games you play at court. Mind that you remember that, Sir Knight-Without-a-Name. Whatever trouble you are in, Elaine is not the answer."

Lancelot was still searching for a suitable rejoinder when Torre stepped out and shut the door. The reason it continued to elude him, he realized, was that there wasn't one.

He walked to the window and gazed out across the fields to the forest, silhouetted against the sky as the sun sank behind the trees. When it rose, he would ride off to the king's tournament. And when it set again, where would he be?

He shivered and turned away from the bloodred sky, his gaze moving over the small chamber that would be his tonight. The bedclothes were patched and mended, the bowl and pitcher of the meanest pottery. Instead of a candle, a rushlight had been placed beside his bed. It seemed that everywhere he looked, he was faced with a fresh reminder of the poverty of the inhabitants.

I should marry Elaine, he thought, *and set this all to rights. That is the least I can do.* He passed a few moments imagining this chamber transformed, but when he pictured Elaine, lying on the bed with her bright hair spread across the pillow, he forgot his noble motives. *Yes, I will marry her, I'll do it. How perfect it will be . . . that is, if she will have me.*

He remembered her scornful words regarding Sir Lancelot, each one of them deserved. *But I am different now,* he thought. *Or am I?* Today he was, but tomorrow he would be du Lac again, up to his neck in trouble with no good end in sight. The best he could manage was to stay the tide by a clever deception suggested by the queen.

Deception. Strange how that word kept cropping up. Or perhaps it was not so strange at that. His entire life was a deception, after all, a glittering edifice built upon a lie. At any moment the whole thing could come crashing down. How could he even think of dragging any lady, let alone Elaine, into such a mire? But now that he had found her, how could he bear to live a life without her in it?

She had a dimple—a single dimple on the left side of her mouth that lent her smile a singular, lopsided charm. And a way of tilting her head, just so, when something puzzled her. He had puzzled her greatly, and while a bit of mystery was said to be no bad thing in love, he did not wish to puzzle her at all. He wanted to tell her everything about himself, beginning with his first memory and going on until he reached the moment she smiled at him in the courtyard of Corbenic and he had experienced that impossible feeling of recognition.

They had not met before. He could never have forgotten her if they had. It was only now, looking at the covered shield propped in a corner, that he caught the memory he'd searched for earlier. He walked over and pulled off the canvas cover, a small sigh escaping him as he regarded his shield.

A ridiculous device, he'd often thought it. Not liking to claim the arms of Benwick while it was still occupied, he'd designed his own. He'd sketched it in a fit of melancholy, a knight (argent) kneeling before a lady (or) upon a field of gules. Though at the time he'd been morbidly pleased with the result, he'd come to hate it since.

Now he touched the cool surface, thinking that there *was* something of Elaine in the proud carriage of the painted head. He wondered what she would say if he told her it had been painted in her likeness, years ago when he had given up all hope of ever finding its model in the flesh. She would laugh at him, no doubt, but he thought she would be pleased. He imagined her blushing, not knowing where to look—

He drew the cover on again. When would he tell her? Not tonight. Tomorrow, then, after the tournament was done and he'd made peace with Arthur? Again, that strange feeling pricked his neck, but he shrugged it off, instead imagining himself returning here and sweeping Elaine off to Camelot. Why should he not? They could be happy— they *would* be happy. He would love her so much that surely she must love him in return, even when she knew everything. And he could change. Elaine was so brave, so strong. She could make of him a different man, a better one; he was certain of it.

Whatever trouble you are in, Elaine is not the answer.

"Touché, indeed," he murmured, lifting his cup to the door through which Torre had just passed. Torre might be a rude young lout, but he was no fool. Elaine deserved better. If he really loved her, he would stay well away from Corbenic in future. Torre might be too proud to accept help, but he should have it nonetheless; it could be done through young Lavaine with no one the wiser. Then Elaine could have a proper dowry and wed some respectable knight.

Lancelot's hands were trembling as he drained his cup, refilled it, and emptied it again, wondering if there was enough left in the flagon so he might drink himself insensible.

But that would hardly be playing the game, though why he should suddenly care about playing the damned game was beyond him. Still, for tonight, at least, he would watch how much he drank, lest he lose control and find himself kneeling at the damsel's feet, her hand in his as he begged her to become his wife. And a neat trick that would be, to pledge his troth to a lady without once mentioning his name.

He drew a shaking breath and passed a hand across his eyes. How strange to think that he had spent so many years longing for a name, and now he wanted only to be rid of it. Life was so interesting that way, he reflected, emptying the mug again, each day filled with such surprising twists and turns.

Today had certainly brought its share. He had woken in his own bed at Camelot, anticipating a pleasant if uneventful journey, and instead he'd been from hell to heaven and back again. Not bad for a day's work.

And then there was tomorrow. That strange pricking of his neck was back, and now, at last, he knew it for what it was.

Sir Lancelot du Lac had fought a hundred jousts. He had known joy and pride and excitement at the thought of entering the lists; once or twice, he had felt anger; more often, simple boredom.

Never until tonight had he known fear.

When a ragged little page came to lead him to the hall, Lancelot sent word that he was too weary to join his host. At least that much was true, for when he cast himself upon his bed, he fell instantly asleep.

Chapter 14

. . .

SOME hours later, Lancelot sighed and opened his eyes, watching the moonlight paint a glowing path across the floor beside his bed. For a moment he had no idea where he was, and while he was still trying to piece it all together, a voice spoke from the darkness.

"Hello, boy."

He sat up, breathing hard, his eyes searching the shadows. "Who's there?"

"What, don't you know me?" It was only when the figure moved that Lancelot could make out the outline of an armored knight. Ice pooled in his gut when moonlight flashed off the gauntlet laid casually upon the windowsill, striking sparks of emerald from the metal. This wasn't real. It couldn't be. He was still dreaming—yes, of course he was. He must be.

"Go away," Lancelot said, forcing himself to lie back. "I need my rest."

"Oh, you'll have plenty of that come tomorrow," the

Green Knight replied, and laughing, pulled off his helm,
setting it on the windowsill beside him. Lancelot could not
help but stare, for he had never before seen the Knight
without his helm. Hair the deep color of pine needles fell to
his shoulders. His skin was lighter, like the first green
leaves of spring. Lancelot had always imagined the Knight
would be hideous, but he was, in his own way, as splendid
as the Lady, his features bold and striking, all sharp angles
and shadowed hollows.

"I warned you," he said. "I told you what would happen,
but you did not believe me. And now it is too late."

"Too late for *what*?" Lancelot demanded, trying to
sound merely annoyed instead of terrified.

"For everything. You've failed, 'tis over—come, don't
tell me you did not know it! Surely even you must have
grasped the import of yesterday's little comedy in the
queen's chamber. How you could have gotten yourself into
such a ridiculous position is beyond me, but you did. Keep
your oath to Arthur and your word to Guinevere is forfeit,
turn it round and it comes out just the same. A broken
promise, lad. You know what that means."

The Lady of the Lake had spoken of this at their parting. She had said Lancelot must be very careful of any oath
he undertook, for his strength lay in his honor, and a broken vow would mean the end of all. Lancelot had listened
with but half an ear, dismissing her advice as the sort of
thing any fond foster mother might say when sending her
son into the world.

He should have known the Lady of the Lake never
wasted words.

"I have served my king and queen with honor—"

"Honor? You do not know the meaning of the word. But
the fault is not altogether yours. 'Twas the Lady who ruined you; you dwelt in Avalon too long. I told her you

weren't human anymore, not in any way that matters. In fact," he laughed, "you're very much like me."

Lancelot stiffened with outrage. "I am nothing like you!"

"You are. But at least I am what I was made to be; you're naught but the Lady's poppet. Oh, you look like a man, but inside—" the Knight tapped his emerald breastplate, "—hollow as a reed."

Lancelot felt his own chest tighten as though the Knight had given him a blow.

The Knight stood and picked up his helm, adding with sudden fury, "By oak and ash let us hope she has learned her lesson this time, for her morbid fascination with mortals has grown beyond all bounds. To actually steal one for herself so she might keep it like some loathsome little pet was more than my patience could withstand. I told her it would all end badly, but did she listen?"

"What do you mean?" Lancelot demanded. "Enough of your hints and riddles—speak plainly or begone."

The Knight glanced over at him, the moonlight limning cheek and brow with silver. "The Lady has no time for a servant who disappoints her, lad, and no use for a champion who has forsworn his vow." His teeth flashed in a grin as he donned his helm. "Work it out yourself."

Resting one mailed hand on the windowsill, he vaulted lightly into the night. Lancelot threw off his coverlet and ran to the window, leaning far out to stare down at the cobbles below, brilliant in the moonlight. They were empty, and nothing moved in the courtyard of Corbenic save the whisper of the wind carrying a stray leaf across the stones.

Chapter 15

. . .

ELAINE sat at her tower window, Lavaine's jupon in her lap, watching the forest take shape against the lightening sky. When she saw Lavaine himself hurry across the courtyard, she rose stiffly and picked up the sleeve from the foot of her bed, turning it in her hands.

At last she covered it with Lavaine's jupon and went down to the hall, wishing she had thought to bring a cloak. The long room was deserted; the housecarls were already up, and the shutters had been taken down, but no one had thought to stir the fire. With an exasperated sigh, Elaine knelt and laid a handful of twigs into the pit, scattering ash as she blew upon the buried coals. When they caught, she added a few logs and sank back upon her heels, holding her hands out to the flame.

"Good morning, Lady Elaine." She started at the sound of the knight's voice close beside her, so stiff and cool that if not for his accent, she would not have known that it was him.

And that, she told herself firmly, is the difference between night and day. Once again he is a knight of Camelot and now the time has come for him to return to his own world. It won't be long—a few more minutes—and you can cry all you like, but for pity's sake don't make a fool of yourself.

"Good day," she answered. "I hope you slept well."

Even before he shook his head, she knew he hadn't. The rosy flush had vanished from his cheeks, and his eyes were sunk in shadowed hollows. When he held out his hand to help her up, she barely touched his cool fingers with her own and sprang nimbly to her feet, making a business of brushing off her skirt.

"No, I dreamed—" He shook his head, smiling with ashen lips. "It was nothing. Lady, may I leave this with you?" He held out his covered shield.

She took it from him, running a finger over the rough canvas surface. "You will send for it?" When he did not answer, she nodded, not daring to lift her eyes from the shield. "It will be safe until your servant comes for it."

"Oh, good, you're ready," Lavaine called from the doorway. He hurried inside, Torre close behind him, planted a smacking kiss on her cheek, then brushed her brow. "What have you been doing? You're all over ash. Is that my jupon?" He seized it from the table and shook it out. "And what is this?" he asked, stooping to retrieve the red sleeve from the floor.

"Nothing," Elaine said curtly.

"'Tis a kind thought, but I don't think it's done to wear a sister's favor in the lists."

"Lavaine, please—" Elaine began, shooting him a fierce look, but Lavaine only danced away, holding it just beyond her reach. She wished that he was just a little younger so she might box his ears.

"Oh, I *see*." Lavaine laughed. "It's not for me at all."

"Give it to me," Torre ordered.

"But why, it can't be yours! And if it isn't mine . . . I wonder who it's meant for?" Lavaine wagged his brows comically at his sister.

Elaine waited for the knight to say that he had asked it of her, but he did not speak a word. Indeed, he did not seem to be listening at all, but was staring past her toward the far end of the hall.

"Lavaine, enough," she said, speaking past the sudden tightness in her throat.

"Wait, I see it now. It must be yours!" Lavaine cried, all high good humor as he tossed the sleeve toward the knight.

Lancelot was only dimly aware of the conversation. His head was aching fiercely, and he could not stop thinking of the dream he'd had the night before. A very odd dream it had been, so vivid—

He stiffened, gazing toward the corner of the hall. There was something in the shadows, he was almost certain of it, but the pounding pressure behind his eyes made it difficult to focus. He started when something hit him in the chest, putting out a hand to catch a small bundle of soft fabric, not daring to take his gaze from the corner, where he was now certain he could make out a pair of green eyes regarding him unblinkingly. He let out a shaking breath when a cat leapt from the trestle table and padded out the door.

It was only then he became aware of the others watching him expectantly, but he had no idea why or what he was supposed to say. Elaine was flushed, Torre scowling. Only Lavaine seemed oblivious to the tension in the room.

"Come, Elly, give me a kiss," he laughed, holding out his arms, "and wish me luck today."

"Good fortune, Lavaine," she murmured, touching her lips to his brow. "And to you, sir," she added stiffly.

Lancelot stared down at the bit of crimson fabric in his hands. It was a sleeve. Her sleeve. The token he had begged of her—had it only been last night? It seemed years ago that they had walked hand in hand into the courtyard, laughing. He could not in honor accept this from her now. Yet he had already accepted it, albeit with something less than courtesy, and was now honor bound to keep it. Or was he? What did he know of honor, after all? The pain in his head made it difficult to think.

Elaine made the decision for him. "May I have that?" She held out her hand. When he saw that it was trembling, his hesitation vanished, and he thrust the sleeve into his belt.

"I will wear it."

"There is no need—"

"But I would like to."

"Oh, for God's sake, Elly, let him have it," Torre snapped. "It's just a sleeve. You have enough to disguise a dozen knights at need. Sir, your horse is waiting." He flashed a contemptuous look at Lancelot and added pointedly, "'Tis past time you were gone."

With that, Torre turned to his brother, flinging an arm across Lavaine's shoulders. With his free hand he gestured Lancelot forward, sweeping them both across the hall. "Now, Lavaine, mind you keep your lance point steady. You have a tendency to dip it at the last."

"I'll remember."

Lancelot looked back. Elaine stood very straight, his shield propped against the smoke-blackened wall beside her. She looked pale today, and older, with her hair scraped back into a thick plait that hung over one shoulder, the edge brushing the plain hempen girdle at her hips. One hand lifted in a gesture of farewell, though she would not meet his eyes.

As he crossed the threshold, he called back, "Lady Elaine, I will come for the shield myself. God keep you until then."

He had one glimpse of her smile before Torre closed the door behind them.

"There is your horse," Torre said. "Get on it. Do it now, without another word, for my patience is as worn out as your welcome. If you want your shield back, send a servant."

Once again, Torre had the better of him. Before Lancelot could begin to imagine a reply, Torre had stepped back into the hall and slammed the door firmly in his face.

Chapter 16

• • •

IF I were king of Benwick, Lancelot mused, *I would make Elaine a queen.* If King Ban's wits had not been scrambled as a morning egg, Benwick would never have been lost. There would have been no flight from the burning castle, no collapse of Benwick's monarch upon some distant shore, no chance for the Lady of the Lake to scoop up Ban's infant son and bear him off to Avalon.

Yet the Lady had said that was Lancelot's destiny. He remembered well their parting at Camelot, when she said his future was foretold.

But what now? If the Green Knight had not been a dream last night—and Lancelot was becoming increasingly convinced that he had not—then the Lady had no use for him anymore. Did that mean he had somehow turned from the path of his destiny into a strange, uncharted landscape where his future was his own to make? If he was not to be du Lac, champion of Avalon, who was he? For a moment he was entirely disoriented, adrift in a world that made no sense, and then he remembered Elaine smiling up at him from the shelter of his arms.

I am still Galahad, he thought. *Elaine is no will o' the wisp to vanish in bright sunlight, but a woman of flesh and blood.* He thought that he could bear it all—the shame, the loss, the failure—if only he had her.

But first he must survive this day.

Twelve hours, he thought. *By then, it will be over, and I can go back to Corbenic. All I have to do is ride in the tournament, Arthur's great tournament, in which his chief knight will play a merry prank upon his lord by riding in disguise. What a good jest it will be!*

Lancelot had never felt less like fighting—or jesting, for that matter. The morning sun shone brightly through a canopy of palest green that danced and shimmered as a small breeze rustled the treetops, yet the day seemed dull and drear. *I must take hold of myself,* he thought. *I must carry this off with style, so Arthur will believe it was a joke. Then he will forgive me for my deception.*

Though the morning air was mild, he shivered. There was that word again. *Deception.*

It was then he knew why he felt so strange. He was *not* himself—not the man he had been yesterday when he awoke in Camelot, before Guinevere had bidden him to her chamber.

He remembered a day when he was very young, no more than five or six. It was one of the rare times the Lady had decided to play at mothering, clad in a simple linen shift with her bright hair all bound up in a coif. She had led him to a hillside where Avalon lay stretched out before them in glittering green and silver, fed him milk and honey with her own hand, and told him stories of Sir Gahmuret, who traveled all the world in errantry and won the love of three queens.

"I will be a great knight, too," Lancelot had cried, tugging at her sleeve.

The Lady smiled down at him. "Indeed you will, my pet. The greatest of all. No earthly knight will defeat you."

His childish heart had swelled with love and pride and a fierce determination to never disappoint her. He had always worked hard—the Green Knight's hand was too heavy to permit slacking—but from that moment on, he redoubled his efforts. When he arrived at Camelot, he found the other squires laughably soft and shoddy. Even when he faced seasoned knights, their skills were so far inferior to his that he felt himself invincible.

Until his match with Sir Gawain.

Gawain had not been soft. Nor had he been inferior. He had been quick and tough, and the blow he had given Lancelot had nearly flung him headlong from his horse.

Nearly. But not quite. Against all hope—against all reason—Lancelot kept his seat. That was when he understood that the Lady's words had not sprung from faith in his abilities. They were merely an announcement of the fate she had decreed: No earthly knight *could* defeat him, however deserving of victory that knight might be.

Gawain, not knowing it was hopeless, defended his title with all the skill and strength he had worked a lifetime to attain. He had taken the best that Lancelot could offer and remained upright in the saddle, not once, but a second time, as well. Only on the third try did Lancelot finally manage to unhorse him.

As Lancelot had ridden through the cheering crowd to accept his victory garland, he had known the truth at last. He was du Lac, made invincible by the Lady's magic so he might serve King Arthur and win glory everlasting. What man would not envy him such a fate?

"You've failed, 'tis over," the Green Knight had said last night, "you know what that means." .

Lancelot did know. He'd known all along, even before the Green Knight appeared, but only now did he believe it. The Lady of the Lake did not dismiss her erring servant with no more than a slap upon the wrist.

Today I die.

"Sir?"

Lancelot started at the touch on his arm. Lavaine was halted beside him, his young face twisted with concern.

"Sir, are you quite well?"

"No. Yes. I am well enough," Lancelot said, forcing a laugh. "Just a bit distracted. I'm sorry, what were you saying?"

"That my friend lives nearby. I often used to visit him when we lived by the river. He's a wondrous learned fellow. I thought—we're nearly there and 'tis so early yet— that we might stop."

"Very well," Lancelot said indifferently. "So long as it does not make us late."

They found the hermit by the river, his robe tucked up into his belt as he checked his lines. "Lavaine!" he called, his broad brown face creasing in a grin as he spied them on the bank. "It has been an age. But as usual, you are just in time to break your fast."

He climbed nimbly up the path and caught Lavaine in a one-armed hug, holding his catch well away from the young knight. "You look well, my child," he said. "And who is your friend?"

"A knight of Arthur's court," Lavaine answered, "he has been our guest at Corbenic."

"God's greeting to you," the hermit said with a friendly nod. "I hope that you are hungry, too. The river has been generous this morning."

Above the wild beard, the man's eyes were kind. "I am afraid we have no time to eat," Lancelot said. "Though I thank you."

"Ah, of course, you two are off to the great tournament. Are you acting as a squire, Lavaine, or should I be addressing you as *sir*?"

"You should not," Lavaine said, hooking his arm through the hermit's with easy familiarity, "though I have been knighted since I saw you last. This is my first tournament, and I thought—that is, if you are not too busy—that you might hear my confession."

"I hope I am never too busy to perform my office," the hermit said. "Come inside."

He stood aside and gestured them to walk into an opening in the hillside. Lancelot stepped in, expecting a dark cave. Instead, he found himself in a lofty chamber, roofed with tree roots and supported by strong columns of stone. Muted sunlight streamed through the opening, bathing the cavern in a cool green glow. The furnishings were simple: two stools, a table, and a pallet of sweet grass.

Lancelot turned slowly round. "How fortunate you were to find such a place as this!"

"God led me here," the hermit said, hanging the fish upon a peg.

"It was nothing but a small cavern then," Lavaine said, "What you see took years of patient labor."

The hermit smiled. "He speaks as one who knows! My little woodland flock worked off many a sin with spade and pick. Digging is a fine penance for rowdy children. Please, sir, sit down. We shan't be long."

He and Lavaine vanished through a second opening, leading to some deeper cavern. Lancelot sat down upon a stool, leaned his elbow on the table, and rested his chin in his hand.

Perhaps he should follow Lavaine's example and make his confession to this kindly priest. But what difference would it make? Arthur might believe he could be washed clean of sin with a few words, but try as he might, Lancelot could not share his faith. What would a Christian priest know of the vow he had made to the Lady of the Lake? Even if he could be brought to understand, he could not change what had been said and done, nor could any man repair a broken oath.

He seized parchment, pen, and ink from a shelf and penned the few lines that would provide for Elaine's future, then folded it, dripped wax upon it from a taper, and impressed it with his seal.

When the hermit and Lavaine returned, he was already mounted. "Father," he said, holding out the parchment, "hold this for me, would you? If I do not return for it within three days, have it taken to King Arthur. Let us go," he added curtly to Lavaine, "the hour grows late."

Lavaine glanced up at him and nodded, his smile vanishing. "Yes, sir, I am ready now."

The hermit laid a hand on Lancelot's knee. "Are you sure you would not like me to hear your confession? I am at your service, sir . . ."

"No, we haven't time."

"Oh, I wouldn't worry about the time," the hermit answered easily. "These tournaments go on all day, and latecomers are always welcomed by the losing side. I have some experience in these matters," he added with a wry smile, "for I was once a knight myself, though it has been many a long year since I took up arms."

He gazed up at Lancelot, his light brown eyes filled with sympathy. *I was once as you are,* he seemed to say, *I know your trials, your hopes and fears. Whatever you might tell me, I will understand.*

But he wouldn't. Not the things that Lancelot could tell him. He shook his head, rejecting the silent offer.

The hermit sighed. "May God be with you, my son, until we meet again."

We will not, Lancelot thought.

The hermit looked at him sharply beneath his tangled brows, then sighed again, his hand falling to his side.

They rode off between the ash and poplar trees, and soon the soothing rush of the river was mingled with the excited voices of the crowd gathered around the tourney field. The two knights dismounted and taking turns to act as squire, donned their helms and armor.

Lavaine's face was so white that every freckle stood out sharply.

"Don't worry," Lancelot said. "Once you're in there, you will be fine."

The boy let out a shaking laugh. "Is it that obvious?"

"All knights feel the same before a battle—even if it is with friends," Lancelot lied. He had never felt the least fear before any sort of encounter. But then, he had never had reason to be afraid . . . until today. Impulsively, he turned to his companion. "Lavaine, you have given me nothing but friendship and courtesy. I know I can trust you to keep my name to yourself." The boy looked at him expectantly. "I am Lancelot du Lac."

Lavaine's jaw dropped. "No! You are—? Oh, sir, I will not say a word. The great du Lac," he whispered, awestruck.

"Not great, just a knight with some small skill. Look there," Lancelot said, pointing over the charging knights to the royal pavilion. It was draped with royal purple, and above the carven throne a single diamond caught the light and threw it back in a thousand glittering facets. "Do you see him there, your king, all robed in red? Look on him and you see greatness."

"Yes," Lavaine whispered. "I see him, the dread Pendragon. Now—oh, sir, if I should be struck blind today, I would not be sorry—no, I wouldn't, not a bit, not now that I have seen . . ." He looked from Arthur to Lancelot, then, blushing, at the earth between his feet.

Despite all, Lancelot nearly laughed. The poor boy was so dreadfully in earnest, yet there was something touching in his innocent regard. All at once Lancelot felt better; the fog of fear and sorrow dissipated, scattered like mist before the sunrise. *I am Lancelot du Lac,* he thought, *a knight of Camelot, and if I am no more, I will give no man cause to say that I was less.* He raised the sleeve to his lips before winding it about his helm.

"While you still have the use of your eyes," he said to Lavaine, trying and failing to repress a grin, "turn them to the engagement and let us see how matters stand."

Lavaine laughed, a little shamefaced, and obeyed. "Look how strong the king's knights are!" he cried. "Those northern lords cannot withstand them. See how they are driven back. Oh, sir, we must hurry, or it will be done before we strike a blow. Come, let us take our place among your friends and kin."

"A paltry adventure that would be!" Lancelot laughed and signed the marshal over. "We shall fight for the northern kings," he said, holding out his spear so the marshal might bind it with a ribbon proclaiming his allegiance. "Come, Lavaine," he urged, "let us join the weaker party and see if we can change their fortune."

Without waiting for an answer, he charged into the fray.

Lavaine followed. No sooner had he taken the field than a knight confronted him, demanding that he proclaim his name and allegiance. "Lavaine of Corbenic. I fight for the northern kings," he managed, the words rasping in his parched mouth.

"Then you shall not pass."

"Who denies me passage?" Lavaine returned.

"Sir Lucando Butler."

The preliminaries over, the two retreated for a space, then charged. To his astonishment, Lavaine found that Lancelot was right. He felt nothing but the keenest excitement as they crashed together—and when he found himself still upon his horse and his opponent on the ground, he laughed aloud and turned to find another challenge.

In the time it had taken Lavaine to ride his first joust, Lancelot had unseated three knights and was preparing to engage a fourth. *The tales are true then,* Lavaine thought, momentarily diverted from the press of heaving horses and clashing armor all around him. Nor was he the only one. Several of Arthur's knights had stopped to watch Lancelot's advance.

"Who is he?" Lavaine heard them cry, one to another, a question none could answer.

Then the press moved closer, and Lavaine was once again in the thick of it, facing his own opponent. Sir Bedivere did not give up easily; it took three charges before the matter was decided. By the time Bedivere was off his horse, Lavaine's charger was winded. Drawing aside to give the beast a moment's respite, he became aware of three knights beside him, passing a waterskin from hand to hand.

"Of course it is him," one said decisively. "It must be. No one rides like Sir Lancelot."

"Yes, Gawain, I believe it is. Lancelot, disguised . . . and bearing a lady's sleeve upon his helm. Well, well, so much for his injury!"

"There is no dishonor in riding with a blank shield," Sir Gawain said reprovingly. "Nor in accepting a lady's favor. But come, our companions have need of us."

He rode off, leaving the others behind. "Look you,

Dinadan," one said to the other, "I have a thought. What if
we—?"

Sir Dinadan shook his head and said something too low
to hear. Both knights turned to look at Lavaine, and then
went off together.

Lavaine watched them for a moment. They rode a short
distance, then separated, though neither returned immediately to the fight. Instead, they rode among the king's
knights, stopping every now and then to speak with one of
their companions. No doubt they were spreading the word
of Lancelot's arrival, Lavaine thought, and then he had no
time for thought as he was challenged once again.

This was his hardest-fought battle. By the time he brought
down his opponent, he was exhausted, and his mount was
lame. Dismounting, he led it aside and looked around to
see Lancelot preparing to ride against another knight—Sir
Gawain, Lavaine realized, judging by the shield. He paused
a moment, eager to see this contest, but before Lancelot
had begun his charge, he was set upon by a band of the
king's knights.

Four—no, five—no, eight charged him from all sides,
and Lavaine's shout of warning was lost in the thunder of
hoofbeats. He strained to see what was happening, but
Lancelot had vanished within the press. A moment later, a
cheer went up from the king's side.

"Unhorsed! He is down!"

Lavaine ran to the nearest knight. "Give me your
horse!" he cried.

"Stand aside, boy," the man, some king of Scotland by
his arms, said, and lifting his shield, he dealt Lavaine a
blow that knocked him sprawling. Lavaine scrambled to his
feet and leapt upon the Scottish king, dragging him from
the saddle. Quite forgetting to draw his sword, he raised his
fist and knocked him to the ground, then mounted his horse

and forced his way through the press, leaping from the horse before it had halted to land beside his fallen friend.

"Sir—" With shaking fingers, he fumbled at the lacings of the helm.

"No." Lancelot's hand shot out and grasped his wrist. "Help me mount again."

"Are you wounded?"

"It is nothing." Lancelot's breath came quick and shallow; his face, beneath his visor, was parchment pale and slicked with sweat.

"But—"

"Get me to my horse!"

Lavaine grasped his hand and pulled him to his feet. It was horrible to watch him drag himself up the side of his great charger, but Lancelot would hear no dissent. King Arthur leaned so far over the balustrade of his pavilion that it seemed he was in danger of tumbling out. Only when Lancelot was on his horse did the king resume his seat. When the knight took up his lance, a great cry went up, not only from his side, but from the stands, as well.

Now the force of Lancelot's charge was redoubled. He fought like one possessed, cutting a swathe through Arthur's knights, and one by one they fell beneath his implacable assault. It seemed no time at all until the marshal threw down a white scarf from his high seat. Trumpets blared, and the knights stilled upon the field.

"Victory," the marshal cried, "to the northern lords. And the diamond to the knight with the red sleeve upon his helm, the knight with the white shield!"

Lavaine cantered to Lancelot's side. He sat unmoving, his helm drooping nearly to his chest. "Sir, you have won!" Lavaine shouted. "Hear how they cry out for you! Sir, look, the king is waiting, you must go to him—"

"No."

Lavaine leaned closer, certain he had not heard aright.

"No," Lancelot repeated hoarsely. "Lavaine, help me—"

Then the others were upon them, pressing close. "Go, sir," they cried, "the diamond is yours!"

"No—" Lancelot gasped, "no diamond—give me air—"

"But you have won it!" they cried. "It is your prize!"

Lancelot raised his head. "My prize—" he drew a hissing breath. "Death," he said clearly, and as the knights drew back, astonished, he set spurs to his charger and burst through them.

Lavaine followed after. Lancelot's horse slowed; at last it stood trembling at the edge of the field.

"Help me. Away from this place. Hurry," Lancelot said, and Lavaine seized the reins of Lancelot's charger and kicked the Scottish horse into a gallop, sweeping past the astonished knights and into the shelter of the trees.

"Farther," Lancelot gasped, "do not let them find us."

Bewildered, Lavaine led him deeper into the forest until Lancelot gave a terrible cry and pitched headlong from his saddle.

Lavaine's hands were shaking so, he could barely unbuckle Lancelot's armor. Blood seeped between the fastenings; his hands slipped upon the straps. When at last he lifted the breastplate, he could only stare in shock at the broken wooden haft protruding from Lancelot's side, the spear tip buried deep within the torn flesh.

"When—how—"

"Bors. Beneath my shield. When they brought me down."

Lancelot made a movement as though to lift himself but fell back with a groan, his hand groping blindly for his helm. He drew the red sleeve from its crest and clenched it in his fist. "Draw it out, Lavaine."

"I cannot!" Lavaine was close to tears. "I will kill you if I draw it—"

"I will die if you do not," Lancelot said steadily, then his face contorted, and he cried, "For God's sake, help me, get it out—"

"Yes, all right—" Lavaine's breath came in gasping sobs as he put two hands on the wooden shaft. "Too much blood—I cannot get a purchase—" He wiped it with the edge of his tunic and tried again. "Now—steady, sir—" He gave a great shout as he pulled the spearhead from Lancelot's flesh.

A gush of blood burst from the wound, soaking Lavaine's hands and spattering his face. With a hoarse cry, he threw the spearhead aside. *God help me,* he thought. *God help me, what do I do now? He needs a surgeon, not me, I know naught of healing.* But there was no surgeon to be found. The small glade was empty save for the two of them.

"You did well, my friend," Lancelot whispered. "Thank you." He brought the sleeve to his side, clasping it hard against the gushing wound, then his head fell back upon the leaves and his eyes closed.

I have killed him, Lavaine thought. *I have killed Sir Lancelot.* With trembling fingers, he touched Lancelot's neck, a sobbing moan bursting from his lips when he found the pulse beating beneath the pallid jaw. Not dead—not yet. But he soon would be.

Stop the bleeding, Lavaine thought, staring transfixed at the spreading pool of blood. *That's what I must do. But how?*

He pressed the sleeve against the wound, staring in terror as it instantly soaked through. *God, don't let him die,* he prayed. *Help me, send someone to find us.*

But no one came.

"It is up to me," Lavaine said aloud. "If I do nothing, he will die. But what am I to do?"

All at once, the answer came to him. He pressed the wadded fabric against the wound, and using his knife, cut strips from his tunic to bind it round the unconscious knight's ribs. A clumsy bandage, soon soaked through, but he daren't think of that. He heaved Lancelot facedown across his horse and led him toward the hermit's dwelling.

Chapter 17

. . .

"AYE, it was Sir Lancelot," Gawain said, throwing his helm across the pavilion and running a hand through his sweat-soaked hair. "I never saw his face, but I am certain 'twas he."

"What went on out there?" Arthur demanded. "Who set upon him like that?"

"Agravaine," Gawain said miserably, "Dinadan, Ector De Maris, Bors—"

"Bors?"

"Aye, but he didn't know 'twas Lancelot himself. Agravaine was saying 'twas some base knight fighting in Sir Lancelot's style, some muddled tale about how this man sought to dishonor Sir Lancelot by mimicking him—I didna catch the most of it, sire."

"And did Agravaine believe this nonsense?"

Gawain could not meet his eyes. "He says he did."

"I see." After a moment, the king said, "How badly was he wounded?"

"He could barely keep his seat. And Bors said—he said his spear is broken, the tip stuck fast in the strange knight."

Arthur walked to the balustrade and looked over the crowd below. "Find him, Gawain," he said without turning. "Find him for me and bring him back."

"Aye, sire, I will."

Chapter 18

• • •

THE village was afire. People fled screaming from their cottages, and the air was thick with smoke shot through with flame. There must have been a battle, Lancelot thought as he fought his way through the press. He could not remember which battle it had been, but that didn't matter now. The village was burning, and he had to find Elaine. As he rounded the corner, he saw the tower of Corbenic, smoke pouring from the highest window.

Wresting the door open, he plunged into the smoke-filled hall, where Torre sat alone at the high table.

"False knight," Torre said, "you stole my youth and strength."

"No—no, it wasn't my fault you weren't good enough—"

"You knew he wasn't good enough," a deep voice said behind him. "No earthly knight can defeat you."

Lancelot spun around and found himself facing the Green Knight.

"Welladay, here we are again," the Green Knight said,

"I had thought to be rid of you by now." He gestured toward the wall of the tower and a portion of stone fell away, revealing a dark passageway. "Go on, manikin, that way is yours."

"Where does it lead?"

"A good question. But I fear you must find the answer for yourself."

Lancelot took a few steps toward the entrance. Far, far away, flames licked against the walls and a faint echo of anguished wails was carried up to him on a searing blast of air, along with the foul stench of rotting flesh.

"I told you the Lady kept you in Avalon too long. You have no soul now."

"I do!" Lancelot drew his sword and advanced on the Knight, but he only laughed and said, "Prove it. Find the Grail."

A whirl of green grew and swirled about the hall. Fire licked at the beams, and from a great distance, Lancelot heard a woman scream.

"Elaine!" he cried, "I will find you—"

And he raced up the stairway to the tower, flames licking at his heels. Through the smoke, he glimpsed Elaine— or no, it was another maiden, holding something in her hands that shimmered with a light too bright to look upon. He flung an elbow across his eyes, shielding them from the terrible beauty of that unbearable light . . . And then the maiden was gone, and he was alone in the burning tower. He turned back, but the steps were gone, there was no way out, he was trapped, choking, burning beams crashing all around, and the floor gave way beneath him.

When he woke again he was cold, so cold that knew he must be dead. He tried to open his eyes, but they were weighted shut. He remembered the corpses in the crypt at Norhaut with coins upon their sunken lids. There lay his tomb, buried in the earth beneath the enormous marble slab he had once lifted with no effort. Now he was inside it, lying on the marble bier, and at his feet was a silver plaque he'd read on the day he had discovered his name. "Here will lie Sir Lancelot du Lac," it proclaimed in letters silver bright, "son of King Ban of Benwick."

This, he thought, *is hell.* Not the fiery pit, but this frozen emptiness where he would dwell alone forevermore.

"Sir Lancelot!" a voice called urgently, but it was too late; Sir Lancelot was dead. Why would they not let him rest? They slapped his cheeks and waved burnt feathers beneath his nose, and though he felt the blows and breathed in the acrid stench, he could not move nor speak. A deep voice intoned unfamiliar words, pausing now and then while they renewed their efforts, urging him to answer questions he did not understand, but in time they gave up and went away.

Chapter 19

· · ·

"IT was meant to be a jest," Guinevere said, the words coming thickly from her numb lips. Her bower was filled with people, all staring with avid curiosity from her face to the king's. Never had they seen Arthur in such a fury. Only rarely did he lose his temper, and then it was a quick, hot flash that soon subsided. And never, never had he been angry with his queen. Guinevere did not know the man who stood before her, his face stern and his light eyes burning with an icy flame.

"A *jest*?"

"You said—his reputation—not fair to the others—do you not remember? And so he wanted to prove . . . We thought you would be amused," she whispered.

"Did you? Well, Guinevere, I would have been far more amused had I been let in upon the joke."

"Lance—he w-wanted to surprise you."

But he hadn't wanted to. That had been Guinevere's idea, not Lancelot's at all.

"Did you give him your sleeve?" Arthur demanded.

"My sleeve?" Guinevere repeated blankly. "No, of course not."

He had not asked for one. He never had. And he surely would not have broken with his custom on the day she'd sent him out to fight disguised. He had been too angry. But she hadn't cared.

"He wore a lady's favor yesterday," Arthur said, but Guinevere scarcely heard him. She was too busy remembering how she had not thought of Lancelot at all, but only of herself and her own need. Now he was wounded, perhaps dead, and she would never have the chance to tell him she was sorry. She had killed him.

And Arthur would never, ever forgive her for it.

The way he was looking at her now, as though he hated her—she had lost him, lost him forever, and through her own selfish folly. She could not bear the cold contempt in his eyes. She raised shaking hands to cover her face, tears sliding between her fingers.

The slam of her bower door told her that Arthur was gone. She rose and stumbled blindly toward her chamber. Most of her women followed, communicating surprise and sympathy and in some cases, satisfaction, in silent glances.

Only one stayed behind. She slipped out the door and found Sir Agravaine waiting in the corridor.

"Well?" he demanded. "How did she take it?"

"She had her story ready," the damsel answered with a shrug, "and not a bad one, either. She managed to shift the blame—or part of it, at least—to the king himself. Apparently he'd made some jest about Sir Lancelot's reputation unmanning his opponents."

Agravaine laughed unwillingly. "Isn't she the clever bitch? And did the king accept her story?"

"He seemed to. He was still angry, but I think she might

have talked him round. But then—" She smiled slowly. "Guinevere made her mistake. Apparently the red sleeve was not hers at all. When the king told her of it, she went dead white and burst into tears."

"Did she? Did she really?"

"And then the king slammed out of there—"

"With a face like thunder," Agravaine finished happily. "You did well, my dear. Very well indeed. I shall remember you to my mother."

"When will Queen Morgause be here?"

"Soon, I think. Once she learns of this, I believe she will decide the time has come to visit Camelot."

Chapter 20

. . .

LORD Pelleas greeted Will Reeve with courtesy. Though they had met only a few days before, when the reeve had come to supper, Pelleas seemed to think he was here this morning to discuss a stallion sent to him for shoeing.

"You must mind the off foreleg," Pelleas said. "He'll bite, you know, if he's handled roughly."

"Father," Elaine began, but Will Reeve was smiling at his overlord.

"Ah," he said. "That would be Jupiter?"

"Yes, of course." Pelleas stared at the reeve as though he'd just stated something too obvious for words. "Jupiter."

"Aye, my lord," Will said. "I know all about that off foreleg. Thass naught for you to be vexed about."

Pelleas nodded and returned to his perusal of the heavy volume open before him on the trestle table.

Elaine regarded the reeve with approval as she gestured the page to fill his cup. From the first, Will's manner to her father had been just right: respectful without a touch of servility, and he had a trick of following Pelleas's rambling conversation with no sign of disturbance or surprise.

"Many's a time I helped my da shoe old Jupiter when I was nobbut a lad," Will said with a reminiscent smile. "A fine, fettlesome stallion that one was."

Elaine waited until he'd taken his first sip before asking, "What of the north field? How long until you are finished?"

"Give it four more days," he said.

The man went up another notch in her esteem. And if he looked a trifle smug, she could not blame him, for she had expected the planting to take at least another week. They must have worked hard to achieve so much in such a short time.

Will cleared his throat and set his ale down. "Lady, what of Planting Day?"

Elaine rested her chin in her palm. It was tradition to mark the end of spring planting with a day of revelry, with food and ale provided by the lord and dancing on the green. The people were within their rights to ask for it. It would put a heavy strain upon their almost nonexistent resources, but that was not what held Elaine back from agreeing.

"I don't know," she said. "After . . ."

She glanced at Torre, seated below the dais on a stool before the fire, his hands busy with a bit of harness he was mending. He did not *seem* to be listening, but one could never be quite sure, and she had been at great pains to keep him in ignorance of what had happened in the fields the week before. The Day, she always thought of it, for it was the day on which her life had changed forever, and the less the Torre knew of it, the better.

Will followed both her glance and her thought. Really, he was most extraordinarily adept at reading the currents running amongst the family of his overlord.

"I say we do it," he declared. "Thass custom, see? Best to keep going on as even as we can. They know they don't deserve it," he added, lowering his voice, "mortal sorry they are, lady, for what befell that day, and they've done their best to show it. 'Twas a kindly thing you did, ordering food for all who worked—and a canny one, as well."

Their eyes met in a conspiratorial glance that brought a warm glow to Elaine's cheeks. It was very pleasant to know that *someone* understood what she had done, and why, and approved of it wholeheartedly.

"Very well, then, if you think it best. Four days until the planting is done; shall we say next—" She broke off, half rising at the sound of a horn winding in the courtyard.

"Is that Lavaine?" Lord Pelleas said, lifting his head and gazing expectantly toward the door.

"No." Torre let the harness fall as he stood, and Elaine realized that like her, he had been waiting. "No, that is not Lavaine's horn."

Elaine's fingers clenched the edge of the trestle table. She wanted to run out into the yard but could not seem to move.

When the door opened at last, she knew at once the knight who stepped inside, for he was so precisely as she'd imagined him: Tall and broad of shoulder, fair of face and noble of bearing, with hair that shone like falling rain. His gray eyes flicked over the hall, across the dais, and fastened upon Elaine.

"Sir Gawain," she said, "you are very welcome here. Please come in and refresh yourself."

"Thank you, lady." He bowed gracefully and stepped before the dais. "I fear I cannot linger; an urgent errand from the king has brought me hither."

Elaine's legs began to tremble. "What—what is it?"

"Five days ago the king held his great tournament—"

"Is it Lavaine?" Pelleas cried. "Is my son—"

"No, my lord," Gawain said quickly. "I have no news of Sir Lavaine. It is Sir Lancelot I seek."

"Why, has he gone missing?" Torre inquired, his tone just short of insolent. "What a pity."

"I fear he has. But—" Gawain ran a hand across his jaw, looking suddenly exhausted. "On second thought, I would be grateful for a cup of ale."

Elaine gestured the page over and turned to Will Reeve. "I think we are finished for the day," she said, softening her dismissal with a strained smile.

"Aye, lady." He touched his brow and stood, looking sideways at Sir Gawain. "Now, don't vex yourself about Planting Day, I'll manage everything."

This time Elaine's smile was more genuine, as were her thanks as she bid the reeve farewell.

Gawain took the seat beside her and drained his cup in a single draught. Only when it had been refilled did she send the page away, bidding him to leave the flagon on the table.

"Now, Sir Gawain, if you would . . ."

He told them briefly of the tournament. "We think the knight was Sir Lancelot," he finished, "but we cannot be certain."

"He was here," Elaine said. "The knight. He stayed with us before the tournament and went off with my brother Lavaine."

Sir Gawain looked at her with new interest, his gaze so searching that Elaine felt herself begin to blush. "The red sleeve . . . ?" he asked.

"Was mine. His name I cannot tell you, but he borrowed Torre's shield and left his own."

Gawain stood. "May I see it?"

"Yes, I have it in my chamber," Elaine said, jumping to her feet. "Come, I'll show—"

"Bring it here," Torre ordered sharply. "Sir Gawain will wait with us."

Torre either had a very low opinion of her morals or a vastly inflated view of her charms, Elaine thought as she ran up the steps to her chamber and seized the covered shield. She focused on the question to hold her fear at bay, and was still undecided whether to be flattered or furious when she arrived breathless in the hall. "Here it is."

Sir Gawain drew off the cover to reveal a device Elaine had seen only once before, on the day Torre met its owner in the lists. She gazed at it in silence, remembering what was said: that the woman was Queen Guinevere; the knight, Sir Lancelot, the device a silent declaration of his love.

Sir Gawain sighed. "Yes. It is Sir Lancelot's."

"So it is," Torre said, coming over to glance at the shield. "Take it to him, will you, Sir Gawain, and save him the trouble of returning for it." He shrugged and turned away. "That is, if he should have need of it again."

Elaine rounded on her brother. "I never thought to be ashamed of you, but I am now. That you could speak so of a brother knight—he who was our guest—"

"The brother knight who did this," Torre said, striking a fist against his leg, "and then made sport of me to his companions! The guest who took advantage of your innocence and refused to give you so much as his name."

"He *could* not. He was sworn—"

"God, Elly, don't be more of a fool than you must. Look!" he cried, pointing toward the shield. "Whose image do you think that is? He *used* you. Can't you understand that even now? He wanted your token—and whatever else he could have of you. Why not? He had nothing to lose, did he? Not even his good name."

"Sir Torre," Gawain put in, "I think you wrong Sir

Lancelot. He has never been accused of trifling with any lady—"

"Well, he trifled with this one," Torre said. "Come, Elaine, is that not so?"

"It is not," she said. "Whatever you imagine went on between us—"

"*Imagine*? Did I *imagine* him kissing you in the courtyard? Did I *imagine* that he begged your favor as though it meant more to him than life itself? He is a deceitful, lying bastard, and if he's dead, I won't pretend that I am sorry."

"You are a fool," Elaine said coldly, "and you understand nothing of Sir Lancelot—or me." Drawing a deep breath, she turned to their guest. "Sir Gawain, I am heartily sorry you had to witness that. Stay a moment while I fetch my cloak, and I will come with you."

"Lady," Gawain began uncomfortably.

"I *will* go," Elaine said, "if not with you, then on my own. I must. If he is wounded—"

"You will *not*," Torre declared hotly. "If you think for one moment that I will allow you to leave this hall—"

"Peace."

They both turned, astonished, to their father. Lord Pelleas raised himself from his seat, palms braced upon the table. "Torre, you forget yourself," he said mildly. "Sir Gawain, please break your fast with us before continuing your search. I would speak with you before you go. Elaine." Pelleas shook his head and sighed. "To you I would speak privately."

He led her to his chamber, piled high with stacks of books and scrolls of parchments, and brushed a sleeping cat from the one stool. "Sit."

Elaine sat. The cat leapt into her lap, turned itself about, and curled up in a ball.

"Often and often I have heard you speak of Sir Lancelot du Lac," Pelleas said. "And never well."

Elaine drew her finger down the cat's spine. "I did not know him then."

"And you do now?"

"A little."

"This man you know—a little—" Pelleas said. "Is it true that he has kissed you?"

"It is."

Pelleas bent to retrieve a piece of vellum from the floor. He made to toss it on the table, then halted and looked down at it. "With your leave?"

"Yes." Elaine waited for some response, but once again, her father seemed to have forgotten her. "Indeed," she added boldly, "with my encouragement."

Pelleas glanced up. "I beg your pardon?"

"It doesn't bear repeating," Elaine said wearily.

"I should think not." Pelleas set the vellum down upon a pile and turned to her, his expression stern. "I never got on well with your mother's father, you know. How strange that after all these years, I should find myself in sympathy with him."

Not now, Elaine thought. *Not another sojourn into the past. I haven't time or patience—*

"But for a moment," Pelleas went on, a twinkle in his light blue eyes, "I could have sworn it was your mother talking. So you are determined to seek out Sir Lancelot?"

"Yes."

"Do you understand what Torre referred to before, the rumors about Sir Lancelot and the queen?"

Elaine nearly fell off her stool, wincing as the cat, alarmed, dug sharp claws into her stomach. She'd had no idea that her father was aware of anything that had happened in Britain since Joseph of Arimethea arrived. "I know of the rumors."

"They may well be true," Pelleas remarked, retrieving

another scrap from the floor. This time, when he examined it, she knew it was merely an excuse to keep from looking at her. "Such things happen far more often than is generally known. A young queen, a handsome knight . . . oh, yes, it happens. It may have happened this time. Would you go to him even so?"

Elaine caught the cat's paw between two fingers and detached it from her kirtle. "I would."

Pelleas leaned against the corner of the table and regarded her for a long moment. She braced herself, expecting some long-winded lecture, but he only said, "Why?"

"Because I love him."

Pelleas shook his head. "No. I'm sorry, Elaine, but—"

"If he is—if he and the queen—I can't believe he would be happy like that. Not knowing how he feels about King Arthur. I think that I could—"

"Change him? Child, if there is one thing I know about men and women, it is that neither can change the other."

"Not change him," Elaine said. "I would not do that."

"Then you would give yourself to a man who loves another?"

"Not that, either. I say I love him, but of course I can't be certain of that yet. Nor can I say if he loves me. But there *was* something between us. I know it sounds absurd when he was here for but a day, yet it was so. And not only on my side, I'm sure of it. Whether it would grow to love, I cannot say, but I do know that if he is lying wounded somewhere I must go to him."

"Very well. You shall go with Sir Gawain. He is an honorable knight. But you will take Mistress Brisen, as well."

Elaine leapt up, spilling the cat from her lap, and threw her arms around her father. "Thank you."

He smiled and kissed her cheek. "I knew your mother for a fortnight when I sued for her hand, but my mind was

set within five minutes of our first meeting. As was hers—
to her father's great distress. I pray God to send you joy,
my child, but for good or ill, this path is yours to follow. I
can only trust that you will not forget your own dear
mother, nor do aught to shame my trust in you."

"I won't," Elaine promised. "But Torre—"

"I will speak with him," Pelleas said, and sighed. "Indeed, 'tis past time I did so. Go, make ready, and leave the
rest to me."

Chapter 21

· · ·

THEY found Lancelot the next day. It happened quite by chance, when they came upon Lavaine in the marketplace, and he related all that had happened after the tournament.

"Sir Lancelot lives," Lavaine assured them, "though he is very ill. No, he can't be moved," he said in answer to Gawain's questions as they turned into the forest, "but he is best where he is. Father Bernard is a notable healer."

Once they reached the cave's entrance, Gawain declared his intention to leave them and ride back to Camelot.

Elaine was sorry to see him go, and a bit puzzled that after searching so long and hard for Sir Lancelot, he would desert them on the very brink of attaining his goal. But Gawain would not be gainsaid, nor would he stay even to accept the meal that Father Bernard offered him.

"Sir Lancelot is in good hands," he said, "and I must return to court. Sir Lavaine, would you ride with me? You can give the king a full account of this matter."

"Oh!" Lavaine flushed. "What do you think, Father? Can you spare me?"

"You go along, Lavaine," the hermit answered, "we shall manage very well."

"Then yes," Lavaine said, "thank you, Sir Gawain."

Gawain smiled at the boy. "Good. I would hear more of your part in the tournament, and I know the king will want to thank you personally for assisting Sir Lancelot."

They went off together, Lavaine looking slightly dazed and very happy as he turned to wave before vanishing between the trees.

Father Bernard led Elaine and Brisen into the cave where Lancelot lay sleeping on a pallet.

Brisen's face grew grim as she made a brief examination. "He's very weak."

Elaine stroked Lancelot's hot, dry brow. She sensed that he was aware of her touch; his eyelids seemed to flicker just a little. She traced the dark, winged brows with her fingertip and smoothed the thick black hair behind his ear.

He lay with his head turned toward her, his face quite still and peaceful, but with a grayish tinge to his skin that frightened her. And he was so thin. Astonishing that he could have lost so much flesh in so short a time. His collarbones stood out, and every bone in his deep-sprung rib cage was visible beneath the bandage wound round his chest. It was clean, she noted hopefully, but when she said as much to Brisen, the dark-eyed healer merely shook her head.

"It isn't draining," she said, and Father Bernard, standing just behind her, nodded his agreement.

"Good evening, Sir Lancelot," Elaine said, watching him closely. Had there been some movement? She thought there was, so subtle that she could not have said just what it was, only that he seemed hear her. Or was she only seeing what she wanted to see?

She took his hand, holding it between both of hers. "Lancelot, can you hear me?" she asked. "I know you cannot speak, but can you show me?"

She searched his face anxiously, but there was no change. The thick black lashes lay unmoving against his pale cheeks, his lips did not seek to form a word or even the ghost of a smile.

"His spirit has fled," Brisen said behind her. She placed a hand upon Lancelot's brow. "Lady, he is far away." She closed her eyes and was silent for so long that Elaine began to wonder if she'd dropped off, but at last she sighed deeply and looked at Elaine, her dark eyes filled with pity.

"What can we do?"

"There is nothing any of us can do now . . . save you, perhaps." Brisen gazed down upon the sleeping knight. "Talk to him. Call him back if you can. And send for me if there is any change."

• • •

AFTER an eternity, the silence was pierced by another voice. Lancelot could not make out the words, but the tone was as soothing as water over stone, beckoning him, drawing him back into the pain and flame.

"No," he tried to say, "no, let me rest," but he could not form the words. Still the voice went on, and still he fought against it. The battle was sharp and brief, but then he knew that he was winning; the pain subsided, the voice faded until he was once again at peace. And then a despairing cry cut through the empty darkness.

"Oh, Galahad, you have to try."

Something stirred in the silence of the crypt. Not du Lac, for he was dead, slain by the will of the Lady of the Lake. It was the Knight of the Red Sleeve who woke and knew it was his lady's voice that called to him.

"He cannot hear you," a deep voice said. "I am sorry, lady, but I fear you've come too late."

Where was she? The darkness was too heavy; he could not find his way. And then she spoke again.

"I will fetch Brisen. She must tell us what to do."

No, no, don't leave, he cried, but she could not hear him. With the greatest effort of his life, he forced his lifeless finger to tighten around hers.

"He does hear!" She took his hand, chafing it between her own, and the warmth of her touch spread up his arm. "You go, Father," she said, "I will stay here."

Her voice was like a silver thread, showing him the way. When she fell silent, he was lost, slipping back, away from her. He squeezed her hand again, silently begging her to go on speaking.

"I would have come sooner," she said, "but I did not know where you were. No one knew. Sir Gawain came to Corbenic looking for you, and told me what had happened at the tourney."

Her words made little sense at first: Gawain, Corbenic— these were familiar, though he felt as though a thousand years had passed since he had heard them. But as she spoke on, images formed in his mind, first dim, then brighter.

"Sir Gawain was terribly upset by what had happened and so ashamed that his brother was one of the knights who set upon you. Apparently it was all a mistake—they thought you were some stranger pretending to be Sir Lancelot in disguise . . . or something of the sort," she added doubtfully. "It didn't make much sense to me."

It made no sense to Lancelot, either. Oh, Agravaine he could understand—he had made an enemy of Gawain's brother back in the days when they were squires. But Bors had been one of the knights—Bors, his cousin, one of the few at Camelot he would have called a friend.

"Has he spoken?" another voice asked, a low, husky voice that was oddly soothing.

"No," Elaine said, "but he hears me."

"Then keep talking, lady."

Lancelot blessed the owner of that voice, though he did not know her name.

"The king is furious with them all and very worried," Elaine said quickly. "He suspected it was really you, and when Sir Gawain saw your shield, he confirmed it. I knew already," she added quietly, stroking the hair back from his brow. "I guessed that night—we all did, really, but of course I couldn't ask. You wouldn't have told me, anyway, so what would have been the point?"

So many lies. But he was free of them now; they were du Lac's lies, and he was dead.

"I left Corbenic with Sir Gawain," Elaine went on, "he was very kind, and so concerned for you . . ."

That is Gawain all over, Lancelot thought with bitter amusement. *He'd rather have his tongue torn out than admit he'd be thrilled to find me dead. Gawain hates me, he did from the first, even before I unseated him and—*

(stole)

—won his title.

"He gave me the diamond," Elaine said, "to give to you. Your prize. He told us all how bravely you fought. And he offered to send to his kinswoman, Lady Morgana, for a healer. I told him that wouldn't be necessary, since Brisen is here, and he said if you have need of anything at all, we must send to him at once."

Why? Why would Gawain offer such a thing for me, a man he has every reason to detest? Surely this was taking hypocrisy to a new level. Or was it hypocrisy at all? Perhaps it was something altogether different that drove Gawain, a thing du Lac could never understand.

"Honor!" The Green Knight had laughed. "You do not know the meaning of the word . . . you're not human anymore, not in any way that matters . . ."

But he was free of the Green Knight, as well, and the Lady—she who had had claimed to love him as a son. But he wouldn't think of the Lady. It was Elaine who mattered now. Elaine, whose sleeve had stanched his wound and saved him from the death decreed by the only mother he had ever known.

"Poor Galahad," she whispered, and he felt her cool lips brush his brow. "Hurry and get stronger so I can take you to Corbenic."

Corbenic. It sprang into his mind, then, so sharp and clear that a sigh of longing escaped his lips. If only he could see it all again, the tumbledown tower and cluttered little courtyard and Elaine laughing in the green grass beside the river.

Du Lac was dead—let him lie there in his tomb. But as Elaine's lips touched his brow again, Lancelot knew that *he* would live.

Chapter 22

. . .

"**D**ON'T leave me."

Elaine started awake. She lay half upon the floor, her head resting on the edge of the pallet. For three days she had not stirred from this spot except for the most necessary errands, and every time she returned, it was to find Lancelot tossing restlessly until she spoke to him. Then he would sleep—a real sleep, Brisen assured her—which was what he needed most. But until now, he had not spoken.

She raised her head, her neck stiff and every muscle aching. Lancelot's eyes were open; they seemed enormous in his fleshless face.

"Don't leave me," he said again, his voice barely more than a whisper.

"I won't." She smiled at him through the tears that stung her eyes. "How are you?"

"Hungry."

She laughed aloud. It was over, then; he would recover after all. Wincing a little as she turned her head, she called for Brisen to bring some broth and bread.

The days passed quickly after that, and each one brought a marked improvement. Elaine, true to her word, sat beside him hour after hour while he slept. As he gained strength, they talked a little. Rather, Elaine talked, and Lancelot listened, prompting her with questions when she faltered. He never asked her of the present or the future, but always of her childhood, which he seemed to find endlessly enchanting.

"Tell me how you found this place," he would ask, or, "What is your favorite memory of your mother?" and Elaine would be off, reliving memories she had thought forgotten. Once, when Father Bernard was changing his bandage—always a painful business—she said, "What of you? Tell me of your childhood!"

"I lost my parents young," Lancelot said, wincing as Father Bernard tugged at the edge of his bandage, "and was brought up by—by my foster mother."

"Did you really not know your name when you arrived at Camelot?" Elaine asked curiously.

"No, it was only later that I learned it."

"But what were you called?"

He shrugged, then drew in a hissing breath as the bandage came free. Elaine could hardly bear to look upon the wound, but Father Bernard nodded as though satisfied. "My . . . tutor called me Boy—when he wasn't calling me other things," Lancelot said with a wry smile. "My foster mother and her household said King's son."

"King's son? So you knew you were a prince?"

"Oh, yes, I always knew that."

"But not your name?"

"The Lady—my foster mother—said I must learn that for myself, when I was older."

"But why?" Elaine asked. "Surely you asked!"

"Many times, but she would never answer, save to say it was my destiny."

"How peculiar! Did she really call her manor Avalon? What sort of place is it?"

"I remember so little now," Lancelot said. "For years, my childhood has been lost to me. Sometimes, though, I can see the lake—that is what I remember best. I used to lie beside it in the tall grass and dream about the future. A courtyard with a fountain." He winced as Father Bernard began to clean the wound, then suddenly he laughed. "The tapestry beside my bed! Yes, of course, how could I have forgotten? It changed—shifted—so every day it showed a new scene from a story. There was a maiden in a tower and . . . and a prince, I think he was, and . . . no, it is gone."

A tapestry that shifted? Elaine brushed her fingers across his wrist; she was not certain whether she was more relieved or alarmed to find it cool.

"Feasting in the hall," Lancelot went on, his eyes wide and dreaming, "pipes and drums beneath the moon, and something—something in the oak grove; I cannot remember what. The Lady, of course, and—and a man who hated me, a knight who went always in green armor."

"The Green Knight?" Elaine asked, relieved to have some solid bit of fact to cling to. "He who visited Camelot to challenge Sir Gawain?"

"Yes. He was my tutor. He always hated me," Lancelot added in a low voice, "I think he would have slain me if he could, but the Lady would not allow it. But that was when I had her favor."

"And you do not now?"

Lancelot closed his eyes and shook his head mutely.

"How did you lose it?" Father Bernard asked, dabbing green ointment on the wound.

"The Lady brought me to Camelot to serve the king. I was her gift to him, her knight she had brought up and trained to his service."

"Her *gift*?" Elaine repeated, but Father Bernard motioned her to silence.

"Go on, Sir Lancelot," he said quietly. "What did you do to so offend your foster mother? Did you not serve the king as she desired?"

Lancelot's head moved restlessly on the pillow. "Yes. I did all she asked—and I was glad to do it, I was proud to serve King Arthur. But then there was Guinevere . . ."

Elaine stiffened. For days she had been braced to hear him call out for the queen in his delirium, but never once had he uttered her name. Now, just when she had relaxed her guard, it cut her like a blade. She must have made some sound, for Lancelot looked sideways at her, then away. "Or, no. I—I misspoke. I am so weary, I hardly know what I am saying."

"Tcha, child," Father Bernard said comfortably, "do not trouble yourself. We are all friends here, you know; you can say anything to us." He looked across the bed at Elaine and nodded toward the opening. When she hesitated, he nodded again, this time more forcefully.

"I shall leave you to your rest," she said to Lancelot, gently removing her hand from his.

"Will you come back?"

"Of course! Sleep, and I will see you later."

• • •

WHEN Elaine was gone, Lancelot closed his eyes, wishing he could recall every word he had spoken. What had he been thinking to go on like that? What must Elaine be thinking now?

"Lancelot," Father Bernard said gently. "You can confide in me. You needn't fear that anything you say will pass beyond these walls. I have taken my own vows and will keep them unto death."

"Forgive me, Father, I have sinned?" Lancelot said with a low, bitter laugh. "No, thank you. I have no faith in your god's powers to put right my wrongs."

"You needn't make a formal confession to be assured of my silence, and your faith is a matter between you and God. But it seems to me you bear a heavy burden. When first we met, before King Arthur's tournament, I sensed that you were troubled—no, more, that you had bid farewell to hope. Was this because the Lady had withdrawn her favor?"

Lancelot looked at him for a long moment, then nodded. "I knew before I rode into the tourney that she meant for me to die."

"Yet here you are, very much alive."

"I should be dead—I was meant to be." Lancelot made an impatient sound. "I know you won't believe me—"

"Why should I not?"

"Because I know how it must sound! And it matters not now—as you say, I am alive. Only . . ." The hermit looked down at the linen he was unrolling, and at last his patience was rewarded. "I have been thinking," Lancelot said in an almost inaudible voice, "about my mother. My true mother. And the Lady of the Lake."

"I once met the Lady of the Lake," Bernard remarked. "I thought her very beautiful and rather terrifying."

"Yes," Lancelot agreed, "she is both. But she was always very kind to me." He looked away, the muscles of his jaw working. "Very kind," he repeated. "Until . . ."

"Was she really?" Father Bernard inquired curiously. "To steal a child—a noble child, a prince—and keep him from his home and kin—"

"But she had to do that," Lancelot interrupted. "It was my destiny."

"Was it your poor mother's destiny to lose both son and husband in one night? She searched for you, my child, throughout that night and for many days after."

Lancelot's eyes shut tight as though in pain. "I know. Lionel—my cousin—told me. He saw her just before she died, and he said she was at peace. He said she was certain I still lived."

Father Bernard laid the new bandage gently on Lancelot's wound. "God granted her that knowledge, and yet that does not absolve the Lady of the Lake of her crime—for it was a crime, you know, and a very wicked thing to do."

"You judge her by our laws, and yet—"

"I do not judge her at all. I leave that to God."

Lancelot shook his head. "You do not understand. She is beyond God's judgment."

"No man—or woman—is beyond God's judgment," Father Bernard said sternly; then all at once he smiled, his eyes warm and sympathetic. "So you have lost her favor. Very well, then, you shall have to live without it. You are still a knight of Camelot. You are still a man."

"But I was never meant to be a man, not like other men. I was meant to be the champion of Avalon. Without the Lady's favor, I can never fulfill my destiny, and then— then . . ."

"Then what?"

"It was all for nothing. My mother's suffering—do you think it means so little to me? I have seen the place she died, forgotten by the world, with my name—*my name*—upon her lips. She died alone, but I could have gone to her. I was already at Camelot, don't you see? I could have gone to her, but I did not know yet who I was. When I learned of it—and of her death—"

"That must have been very difficult to bear," Bernard said neutrally.

Lancelot nodded, his throat working as he swallowed hard. "The only way I could make sense of it was to tell myself it was meant to happen. That it was all part of my great destiny. It would all be redeemed, all the suffering and loss and pain, and then—then I wouldn't feel so—so angry. So *used*."

"Such feelings are natural. The Lady and her knight were very wrong to—"

Lancelot shook his head. "You do not understand. *I* am the one at fault, *I* am the one who threw away the chance to give meaning to my mother's death."

"You have made mistakes—terrible mistakes—as have each one of us. And as sorry as you might be now, they cannot be undone."

Lancelot's chin jerked in a nod.

"It is not an easy thing to admit your own mistakes," Bernard went on thoughtfully, "and I admire you for doing it. But it is important that you not allow guilt to cloud your judgment. Your childhood is lost to you, you say, but I would put it differently. I would say that it was stolen. You *were* used, Lancelot, most infamously used, and you have every right to your anger. No matter what you have been told, your destiny is yours alone to make. You say that you have lost the Lady's favor—I say you have been given a new chance. Offer your life to God's service, for He alone can redeem all suffering."

"The Green Knight said—he said I am empty—hollow as a reed. He said I have no soul."

For the first time, the hermit looked genuinely angry. "He lied. I swear to you, he lied. You are God's child, Lancelot, and if you but seek Him, He will come to meet you."

Chapter 23

. . .

ELAINE found Father Bernard in his outdoor work-room tucked against the hillside, a long shelf beneath a slanting roof, open on three sides.

"Come in, child," the hermit said, not looking up from his work. "You were disturbed earlier, were you not?"

"Yes."

Bernard nodded, his hands moving swiftly over the flasks and bowls of herbs, adding a drop of this, a pinch of that to the fragrant mixture in the low wooden bowl.

"I am not surprised. Would you hand me that beaker?"

He tilted the beaker over the mixture. The faint, spicy scent of gillyflowers drifted through the air, reminding her of the garden at Corbenic through which she and Lancelot had walked hand in hand.

"It is . . . a strange thing," she said slowly, "not to remember one's childhood."

"Perhaps it is not so much that he cannot remember it," Bernard answered carefully, "but that he does not want to."

"Why would he not?" she asked, surprised.

"It happens sometimes." He stoppered the flask and set it on the shelf. "Memories which are too painful can be put aside, tucked away safely out of reach."

He pulled two stools from beneath his workbench and offered one to Elaine. When they were seated, he said, "The tale runs that the Lady of the Lake is some mystical being who dwells in the enchanted realm of Avalon." He waited, looking at her as he used to do when questioning her on her catechism, one brow raised in silent question.

"I have heard that, too," she answered. "Now tell me who she really is."

He smiled his approval. "This land is old, and there are some who do not accept King Arthur's Christian rule. It is rumored that they call their chief stronghold Avalon, no doubt inspired by the old tales. The location is a closely guarded secret, but it is a real place, and those who dwell there are flesh and blood. And it is not unknown for heathens to steal infants to use in their rituals."

Elaine leaned upon the bench, feeling suddenly ill. "And you think—you believe—"

"—that Sir Lancelot was one of those poor children," he finished with a nod. "You marked, perhaps, that the knight was hostile to Sir Lancelot, his menace held in check only by the Lady, while she was kindness itself. That is an old trick, Elaine, oft used to break a captive's spirit."

Elaine stared at him, appalled.

"Which is not to say," Bernard added, "that they entirely succeeded."

"But—but the tapestry," Elaine faltered. "He said it moved."

Bernard nodded gravely. "Do you see now how they worked? He was so confounded that even today he cannot distinguish between illusion and the truth. Don't look so surprised, child. The world is full of folk who employ all manner of cunning arts to convince people they are seeing the impossible. To practice such deceptions upon a helpless child—to convince him that pictures upon a tapestry could shift, or that in doing their will he was fulfilling some great destiny—"

"You think that is what the Lady is? A charlatan?" Elaine interrupted. "And when Sir Gawain struck off the Green Knight's head—they say the knight picked it up, his own head, and galloped off—'twas but a mummer's trick?"

"I doubt it was a miracle," Father Bernard answered dryly. "Though he went to great pains to make it look like one."

"I knew it could not be as they said it was. And yet," she went on, troubled, "by all accounts, the Lady of the Lake is King Arthur's friend."

"At one time she may have been. But I hear things even here, and they say that those of Avalon have turned against King Arthur."

"Not Sir Lancelot," Elaine said at once. "There is no more loyal knight than he."

"So he has said. And I believe that *he* believes it. Yet the fact that he remembers so little before he arrived at Camelot is troubling."

"Do you think—oh, Father, is he mad?"

Bernard frowned down at his folded hands. "No," he said at last, "I do not believe he is. I fear, Elaine, that someone took steps to ensure that he would not remember certain orders he was given. Such things are possible, and they had him from his infancy. Having met the king, Sir Lancelot's natural inclination was to love him and serve him with all honor. And yet . . . there are distressing rumors coming from Camelot. You know of what I speak?"

"Yes. And . . . and do you think they are true?"

"True or false, they still exist. And they are all concerned with Sir Lancelot himself. Is this chance? Or is it part of a larger plan to discredit King Arthur's rule?"

"This is all supposition," Elaine began.

"Oh, I know," the hermit agreed instantly. "And believe me, I do not seek to cast blame upon Sir Lancelot—quite the contrary. If what I suspect is true, he is in peril."

"From the . . . folk . . . of Avalon?"

"Very possibly, though there is another danger, too. I have no doubt that Sir Lancelot has served King Arthur to the best of his ability. But if this is contrary to what he was sent forth from Avalon to accomplish—" He broke off, frowning. "I cannot say more, only that such a conflict, unresolved, could break his mind asunder."

"What can I do?" she asked. "How can I help him?"

Bernard shot her a keen look from beneath his bushy brows. "I have never known you to shrink from a challenge, but I want you to be careful here. I believe Sir Lancelot to be a good man, but there are forces at work—both within him and around him—that could well bring you into danger."

"Do you think that matters to me?" Elaine cried.

"No, I don't suppose it would. And that," the hermit said with a trace of his old tartness, "is because you are in love, and therefore impervious to reason. I implore you to do nothing hastily. But—" he added, raising a finger to still her protest, "—if you will not be dissuaded, the best thing you could do for him would be to take him to Corbenic and keep him close." He covered her hand briefly with his own. "He is a very fortunate young man, Elaine. If he has any sense at all, then time—and God—will do the rest."

Chapter 24

. . .

DURING the next fortnight, Elaine could see no sign of madness in Lancelot, only a very natural irritability at being kept abed as his strength returned.

"Why don't you go out and get some air?" he said to her one fine afternoon, when the scents of rain-washed earth and apple blossoms drifted through the open doorway. "You've been cooped up here long enough, and I'm no fit company for anyone. Run along," he urged her when she hesitated. "I will be fine."

Elaine emerged from the dim cave, blinking in the sunlight. She lingered for a while by the river, breathing in the cool, fresh air and chatting with Father Bernard as he checked his lines. She took the catch of fish and started back toward the cave, halting behind a broad oak when she heard voices in the clearing.

Peering cautiously around the tree, she spied two riders who had halted their steeds at the cave's entrance. She could see at once they were brothers, for they were much alike, both good-looking young men with distinctive high-arched brows and angular faces. One had hair of chestnut brown, drawn back severely from his face, while the other's tawny mane curled about his shoulders.

"This isn't it," the tawny one said decidedly. "I *told* you we should have taken the left-hand turn back at the marker."

"If you hadn't insisted on going off after that maiden, we wouldn't have lost the path in the first place," the other replied sharply.

"What was I supposed to do when she cried out for help?"

"She wasn't crying out for help, she was calling back to her companion to make haste."

"Yes, well, I didn't know that then, did I?" the tawny brother muttered. "And nor did you. She might have needed our assistance—"

"But she did not." The dark one shook his head, frowning. "You're such a scatterbrain, Lionel, running hither and yon to chase every new adventure! A true knight is steadfast to his purpose."

Elaine studied the knights with interest. Lionel was Lancelot's cousin, which meant the dark young man must be Sir Bors, who had so nearly killed his kinsman Lancelot in the tournament.

"A *true* knight will always take the unknown path," Lionel retorted hotly. "Only cowards turn from an adventure!"

"And only silly, stupid children can't keep a thought in their head for longer than a moment."

"Be damned to your infernal caution!" Lionel cried. "Everyone knows a knight is honor bound to assist any lady in distress!"

"Don't swear," Bors said tightly. "How many times have I told you that swearing is—"

"Be damned to swearing, too! I *said* I was sorry that we

lost our way. I admitted I was wrong! And *you* said you forgave me!"

"So I did."

"Well, if this is your forgiveness, I'd hate to see you
bear a grudge."

Elaine stepped out from behind the tree. "Good day, Sir
Knights," she said, raising her voice to be heard over their
argument. They broke off at once, staring at her.

"Good day, demoiselle," Lionel said, shooting her a
melting smile. "I fear we have lost our way in this wood."

"Oh, I shouldn't think so, Sir Lionel. That is, if you
have come to see your kinsman. Sir Lancelot lies within."

They dismounted instantly and bowed. "You must be
Elaine of Corbenic," Lionel said, his eyes moving over her
with interest. "The Lady of the Red Sleeve. Gawain said
you were lovely."

Hot color rushed to Elaine's cheeks. "Sir Gawain is
very kind," she murmured awkwardly.

Bors lingered beside his horse, twisting the reins about
his hands. "Is Lance—how does he fare?" he asked, not
looking at her.

"Much better," Elaine said, "though still weak."

"Will you tell him I am here?" Bors asked.

"I'll take you to him now."

"He might not want to see me . . ."

"Of course he will. I'm sure he will be very glad that
you are here."

She led the way to the entrance of the cave, the brothers
falling into step behind her.

"See, Bors? I *told* you we would find him."

"No thanks to you. Take the left-hand path, you said, the
other *feels* wrong."

"What if I did? We're here now, aren't we? Must you
throw every mistake into my teeth?"

Laughter, faint but genuine, met them at the door to Lancelot's rough chamber. "It must be Bors and Lionel," he said. "Is this the same argument you were having the last time I saw you, or a new one?"

"A new one," Lionel said, grinning, as he ducked through the low entrance to the chamber. "We laid the old one aside so we could come and see you." He stopped before the pallet. "You look like a plucked chicken, Lance. Haven't they been feeding you?"

"They say they are, but 'tis all gruel and pap."

"You may have some fish tonight," Elaine said, raising the string. "There will be plenty for all. You will stay the night, won't you?" she added to Lionel.

Lionel did not answer at once. He looked to his brother, who still hovered half-in, half-out of the doorway, staring down at his feet.

"They will," Lancelot said. "Unless Bors was planning to sneak off without so much as greeting me. What are you doing out there?"

Bors raised his head; his gray eyes were shimmering with moisture. "Lance, I am so sorry. Can you ever forgive me? I didn't realize it was you—"

"I know, Bors," Lancelot said. "That is the whole point of riding in disguise."

Bors crossed the floor in two steps to fall on his knees beside the pallet and embrace his cousin in the Gaulish fashion, kissing him on either cheek. "I thought I'd killed you," he said.

"Well, you did not. Even if you had, I wouldn't take it personally." He hooked an arm briefly around Bors's neck before falling back upon the pillow.

"See, Bors?" Lionel remarked, "I told you he'd forgive you."

Bors gave a choked laugh as he sat back on his heels

and wiped his eyes. "He didn't, you know," he said to Lancelot, "he said you'd never speak to me again."

"No, I said *I* would never speak to you again. And I meant it. But he was so miserable about the whole thing," Lionel added to Lancelot, sitting cross-legged on the far side of the pallet, "that I relented."

"I'm sorry you were miserable," Lancelot said.

Bors smiled. "Now that I've seen you, I feel much better."

"Everyone has been horrid to him," Lionel said. He took Lancelot's knife from the bedside table and tossed it in the air so it landed point down in the earthen floor. "He took it well—probably considered it a penance—but even Bors has limits. He lost his temper in the end, and of all people, with the queen."

Elaine, watching from the doorway, saw that both Bors and Lancelot grew very still. "Bors shouted at her," Lionel went on, laughing. "Can you believe it? But it's true, I heard it for myself. Well, I could hardly help it, could I? We all heard, a whole crowd of us who were in the queen's antechamber, waiting for her to come out hunting. No one even knew that Bors was in there until the door flew open and there he was, shouting that he couldn't stop people saying things."

Elaine looked to Lancelot, who stared fixedly at the rushlight burning at his bedside. Bors was scowling at his brother, but Lionel was focused on the knife, which he flipped again, this time so it turned twice in the air before sticking in the floor.

"The queen came after him, crying, 'But is it true that Sir Lancelot—' And then she saw us. It was an awkward moment, to be sure, but before anyone could say a word, she slammed the door in our faces. Bors, of course, won't tell me anything, but I reckon she'd been at him about the latest rumor going round."

"I'm not interested in rumors," Lancelot said evenly.

"Oh, I don't mean the one about—" Lionel broke off, glancing quickly toward Elaine. "I mean, it has nothing to do with the—with—" He floundered to a halt and cast a pleading look to his brother.

Bors had gone nearly as white as Lancelot. He opened his mouth as though to speak but shut it again without uttering a sound.

"They were saying Bors murdered you so he might inherit Benwick," Lionel said rapidly. "Have you ever heard anything so ridiculous? I mean, Benwick isn't even yours, no more than Ganis is ours, since that bastard Lucius holds them both. Not that Bors would murder you even if it was," he added with an awkward laugh. "I mean—that is to say—"

At last Bors found his tongue. "Shut up, Lionel."

"Yes. Yes, perhaps I should." Lionel tossed the knife back on the table. "We'd better go and let you rest a bit, Lance."

He rose to his feet and held a hand out to help Bors up. "I'm sorry if I tired you," he said to Lancelot. "My tongue ran away with me again. But I didn't—I wasn't talking about—"

"Lady," Bors said to Elaine, "is there somewhere I might put my brother? Some dank, dark cell, perhaps, where he won't trouble anyone?"

"Yes," Elaine said. "That is, no—but why don't you come out and meet Father Bernard and have something to drink while I take these to my woman?"

"Elaine." Lancelot spoke from the bed. "You stay."

"But—"

"Allow me," Bors said, taking the fish from her hands. "We will find the good Father for ourselves."

Chapter 25

• • •

Elaine wiped her palms upon her skirt, miserably aware of the scent of fish that clung to her, the hair straggling down her back, the mud spattering her ankles. She had, she realized now, been living in a dream. Lancelot had needed her when he was ill, but he was better now. Had she really believed he would come with her to Corbenic? Perhaps he had meant to, but now everything had changed. He would—he must—go back to Camelot where the queen waited, distraught, for his return.

Guinevere. The very name, so sweetly musical, had the power to drain all light and happiness from the day. Guinevere, the most beautiful woman in Britain—some said in all the world. Guinevere, so charming and witty and merry, the radiant young queen no man could look upon without desiring.

Guinevere, who had eyes for only one man. The one who lay before her now, naked save for the coverlet over his hips, one long leg stretched out, the other bent slightly at the

knee. His dark hair—had she really combed it just this
morning?—curled over his shoulders, brushing the collarbones that still stood out too sharply. Every spare ounce of
flesh had been stripped from his face, revealing the perfect
harmony of brow and cheek and jaw. His was a bone-deep
beauty that even his long illness could not mar. It was no
wonder Guinevere desired him. Any woman would. As so
many had before, to their eternal sorrow. Deadlier than the
plague, Brisen had named him, what with all those maidens
pining themselves into the grave for love of him.

Not me, Elaine thought with rising anger. *I refuse to be
reduced to some pathetic footnote in the tale of Lancelot
and Guinevere, just one more maiden who could not face
life without the great du Lac.*

"Lionel is a fool," Lancelot said abruptly.

"He is a young man who finds it impossible to dissem-
ble," Elaine replied evenly. "You may call that foolish; I
thought him rather charming."

Lancelot smiled grimly. "Have you ever tried to stop a
rumor? Stay silent, and you are damned—protest, and you
are damned twice over. I have enemies at court. They dare
not challenge me directly, so instead they choose to
blacken my name."

With the truth? The question trembled on Elaine's lips,
but she feared she already knew the answer. "I was sent to
serve King Arthur," Lancelot had said, "but then there was
Guinevere . . ."

What more was there to say?

Elaine nodded. "I see. Well, Lancelot, 'tis time you took
some rest. Supper should be ready—"

"The queen and I came to court at about the same time,"
Lancelot said rapidly, "we are of an age, and were often
thrown together in our duties to the king. That, and some
similarities in temperament—I don't deny that I count the

queen a friend. We laughed at the same things—court life is often quite ridiculous—and now I realize we were not always discreet in our amusement."

Elaine remembered the day she had first met Lancelot, and he had exercised his wit at Sir Gawain's expense. Now, having met Sir Gawain herself, she knew Lancelot, had been not only unkind but unjust. If the queen was of a like mind, she could see quite well how the pair of them had managed to make dangerous enemies.

"Elaine, I am ashamed that that these rumors began in the first place," he said earnestly. "My only excuse is that I was young and foolish, and life at court was strange to me."

She longed to believe him, wanted it so much that it frightened her. "There is no need to tell me these things," she said. "When you return to court—"

"But I thought—you said—" He looked down, his long lashes veiling his expression. "Ah. You have reconsidered your invitation."

"No, of course not. You are still welcome at Corbenic. But once you are well—"

He looked up at her. "I'm not going back to court."

"But your duty to the king—"

"Britain is at peace; the king has no real need of me. Save in times of war, he cannot compel my service—and he would not, even if he could."

He wasn't going back to court—to Guinevere. Her heart leapt, but she dared not believe he meant more than he had said.

"Will you return to Benwick?"

He sighed. "I suppose I should do something about Benwick, but in all honesty, I would be hard put to care less about the place. No, I have a castle—at Norhaut, that was once called Dolorous Gard. 'Tis my own; I won it years ago and have not set foot in it since. I had hoped," he added diffidently, "to show it to you. If you would like to see it."

It was impossible to mistake his meaning now. He wanted to share something with her that he had never shared with anyone before.

Something he could never share with Guinevere.

Elaine could accept that he had loved before. Perhaps she was not Guinevere's equal in grace or charm or beauty, but she could make Lancelot a home, bear his children, give him the settled security he craved. He cared for her, she was certain of that much, and in time, the memory of his youthful folly would fade.

"Yes," she said, "I would like to see it. But not until you are well again. Sleep now, and I will wake you when 'tis time to eat."

Chapter 26

• • •

*T*HAT *didn't go too badly,* Lancelot thought. He reached for the water at his bedside, though his hand was shaking so that some slopped over on the table. Abandoning the effort, he lay back against the pillow. Elaine hadn't quite believed him, but she was prepared to let the matter rest.

He had not lied—he had promised himself he would never lie to Elaine—yet he had not betrayed Guinevere. Poor Guinevere. How would she cope without him? Apparently she was not doing very well so far, but he could not help her now. She would have to rely upon herself . . . and Arthur.

Something was very wrong in their marriage, though Lancelot had no idea what it was. Arthur had been delighted with his bride, and Guinevere had been half in love with him already before they wed. They had met some months before their wedding, for Arthur had ridden to King Leodegrance's aid when Cameliard was attacked.

"Tell me everything about him!" Guinevere had demanded of Lancelot during her bridal journey to Camelot. "I want to hear it all."

"King Arthur is . . ." Lancelot lifted one hand in a gesture of futility. "He is . . ."

"The king. Yes, so I've heard. But what of the man? What are his likes and dislikes, his pastimes, his passions? Oh, I know he's a great warrior, but does he care for music? Can he dance? Have you heard him sing or play upon an instrument?"

"No, but there had been little opportunity—"

"Is he learned or one of those men who scorns the written word? What is his favorite dish?"

"How should I know?" Lancelot demanded, laughing. "Why did you not ask him all this nonsense yourself?"

"There wasn't time! I met him twice—well, only once to speak to—and then he was sore wounded. And I did not know then that he—that we were to be—"

"Ah. I see it now. You were too dazzled by his skill at arms to ply him with impertinent questions. Very wise of you, I'm sure." He laughed. "And now you are blushing! Don't tell me you are in love with him already?"

"Of course not." Guinevere sniffed delicately. "How could I be on the strength of one meeting?"

"You said two," Lancelot pointed out. "What was the first one?"

"Oh, it was nothing. I only saw him from the battlements one evening. I did not know then who he was—nor did he know me." Guinevere blushed and bent her head, making a show of straightening the folds of her cloak. "It was just a look, no more," she added in a would-be careless voice. "Completely unimportant. I can't imagine why I mentioned it."

"Hmm. It all sounds suspiciously romantic to me. Now,

if you can just stay silent until the vows are spoken, he'll never know what a silly wench you are until it is too late."

There was something wrong in the silence that followed. He leaned closer, trying to peer into her face. "I was only joking. You're not so bad. I daresay he'll resign himself in time."

She laughed, but it was not natural, and turned her face away.

"What?" he demanded. "Tell me what is wrong."

"Oh, 'tis naught. Only—well, I had a rather dreadful scene with Father before I left."

Lancelot fell silent. He could well imagine what the scene had been about. He'd had a rather dreadful scene with King Leodegrance himself, when he had arrived at Cameliard to escort Arthur's bride to court. Leodegrance, upon learning Lancelot's identity, had seemed to go mad. Seizing his sword, he'd made a blundering attempt to run Lancelot through, and failing in that, to turn the blade upon himself. Once disarmed, he wept—it had been horrible to see—and a very nasty tale had come out.

Apparently Leodegrance, a young man newly wed, had gone to Gaul to visit King Ban, his dear and trusted friend. When he'd been summoned back to Britain by Uther Pendragon, he left his bride in Ban's care, expecting to return in a matter of weeks. But the Saxons had attacked, Leodegrance stayed to fight, and by the time he returned a year later, it was to find his lady heavy with child. Rather than cast herself upon his mercy—which would not in any case have been forthcoming—she'd had the audacity to beg him to leave her as she was, claiming wildly that she would rather be Ban's leman than Leodegrance's wedded wife.

Luckily, Leodegrance had said, his lady did not survive the birth. The child, Guinevere—which he admitted openly he planned to smother had she been born a male—was instead packed off, first to the nursery and later to a convent.

Leodegrance immediately wed again. And again. Three dead queens later and without an heir to his name, he found his grown daughter upon his doorstep. Before he could decide what was to be done with her, Cameliard was attacked. King Arthur saw the chit and fancied her, throwing Leodegrance into a quandary of conscience. Only with the greatest reluctance had he agreed to the marriage between Guinevere and the high king.

Lancelot had listened to these drunken ramblings with a distaste that soon turned to bored revulsion. Why should he care what two strangers—both dead now—had gotten up to before he was even born? Why should anyone care? What difference did it make who had fathered the girl so long as Arthur wanted her? As for Guinevere, he hadn't regarded her at all. He had certainly felt no connection to her.

Until they met.

Lancelot had told Elaine that he and Guinevere were similar in temperament, and that, though true, did not begin to explain it. Within an hour of meeting, he and Guinevere were finishing each other's sentences. Soon they had no need for words at all. The lift of a brow, the motion of a hand was enough to communicate volumes.

By the time they reached Camelot it seemed that Lancelot had always known her. She could be—and often was—haughty and impatient, but as these were flaws he shared, he regarded them with amused indulgence. Or he had at first. Later, he'd realized just how willful she could be—and how reckless. But by then it was too late, for he was bound to her by oaths unbreakable. Bound to silence. Bound to obedience. Bound to stand by while she laid waste to his friendship with Arthur.

What had gone wrong in their marriage? Arthur would

never breathe a word of such private matters to any man—
save perhaps his confessor—and Guinevere refused to admit
that anything was amiss. But the signs were there. Her laughter was too shrill, her eyes too bright, her entertainments so
lavish as to be absurd. She flirted shamelessly with every
knight at court, and though most of the poor fools fell under
her spell, a few found her both unseemly and ridiculous.

It finally occurred to Lancelot that there was only one
man she was trying to impress, and she was going about it
in precisely the wrong fashion. Arthur cared nothing for
glittering pageantry and extravagant entertainments. The
harder Guinevere tried to win his notice, the more he with-
drew from the beautiful, volatile, altogether puzzling creature he had wed. So Guinevere had turned to her one
friend—the word *brother* was never so much as whispered
between them—to fill the emptiness.

Lancelot could not help but respond. He was intensely
protective of her, even as he lived in dread of her next act
of folly. The one thing he found impossible to forgive was
that she had poisoned his relationship with Arthur, the
brother he had always longed for, the father he had never
known, the best friend any man could want.

But maybe, without Lancelot in the picture, they would
turn to one another.

When Elaine looked in a little later with a dish of fresh
fish and greens, he pretended to be sleeping. He saw no
one until the next day when Bors came to say farewell.

"Leaving so soon?" Lancelot asked, though in truth he
was relieved.

"I promised the king I'd go straight back once I knew
how you fared. He has been very worried," he added mildly.

"I know. Tell him I am mending."

Bors nodded and drew on his gloves. "He will be glad to
hear it." He was silent for a time, waiting, but at last he

voiced the unspoken question hanging in the air. "When can I tell him to expect you?"

"It is better," Lancelot said carefully, "if he does not."

"I know it's difficult to say—Father Bernard thinks it will be some weeks yet before you are returned to full strength. But the king will want to know. Say a month?" Lancelot shook his head. "Six weeks, then?"

In time, Arthur would understand he was not coming back at all. Let the knowledge steal upon him gradually; it would be easier that way.

"Give him my greeting, Bors."

Bors nodded, as though he had heard the words Lancelot could not bring himself to speak. "And the queen?" he asked quietly. "Will you send no word to her?"

Nothing Lancelot wanted to say to her could be sent by such a messenger, or indeed by any messenger at all. And perhaps that, too, was for the best. "Say to the queen," he managed, "that I commend myself to her."

Exhausted, he turned his head upon the pillow and closed his eyes.

"All right, Lance." Bors walked to the entrance; there his footsteps halted. "You're doing the right thing," he said. "God will reward you for it."

"You might mention that in your prayers."

"It would be better coming from you. He does listen, you know, if you would only talk to Him."

Lancelot managed a weak smile. "You do it for me, Bors."

"I always do," Bors answered on a sigh. "Farewell."

Chapter 27

· · ·

"LADY, may I . . . ?" Mab, one of the Corbenic serving girls, gestured vaguely toward the privy.

"Of course." Exasperated, Elaine turned to Brisen, who
was tossing handfuls of wood ash into the cauldron bubbling
in the center of the courtyard. "What ails these wenches?"
Elaine demanded. "Is there some sickness going round?"

Brisen burst out laughing. "You could call it that. Green
sickness, at any rate. Sir Lancelot is practicing in the yard."

"Is he?" Elaine glanced toward the practice yard, then
turned her attention firmly to the work at hand. "Here, now,"
she called sharply. "You're dragging that sheet through the
mud!"

Giggling wildly, the three girls gathered up the dripping sheet and flung it over a shrub, their heads bent close
together. The day was fine and breezy, a perfect opportunity to turn out all the bedding, the mattresses to be
picked and aired, the linen washed and hung in the sun to
bleach.

"Do you think he should?" Elaine asked Brisen. "It's very soon, isn't it?"

"I should hope he'll have the sense to leave off if he's in pain," Brisen said. "But perhaps you should go and see how he gets on."

"Yes. Perhaps I should."

"You might want to leave the apron here," Brisen suggested blandly.

"Wench," Elaine muttered, but she did as Brisen bade her. leaving the sacking apron folded neatly over a stool. "I'll be right back," she added loudly. "Keep on with your work."

She found not only Lancelot but Torre in the yard. Torre was astride his charger, and Lancelot bent over the stirrup. "Try it now," he said.

To her surprise, Elaine saw that the quintain had been set up in the center of the yard. She leaned against the wooden railing of the fence and watched Torre charge it with a practice lance. He hit it true, and the arm swung round with a squeak, catching him a glancing blow upon the shoulder. He kept his seat, though, and trotted over to Lancelot.

"Not bad," he said grudgingly. "Where did you come up with that?"

"Sir Kay's stirrup is built up and seems to serve him well."

"Thank you," Torre said gruffly.

Lancelot picked up a wooden practice sword and swung it. "Care to join me?" he asked Torre.

Torre hesitated, then said with a passable attempt at carelessness, "Why not?"

Elaine retreated a little farther into the shadow of the stable as Torre dismounted. Lancelot demonstrated a complicated series of moves; Torre, after one or two false starts, followed his example. He managed surprisingly well, Elaine thought; his bad leg threw him off, but not as badly as she'd feared. Of course he could not compare to Lancelot, who moved with the ease of long practice. After half a dozen repetitions, Torre stumbled and dropped the sword.

"You do this often?" he asked, limping heavily to the bucket hanging by the gate.

"Every day." Lunge, withdraw, lunge, and turn; Lancelot swung the practice sword in an arc above his head then dropped into a crouch, rising smoothly to lunge again at the straw target. He rested on his sword, his chest rising and falling deeply. "One hundred is the usual. More than that begins to waste the muscle. But I'll be lucky to make twenty today."

"Who trained you?" Torre asked, offering him the ladle.

Lancelot rinsed his mouth and spat into the dust, then poured the remainder of the water over his head. "A kinsman of my foster mother. He'd laugh himself sick to see me now."

His threadbare linen shirt was rolled up at the sleeves and hung open at the neck, the fabric plastered to his body, revealing the hard muscle of his chest and shoulders. Hearing a giggle nearby, Elaine turned to find several of the maids hanging over the fence. Torre looked over, too, and scowled.

"That's enough," she said, shooing them toward the courtyard. "Get back to your work. And that is enough for you, as well," she called to Lancelot.

"I would argue the point, but I'm weak as a kitten," he said wryly.

"Get you to the river, then," she advised. "You've earned a rest."

"Only if you come, too."

"*Some* of us have work to do. Perhaps when I am finished."

"With food?" Lancelot asked hopefully.

She smiled at him. "Possibly."

"Coming, Torre?" Lancelot asked, propping the sword against the fence.

"No." Torre swung himself onto his horse. "I've . . . business in the vill." With a mocking bow to Elaine, he rode off.

"Business," she muttered. "In the alehouse, I'll be bound."

"More likely in the back room." Lancelot, his eyes narrowed against the sun, watched Torre vanish down the path. "What he needs," he said thoughtfully, "is a dragon."

"If you find one, let him know."

Lancelot shook the sweat-soaked hair out of his eyes. "That wouldn't serve. I don't think your brother likes me much, Elaine."

"He'll come round."

Lancelot grinned. "What he *really* needs," he said, "is a woman."

"Oh, he has plenty of those."

"I should have said a lady. Someone like . . . well, like Mistress Brisen. She's rather taken with him, isn't she?"

Elaine sighed. "You noticed, did you? I think Torre is the only one who hasn't."

"Or he's not interested," Lancelot remarked, shutting the gate behind him. He and Elaine fell into step as she headed back to the courtyard. "A pity; she would do him good."

"And since when have men wanted what is good for them?"

Lancelot tipped her face up to his. "We're not all fools, you know. You will come down to the river, won't you?"

"Yes," she answered quickly, turning away to hide her sudden confusion. "The moment I am free."

• • •

LANCELOT plunged naked into the river, crying out his shock as the icy water hit his skin. He was a strong swimmer, but today he tired quickly. Just the small amount of practice had done him in. But at least it was a start.

Leading where? he wondered as he pulled himself up upon the tiny dock and stretched out in a patch of sunlight. The questions he had put off these past weeks now rushed into his mind, demanding answers. Where would he go now? What would he do? His time as a knight was finished. Arthur had accepted his absence with a silence that said more than any words. And having served King Arthur, Lancelot had no desire to offer his sword—whatever it was worth now—to any lesser man. To raise an army and march into Benwick was a hopeless dream without Arthur's help, and he refused to return to Camelot a beggar.

He knew naught of husbandry or farming, even less about the management of an estate. The thought of returning to Dolorous Gard reduced him to despair. What would he *do* there? How would he fill his days?

Unless . . . unless Elaine was with him.

Which brought him face-to-face with the decision he had avoided making for too long.

He had been waiting, though for what he did not know, letting day after day slip by while he basked in her attention. He loved her. Of that he had no doubt. And he thought that she loved him. But did she love him enough to accept him as he was?

Or did she only love the man she believed him to be?

As he dressed, he wondered what she would say if she knew the truth about the great du Lac. That his victories—particularly his victory over her beloved Sir Gawain—had not been his at all but the sorcery of the Lady of the Lake, who had now cast him off in disgust.

And had she not been right to do so? Would Elaine not

be right to do the same? He was a sham, as hollow as the Green Knight had named him. Through his own folly he had thrown away his one chance at greatness, and his mother's long suffering and lonely death could now never be redeemed. Arthur, who had given him so much, had been deprived of the magical protector bestowed upon him by the Lady of the Lake.

Lancelot turned and buried his face in his arms, but he could not blot out the truth. He had been given the chance to do something extraordinary, to serve the greatest king the world had ever known in a way no one else could ever do. It was a glorious destiny, just as the Lady said, surely the finest ever offered to a mortal man. But he had not been able to hold onto it.

He had lost everything . . . save Elaine. If she refused him now, he would be finished.

Coward, he thought. *Tonight you will ask her and have done with it.* If she said no—but he would not think of that. Instead he imagined an end to the torture of being so near her every day, yet not daring to so much as kiss her lest he lose all control and beg her to be his wife.

He pictured her as she had been that day by the river, all rosy and tumbled in his arms, until his thoughts slipped into dreams.

• • •

IT was nearly dusk before Elaine was able to escape, a heavy basket over her arm. She was thoughtful as she walked beneath the trees, remembering what Lancelot had said to her before.

She found him sleeping on the dock before the boat-house, a faint smile curving his lips. As she approached, he stirred and stretched luxuriously, his smile deepening when he caught sight of her.

"So you've come at last. I thought I would starve to death!"

She set the food out between them: a loaf of brown bread, cheese, a small pot of honey, and half a cold roasted capon.

"A feast!" he declared, helping himself to a leg of the capon.

She shook her head, smiling as she spread a bit of bread with honey. "You are accustomed to far finer fare than this. At court, I mean. They serve all manner of wonderful dishes, don't they?"

"I suppose so," he said, accepting the bread with a smile. "I know that Arthur is forever complaining that he cannot stomach the concoctions they keep bringing him. He used to ask for plain meat and bread, but Sir Kay—his foster brother and seneschal—was so insulted that Arthur finally gave it up. Do you know—" Lancelot laughed. "Once I found him in the kitchens, very early, entreating the spit boy to cut him a slice from the roast before it could be spiced and sauced."

"I think I would like the king."

"You would. I know he would like you." Lancelot stilled, the bread halfway to his lips, the merriment fading from his face. Once again, he wore the look Elaine had come to know too well, so sad, so . . . lost that just to see it hurt her.

"But you," she went on after a time, "you enjoy rich foods. I remember when you were ill, you used to long for goose liver and iced cakes, sweetbreads and roast peacock."

"Yes, but I couldn't have eaten them."

"You could now," she pointed out.

"What is this about, Elaine? Are you planning me a feast?"

"Would you like one?"

"Not particularly, no. I'd rather eat out here, with you."

She smiled tightly. "Because you know what is good for you?"

The sun lingered on the tops of the trees, painting them with gold, but the river was in shadow. She could scarce make out the far bank now, though Lancelot's hand, resting casually on the bleached wood of the dock, was very clear.

"I do know," he said. "Is there something wrong in that?"

"Of course not. No one can exist forever upon cake and peacock. But having once tasted such dishes, the longing will always be there, won't it?"

There was a muffled splash as he swept his arm across the space between them, tipping bread and bones and honeypot into the water. A moment later he was on his knees before her, his arms around her neck as he drew her forward.

"You," he said, "are sweeter than iced cakes. Intoxicating as the richest wine of Gascony. You are far more exotic than any peacock I've ever tasted," he said, dropping a honeyed kiss upon her lips. "And—" He drew back and regarded her with amusement. "—as silly as a peahen! What put such foolish thoughts into your head?"

She laughed, resting her brow against his arm. "It was nothing. Only, when you said before—about Torre—"

"You mean when *you* said that men never want what is good for them? But what if what is good for them is the thing they desire above all?"

Did he desire her? Tonight was the first time he had kissed her since they returned to Corbenic, but before she could put her arms around him, he had drawn away, leaving her confused and trembling. *It must not be that sort of desire he spoke of,* she thought, *not the same sort I feel for him. Else he could not hold back as he is doing now.*

"What then, Elaine?" he insisted gently. "Or was that your way of suggesting I return to court?"

Do you want to? Is it Guinevere who makes you look so

sad? When you kiss me, do you think of her? "Now it is you who is being foolish," she said, and in her effort to keep her voice from shaking, it sounded stiff and stilted. "You know you are welcome here for as long as you want to stay."

"Thank you," he said, and though he smiled, his voice was oddly flat. "Well, then, should we be starting back?"

He took her hand as he helped her from the dock onto the shore, and kept it in his as they started down the path. "I should never have kept you out so late," he said contritely as the darkness of the forest closed around them.

"I'm not afraid," she answered, and it was true. Nothing could harm her as long as he was here. But how long would he stay?

They had gone about half the distance to Corbenic when Lancelot stopped abruptly, lifting his head as though straining to make out some sound beyond the edge of hearing.

"What is it?" Elaine asked.

"Listen. Listen, do you not hear the horns?"

Elaine felt a chill wind down her back. "I hear the wind in the trees," she whispered. "No more."

"What night is this?" he asked, gripping her hands hard. "Is it—of course, 'tis Midsummer's Eve. We should not be out here, not tonight when they are hunting."

"Lancelot, don't," she cried, "you look so strange."

"Do I?" He laughed a little wildly. "I feel strange—" He caught her close, burying his face against her neck. "Hold me, Elaine, talk to me of—of the harvest or the new bull."

"Hush," she said, stroking his hair with wild tenderness. "All is well, it is only the wind in the trees, no more—"

He lifted his head. "They are close now, do you hear them? Elaine, you must! Tell me that you hear the horns and the baying of hounds!"

"No," she cried. "I do not. There is nothing there, nothing that can harm you." Looking into his face, she cried,

"Or is it that you *want* to hear them? Oh, Lancelot, are you not happy here, with me?"

"Yes. Yes, I am happy, you know I am. 'Tis only sometimes—Elaine, do you remember when I told you I thought I would be a great knight?"

"Yes, and you are. You are First Knight of Britain!"

"No! I didn't mean the best in Camelot or Britain or even in the world, but the best that ever was or ever would be. I told you how I was when first I came to Camelot," Lancelot went on, speaking very quickly, "how proud and rude. But there was so much I didn't know. I didn't understand about family or loyalty or even simple courtesy. I had no idea how to carry on a conversation. No one had ever told me of those things, Elaine, no one had ever shown me how to live among people. I had always been alone, but I told myself I didn't care because I knew what I would achieve. And now . . ." His voice broke, and he held out his hands, palms upward.

She placed her own in them, holding him tightly. "What was done to you was very wrong, but it cannot be changed. The only thing that matters is what you do now. What is it to be, Lancelot? Will you go back to Camelot? Is that what you want?"

"It is too late. I can never go back." He bent and kissed her hands. "But it is all right as long as I have you. Then nothing else matters."

Even before he raised his head, she heard the sound. It could have been the wind in the treetops—had any wind been blowing—or a nightingale's call carried from the wood . . . or the faint, far-off sound of a horn winding in the distance. The moonlight on Lancelot's face lent him an unearthly beauty as he stood poised upon the brink of flight. She clasped him round the neck and dragged his mouth down to hers.

He kissed her as he'd never done before, with a fierce, possessive wildness that set fire to her blood. He parted her lips and plundered her mouth, one hand tangled in her hair, the other boldly stroking her breast through the thin wool of her kirtle, teasing the taut peak until she moaned aloud. His hands moved down her spine and, grasping her hips, he pulled her close against him, letting her feel the hard length of his arousal. He dragged his mouth away, his eyes burning into hers.

Yes. She never knew if she'd said the word aloud or only thought it. It did not matter. The question had been asked and answered, and there was no time for thought, no chance for regret. His mouth found hers again, and she sank deep into the sweet darkness of his kiss, surrendering herself to the magic of his touch.

She was trembling as they lay down together—with excitement, with anticipation of his next touch, and with fear. Yet in the next moment she forgot her fear, for their urgent fumblings with ties and laces were interspersed with bursts of laughter. It was only when the last garment was cast aside and the two of them were naked on the cool grass that all merriment died.

With heart-stopping suddenness he was poised above her. Moonlight gilded the corded muscles of his arms and cast eerie, flickering shadows round his head. At one moment it seemed that he was haloed like an angel; in the next he wore the antlers of a stag. His eyes were fathomless pools of darkness as he waited, perfectly still yet every muscle trembling.

He was hers now, hers alone. She smiled, drawing out the moment, tracing a fingertip down his sweat-slicked cheek and drinking in his groan, ripped from the very depths of his soul. He would wait. No matter what it cost him, he would wait, for he existed only for her command. Each bead of sweat upon his brow, each shaking breath was new proof of her power. At last she moved her hips upward, taking him inside her with a cry of mingled pain and triumph.

He thrust deep within her, so deep that she feared that she would shatter, and her triumph turned to fear. "Shh, Elaine," he murmured against her hair, "don't be afraid, I would not hurt you—" He thrust again and she stiffened, her fists clenched in his hair. "Oh, God, Elaine, I cannot— yes, love, yes—"

For a moment she was certain she would die, then abruptly he relaxed, lying like a dead man with his cheek against her breasts. Was it over? God be thanked, it was. He wasn't moving, and she had no intention of disturbing him just yet, lest he start it all again. She was quite sure she could not survive a second bout.

She hardly dared to breathe until he slipped away from her, and she was certain it was finished. Relief washed through her, though it was tinged with disappointment, too. She must be one of those women who did not take pleasure in physical love. She'd never expected to be one of them; was, in fact, surprised to find herself in their company, for she'd always imagined that the difference lay in choice. She'd chosen Lancelot. She had certainly desired him. But it seemed desire played no part in satisfaction.

Still, it was rather pleasant having him so close. She felt an uprush of tenderness as she smoothed the hair back from his brow.

His beard rasped painfully against her skin, but his lips were soft and warm when he kissed the sensitive underside of her breast, his mouth lingering against her skin as it traveled upward to the nipple, which tightened almost painfully. She shivered, moving restlessly against him, the ache between her legs pulsing in rhythm to her heartbeat as he tongued her nipple, then took it in his mouth. She cried out, arching upward when she felt his hand caress her inner thigh. When his fingertip traced the soft folds between her legs, she went very still, incapable of speech or movement.

Please, she thought, *please,* though she had no idea what she longed for—until he touched the throbbing bud at the center of her being. His touch was delicate, and now his lips were on hers, his tongue delving into her mouth and out again, echoing the rhythm of his fingers, quickening in response to the movement of her hips.

"Please," she cried quietly, "please, please—Lancelot—yes!" her words taking up the rhythm, urging him on and on until all her words were lost as her world exploded in a burst of white-hot flame.

"And to think," she said dreamily some time later, when she was capable of speech, "that I had just decided I was incapable of physical pleasure."

He laughed softly. "I don't think we need worry about that." Raising himself on one elbow, he looked down at her. "Will you marry me, Elaine?"

"Oh, yes." She traced the outline of his lips. "You have such a lovely mouth. Did I ever tell you that?"

"No, you must have forgotten. Your breasts are beautiful," he said, bending to kiss them each in turn. "And I'm quite sure I haven't mentioned *that* before. But I've often thought they would be. When you would sit by my bed and put cool cloths on my head, I used to wonder what you would look like just as you are now."

"You *did*?"

"You didn't guess? I thought you must have, I was always—well," he said, guiding her hand downward. "Every time you touched me, it was difficult—impossible—not to respond."

She laughed, looking down at him. "As you are now?"

"Just so. A bit embarrassing."

"I never noticed," she said, then dissolved in laughter at the pained expression on his face. "I didn't think to look. Even if I had, I wouldn't have known what I was seeing. It's quite extraordinary, isn't it?" she added, reaching out to touch him once again, "the way it . . . goodness! No wonder it hurt."

"I'm sorry. Was it awful? I've heard the first time is painful for a lady—"

"Mmm. But what of you? What was it like?"

"Not painful. Just . . . oh, God, Elaine, wait, you'd better stop." He caught her hand and raised it to his lips. "There was a moment when I did think I might die, but honestly, I didn't care. Did you feel—was it anything like that?"

"Well," she said, lying back against his chest, "I thought I would die, too—but that was because it seemed impossible that you could . . . fit. But after, when you—" She buried her face against him. "It was more like flying," she mumbled against his shoulder.

He laughed and kissed her hair. "That's something to go on with, isn't it? In time we will fit more easily together. And we'll have all the time we need when we are wed."

When we are wed. She shivered as she lay beside him, gently tracing the scar beneath his ribs as his breathing slowed and deepened. Had he really asked her to marry him? It seemed so natural at the moment that she'd accepted him without thinking. It was only now she realized what that meant.

She sat up, her legs crossed beneath her. Lancelot lay upon the grass, one arm crooked beneath his head, moonlight bathing the hard contours of his body in a silver glow. A smile still lingered upon his lips, those precisely chiseled lips that she had always so admired. Impulsively, she leaned over and kissed them lightly so as not to wake him.

His brows were thicker above his nose, tapering as they arched. The left one had a tiny scar running through its outer edge, marring their perfect symmetry. She kissed the scar, as well, and then the tip of his nose, and then his lips once more because she could not resist them. Sitting back, she admired him shamelessly, her eyes tracing the bold contours of his wide jaw and high cheekbones, lingering on the deep, enchanting hollows in between.

Would she ever grow weary of looking at his face? In ten years, twenty—no, even then she could not imagine such a thing could ever happen.

A rustle in the wood behind her shattered her reverie. She shook her hair over her shoulders, shielding breasts and belly before she turned, blushing yet defiant, to face whoever had disturbed them.

Only to find the glade empty. She could still hear muffled sounds, yet she could not see what might be making them. She gasped aloud when she saw the high grass bend as though beneath a footstep. For a moment it seemed someone was there with them—she had the impression of the hem of a glittering gown sweeping across the grass, a high-arched foot encased in a jeweled slipper. When she tried to see more, the image wavered and was gone. All that remained were two patches of flattened grass, a swirling darkness between her and the trees, a rustle in the undergrowth and the occasional green glint of eyes, as though a score of tiny animals had gathered at the clearing's edge.

"Who is there?" she cried, her voice high and thin with fear.

Lancelot started awake, lifting himself on his elbows. "Elaine? What—" He looked past her, and his eyes widened.

"Who is it?" Elaine cried, turning to search the empty clearing. "What do you see?"

"Nothing," Lancelot said. "There is no one there . . . now. It is all right, Elaine. I swear it."

When he drew her to him again, she went, trusting him completely as she lost herself in his embrace.

Chapter 28

• • •

"**B**UT what if it doesn't stop?" Elaine asked, peering from the doorway of the barn as the rain beat upon the fields beyond. "We'll have to bring the hay in—"

"Nay, lady," Will Reeve said decidedly, dragging a bony wrist across his streaming brow. "That'll mean fire sure enough. Damp hay—" He shook his head. "It just won't do. We can only hope this rain don't bide."

"My scar was a-paining me yestere'en," Lancelot said suddenly from her other side, in such a dead-on imitation of the reeve that Elaine was forced to manufacture a hasty coughing fit. "And thass a certain sign of rain. 'Twere but a middling sort o' pain, though, nobbut a shower's worth, I'll vow. But then," he paused dramatically, "this morning I found a spider in my porridge."

"I hope you didn't kill it," Elaine said severely, giving him a sharp dig with her elbow.

"Nah, lady, not I!" Lancelot declared. "'Twere a rare fool—"

"—that'd kill a spider at hay-making time," Will Reeve finished flatly. The two men eyed each other over her head. "Well, lad, at least ye listen."

"Always," Lancelot assured him.

"Even if ye are a scamp," Will said, his face lighting with a rare smile.

"I am," Lancelot said humbly. "And I'm sorry for it."

"Bullocks," Will declared. "But thass all right, we can all use a bit o' merriment."

Elaine grinned as Will vanished into the barn behind them, where the rest of the villeins had fled the sudden storm. "Very good," she said approvingly, "we'll make a farmer of you yet."

"You," Lancelot said, "can make me anything you like."

He stood in the doorway of the barn with the rain beating down behind him, one hand braced above his head and his damp hair curling about his brow.

"Will," he called, not turning from Elaine, "what say we give the lads a rest? Say an hour . . . or no, let us make it two."

Within moments the barn was empty save for the two of them. "I could not sleep last night," Lancelot said.

"Warm milk is said to be effective in such cases," Elaine retorted primly, though her heart was pounding so hard and fast that she was certain he must hear it. So it always was when he looked at her that way, as though the world and everything in it had ceased to exist—save her.

"It was not warm milk I wanted." He lowered his arm and stepped forward until they stood toe-to-toe, barely an inch between them. He tugged the coif from her head and let it fall to the floor. "I lay in bed, watching the moon, remembering sunset at the mill and a certain sound you made . . ."

He deftly unwound her braid and ran a hand through her

hair, spreading his fingers so the strands gleamed against his skin. "Do you know the one I mean? It was when I—"

"Yes, I know," she said quickly, her cheeks warming as she remembered the flock of swallows bursting from the ruined mill with a clap of wings, startled from their perches by her cry. She had laughed, then, watching the black shapes wheel against the red-streaked sky, her arms wound around her lover's neck and his breath warm and quick against her neck.

"I liked that sound," he went on, his face thoughtful as he wound a golden lock about his wrist, "oh, I liked it very much, Elaine. The more I thought of it, the more I longed to hear it once again."

He tugged her hair, drawing her closer until she could feel the beating of his heart. "Do you think I might?"

"Perhaps. I cannot promise . . ."

"Is that a challenge?"

Before she knew what he meant to do, he bent and seized her about the knees, tossing her over one shoulder and striding toward the wooden ladder leading to the hayloft. "Put me down—you'll do yourself a damage—"

"Too late," he said, dropping to his knees and laying her down in the deep straw. He bent to her, and the rain pounded on the roof as he explored her with lips and tongue and hands, greeting each response as a revelation.

"This?"

She moaned softly as he trailed a path of soft kisses from the peak of her breast to her navel. "Or . . . this?" He dipped lower, and when she gasped, he raised his head to look at her through half-closed eyes. "No? Or was that a yes?"

Before she could collect herself to answer, he bent to her again, his explorations growing bolder. When she cried out, her body arching toward him, he laughed aloud. "Oh, that was assuredly a yes. What's this?" he said with mock sternness as she clamped her legs together, stammering an incoherent and much belated protest. "No, I will not have it, indeed I will not."

So it always was when they lay together and with endless patience he sought her deepest pleasure. All he asked of her was honesty, which she could not have refused him if she would.

At last he came to her, and they strained together, rising, rising toward some distant peak. As one they reached it, hung poised for a heart-stopping moment, then her cry woke the echoes in the rafters above their heads before she tumbled headlong into oblivion.

"Mmm . . ." Lancelot murmured sometime later, rousing her from a doze. "Just think, only a fortnight, and you will be mine forever."

"What then?" she murmured sleepily.

"Then we can make love in a proper bed. With pillows."

She laughed, remembering their visit to his castle and the hour they'd spent in the lord's bedchamber. There had been many pillows on the great bed. A tiny cloud of dust had burst from the one she had used to attack him by surprise. What had started as a romp soon took some very interesting turns.

She sighed. "I do like pillows. Yes, we must have dozens. But . . . where are we to live?"

"I had thought at Joyous Gard," he answered, his hands moving lazily up and down her back.

She smiled, remembering the moment when he so named it, as they stood together on the battlements, her body glowing from their bed play and the wind whipping through her hair.

"Did it not please you?" he added.

"Oh, it did, very much. It's lovely. Only . . . I would like to see the crop in."

"Then we shall. Joyous Gard isn't going anywhere."

"Do you mean it?"

One broad shoulder moved in a shrug, making the muscles move like liquid beneath his sun-browned skin. "I'm in no particular hurry to take up residence. After all, it's where I'll spend eternity."

"What do you mean?"

"My tomb is already built, complete with a plaque that bears my name and lineage."

She drew back a little, a chill touching her neck. "You've constructed your tomb?" He hadn't had anything else done to the keep or lands; indeed, she'd been a little shocked at how run-down the castle was. She covered her discomfort with a laugh. "How frightfully practical."

"Practical? Me?" One dark brow lifted. "No, it was there already."

"But if you did not—then who made it? Why?"

He smiled, drawing her down so her head rested against his shoulder. She traced a finger across the curling dark hair upon his chest, listening to the steady beating of his heart.

"I've told you before that when I came to Camelot," he said, "I did not know my own name or who my parents were. The Lady presented me to King Arthur and asked him to make me one of his knights. He agreed—though he didn't look very happy about the whole business. I was quick to take offense in those days, so I said he needn't bother until I could present myself to him properly."

Elaine nodded, lulled by the music of his voice. This was nothing she hadn't heard before, but it was the first time since he had been ill that he had spoken of the past at all.

"Instead, I asked for an adventure," he went on, "and soon enough he found me one—a good thing, too, as I wasn't getting on very well with the other squires. Well, that adventure led to another, and so at length I found myself riding to Norhaut to aid a lady in distress."

Elaine knew *this* tale; she doubted there was a person in all of Britain who did not. It was Lancelot's first adventure, the deed that won him both spurs and fame . . . and by the time it made its way to Corbenic, it had been so twisted and embroidered as to be completely unbelievable. Elaine had a hundred questions, but the first one springing to her lips was the foremost in her mind. "Was she a beautiful lady?"

"Not as beautiful as you," he said, his lips brushing her temple. "But passing fair. Well, once the battle was over—"

"Wait!" Elaine interrupted, laughing. "You can't just say, 'once the battle was over'!"

"Another time—"

"But that is what you always say! You never talk about your adventures, and I've heard such fanciful things—you would laugh if you knew what they said of this one. I want to know what it was really like."

He heaved a martyred sigh that she thought was only part in jest. Her small pang of guilt was quickly stifled by her curiosity, and she promised herself she would not laugh, no matter how far the truth varied from the tale. "Very well," he said. "What do you want to know?"

"Everything! To begin, how many knights fought with you?"

He gazed up at her, his expression as resigned as a man who had just offered himself to be tied upon the rack. "None."

"You had the sole command? But you were just a lad!"

"Yes, but I had been preparing all my life."

"Still, an untried squire?" Elaine shook her head. "Poor lady, she must have been quite desperate."

"She was that," Lancelot agreed.

"How many foot soldiers did she have?"

"There were none." She gave him a sharp look, but he merely shrugged. "Men-at-arms?" He shook his head. "Squires? Not even a one-legged soldier or an incredibly brave page?"

"Norhaut had been occupied for years," he explained. "The defenders had all been killed or run off long ago. I fought alone that day."

"Oh." Elaine regarded him in silence, half expecting him to burst out laughing. But he merely went on watching her with patient resignation, as though he knew how ridiculous the whole thing sounded, and was sorry, but could not do anything about it.

If she could have dropped the subject there and then, she would have done it. But she had gone too far to retreat; no matter how little she might like the answers to her questions, she had been the one who insisted on asking them. "Next you'll tell me there really were two giants," she said, trying to speak lightly. "And six score knights defending the gates."

Then, at last, he smiled. "Of course not," he said, and she laughed, a bit surprised at the strength of her relief.

"There was only one giant," he went on. "Poor fellow, he wasn't very quick—and three score knights, not six, none of them particularly brave or skilled."

Elaine stopped laughing. "You—wait a moment, I want to be sure I understand you. You defeated a giant and three score knights? Without any help at all?"

"Oh, no, I did have help. Just before I reached Norhaut, I met a damsel—"

"Another one?" Elaine smiled to show she was not jealous in the least, though she feared her smile wasn't terribly convincing.

"This one came from the Lady of the Lake. She gave me three shields; each was meant to increase my strength by ten."

Elaine was starting to feel ill. She'd forgotten the shields, which had figured largely in the tale. "Why didn't you say so earlier?" she said with a brittle laugh. "Let's see . . . thirty times your strength against sixty knights, is that it? So really, it was two to one, almost an even match. That's leaving the giant aside, of course, but we're not counting him."

"I used two of the shields," he said, his face as stony as if she'd just given the rack another twist. "The third I cast aside."

Now she had joined him on the rack. His story was absurd, impossible. Elaine might not understand much about knights or battles or giants, either swift or slow, but what she knew, she *knew*. And included among those few, indisputable facts was that a shield was only as good as the materials that went into its making and the strength of the man who wielded it. To believe otherwise was folly . . . or . . .

"Why did you cast it aside?" she asked quickly, before she could follow that line of thought to its logical conclusion.

"I did not need it. The giant was no trouble; as I said, he was dreadfully slow. And many of the knights turned tail and fled. I doubt I fought more than half of them."

Ah, well, that explained it. How foolish she had been to doubt! Single-handed, he had defeated only *thirty* knights, not sixty. No wonder he had tossed the last shield away!

Had it been anyone else, she would have laughed, certain he was either a braggart or a liar. But she refused to believe that Lancelot would lie to her, and he had never once attempted to impress her with his deeds. Even now, he had done his best to avoid the subject, and she was quite sure he wasn't jesting. Which meant that he was telling her the truth.

And still it was impossible.

"Lancelot," she said carefully, "are you quite certain that is how it was? Not that I doubt you," she added quickly, "I'm sure you fought bravely that day. 'Tis only . . ."

"Only what?" He sat up and brushed straw from his damp skin.

"Well . . ." she drew a swift breath and plunged ahead. "No boy of eighteen years, however doughty he might be, could possibly defeat thirty knights. Even if they were hopeless, utterly unskilled, and cowardly into the bargain, the sheer numbers would have been enough to overcome a single challenger."

"Yes, but I had the shields."

"The shield does not exist that can increase its owner's strength tenfold! It simply isn't possible; it isn't in the natural order of things! Listen to me," she said urgently, sitting up to face him. "The sun rises each morning in the east. Every night it sinks into the west. That is God's ordering of the world; it can never change, no more than a seed of rye, planted in a field, might yield a turnip—or an onion or a rose—if rain falls upon a Tuesday or the wind blows from the north!"

"Or that killing a spider at harvest time brings rain?"

"Of course it doesn't! That is just a silly superstition, and only the ignorant believe it!"

"So I am ignorant?" he retorted, his eyes flashing.

"No!"

"Oh, I am a liar, then!"

"Not that, either. Please don't be angry, I only want to help. The Lady of the Lake—she isn't who you think she is." Quickly she told him of her conversation with Father Bernard. Lancelot did not interrupt but sat quietly, his head bent. "So you see," she finished, "it isn't your fault at all. You were just a child; of course you believed everything they told you."

At last he raised his head. "So what you are saying," he said slowly, "is that I am mad."

She flinched as though he'd struck her. "No! You are . . .

confused. Mistaken. Oh, Lancelot, there is no such thing as magic."

"No such thing as *magic*!" He laughed a little wildly. "Do you honestly believe that?"

"It is not a matter of belief; I know it for a certainty. My love, I would not lie to you, not about anything and surely not about this. If only you will trust me, together we can find the truth."

He stared at her as though he had never really seen her before. "Then what do you think happened in Norhaut?" he said at last.

"You fought and won a battle. That much we can be certain of, as the castle is now yours. As for the rest, it could be that the damsel—the one from the Lady of the Lake—made you believe things that were not real. Father Bernard told me once such a thing was possible, he had seen it for himself in his travels to the east, in the days he was a knight."

Lancelot shook his head, not in denial but as though to clear it. "Elaine, if what you say is true . . . then I *am* mad, for I remember fighting every moment of that battle. And my time in Avalon—it was not as you say."

"Are you sure?" she asked gently.

"Yes." He put a hand to his head, rubbing the space between his brows. "Or . . . how can I be sure of anything?"

"You can be sure of me," she answered, resting her hand upon his shoulder. He seized it in his own and brought it to his lips.

"Yes. I am sure of you, Elaine."

"Then all will be well," she said simply. "Now, tell me what happened after the battle."

"When it was finished, the lady who had brought me there said the castle was to be mine. Apparently some old seer had predicted the whole thing, and it was writ upon a scroll."

"There, you see? That is quite impossible."

"I saw the scroll, Elaine. It is still in Joyous Gard if you care to examine it yourself."

"Oh, I don't doubt it exists. But it must have been some sort of trick, or—"

"A lucky guess? I suppose it could have been either, though why they would go to so much trouble to present me with a castle is a mystery. Still, let's call it a guess—a particularly lucky one, for the scroll specified a nameless knight as their savior from the tyrant. It went on to say that this knight would find his name inscribed below the castle. Before you ask, the ink was dry," he added wryly. "I checked. In fact, the scroll appeared to be quite old, though I imagine there are ways to manufacture the appearance of age. But again, why would they bother?"

"I don't know," Elaine admitted. Frightened, she reached for his hand. "It's such a very odd thing to do."

"Not nearly as odd as what happened next. The lady led me down through the crypts. Do you know, I'd never seen a crypt before, or a corpse—save for men new slain in battle, which isn't the same thing at all . . ."

He was silent for a moment, his eyes dark with some deeply unpleasant memory, then went on, "She took me to a marble slab set into the floor. I lifted the slab—easily, though it must have weighed half a ton—and went down the steps beneath. It was all dust and cobwebs, and at the bottom was a small chamber with a marble bier. At the foot was a plaque that read, 'Here will lie Sir Lancelot du Lac, son of King Ban of Benwick.' "

Elaine frowned. "I don't believe it."

"I assure you it is there. I will show it to you if—"

"Oh, I believe *you*. But someone arranged it—they must have."

"Yes, of course. The Lady of the Lake."

Elaine shivered, wondering at the mind that could plan such a thing so far in advance. "How cruel!" she said, very low. "And to what purpose?"

"That I cannot say." He lay back in the straw as though exhausted. "I only brought it up in the first place because I wanted you to understand that Joyous Gard is not a place to which I am overly attached. In fact, I haven't been back since that first time until we went together. It is only joyous when *you* are in it, Elaine." He cupped her chin in one hard palm and turned her face to his. "I would as lief stay here, an it pleases you."

"Thank you." She kissed him gently and lay down again, their bodies curling together. "But Lancelot," she said after a time, "I wonder what purpose it served to keep you in ignorance of your identity for so many years? And why choose such a complicated way to—"

His mouth came down on hers, silencing her questions. When his hand moved down her neck to cup her breast, she decided they could wait. Only later, when they lay entwined again, the sweat cooling on Elaine's body, did she remember what she had meant to ask.

"Lancelot," she began, and when he did not answer, she raised herself on an elbow to find he was asleep. Sighing, she lay down beside him and rested her head on his chest.

There was something very peculiar going on. Not magical, of course, though someone had gone to a good deal of trouble to make it look like magic. This was some complex web of intrigue, carefully planned, meticulously executed— but to what end?

She was certain of only one thing: Lancelot was an unwitting participant in whatever intrigue was being carried out. He looked so young, so innocent, with his hair curling round his sleep-flushed cheeks. For a moment she could see the child he had been, stolen from his grieving mother and denied even the knowledge of his name. All part of a plan, she thought, and suddenly she knew that they—no, *she*, the Lady of the Lake—was not finished with him yet.

"You shan't have him," she said aloud. "He is mine."

She hadn't noticed how very silent the barn was until she spoke. Though her voice had been little more than a whisper, her last word lingered in the stillness. *Mine.* The air was strangely heavy, as happened in the moment before a storm, though now the sun shone through the little chinks in the walls, bits of chaff suspended in the beams like faery dust.

Elaine sat up, every muscle tensed and all her senses straining. As the silence lengthened, she became aware of her own heart thudding audibly and the rasping of her breath. When a gust of wind shook the barn, she started with a little cry. It whistled shrilly through the walls with a sound like mocking laughter.

Chapter 29

· · ·

"WAKE up," Elaine said urgently. "We must go."

Lancelot opened one eye. "Not yet."

"Yes, now." She rummaged in the straw and found his shirt. Tossing it to him, she dragged her shift over her head. "Hurry."

"Why?"

A logical question, and one for which she had no answer. There was no explaining her sudden panic, the feeling that they had to get away at once. "Just do as I say," she snapped, and he sat up, brows raised.

"Where are we going?"

"To—to the fields. We must turn the hay while the sun is strong."

"If you like," he said agreeably. "You've got your kirtle on back to front. Here, let me, you're all in a tangle."

"I can do it." She jerked it off with shaking hands and twisted it around. "Please, just—"

And then she heard it, the sound she now realized she'd been waiting for. The sound of hoofbeats on the road.

Lancelot hadn't noticed. He pulled on his boots and looked at her, still sitting in her shift with her kirtle clutched before her. "Well? Are you coming?"

He hadn't bothered with his jerkin, still damp from the storm, and wore only a pair of faded trews with a linen shirt, splashed with drying mud. It was open at the neck, revealing the strong brown column of his throat, and bits of hay were caught among his raven curls. When he smiled and held out a hand to her, tears started to her eyes. "Too late," she whispered.

"Too late for—?" He stiffened, looking toward the door.

The rider had stopped and was calling to someone—Torre, perhaps—asking for Sir Lancelot.

"That sounds like—"

"Sir Bors," Elaine said.

"Yes, you're right, it does."

Lancelot swung himself over the side of the hayloft and dropped lightly to the ground, calling over his shoulder for her to hurry before he vanished out the door. Elaine pulled on her kirtle and ran her fingers through her hair, dislodging as much hay as she could, then twisted it into an untidy braid. Her hands were steady now, her eyes dry, though she felt as stiff as an old woman as she went carefully down the ladder. When she reached the doorway, she looked back. All was peaceful, utterly serene. Tiny beams of sunlight turned straw to gold, and the air was fragrant with crushed flowers.

Damn you.

She did not speak the words aloud, for of course there was no one there to hear her. No one at all. Slowly, still moving with that odd, jerky stiffness, she opened the door and stepped outside.

"Elaine!" Lancelot called, gesturing her over to where

he stood with Torre and another young man, who turned quickly, smiling as she approached. "Look, it *is* Bors!"

"Lady Elaine." Bors bowed. "I am so pleased to see you again." His eyes went from her to Lancelot, taking in their crumpled clothing, liberally bedecked with chaff and straw, and a quick blush stained his cheeks.

"Yes, she's quite a sight," Torre drawled, and though Elaine knew she should be mortified, she could not find the energy to care.

"Welcome to Corbenic, Sir Bors," she said. "Won't you come inside?"

"I'm sorry, but I cannot stop. I am on an errand from the king."

Elaine put out a hand to grasp the fence post behind her.

"Lance," Bors went on, turning to his cousin, "we're off to settle this Claudus. The king bade me find you. Here, he sent you this."

Lancelot took the square of parchment and turned it in his hands, breaking the seal with such eagerness that the parchment tore a little.

"Claudus?" Elaine said.

"Claudus set himself up as Emperor of Rome some time ago and demanded tribute of King Arthur. Of course he was refused, but the king has been keeping an eye on him ever since."

After his haste to unseal the letter, Lancelot was showing a strange reluctance to read it. He held the folded square in his hands as Bors went on about Claudus, almost as if he feared to see what was within. At last he unfolded it and read, his expression deeply wary. A moment later he smiled, just a little, then his smile widened to a grin, and at last he laughed aloud.

"It is good news?" Elaine asked.

"Yes. It's all right, he isn't angry. He said he's sorry to

disturb my convalescence, but needs must. And he sent you, Bors, because he knows the man who could leave his spear tip in my ribs and live to tell the tale is one I love too well to refuse."

Bors blushed again. "He is jesting—"

"Yes, but it is true," Lancelot said. He looked very merry, but Elaine fancied there was a hard brilliance to his humor. When he looked at her, his eyes seemed fever bright.

"He remembers you, too, Elaine. Listen. 'Give the Lady Elaine our thanks for her care of you, and her patience in bearing with your company. She must be a very saint, and if her beauty is even half what rumor makes it, 'tis no wonder we have not seen your face in Camelot. Say to her—or not, as your discretion bids you—that we shall keep you but a little while, and with God's help, return you all the better for your adventure.' "

"He is very kind," Elaine said.

"Always." Lancelot folded the letter carefully. "I must go, Elaine."

"Of course you must," she said.

In the act of tucking the letter into his belt, Lancelot halted. He wore the look of someone trying very hard to remember something . . . or a man straining to make out a distant sound inaudible to any but himself.

"The ships are provisioned and waiting . . ." Bors went on, but Elaine was not listening.

Lancelot's eyes widened. His lips parted slightly, as though he was about to cry out in surprise, but then he checked himself and made no sound save a sharply indrawn breath.

"I waited until the last to come to you," Bors finished, "and so I'm afraid we'll have to go at once."

"At once," Lancelot repeated distractedly. "Yes. I—a moment, Bors, I think I left something . . ."

He ran to the barn, pulled open the door, and vanished inside. Torre glanced at Elaine, brows raised. She shrugged as though nothing were amiss. "How is Sir Lionel?" she asked.

Bors grimaced. "Still Lionel, I fear."

They passed a few minutes laughing at Lionel's latest scrape, but soon the subject was exhausted, and Lancelot had not returned.

After a rather awkward time, when the three of them stood looking at anything but one another, Torre said abruptly, "Do you think he ran off?"

Bors laughed. "Lance, run from a fight?"

Elaine laughed, too, albeit a trifle wanly. Another minute passed before Lancelot emerged from the barn, and she knew at once that something had happened. He was once again the knight who had first arrived at Corbenic. Even dressed as he was in his mud-spattered shirt and old trews, he stood apart from the common run of men. He did not glow; such a word was too tame for the fire that consumed him from within. When he reached them, the others seemed to fade, while Lancelot stood out in sharp relief.

"Sorry," he said, "I couldn't find it at once. Bors, I need a few minutes with Elaine. Come, man," he added with an edge of his old arrogance, "the ship won't sail without *me*."

Bors glanced at him, surprised, then back to Elaine. "Perhaps I do have time for ale before we ride. Sir Torre, if you would be so kind . . ."

"Elaine, I'm sorry for this," Lancelot said the moment they were alone, though he did not look sorry in the least. He looked . . . happy, a little stunned, as though he had received an unexpected gift of great magnificence.

She had seen that look before, though for a moment she could not imagine when or where. And then it came to her. With a cold shock she remembered seeing just that expression on his face the first time they lay together.

"The timing is wretched, I know," he went on, and though he did his best to look concerned, his glowing eyes and ruddy cheeks gave him the lie, "but it shouldn't take too long."

She nodded, not trusting herself to speak, and he took two steps forward to lay his hands upon her shoulders. "Say something; don't just look at me as though I've killed the cat!"

"You—you are pleased," she faltered, the words not quite a question.

"Not pleased to leave you, no—but, Elaine, the king has sent for me. I cannot deny that brings me joy."

But it was not the king's message that had given him that unseely glow. No, that had come after. What had he heard upon the wind? Who had been waiting in the barn?

She shivered. "Lancelot, I'm frightened."

"There is no need. As soon as this is settled, I'll be back. Do you hear me, Elaine?" he said, giving her a little shake. "I will be back."

"You cannot be certain—"

"But I am. It's all right now, I've been given another chance."

Oh, God, she thought, *sweet Jesu, let him not mean what I think he does.* "By the king?" she asked, her voice seeming to come from very far away.

His hesitation lasted but a moment, though it was long enough for her to read the answer in his eyes. "Yes," he said too quickly. "Yes, by the king. All is as it was before, and this time—this time I will do better. So you see, there is no need to worry."

But all she saw was a man in the grip of a dangerous delusion.

"Lancelot," she said, choosing each word with care, "do nothing reckless, I beg you. Remember your wound."

"I'll remember it," he promised solemnly, "every time it rains. And I am never reckless—well, almost never." He drew a finger down her cheek. "Don't fear, love; no harm will come to me."

"You sound so sure. How can you know such a thing?" she asked, striving to sound merely curious.

He smiled down at her and tucked a lock of hair behind her ear. "I *have* fought before, you know. They say I'm rather good at it."

There was no one in the barn, she told herself. *There is no such thing as a magical lady who can appear and disappear at will. He is confused—mistaken—his mind was twisted when he was just a child. Not his fault. Not madness. He was better, much better until today.*

"Is it . . ." She drew a breath and finished in a rush. "Is it because the Lady of the Lake has said so?"

His dark brows drew together in a scowl. "Leave off, Elaine. You would not understand. But in the end, it makes no difference. The king commands; I must, perforce, obey. That is how it is with me, how it will always be. Before all I am the king's man."

"Yes, of course," she said, "I understand that much."

"Then you know everything that matters."

But she knew nothing at all, save that he had changed in the space of a few moments. He seemed a stranger—the great du Lac—not her Lancelot at all. Helplessly, hating herself, Elaine began to cry. "This Lady—whoever or whatever she may be—is using you. Can you not see that?"

He frowned, rubbed absently at the space between his eyes. "Leave off, Elaine, I beg you. You know nothing of the Lady, and I do not want to quarrel with you now."

"What has she offered you, Lancelot?" Elaine cried. "What payment for your services?"

He whitened to the lips. "I said leave *off*!"

He was slipping away from her, so quickly that she could scarce accept what was happening. His smile looked strained as he held out his hand. "Elaine, I don't want to go like this. Come, kiss me farewell; Bors is waiting."

But when he bent to her, she turned her face away. "Tell me one thing more," she said, her voice shaking. "Will you see the queen before you sail?"

"Oak and ash, not *that* again!" he said impatiently. "I have no idea where the queen is now. Belike she is in Camelot, though she may have gone to the ships with—"

"Swear that you will have no private speech with Guinevere before you leave. Give me your oath upon it!"

Who is this woman with the shrill, ugly voice? Not me, Elaine thought, appalled, *no, this isn't me, it can't be—*

"How dare you tell me who I may or may not speak to?" he demanded. "I have said I love you—I have offered you marriage. What more do you want of me?" He turned away, adding bitterly, "If you really loved me, you would trust me."

"I want to trust you, but how can I?"

"That is a question only you can answer. I suggest," he added coldly, "that you think well on it while I am gone. God keep you until we meet again."

"And you," she answered steadily, but did not trust herself to say more. She watched him walk away, part of her longing to go after him and beg his forgiveness—

For what? For asking him to speak the truth? No, it was he who was wrong—wrong to keep these secrets from her, wrong to always put the Lady first, wrong to ride off to the queen and leave her all alone when she—she—

All at once Brisen stood beside her, her arm around Elaine's trembling shoulders. "Did you tell him?"

"Tell him what?"

"That you bear his child. Oh, lady don't deny it, I know a breeding woman when I see one. Did you tell him?"

Elaine shook her head. "I wanted to be sure before I spoke."

They stood together watching Bors and Lancelot emerge from the stable. She fancied that Lancelot hesitated before mounting, his face turned to the place where she and Brisen stood. She nearly went to him then, but Brisen halted her.

"Don't," she said. "It is too late. You'll only make it worse for him—and for yourself. Besides," she added bracingly, "you want him back whole, don't you? There's no worse luck for a man riding into battle than to leave behind a weeping woman."

"Then we must pray," Elaine said bitterly, "that he does not see the queen before he goes."

Chapter 30

• • •

R AIN lashed against the shutters of the hall. The air
was thick with smoke from the damp wood smolder-
ing in the central fire and the rushlight burning on the trestle table. The baby wailed fitfully at Elaine's feet as she
squinted at the column of figures, then threw down her
quill and dropped her head into her hands, her stiff fingers
massaging her throbbing temples.

"Brisen," she said carefully, fearing her skull would
shatter if she raised her voice. "Brisen, Galahad is hungry.
Send for his nurse."

"Aye, lady," Brisen said, scooping up the crying child.
"And you should lie down for a time."

As if Elaine hadn't spent enough time in bed. Six weeks
she'd lain there after Galahad was born, and though the first
fortnight had passed in a blur of pain and fever, the rest had
dragged by interminably as she waited vainly for her
strength and spirits to return. After a solid month of staring at the ceiling and choking down Brisen's bitter brews,

she'd had enough of waiting. There was still work to be done.

Galahad's nurse arrived, a plump, cheerful lass who'd borne a daughter a mere fortnight before Galahad's birth. Brisen surrendered the infant to her reluctantly.

Elaine leaned her head in her hand and watched Galahad suckle noisily, his tiny fists flailing, feeling a dull twinge in her own flaccid breasts. The birth had been hard; by the time she'd regained her senses, Galahad was accustomed to his wet nurse. Elaine had made one or two attempts to feed him herself, but it was hopeless from the start.

And it was better this way. She had far too much to do and little enough energy with which to do it, without a nursing child to distract her. Yet still she sat, her cheek resting in her palm, watching Lotte grasp one of Galahad's waving fists and fold it gently in her own palm before raising it to her lips.

They were lucky to have found such a kind, healthy lass. When Lotte placed the full and sleeping child in his basket and slipped away, Elaine resolved yet again to make her a goodly gift when her service to Galahad was finished.

If, she thought, gazing down at the column of figures, they had anything to give.

Lancelot had been generous. In fairness, she must give him that. He'd left a purse with Torre, and before he'd sailed, he'd found the time to send two dozen ewes and a ram—the black-faced, long-legged kind she'd always longed to try—complete with a shepherd accustomed to their ways. A fortnight later had brought three sows, two in pig, and a man to tend them. Later still had come a bolt of Arabian silk of peacock blue shot through with golden threads. But no letter. No message explaining if these gifts were a promise of his eventual return or a farewell.

And then the gifts had stopped. As though that had been some sort of signal, the ones he had given began to vanish like faery gold in sunlight, a parallel Elaine did not like, but one she could not escape.

First the sheep sickened. One slipped her lamb and died upon the snow-swept hillside, then another and another, not only the black-faced sheep, but their own as well. Now only three ewes and the two rams remained. The pigs lasted a bit longer, until a swine fever swept the countryside. The swineherd ran off with their best dairymaid and was never seen again.

All that was left were a few coins and the bolt of silk that Elaine could not quite make up her mind to sell.

And Galahad.

After his birth, Elaine had been seized by the morbid certainty that he, too, would be snatched away, a fear that even now had not quite left her. He was an extraordinarily beautiful baby, though he bore no resemblance to his father. Galahad's hair was like spun gold, his eyes a very clear, light blue. He was a son any man would be proud to acknowledge . . . any man save Lancelot, who did not even know of Galahad's existence.

Despite the fact that the king had returned to Camelot six weeks before.

Lavaine's squire, Gaspard, had brought the news. He was a Spanish lad who had attached himself to Lavaine somewhere in Picardy, and had been sent to Corbenic so he might recover from a festering wound. Now he sat by the smoking fire, whittling a toy for Galahad, to whom he was devoted. He spoke their language a little, enough to give them halting accounts of battles fought across the sea, in which Lancelot's name figured prominently.

"He ees the finest," Gaspard had assured them, his black eyes shining, "the bravest, the noblest, the—how you say?—"

"I don't," Torre growled. "Where is Sir Lancelot now?"

Gaspard shrugged his bony shoulders. "With hees king, no? Where else would he be?"

Where else, indeed?

• • •

FOR the next fortnight, Elaine had gone about in a daze, leaving a trail of tasks half finished when she started up and flew to the nearest window at each imagined sound. Now that another month had passed, she'd finally accepted that Lancelot wasn't coming back.

So she did not rush to the door when a horse clattered into the courtyard, leaving Torre to investigate. When he called her name a moment later, she did not at first recognize the tall young man beside him.

"Well, Elly?" he said, holding out his arms. "Is this the greeting I get?"

And then she knew him. "Lavaine," she cried, leaping from her seat to run to him. He caught her up and spun her around before setting her on her feet. "Oh, Lavaine, I'm so glad to see you."

He was broader across the shoulders, deeper in the chest, and he moved with a new grace, as though he'd finally grown accustomed to the length of his arms and legs. He smelled of rain and horses, and when he smiled down at her, she realized the boy who'd left them had returned a man.

"How fare you, Elly?" he asked, his eyes darkening with concern. "Have you been ill?"

"A little, but I'm better now," she said, leading him over to the fire.

"Gaspard!" Lavaine said to his squire, "I can see you're in fine fettle! Have they been spoiling you?"

"*Sí*, sir," Gaspard admitted with a grin. "Much spoiled."

"Well, you can go stable my horse, you lazy dog,"

Lavaine said, laughing. "And see to my armor before it rusts through."

"Here," Elaine said, "give me your cloak—Brisen, look! Lavaine is home."

"Hello, Brisen," Lavaine said, sinking down on the settle and stretching his long legs toward the sullen little blaze. "Pretty as ever, I see."

"For that, you shall have a honey cake with your wine," Brisen said, bending to drop a kiss on the top of his head.

"Do I get one, too?" Torre asked.

Brisen regarded him through narrowed eyes. "One what?"

"A honey cake. Please," he added with a smile.

"No." Brisen's eyes flashed and she whirled, her skirts flying as she ran swiftly from the hall.

"Well, that's nice!" Torre said, shaking his head as he stared after her.

"I always was her favorite," Lavaine said smugly.

Torre cuffed his brother lightly before taking the seat beside him, and though he laughed, a small frown creased his brow as he stared at the doorway though which Brisen had just passed.

"Tell us everything, Lavaine," Elaine urged, squeezing onto the settle on Lavaine's other side and taking her brother's arm.

And he did. Battle by battle, he described King Arthur's victory over Claudus, stopping only to embrace his father when Pelleas arrived. By the time he'd finished, the flagon was empty and the plate of honey cakes nearly gone.

"A few of us remained behind in Gaul—we reached Camelot last night. I thought to stay a few days for the feasting, but I woke early and decided to come home. The path was flooded out, just by—" He broke off, looking over his shoulder. "What is that?"

"That," Elaine said, hurrying over to the basket beneath the trestle table, "is your nephew."

Lavaine turned to Torre. "When did you—"

Torre shook his head. "Not mine."

"Not—? Oh, Elly, I had no idea! Why didn't you tell me you'd been wed? Who—"

Elaine plopped the baby in Lavaine's arms. "You do know how to hold him, don't you? Watch his head—that's right, put your hand there—"

Lavaine gazed down at the child. Galahad looked back, his blue eyes wide and solemn.

"Hello, nephew." Lavaine tickled Galahad's belly, making the silly faces men always made when confronted with an infant. "God's beard, Elly, is he always this serious? He looks like he's about to start lecturing me on my sins. What is his name?"

"Galahad."

"He's a fine boy," Lavaine said. "Congratulations. When were you—?" He broke off when Torre caught his eye and shook his head. "Oh. I see." He stroked Galahad's hair with one finger, his face grim. "How—who—?"

"I would think by your age you would know *how*," Elaine snapped. "As for who—" Her throat tightened, and she looked helplessly at Torre.

"His father is Sir Lancelot du Lac," Pelleas put in unexpectedly. "A noble lineage—young Galahad stands but in the seventh degree from—"

"Sir Lancelot?" Lavaine interrupted. His cheeks flushed a brilliant red. "But—but I fought with him; we were together constantly—he never said—"

"Did he not speak of me at all?" Elaine asked, taking Galahad from her brother and settling him in the crook of her arm.

"Yes, he did, often—and always with the greatest re-

spect. He said how kind you'd been when he spent those
months here at Corbenic—" Lavaine's eyes flashed. "But
he never said *how* he had spent them. By God, I'll—I'll—"

"You'll wait your turn is what you'll do," Torre cut in
sharply. "Once I'm finished, you can have whatever's left."

"Neither of you will fight him," Elaine said. "I forbid it."

"Elly, we're your brothers—"

"I don't care who you are," she said fiercely. "I will han-
dle this in my own way—in my own time."

How and when that would be, she did not know. So far
she'd been incapable of anything but hoping Lancelot
would return, and when hope was gone, waiting passively to
see what happened next. The only thing she knew for certain was that she did not want her brothers to issue Lancelot
a challenge. The very thought made her stomach churn.

"He'd make mincemeat of the both of you, anyway,"
Brisen said tartly, sweeping the dish and flagon from the
table before turning to fix Torre with an icy glare. "And if
you think I'll put you back together a second time, you are
mistaken."

Torre looked so taken aback that Elaine almost laughed.
"Who asked you to?"

"Not you, that's certain," Brisen retorted. "You never
ask me for anything, do you? You just ignore me or order
me about."

"Why, you daft besom, I asked you for something
earlier—asked nicely, too, for all the good it did me."

"Right. So you did." Brisen picked up the last, half-
eaten cake from the plate and flung it in his face. "There. I
hope you choke on it."

Torre shot to his feet. "Did you see what she just did?"
he demanded of his siblings. "What the devil can she mean
by it?"

"Why don't you ask her?" Lavaine suggested. He

picked up the half-eaten cake from the floor, brushed it with his sleeve, then sighed and tossed it into the fire.

"You," Brisen said, stabbing a finger into Torre's chest, "are a selfish, idle wastrel. I wish you *would* fight Sir Lancelot—mayhap this time he'll finish you!"

Torre batted her hand away. "You're mad."

"Not anymore." Brisen's dark eyes shone briefly before she turned and walked away.

"Mistress Brisen seems upset," Lord Pelleas remarked.

"She's daft." Torre laughed uncomfortably. "Raving."

"She seemed sane enough to me," Lavaine said. "Just angry. What have you been getting up to, Torre? Brisen is a good sort—I mean, she saved your life and all, wore herself to a shadow sitting up for weeks on end—and now, if you've been trifling with her—"

"Trifling? With *Brisen*? I've never even thought of it!"

Lavaine's brows shot up. "You haven't?" He shook his head, a grin quirking the corner of his mouth. "Well, that explains it."

"Explains *what*?"

"Ask her yourself," Lavaine said.

"I will." Torre stood a moment, staring at the doorway, then abruptly resumed his seat. "Later. First we need to settle this, we've put it off too long already. I mean to speak to Sir Lancelot."

Lavaine frowned at his nephew. "Elly, does Lancelot even know?"

She shook her head. "Not yet."

"What difference does it make?" Torre said impatiently. "He must have known there was a chance this would happen, and he's had well over a month to come and see—"

"He hasn't," Lavaine said. "He only returned to Camelot last night, with me."

For one brief, terrible moment Elaine feared that she

might swoon. The hall seemed to darken, and a sound like
rushing water filled her ears. She managed to drag in one
gasping breath, and then another, and the rushing subsided
in time for her to hear Torre say, "Well, *you're* here, aren't
you? He could have come, as well."

"Not this morning. He was meant to see the king."

Elaine bent to put Galahad in his basket, taking her time
adjusting his coverlet. *Not again,* she thought. *Please, God,
I cannot do it all again.* Only in the past few days had she
felt anything like herself, and now that hard-won peace had
been demolished by a few words from Lavaine. Already
she could feel it starting, the sickening jolt between exulta-
tion and despair.

At one moment she was certain Lancelot was on his
way, utterly convinced of his love. In the next, she was
equally certain she had lost him forever. Back and forth, up
and down, going over every word they'd ever spoken, reliving each sigh and touch and kiss, replaying their last
quarrel and trying to pinpoint the precise moment when it
had all gone so wrong, searching for the words she could
have used to make it come out differently.

When she was not dwelling in the past, her mind was
racing toward the future, imagining how and when Lancelot
would learn of Galahad's existence. From Lavaine? Torre?
Or would some stray bit of gossip reach him before her
brothers did? What would he say? What would he feel? Re-
morse? Annoyance? Pity?

Holy Mother, I cannot, she thought, I *cannot do that
again.*

And I will not.

She raised her head. "I am going to Camelot."

"What?" Torre demanded.

"Oh, Elly, you can't!" Lavaine cried.

"I can. I shall. Sir Lancelot deserves to know he has a son, and I will be the one to tell him."

Torre slammed his fist upon the table. "I will not let you humble yourself to that—that—"

"I have no intention of doing so," she answered coolly. "Galahad cannot be hidden forever. Sir Lancelot may acknowledge him or not—that will be his decision. But I refuse to sit here, hands folded, and wait for him to make it."

"But Elly," Lavaine protested, "don't you see how it would look? You can't expose yourself like that—you don't know what it's like at court!"

"He's right," Torre said. "I will go."

"And I!" Lavaine cried.

"Yes," Lord Pelleas said. His eyes met Elaine's, and he smiled. "I think you should both accompany your sister."

Elaine walked over to her father and kissed his brow. "Thank you. For . . ."

For loving me. For loving Galahad. For never treating either of us as though we had disgraced the family name.

". . . for everything," she finished.

"That's quite all right, my dear," he said, reaching up to pat her cheek. "I'm very proud of you. Always have been."

Elaine turned to her brothers. "To Camelot, then. We leave at dawn."

Chapter 31

. . .

THE feast was a success, Guinevere thought, trying very hard to care. She forced herself to smile at Arthur, to sip from the cup they shared, and chat lightly of the latest gossip. But all the while she was conscious of the dull ache beneath her girdle. This afternoon she had woken to the knowledge that there was no baby after all, no new life growing within her. There never had been, she told herself. *I was late, that's all, it means nothing. Next month, perhaps . . .*

Having consumed every morsel amid a babble of excited talk and laughter, her guests had reached the state of satiety. Guinevere, judging the moment right, caught Sir Tristan's eye and nodded.

Tristan bowed to Guinevere and smiled, which did nothing to dispel his air of melancholy, for though his lips curved charmingly, his eyes remained as they ever were, large dark pools of sorrow. Two pages hurried over with his harp and a cushion, and he sank down with a heavy sigh. Tristan did not merely sit, he drooped—and most becomingly, Guinevere noted cynically, before she dismissed the thought as unworthy. With an awareness sharpened by her own loss—which had been no loss at all, she told herself fiercely, but merely a mistake—she knew Tristan innocent of artifice.

It was almost impossible to reconcile his fine-drawn features and slender form with the stories of his ferocity in battle, yet Arthur had assured her that the tales were not exaggerated.

"Well, you've seen him joust," Arthur had said. "Granted, he seems to do it in his sleep, but you'll note he stands third in the ranking. 'Tis the same in battle. Right up until the action starts, he seems only half awake, but once it begins, there is no one—save Lance and Gawain, of course—I'd rather have beside me. It's good to have them all back again, isn't it?"

Lancelot had returned two days before and still looked weary from the journey. He sat across the hall with his fellow knights while a steady stream of pages approached him. Guinevere amused herself by identifying the ladies who had sent them, watching their faces fall as the pages returned, still bearing the rejected glove or ring.

Once Lance would have laughed, reveling in the attention, but today he scarcely seemed to notice. Dinadan, sitting beside him, was smiling as he leaned on Lance's shoulder, no doubt providing one of his acidly amusing commentaries on the offerings. Gawain, seated nearby, watched the procession with stony disapproval. Yet it was said that Gawain had received scores of such invitations—and accepted a good many of them, too, before his adventure with the Green Knight turned him priggish as a monk.

Dinadan managed to win the occasional smile from Lancelot, but for the most part, he looked miserable in the midst of what should have been his triumph. This feast was in his honor, after all, as he had missed the king's home-coming celebrations.

When Arthur had stood and raised his goblet, praising Lancelot's courage on the field, the entire company rose to their feet, crying out, "Du Lac! Du Lac!" until the very rafters echoed with his praise. Lancelot had bowed and smiled, yet even then his eyes darted from door to window, like an animal caught fast in a trap.

What could be the matter with him? Guinevere wondered yet again, bending forward to look past Arthur, vainly trying to catch his eye. No one loved a feast as much as Lance, particularly when he was the center of attention. He should be laughing now, not slouching in his seat as though ashamed. He finally glanced at her, but only fleetingly, with a quick smile and half shrug meant to reassure her, then he fixed his eyes on Tristan as though willing the entire company to do the same.

The ladies, at least, obliged, temporarily diverted by the rare spectacle of Tristan preparing to give them a song. Watching their faces, Guinevere knew just what they were thinking, for she'd often heard them ask aloud: What could make such a fair young man so very sad? She knew, as well, what they thought but did not say: Given half a chance, *I* could make him happy.

That much, she doubted. Tristan's heart was set upon Isolde of Cornwall, wed to his own uncle. Once Guinevere would have thought him ridiculous to persist in an impossible love when so many perfectly good ladies wanted nothing but to console him, but now she understood a heart once fixed could not be moved by such a puny tool as reason.

Arthur looked over the assembled company, enjoying their anticipation, for he liked nothing better than for those around him to be happy. He was pleased, too, that Tristan—who seldom sang publicly—was making such an effort to rouse Lancelot from whatever ill humor had him in its grip.

As his king, it was his duty to censure Tristan, Arthur mused. By all accounts, the lad had gotten himself into the devil of a mess in Cornwall. But Tristan was in many ways so innocent, and possessed such a sweet generosity of spirit, that Arthur could find no room in his heart for anything but pity. *It is so hard to be young,* Arthur reflected with a sigh, feeling as though an age separated his own thirty-two years from Tristan's twenty.

When all eyes were riveted upon Tristan, Arthur spied a slender, auburn-haired woman slip though the doorway and sink unobtrusively into an empty seat. She glanced around and met Arthur's gaze.

Morgause. What was *she* doing here? It must be three years or more since Arthur's half sister had come to court, and Gawain had given no hint that she planned a visit. Likely Gawain hadn't known; if he had, he would have made some excuse to absent himself before his mother arrived. The two were barely on speaking terms these days. Arthur wrested his gaze from hers and turned determinedly to the front of the hall as Tristan's long, pale fingers struck the first chord on his harp. A moment later he had forgotten Morgause completely.

When Tristan began to sing, the hall fell silent. Not a single person spoke or even moved. From the lowest scullion who had crept into some shadowed corner of the hall to the king himself, all were transfixed.

His song was a simple one. It told of green meadows and birds upon the wing, butterflies among the blossoms on the wold. He sang of summer's end, when chill winds sent bright petals dancing over stubbled harvest fields.

Youth and hope and innocence—gone, all gone, fled like springtime's promise before an autumn gale.

Arthur stared straight ahead, no longer seeing Tristan but the long spring of his childhood, when the world was new and each day a marvelous adventure. He thought of running bare-legged in the fields, the hounds jumping and barking all around him. He thought of Sir Ector, dead this past spring, red-faced and laughing in the first snowfall of the year, while his lady, Orma, scolded her husband and sons to come in from the cold before they took an ague. Ector had seized her around her solid waist and whirled her into the courtyard, planting a smacking kiss upon her rosy cheek. How they had all laughed! Even Merlin, leaning in the doorway, had been smiling his rare sweet smile as he watched them dancing in the snow.

Could I have really been so happy? Arthur wondered. *Yes,* his heart cried, *I wanted nothing but to be Kay's squire and steward of his lands. Never, never did I think to leave the home and fields and family that I loved. But then Kay forgot his sword, and I ran off to fetch it . . .*

Sometimes, even now, all that had happened since seemed like a dream. The wars and deaths and treaties and betrayals, the kingdom under his command and the thousand weighty matters awaiting his decision were insubstantial as a puff of thistledown. At such times, Arthur was certain he would wake to find himself curled up beside the fire in Sir Ector's hall with half a dozen hounds beside him, Kay arguing good-naturedly with Merlin over some lesson he had skimped, while Dame Orma sewed their shirts and threatened to make them do their own mending if they couldn't be more careful of her handiwork.

But now I am a king, he thought. *A great king—or so they tell me. I have a dozen shirts and no one dares to scold me when I tear one. Britain is secure, the people safe to till their fields. We make music in my beautiful castle, filled with the bravest knights in all the world, presided over by the loveliest queen who ever graced a table. I lack nothing for perfect happiness. Therefore, as Merlin would have said, logic dictates that I must be happy.*

Muttering a quick excuse, Arthur stood and left the hall, half blinded by the illogical tears welling in his eyes.

Guinevere was dry-eyed as Tristan's song faded into silence, one hand resting lightly on her girdle. *Spring will come again,* she thought, *but not this spring. Never this moment, this month, this . . .*

Tomorrow she would remember how desperately she needed an heir. Now she only thought of the spark of life of which she'd dreamed so vividly the night before—the son with Arthur's light blue eyes and sunny smile who called her "Mother" and brought her crumpled flowers—snuffed out before he ever had the chance to live.

She turned her head just as Lancelot turned his, and their eyes met across the hall.

"Oh, what is it?" she cried softly, startled out of her unhappiness by the naked misery in his eyes. "What is wrong?"

As though he'd heard her words, he shrugged again and looked away, picked up his goblet, and set it down again untasted. Dinadan leaned toward him, drawing his attention to a page who hovered at his elbow, holding out a scarf. He was a handsome little lad, with light hair and a merry, gap-toothed smile. *His mother must be so proud of him,* Guinevere thought, her throat aching with a wild pain. *How could she bear to send him from her side?*

Lancelot stood abruptly and walked from the hall, leaving the company to stare after him in shock. It lasted but a moment before the talk broke out, voices rising in excited speculation as they stared after the First Knight, then toward the queen, sitting all alone at the high table and staring at the seat Lancelot had abandoned, tears sliding down her cheeks.

Chapter 32

· · ·

LANCELOT was halfway to the stable before he stopped himself. He turned back to the hall, gave a sharp exclamation of disgust, and began to pace the small garden. Twelve steps carried him from end to end, twelve steps and he was back where he had started.

"Elaine," he said, hoping that to speak her name aloud would ease some of the terrible pressure inside him. "Elaine," he said again, the word ripped from him on a groan.

He would go to her, he thought, beg her to forgive him—but for what? For being what he was, what he could not help but be? No, Elaine was lost to him. He had made his choice in the hay-scented barn in Corbenic, though at the time he had foolishly believed it was no choice at all. He only realized what he'd done when he faced his first opponent on the battlefield.

The Green Knight had spoken truly: du Lac had no soul, no hope of heaven, and honor was something he could never know. That belonged to his companions, who rode laughing into battles from which they knew well they might not return. He had seen it, too, in the eyes of the men he himself had slain. Their faces haunted his dreams: grim campaigners with years of experience carved upon their brows, merry-hearted lads still bearing their first shield. They were all dead now, gone forever from this middle earth, struck down by a force against which no amount of skill or courage could avail them.

The great du Lac. The Lady's poppet. A manikin who'd once dreamed it was a man.

There was no place for such as him in Elaine's world, where the sun rose always in the east and set into the west. She would never believe that he had dwelt in a land beyond the sun, where night and day were subject to the Lady's whim.

Nor did he want her to believe it. He wanted her to stay exactly as she was, untouched by the dark magic that ruled him. *Let her go,* he told himself. *You have no right to so fine and fair a woman when all you have to offer is an empty shell.*

His place was here, at Camelot. For this he had been born, his path laid out for him before ever he drew breath. To go on fighting the inevitable would only drive him mad.

"Lance?"

He jumped, then turned to find Arthur just beside him. "You startled me," he said with an unconvincing laugh.

"I called you twice. Why aren't you inside? Are you ill?"

"No. It was just the crowd—the noise. But why are you out here?"

"Tristan's song." Arthur grimaced wryly. "Looking back is a pastime for old men. I'll come to it soon enough, no doubt—but not today."

"I should think you would enjoy looking back," Lancelot said. "Surely you have nothing to regret."

"Of course I have regrets," Arthur snapped. "You know I hate it when you talk like that, as though I am some sort of saint."

Lancelot stared down at the ground. All at once he was tired, so weary that he wanted nothing but to cast himself upon his bed and sleep. "I am sorry," he began.

"And don't apologize for my bad humor."

"I—" Lancelot clamped his lips shut before he could apologize again.

Arthur passed a hand over his face and sighed. "Forgive me. I am a beast today, but 'tis no fault of yours. Shall I leave you to your peace and quiet?"

"No," Lancelot said. "Stay."

Arthur smiled. "Good. We've hardly had a chance to talk since you returned. King Bagdemagus sent me a gyrfalcon. Would you like to see her?"

Lancelot returned his smile. "Yes."

"I hear you saved Agravaine's life in battle," Arthur remarked as they walked together toward the mews. "That was the second time, wasn't it?"

"Bad luck, isn't it?"

Arthur lifted one brow. "For him or you?"

"A bit of both," Lancelot answered with a halfhearted grin, "though I was talking about Agravaine. From the look on his face, I think he'd rather I'd left him as he was."

"He didn't thank you, I suppose." Arthur sighed. "Poor Agravaine. He seems to think you do it a-purpose, just to embarrass him."

Lancelot gave a short laugh. "Does he imagine I follow him about, waiting until he gets into trouble so I can get him out again?"

"No, that is Gawain's job. Between Agravaine and Gaheris, they keep him very busy."

Lancelot knew what was coming next, and before

Arthur could ask yet again why he and Gawain could not seem to get along, he said quickly, "I like Gaheris. We rode together for a time in Gaul."

"I like him, too," Arthur said.

They walked in silence down the pathway to the mews. But while their silences were usually comfortable, Lancelot suddenly felt he could not bear this one a moment longer.

"There is another brother, isn't there?" he asked. "A year or two younger than Gaheris?"

"Gareth."

"Yes, that's right."

"I'm looking forward to having him here," Arthur said.

Before that terrible silence could fall again, Lancelot made another effort. "Gaheris said that Gareth can hardly wait to come, but Queen Morgause doesn't want to let him go just yet."

Arthur stopped to examine a climbing rose. "So I've heard."

"I suppose it's only natural. He is her last, isn't he?"

"No," Arthur said, leaning forward to inhale the blossom's scent. "Not the last. There is one more after Gareth."

"What's that one called?" Lancelot asked.

"Mordred," Arthur said softly, reaching out to pluck the rose. "She called him Mordred."

"Is he—"

Arthur drew back his hand with a sharp hiss of pain.

"Are you bleeding?" Lancelot asked.

"It's nothing." Arthur shook his hand out. "Stupid of me. Listen, Lance," he said, suddenly brisk and businesslike, "I meant to tell you that there's a rumor Sir Turquine is up to his old tricks."

"I'll go have a look," Lancelot offered.

That should keep him busy for a time. By then, with any

luck, something else would have come up. He'd heard the Saxon treaty troops had grown restless while Arthur was away. Perhaps Arthur would send him there, as well. He'd always gotten along surprisingly well with the Saxons.

Yes, that was the way, do one thing, then the next, and hope that in time he could—not forget Elaine, he knew that was impossible—but learn to live with this pain that seemed unbearable. Yet it must be borne, and to wallow in his misery was contemptible. So long as he did not look back, or allow himself to hope, or wish for what could never be, he could still be of use to Arthur.

"Lance!"

Lancelot realized they had reached the mews. Arthur stood by the open door, waiting for him to pass.

"What is it?" Arthur asked, looking at him with concern. "Are you sure you aren't ill?"

"No. No, I'm fine."

"You're not." Arthur put a hand on his shoulder. "You're shaking, Lance, and pale as a wraith. What is the trouble?"

Lancelot twisted away. "Don't," he said in a low voice. "Just . . . don't. Please."

"Don't what?" Arthur asked quietly.

"Don't ask me questions—and don't look at me like that! I've said I'm fine, and I am."

"'Ere now, who's shouting out there?" a voice called from within the mews. "You're upsetting the king's gyrfalcon."

Lancelot passed a hand across his face. "I'm sorry. I— I'd better go."

Before Arthur could comment, he turned and fled back the way they'd come.

Chapter 33

• • •

THE herald, having blown his trumpet and announced the arrival of Sir Torre, Sir Lavaine, and Lady Elaine of Corbenic, stood back for them to enter the hall of Camelot.

Elaine had hoped to slip in unnoticed and send word to Lancelot, but there was no chance of that now that they'd managed to arrive in the middle of a feast. After the brightness of the afternoon, the hall was too dim for her to make out individual faces. All she could see was a sea of eyes turned toward them as they hovered uncertainly just inside the doorway in a patch of pale yellow sunshine.

"Lady *who*?" the people whispered, loud enough for her to hear. "Could it be—no, not her, 'tis impossible. *She* cannot be the Lady of the Red Sleeve!"

"Well, this is rotten luck," Lavaine murmured, and much to Elaine's surprise, she laughed.

"That's the way," Brisen said, warmly approving. "Don't mind them."

"I don't. Here, give him to me."

Elaine took her son in her arms and smiled sweetly at the assembled company, who fell abruptly silent. "Kind people," she began, "can someone tell me—"

"Good day, Lady Elaine," a low voice interrupted her. "Welcome to Camelot."

Elaine found herself looking into a pair of violet eyes framed by thick, sooty lashes, large and luminous eyes that shone more brilliantly than the jewels flashing on the high brow of Britain's queen.

"Madam," she murmured, making the queen a reverence.

"We did not expect you," Guinevere said.

"No." Elaine smiled blandly as she straightened. "May I present my brothers, Sir Torre and Sir Lavaine."

"Sir Lavaine is no stranger here," Guinevere said, casting Lavaine a smile that brought a warm blush to his cheeks. "Sir Torre, you are very welcome."

"Mistress Brisen," Elaine went on, "late of the Duchess of Cornwall's service."

Guinevere nodded graciously. "I believe we met once before, Mistress Brisen, when my lord took a summer fever."

"I am honored that you remember," Brisen said, sinking gracefully to the floor.

And then there were no more distractions. Guinevere looked at the baby in Elaine's arms. Her lovely face grew chill.

"My son." Elaine met the queen's eyes. "Galahad."

Guinevere's expression did not alter. Only the sudden dilation of her pupils betrayed her shock.

"Madam, I apologize for disturbing your revelry," Elaine went on steadily. "Can you tell me where I might find Sir Lancelot?"

A heated buzz broke out amongst those nearest to the door, spreading like wildfire across the hall.

"Sir Lancelot is not here at the moment," Guinevere said. "I shall have him sent for."

She turned and walked back to the high table.

"What, we're not to sit down?" Torre muttered.

"Apparently not," Brisen said.

People seated in the back of the hall were standing, craning their necks to get a glimpse of this fascinating new diversion. Elaine kept her head high, though she felt a hot blush creeping from her neck to her forehead. Galahad woke and began to fuss.

"Shall I . . . ?" Brisen said.

"No. Thank you." Elaine's lips were oddly stiff; she compressed them into a tight line to still their trembling.

She had not slept the night before; her mind had been too busy conjuring a hundred different versions of her arrival at Camelot. Many of them had been unpleasant, but not even the worst could begin to compare to this reality. Galahad, who seldom cried save when he was hungry, let out a piercing wail. When a ripple of laughter passed across the hall, the courage that had carried Elaine this far began to waver, then collapsed. She bent her head and stared helplessly at the stones beneath her feet, wishing they would open up and swallow her.

"Lady Elaine."

Sir Gawain stood before her, resplendent in a robe of blue and silver, his face rigid and his gray eyes burning. He held out his hand, and Elaine, shifting Galahad, took it. He raised it to his lips and made her a deep bow.

"I am so pleased to see you again," he said. "Sir Torre, Lavaine," he nodded to them courteously as he offered Elaine his arm, "would you like to wait in the garden? I was just going there myself. The air in here," he added, flashing a look of icy contempt across the hall, "does not agree with me."

It was only when the door was closed behind them that Elaine began to shake.

"Thank you," she said, "that was a bit . . . awkward."

Gawain's lips twitched. "A bit, yes. Here, step inside," he said, unlatching a low gate leading to a small pleasance nestled between two wings of the castle. Roses overhung a stone wall that overlooked the forest below. A small fountain bubbled into a marble pool where golden fins flashed between water lilies.

"Sir Torre." Gawain gestured toward a group of stone benches. Torre looked to Elaine, who nodded, then moved off toward the benches with Lavaine and Brisen. Galahad squirmed, crying fitfully, and Elaine bounced him in her arms as she walked toward the low wall, crooning nonsense syllables.

"May I?" Gawain said, and scooped the child into one arm with practiced ease. "That's enough, now, we've all heard you. You've nothing to complain about."

Galahad stilled. The two studied each other with mutual interest.

"Well, you're a handsome fellow, aren't you?" Gawain said. He sat down on the wall and held out a finger that Galahad seized in one small fist. "A good grip, as well. The king will be pleased to have you at his table in a few years."

Galahad let out a gurgle of delighted laughter. For the first time in what seemed like days, Elaine smiled. "You're very good with him."

"He's a fine lad," Gawain said. "You must be very proud of him."

"Yes. Thank you." Elaine's eyes filled, and she looked away quickly, hoping he hadn't noticed.

"Now, here is what I suggest," Gawain said, suddenly very brisk. "Sit down and rest yourself—no one should disturb you here—and I will arrange for some refreshment.

Sir Lancelot went off after the king; likely they're down in the mews. I will see he joins you shortly. Would you like your brothers to stay, or shall I—"

But Elaine was no longer listening. Over his shoulder she had seen a man walk out of the shadow of the trees. He moved slowly, his dark head bent, but even before he looked up, she knew that it was Lancelot. He did not see her; he was staring straight ahead.

Gawain turned to look over his shoulder. "Ah," he said, his voice neutral. "Here he is now."

Elaine took a step forward, her hands clenched between her breasts, every muscle trembling. She tried to call out to him, but no sound came from her lips.

Lancelot turned as if he meant to walk into the orchard. But he stopped at the first tree, braced a palm upon its bark, and rested his brow against his outstretched arm, every line of his body etched with despair.

"Shall I . . . ?" Gawain asked in a low voice, but before Elaine could answer, Lancelot turned his head, and their eyes met.

For one terrible moment, she was sure he had not recognized her. His expression did not change nor did he move. Then his arm fell slowly to his side; he straightened, the dark wings of his brows drawing together in a frown. Elaine's heart lurched—the air left her body in a sickening rush. Lancelot's eyes grew very wide. Then he was running up the slope, a blur of gold and crimson against the green grass. He vaulted lightly over the wall, only to halt half a dozen paces from her.

"Elaine?" he said, as though even now he was not quite certain she was really there.

She nodded helplessly, and before she stopped to think, her arms rose, reaching for him. He did not move, or smile, or speak again. A blazing rush of heat suffused her face, and her arms fell stiffly to her sides. She was aware of Gawain rising to his feet beside her, of Torre and Lavaine moving forward, and she knew that she must speak, say something, anything to defuse this unbearable tension, but before she could force her numb lips to move, Lancelot took a few steps forward, one hand outstretched.

"Elaine?" he said again, and she saw his hand was shaking as he reached out and touched her cheek, his callused fingertips rough against her skin. "You—it really *is* you—" he said, and then he made a sound that was only half laughter and seized her in his arms, crushing her against him, burying his face against her neck.

"Of course it's me," she said. "Did you think I was a wraith?"

"I thought I was—it doesn't matter now, you're here—" He drew back and looked into her face as though assuring himself that this was true, and then he laughed and kissed her cheeks and brow and eyes before his lips found hers.

Elaine forgot the others. She forgot everything in the wild rush of joy sweeping through her. How could she have ever doubted him?

"Lancelot," she said at last, drawing away. "Lancelot, wait—no, wait, look at me, I have to tell you something."

Galahad, ignored by everyone, gave a sharp, demanding wail.

Lancelot raised his head. "What—"

He looked around, bewildered, his eyes narrowing when he noticed Gawain, who immediately thrust the baby into Elaine's arms. "Forgive me," he said, "I did not mean to intrude."

"Who—?" Lancelot said, staring from Galahad to Gawain. "What—?"

"Lancelot," Elaine said swiftly, "this is your son."

The moment the words were spoken, she wished them back again. This was not how she had meant to tell him. Every trace of color drained from his face, and she instinctively tightened her hold on Galahad, gripping him so fiercely that he let out an indignant squeak.

"My son?" Lancelot repeated hoarsely. "My . . . ?"

"Ours," Elaine rushed on. "He was born just before Easter. His name is Galahad."

"Galahad?" Lancelot raised his eyes to her; they were shimmering with tears. "Our—oh, Elaine," he whispered, "is it so?"

She nodded silently.

"You were—and I left—why did you not tell me?"

"I did not know."

Lancelot touched one of Galahad's curls, then pulled his hand away. "Look at him, Elaine," he breathed, "is he not beautiful?"

"Yes," she said, laughing through her tears. "He is. Do you want to hold him?"

Lancelot drew back. "Oh, no—do you think I should? He's so small."

"Nonsense, he's enormous. Take him—he won't break, I assure you. Just put your hands here—and here—that's right." He held Galahad stiffly before him, an expression of such mingled pride and terror on his face that even Torre, who had been regarding Lancelot with wary disapproval, burst out laughing.

Then they were all laughing, standing among the roses with the fountain singing and the sunshine warm upon their heads. Slowly, carefully, Lancelot drew his son closer until Galahad's bright curls rested on his heart. Elaine leaned against him, her cheek upon his shoulder, as they gazed down on their child.

The others fell silent, and as one they turned and left the garden. Torre was last, and as he shut the gate behind him, he blinked, a little dazed, as though he had stared too long into the sun.

Chapter 34

• • •

IT was only much later, as she and Lancelot lay entwined, that Elaine realized they had not spoken a word since they left the garden. Brisen had been waiting at the gate to take Galahad to his wet nurse, who they had lodged in a small tavern in the village. Lavaine and Torre were nowhere to be seen. Lancelot had simply led her to his chamber and just as simply she had gone, moving as if in a dream.

The dream had shattered only once, when he untied the laces of her gown with shaking fingers.

Galahad's birth had altered her in ways that went far beyond the physical, though it was the outward changes that were uppermost in her mind as Lancelot eased her gown from her shoulders and bent to her. Even as she gasped at the piercing sweet sensation of his lips against her breasts, a small part of her was aware that they were not as firm and high as they had been the last time Lancelot kissed them.

She tried to lose herself in the pleasure of the moment,

yet when he sought to remove her shift, she resisted, knowing too well what he would find. During the weeks following Galahad's birth, the flesh had melted from her bones, sharpening cheek and chin and digging hollows above her collarbones. Her hipbones jutted outward, yet between them, the soft skin of her belly sagged like an empty wineskin. It helped matters not at all that their separation had only heightened his beauty. For the first time she saw him as the warrior he was, the muscles of his arms and thighs and belly as sharply defined as though they had been cast in bronze. But he was so sweetly insistent that at last she allowed him to draw off the shift.

As she stood naked before him, she tried to steel herself against his disappointment, masked though it might be by concern. As the silence lengthened, she grew a bit indignant—after all, it was in bearing *his* son that she had changed. She stole a glance at him beneath her lashes, searching his face for any sign of disappointment and finding none. But surely he must notice! How could he not when was devouring every inch of her, first with his coal-bright eyes, then with feather-light touches of his callused fingertips and finally—God help her—with his mouth?

It was then her self-consciousness vanished. She was as she was—and, sweet blessed Lady, what she was, had always been and always would be: his. And he was hers to do with as she would.

His skin was warm and smooth as he slid onto the bed to lie beside her. He cupped her face in his hands, looking deep into her eyes as he had done so many times before, as though seeking something he could never bring himself to ask for.

There was nothing she could give him but herself, but that she offered without reservation, and it was enough. Slowly, his eyes never leaving hers, he joined with her.

When they were one, his smile wrenched her heart, it was so filled with astonishment and gratitude, as though he could not quite believe that anything so wonderful could possibly be happening to him. It fit so precisely with her own feelings that once again she knew beyond a doubt that the two of them had been fashioned for each other.

What need had they of words? *None*, she thought dizzily as he began to move within her, first slowly and then with a gathering urgency as his lips brushed hers in a kiss made all the sweeter for its uncertainty. What they shared could never be explained. It simply was, as natural as the soft rain tapping against the windows and as much of a miracle as the child they had created.

"The birth," he said at last, drawing her more closely into his arms, "was it . . . ?"

"Rather awful," Elaine said. "It went on and on—in the end, Brisen had to turn him." She shuddered at the memory, and his arms tightened around her.

"I'm sorry. I wish I'd been there."

"Better you were not. I wasn't feeling very kindly toward you at the time."

"Elaine, if I had known—"

"You would still have had to go. And even if you'd been with me, there was naught you could have done. I think it is the same for all women at such times," she added, smiling as she touched his cheek. "Men have all the pleasure and none of the pain . . ."

"*All* the pleasure?"

"Well, half," she amended.

"Just now, was it . . . all right?"

"Not bad," she said carelessly, then laughed. "It was wonderful, you noddy."

"You got my gifts?" he asked. "The sheep and swine and—why are you laughing?"

"I'll tell you later. The gifts were very thoughtful. But I would rather have had a message."

"I did not know what to say," he admitted. "I hated leaving you like that. And after the way we quarreled, I wasn't sure you'd want to hear from me. I am so sorry—"

"So am I. Let's not talk of it. Tell me of the battles!"

He grimaced. "They were battles. The king won. That's what matters."

"You haven't changed, have you?" she asked, laughing. "At least I cannot accuse you of conceit!"

"I would much rather hear about you," he said swiftly. "Are you sure you are well?"

"Do I look so very different?"

"Yes. You are far more beautiful than I remembered, which I would have sworn impossible. But I would like to see a bit more flesh upon your bones."

"Then you will have to let me up so I can eat."

He heaved a sigh. "Yes, I suppose . . . or no, I'll have something brought to us. If you would like."

"Mmm, yes, I would." She stretched, feeling every muscle thrill with pleasure. "Wake me when there's food," she said, and turning on her side, fell instantly asleep.

Lancelot pulled on a chamber robe and belted it loosely around his waist. Elaine lay upon her side with one knee drawn up and one hand extended, palm upward. He stood by the bed, watching her, then went down upon one knee and took a lock of her hair between his fingers, gently so as not to wake her. He raised it to his lips and inhaled the scent he had dreamed of for so long.

He could not lose her. Not again. Nothing had changed; all the reasons he had given himself to stay away were as true as they had been before, yet everything was different. There was more at stake than his broken heart or even Elaine's sorrow if they were to part. He was a father. Elaine had given him a son. The three of them were bound by ties even death could not dissolve.

I will be careful, Lancelot vowed. *Elaine will never know that I have changed. No darkness will touch her or Galahad, I swear it. Please, God,* he pleaded silently, *please protect them from all harm.*

Think you God will heed any prayer you utter? A mocking voice demanded in his mind. He thought again of the knights he had slaughtered during the campaign, the others he had struck down in the lists with his inhuman strength. Torre, Gawain . . . Gawain upon the battlefield, singing as he challenged death; Gawain, whose courage could no more be doubted than his honor—or his kindness, as he had proved again today. Oh, Lancelot had wronged him, creeping into Camelot like a thief in the night to steal the glory Gawain had worked so hard and long to earn.

No, Elaine must never know. And she would not. *Even if I tried to tell her,* Lancelot thought, *she would not believe me. She would think me mad.* God knew he had felt close to madness this past year, mad with misery and shame as Arthur heaped honor upon honor on his head. Today's feast had seemed the final blow.

I will not go mad, Lancelot vowed. *Elaine's love will protect me, just as her token did. So long as she believes in me, all will be well.* His eyes stung as he bent to kiss her brow.

No pages lingered in the passageway, so he started for the stairway where they often sat in a small alcove at the top. Finding no one on duty there, either, he realized it must be far later than he'd thought. But surely someone would still be in the kitchens.

He went down the twisting stairway, the stone cold against his bare feet. He briefly considered turning back to dress, but what were the odds of meeting anyone at this hour?

He passed through the darkened hall, quietly so as not to disturb the servants and guests sleeping on the floor. On the far side, he went through a curtained doorway into another corridor that led toward the kitchens. The stone was rougher here, interspersed with pools of shadow where tiny alcoves had been set into the walls. These were often used for assignations, though now they held various cooks and stewards, gently snoring. It must be very late indeed, he thought, then shrugged, thinking he was surely capable of cobbling together some sort of meal without assistance.

He was just wondering if there would be any plums—Elaine had a fondness for them—when a figure stepped out from one of the alcoves and stood before him. He started back, and the woman—for it was a woman, he saw now, near as tall as he was—leapt in the opposite direction.

"I'm sorry," Lancelot said, half laughing, though his heart thudded painfully in his chest.

"No, no, it is I who should apologize," she said, her sweet, rather husky voice pitched low. "I did not expect to meet anyone."

"Nor did I." He flattened himself against the wall to let her by, and she brushed against him—deliberately, he thought, for there was more than enough room for her to pass—in a wave of sweet, heavy scent.

"Why, it is Sir Lancelot!" she said, pausing just in front of him.

"Yes," he answered, not altogether pleased at being recognized and surprised that any lady caught in such a compromising position would want to linger. With a touch of malice, he said, "I don't believe I've had the honor . . . ?"

She moved so the flickering torchlight fell upon her face. "Morgause of Orkney. We've met before," she purred, "do you not remember?"

He remembered very well indeed. It had been several years ago. He had nearly fallen from his seat when she glided into Arthur's chamber and the king introduced her as his half sister, the queen of Orkney. It was not that she looked far too young to have borne Gawain, let alone Gawain's numerous brothers. Nor was it her beauty that struck him dumb, though she was very beautiful indeed. What had rendered him nearly incoherent with embarrassment was that he had already met her once before, though at the time he had dismissed their meeting as a dream.

Some months before Queen Morgause walked into Arthur's chamber unannounced, Lancelot had been out adventuring. The day was hot, the sun shimmering over the fields, and a few bright butterflies danced among the wildflowers. He had lain down in the shadow of a hedgerow and plunged into a heavy sleep.

He woke—or dreamed he woke—to find four ladies standing over him, shaded by a canopy of purple silk. It seemed they had been there for some time, for cloths had been laid upon the grass behind them, spread with a feast of great magnificence. The ladies were all crowned, and each of them was exquisitely garbed and jeweled. They introduced themselves as the queens of Northgalis, the Outer Isles, Wales, and Orkney, and said he must choose one of them as a paramour.

Though the dream was utterly fantastical, it was oddly realistic in its details. Lancelot had been befuddled, grittyeyed, and clammy with sweat, his mouth parched with thirst. The ladies' faces were all beautiful, but frightening, too, for the canopy cast eerie violet shadows upon their features.

"I—I—" he stammered thickly, "forgive me, did you say . . . ?"

"We would like to lie with you," one of the queens—she had brown hair and blue eyes—explained kindly.

"To swive you," a black-haired, green-eyed beauty clarified, as he continued to gape at them in silence. She turned to the others and said, "I don't think he understands."

A tall, auburn-haired lady leaned down and grasped him firmly between the legs. "Oh, I rather think he does." She stroked him, her long, white fingers trailing over his swelling manhood in a lingering caress. "Mmm," she said, straightening. "I think *he* could serve us all."

"But that was not the wager," the last queen, who had a wealth of butter-yellow hair, protested. "He has to choose. You shouldn't have touched him, Morgause," she added reproachfully, "it isn't fair now."

The queen thus addressed shrugged. "It's fair if you do the same. He won't mind," she added, gazing at Lancelot through half-closed eyes. Her face was wide across the cheekbones, tapering to a small, pointed chin. When she smiled, she looked like a cat.

Lancelot sat up, vainly hoping to hide the evidence of his arousal. "Madam," he said, "Such a choice as you require of me is one I cannot make."

"Ooh, he does want us all!" The green-eyed lady laughed and reached for him.

Lancelot scrambled back, very much aware of the hedgerow behind him catching his hair and digging into his neck. "You mistake me," he said with as much dignity as he could muster. "I am sorry if this sounds discourteous, but you have forced me. I will have none of you."

"That," the auburn-haired queen said with another cat-like smile, "is not a choice available to you."

"It is, however, my decision."

"Then, sweet Lancelot," the yellow-haired lady sighed, "you must think again."

"I could think from now 'til—" he began, twisting away as she put out a hand as though to stroke his face. Then her fingertip touched the space between his eyes, and the world vanished.

When he awoke—for the first or second time, he didn't know—it was to find himself in a dungeon. Soon after, a pretty serving maid who either did not know or would not say who had imprisoned him, helped him to escape on the condition that he fight in a tournament for her father. In the ensuing excitement, Lancelot had convinced himself that the four queens were nothing but a strange dream.

So when Queen Morgause of Orkney had strolled into King Arthur's chamber some months later, looking just as she had that day beside the hedgerow, Lancelot had been thrown into confusion.

And now, facing her in the twisting passageway leading to Camelot's kitchens, he was once again at a loss.

"Don't tell me you have forgotten me?" she inquired, laughing.

"No, of course not, madam." He bowed briefly. "We met in the chamber of the king, your brother—"

"Half brother," she amended sharply. "*My* father was Duke Gorlois of Cornwall."

A man walked out of an alcove, fastening the brooch clasp at his shoulder. When he saw Lancelot he immediately stepped back into the shadows.

"Lamorak!" Morgause called imperiously. "Come out and greet Sir Lancelot."

Lamorak had been with them this past year; he'd been knighted on the field. He must be all of nineteen, Lancelot thought, though he looked even younger with a blush staining his cheeks.

"Good evening, Sir Lamorak," Lancelot said, rigid with embarrassment.

"Sir Lancelot," the boy mumbled, staring down at his feet.

"What, has Camelot become a monastery?" Morgause

inquired with a mocking laugh. "It wasn't so in Uther's day! Come, Lamorak, hold your head up. Sir Lancelot is in no position to sit in judgment on you. Stay," she ordered sharply as Lancelot turned to leave. "Tell me about that wench who burst into the hall earlier."

Lancelot had no intention of answering, no more than he'd meant to halt at her command. Yet here he stood, saying, "She is—" before he clamped his lips shut. Morgause's brows rose.

"Tell me," she said again, this time in honeyed tones.

And suddenly he wanted to. He wanted to tell her everything about himself and Elaine, for it seemed clear that Morgause would understand as no one else could. Indeed, he had to tell her; it would be churlish to refuse when she had every right to know . . . only he did not think he'd tell her just this moment. When he came to think of it—which wasn't easy, for the effort made his head pound—he realized he would prefer not to tell her anything at all.

"It is late, madam," he said, relieved to hear the words come out so firmly. "I don't want to keep you here."

She laughed, surprising him. "Well done! There is more to you than meets the eye. I suspected as much, and I'm sure you will forgive me for my little test. Certes, I have no wish to meddle with the Lady of the Lake, or her . . ." She paused delicately, but when Lancelot made no answer, she merely laughed again. "Well, she has excellent taste—as do I," she said, smiling as she stroked Lamorak's cheek. "Run along, my sweet," she said to the young man. "You need your rest." He obediently kissed her offered cheek, bowed to Lancelot, and vanished down the corridor.

Before Lancelot could follow his example, Morgause laid a hand on his arm. "But come, do tell me of that chit who arrived earlier, a squalling brat in arms and your name upon her lips!"

Lancelot forced his gaze to remain steady. He would not give this woman the satisfaction of knowing how deeply her words had angered him. "The child you refer to is Galahad, my son, born while I was away in the king's service. Lady Elaine and I shall be wed as soon as possible, of course."

"Of course." Morgause adjusted the collar of his robe. "That *is* handsome of you, Lance—may I call you Lance?" Without waiting for an answer, she went on, "But I feel it is my duty to give you just a word of warning. These forced matches, no matter how nobly undertaken, have a way of ending badly. Pay her off—I daresay you can afford it—and send her back to Carbuncle or whatever it is she comes from. When the boy is of age, you can make some provision for him. Knowing my half brother, Arthur will be pleased to take any number of your by-blows into his service."

"Madam, you mistake me," Lancelot said, and when their eyes met, he knew his dream had been no dream at all. "Lady Elaine and I were betrothed before the king summoned me away. Our marriage is something I have longed for since duty called me from her side."

"Ah. Yes, I see." Morgause smiled in a fashion that raised the hairs on his neck. "*Very* handsome. But who would expect less from the great du Lac! I only wonder," she said, tipping her head to one side and examining him curiously, "how your lady will feel about sharing you with the queen . . . and the king. But there, I'm sure she'll let you know precisely what she thinks. She doesn't lack for courage, does she? The way she faced the queen earlier—it is a good thing that looks cannot really kill, or the two of them would have lain dead upon the floor!"

Lancelot could only stare at her, utterly nonplussed, as her gaze moved slowly over his gaping chamber robe. "I daresay you and Guinevere have made up any little quarrel that resulted." She looked back the way he'd come, a knowing smile curving her red lips, as though expecting Guinevere to step from one of the shadowed alcoves.

"Madam, I beg you to excuse me. Lady Elaine awaits," Lancelot said coldly.

Morgause laughed. "Ah, you young knights! Such stamina! Well, be off with you, then."

Before he could reply, she walked away and was swallowed by the darkness.

Forgetting his errand, Lancelot raced back through the hall and up the stairway to his chamber, where Elaine still slept. He sat beside her, as if his presence could somehow protect her from the dark magic Morgause exuded like a noxious fume.

"There is no such thing as magic," Elaine had assured him solemnly. If there was a God at all, she would go on believing that. He touched her warm cheek and smiled to see her smile when her fingers twined with his.

"Where is the food?" she murmured without opening her eyes.

"I've brought you something better." Shrugging off his robe, he slid beneath the coverlet to catch her laughter on his lips.

Chapter 35

. . .

"YOU have to face them some time," Brisen said, tucking the last ribbon into Elaine's hair and standing back to examine her handiwork. "Come, lady, you don't want to keep Sir Lancelot waiting."

"No." Hearing the reluctance in her voice, Elaine stood and smoothed her skirts. "No, of course not." That was better; she sounded firm and purposeful, but a moment later she spoiled it by adding piteously, "You will come with me, won't you?"

"Of course. And your brothers should be there, as well."

Elaine wasn't sure if that was comforting or not; given Torre's aptitude for saying precisely what he thought, she rather thought it wasn't.

"Sir Torre has promised to be on his best behavior," Brisen said as they started down the passageway.

"I thought you weren't speaking to him."

"I'm not. But I made an exception for your sake."

"What devotion," Elaine said lightly. "Thank you. What exactly did he do to get in your bad graces?"

"Nothing he hadn't done a hundred times before," Brisen admitted with a wry smile. "But I walked in on him with that Bette from the vill—you know the one I mean, her father owns the alehouse—and suddenly I realized what a fool I'd been. Ah, well," she added with a brittle laugh, "it happens to us all. Not you, lady," she amended quickly, "I didn't mean—"

"I know what you meant, and you're quite right. But I'm sorry Torre is such a thick-headed idiot."

"That's very kind of you."

Halfway down the stairs, they met a lady coming up. Elaine stopped to let her by. "Why, it's Mistress Brisen, isn't it?" the lady said.

"Madam." Brisen made her a brief curtsy.

"Morgana has missed you dreadfully, you know, she was saying so just the other day."

"I have been in Corbenic," Brisen said. "Queen Morgause of Orkney, may I present my mistress, Lady Elaine of Corbenic."

Elaine nodded. "Madam."

The lady's bright blue eyes widened. "My dear!" she cried, "I have so longed to meet you!" She turned back the way she'd come, slipping her arm through Elaine's and drawing her down the stairway. "Sir Lancelot speaks so highly of you—and congratulations on the birth of your son. Galahad, isn't it? I only caught a glimpse of him yesterday, but he seems a fine, healthy lad. Does he take after his father?"

"No," Elaine said, bemused by this outpouring. "I'm afraid he takes after me."

"Then he must be a very handsome boy—now, my dear,

don't bother to blush, you must know you're lovely. Come, let me introduce you to everyone. Run along, Brisen," she added over her shoulder, "I shall take good care of your lady."

Before Elaine could protest, she was swept forward toward a small chamber off the hall. "Let's begin with the queen's ladies; a sillier bunch of maidens I've never met, but I'm sure they—"

They halted at the half-open door, where a girlish voice exclaimed, "—a most vile trick! Apparently her serving maid is a witch—trained up by the Duchess of Cornwall, and you know what *she* is like—and together they plotted to get Sir Lancelot into the lady's bed."

"The maid gave him a handkerchief bearing the queen's scent," another voice went on in a piercing whisper, "and kept the chamber darkened so he would not know the difference."

Not know the difference? Elaine made a low sound, half amusement and half disgust. *That doesn't say much for the great du Lac's powers of perception!*

"He was quite mad with lust, of course—"

At least they'd gotten that much right, Elaine thought dryly as a small silence fell within the chamber, followed by a collective sigh before the first voice took up the tale again.

"—for the maid had slipped him a love potion. When he discovered the ruse—the next morning, it was, when the deed was done—he drew his sword and threatened to cut off her head! But of course he didn't. He is too fine to use any lady ill, even one so false."

"Poor Sir Lancelot!" a high voice cried, "to be so cruelly used!"

Elaine had heard enough. She whirled, forgetting that Morgause had hold of her arm. "Running is no good," Morgause said, and though her expression was one of deep concern, her eyes glittered. For a moment Elaine wondered if she had led her here a-purpose, but the next moment Morgause had all but dragged her into the bower.

"Ladies," she cried, "look who is here! 'Tis Lady Elaine of Corbenic—or, as some would call her, the Lady of the Red Sleeve."

A rather dreadful silence fell, during which the girls—for they seemed girls to Elaine, even those few who were her own age—blushed painfully, guilty glances flying in all directions.

"Good day," Elaine said stiffly to each one in turn as Morgause named them. When at last it was finished, she said, "And now I must be going. Sir Lancelot is waiting." She knew the last was childish, and it was that, rather than anything they'd said, that shamed her.

The moment she'd left the chamber, a buzz of talk broke out. "Do you think she heard? So what if she did? After what she did to poor Sir Lancelot . . ."

Morgause, who had followed her from the chamber, laughed. "Don't take it too much to heart. Any one of them would have done the same had Sir Lancelot looked twice at her."

"The same? I assure you, madam, that I did not trick Sir Lancelot—"

"Of course you didn't!" Morgause said warmly. "Why, a lass like you would have no need of magic to woo any man to her bed—even the great du Lac! Come, now, dry your eyes, you mustn't let on that you're upset."

Elaine recognized the sense of that advice and obeyed as they walked together to the hall. Yesterday Elaine had not noticed its beauty, but now she hesitated in the doorway, staring about in wonder.

"You go ahead," she said to Morgause. "I must wait for Sir Lancelot."

Light fell through a high-arched window set with small panes of colored glass. Amethyst, emerald, carnelian, topaz—she had never seen anything so beautiful. Tapestries adorned the walls, not merely one or two, but dozens, each woven in the same glowing jewel tones as the window. Apparently she was early, for most of the company had not yet arrived, and Lancelot was not among the few who gathered in small groups, chatting easily. The high table was set with gleaming silver, and at its center sat a man in a high-backed chair.

The crown sat solidly on his high brow, and light hair fell to his broad shoulders. He looked kind, Elaine thought, as he bent forward to speak to a serving lad with a tray perched on one shoulder. The boy made some remark, and Arthur laughed, waving him away and relaxing back in his seat. His gaze drifted across the hall and fastened upon Elaine, hovering half-in, half-out of the doorway. His brows lifted, and then he smiled and gestured her toward him.

"Lady Elaine?" he asked when she had made her reverence.

"Yes, sire."

The king gestured toward the seat at his left hand. "Come and join me if you would."

Elaine took the offered seat and accepted the goblet the king handed to her. "Welcome to Camelot," he said, and she could only nod her thanks, too overawed to answer.

They sat in silence while the hall filled. At last, when it seemed that Guinevere and Lancelot were the only ones missing from their places, the king lifted his hand. A clear trumpet sounded, and a young page immediately knelt to present Elaine with a silver basin of water with rose petals scattered across its surface. She dipped her fingers, dried them, and turned to the king.

"Congratulations on your victory, sire," she said.

"Thank you," he said absently, his eyes turned toward the doorway. She followed his gaze, praying it was Lancelot, but some other knight walked in and took a seat. The king glanced over at her, and with an obvious effort, said, "I trust your journey was pleasant?"

"Yes, very."

Silence fell again. Elaine picked up a bit of meat and dipped it in a small bowl of sauce. After one bite that burned her tongue, she set it down again.

"Corbenic," the king said suddenly. "I remember now. The Saxons took it, didn't they?"

"And you restored it to us four years ago," Elaine agreed.

"Gawain did most of it," Arthur said. "He fought that fellow—what was his name?"

"Binric."

"Yes, that's right. The land was in poor condition," the king said. "How have you fared?"

"It was . . . difficult at first," Elaine admitted, "but this year our harvest was a good one."

"And your villeins?" Arthur asked casually. "Any trouble from that quarter?"

Elaine's cheeks warmed. "We did have some," she said. "I believe my uncle Ulfric wrote to you with a complaint—"

"Poaching, wasn't it? He mentioned something of the sort when we were in Gaul. A good man, Ulfric," the king said thoughtfully. "I can always count on him to send me soldiers, not just a pack of peasants armed all anyhow and ready to bolt at the first charge."

"A good man . . . and a careful one," Elaine murmured. "But as I said, we are doing better now. I assure you my uncle will have no further cause for complaint."

"My dear, it isn't only Ulfric who concerns me. If your

father is having difficulty, he should have come to me. I told him so when he returned to his demesne. I could see then that he had troublesome times ahead, and he wasn't quite . . . himself. Perhaps I should send a man to speak with him and offer our assistance."

"Please don't, sire," Elaine said. "Father would only be upset, and he wouldn't understand." When Arthur nodded sympathetically, she hurried on, "We have a new reeve now, he's very able, and Sir Lancelot—" Her voice caught a little on his name. "—has been most . . . generous."

"Has he? Well, then, we'll say no more. But if you ever do need help," the king said, looking straight into her eyes, "I hope you will not be too proud to ask."

"No, sire," Elaine promised, "I won't. And thank you."

"Ah," Arthur said, "here is that boy at last with some real food. I can't abide all this sauce and spice," he added confidentially. "Would you care for a bit of plain meat?"

"Yes, I would," Elaine said, and soon she was sharing the king's trencher as well as his goblet, their heads bent together as they discussed Corbenic, which the king remembered well. He gave her several excellent suggestions about draining the southwest field.

"What became of those sheep Lance sent?" he asked unexpectedly. "I told him it was a mistake—Corbenic is too low-lying for sheep to thrive, particularly those long-legged ones, but he insisted."

"I was the one who wanted to try them. But alas, I fear you had the right of it, sire."

"Foot rot?"

"Among other diseases, some of which the shepherd swore were hitherto unknown."

When Arthur laughed, she found herself laughing, too, though at the time the incident had been anything but amusing.

"I'm off to try my new gyrfalcon," he said when the trencher was empty. "Would you care to join me?"

Elaine looked around, noting with some surprise that the meal was over. Lancelot had not appeared—nor had the queen. What that might mean, she did not know, nor did she want to think too deeply on the matter.

"Will you be riding out?"

"No, I'll just fly her on the creance today." He held out his arm to her and called down the table, "To the mews!"

A small crowd of knights and ladies left the hall. Elaine walked at their head, her hand tucked into the king's elbow.

Chapter 36

· · ·

"YOU'VE come to scold me, haven't you?" Guinevere said, after she had dismissed her women and she and Lancelot were alone. "And I deserve it. I was horrid to your Elaine."

Scold her? Lancelot wanted nothing of the sort. What he wanted was to shake her hard, as though that might force some sense into her empty head.

"Why?" he demanded furiously.

"I was . . . upset. That's no excuse, of course—I'll beg her pardon, I swear I will, only . . ." Her voice trembled and she swallowed hard. "Only don't be angry with me."

Only yesterday, Guinevere had seemed quite well—better, in fact, than Lancelot had seen her for some time. He had breakfasted with her and Arthur, and she had kept them both laughing with her complaints about King Bagdemagus's boorish son, who, among his many sins, had committed the unpardonable offense of belching in the presence of his queen without apology.

Today her glow had faded. She looked weary and distraught as she plucked restlessly at the folds of her gown. But that, Lancelot reminded himself firmly, was none of his affair. Guinevere was a woman grown, a queen, and she must learn to help herself.

"If you apologize, we shall forget the whole incident," he said.

"Very well, Lance," she said so meekly that his anger began to fade into the familiar dead weight of pity. "Let me just fix my hair, and I will go down with you. Have you heard the latest on Tristan and his lady love?" she said with a smile as false as it was brilliant as she pinned a flower among her raven braids. "King Mark is suspicious, but that is nothing new! Why he doesn't simply banish Tristan from Cornwall is beyond me. You should talk to Tristan, Lance, before he goes back there, convince him to give her up before something dreadful happens."

"Even if I could bring myself to such impertinence, I doubt he'd listen," Lancelot answered coolly.

"No, I don't suppose he would," Guinevere agreed. "He truly loves her. Did I tell you that I met her?" she went on quickly, plucking at a lock of hair, "the fair Isolde? She was here two weeks ago with Mark, and as lovely as we've heard, though just between the two of us, she's wretched company. All she does is sigh and droop and turn those great sad eyes to Tristan—and he's no better; he just looks back at her with his whole heart in his face, and it really is a shame, because anyone can see they only live for one another."

"It is an unfortunate situation," Lancelot said neutrally, holding open the door so she might pass through. They went together toward the hall, Guinevere taking two steps to his one, her eyes anxious as she searched his face.

"Yes, it is unfortunate. And the worst of it is that they seem to revel in their misery. Oh, I know what they say about the two of them swallowing a love potion and all, but, honestly, Lance, even if Tristan can't help himself, *she* could make some effort. Mark isn't so bad. Of course he isn't as good-looking as Tristan, but he can be quite sweet. Why, just before he left, he said to me—"

"I don't want to hear about King Mark," Lancelot said, cutting off the flow of words. "Or his queen, or poor benighted Tristan."

Guinevere laughed as though he'd made a jest, the skin tightening about her eyes. "No, of course you don't. I'm sorry. But there's so little else to talk about. It's just the same thing every day, you know, laundresses and seamstresses and Sir Kay with his menus and the mischief that my ladies get up to every time I turn my head. Such a lot of geese they are, and what with all the marriages I must arrange to rescue their good names, I scarce have a moment to draw breath! The Blessed Lady be praised that so far I have got them all well settled, though, honestly, I never imagined maidens so gently reared could be so rowdy. And the knights! Why, just the other day, I came into the bower and found Sir Dinadan behind the tapestry with . . . with . . ."

They had reached the doorway to the hall. Guinevere stood, one hand pressed to her throat, her eyes fixed on the high table. Arthur had already welcomed Elaine, Lancelot saw with quick relief. They looked quite companionable, chatting away, sharing a goblet and trencher. As Lancelot watched, Arthur laughed. It was a real laugh, not a mere politeness, and a moment later Elaine burst into a laugh as merry as his own.

"I—I feel unwell," Guinevere said in a high, strained voice. "I must . . . make my excuses, Lance . . ."

Lancelot turned to see her stumbling back up the passageway, one hand to her face, the other outstretched to guide herself along the wall.

Let her go, he thought. *Whatever her trouble, she must bear it alone or confide it to her lord.* He forced himself to take another step into the hall, then with a muttered curse, he turned and followed Guinevere, catching up to her in the corridor outside her chamber door.

"Guinevere," Lancelot called, "stop."

"Go back," she said, fumbling at the latch. "It is all right, I was just a bit . . . but I am better . . ."

He followed her inside and shut the door, glancing about quickly to make sure they were alone.

"Look at me," he ordered. "No, don't turn away. Now, tell me what the matter is."

"Can I really? Will you promise not to say a word?"

"When have I ever betrayed your confidence?"

"Yes, of course. Well, then . . ." Guinevere drew a long breath, then burst out in a rush, "Yesterday—well, before that, I thought I was—I hoped—" She shook her head. "No, it was more than just a hope. I had conceived. I meant to tell Arthur last night, before the feast, but then—then—" her slight frame shook with sobs. "He would have been so happy!"

"Oh, Guinevere," he said helplessly. "Are you sure you were not mistaken?"

"Not this time. I was sure—women know these things—but I could not hold onto it. Why?" She began to pace the chamber. "I've asked myself a thousand times, why? What am I doing wrong that I cannot keep a child?"

"But—sit down, you aren't well, you must rest. Here, now, take this wine." He sat down on a hassock beside her chair. "These things happen. But it doesn't mean you can't—that you won't do better next time," he finished lamely.

"That is what I told myself the first time," she said, dragging a hanging sleeve across her eyes. "And the next. But now . . . I thought the third—they say it is a charm, but—" She raised the cup and sipped, then with a sudden gesture threw it against the wall and leapt to her feet. "God damn him!" she cried. "He cursed me, and now I am barren!"

"He? Who cursed you?"

"My fa—King Leodegrance," she spat. "When he told me who—what I really am."

Lancelot could only stare at her in shock. Never once, in all the years that had passed since they set out for Camelot upon Guinevere's wedding journey, had they referred to Guinevere's parentage. That she would do so now revealed a disturbance that frightened him.

"I always knew he hated me," she went on, her train whipping behind her as she whirled. "Always. But I never knew how much. And then he told me. He told me everything, all about my mother and King Ban, things I did not want to hear. I couldn't bear it; it was all so horrible, so—sordid."

"I know," Lancelot said. When Leodegrance had told him the same tale, he hadn't thought it of much importance. Now, after years at court, he understood far better. If the truth were ever known, Guinevere and Arthur would never recover from the scandal.

"Before we left for Camelot," she went on slowly, "Leodegrance said he had reconsidered. He swore he would tell Arthur, break our betrothal, shut me away in a nunnery forever. I begged him—" She wrapped her arms around her middle, shaking. "At last he said he would keep silent—for the honor of his *house*. But he said he would be damned for foisting a base-born whore upon his king, and if God was just, I would never bear my lord a child."

"That is nonsense," Lancelot said. "If God granted every prayer made in anger—"

"But he was right," she said, tears welling in her eyes.

"He *is* damned—and so am I, for not telling my lord the truth about my birth."

"Then why don't you just tell him?" Lancelot burst out. "I've begged you to before, and now—"

"I can't! He would annul our marriage, send me away, lock me up forever—"

"Of course he wouldn't," Lancelot said. "You are being very foolish."

"No, I am not. Just think, Lance. What good is a queen who cannot give her lord an heir? Now Arthur feels honor bound to keep me, but if he knew I had deceived him, he would have the perfect excuse to cast me off and seek another bride."

"What folly! He would never put you aside!"

"If you believe that, *you* are the fool!" Guinevere cried. "He would do what is best for Britain."

Lancelot was silenced. Arthur could well do such a thing if he believed it would serve the interests of the realm. Indeed, Arthur might feel he had no choice.

"Even if he did annul the marriage," Lancelot said, "I'm sure he would allow you to go home."

"Home? To Cameliard? Where Leodegrance still reigns? I couldn't bear it! No, I'd rather die. And I would. I'd jump from the tower before I let him send me back there—or pack me off to a nunnery. I won't leave him, I can't, I couldn't bear it—"

"Stop it," Lancelot ordered sharply. "You will not jump from any tower. Never say such a thing again. Now sit down and drink this," he ordered, pouring a cup of wine and thrusting it into her hands.

Apparently this was the right approach. She raised the cup in shaking hands, splashing wine onto her gown, but Lancelot saw her throat work as she swallowed.

"Drink it all," he said sternly, and she obeyed. "Now, are you more reasonable?"

"Yes," she said meekly.

"You are still a young woman, Guinevere, with years before you in which to give your lord an heir. And look at the other things you have accomplished! Everywhere I go, the people talk of the good works you've done, your kindness and your charity. They are proud of you; you bring joy into their lives. Even your foolish pageants make them laugh, though they may never see them. All of Britain loves you."

She turned her head to gaze out the open window. "Not quite all," she whispered.

Following her gaze, Lancelot saw a group of knights and ladies gathered in the courtyard. Among them, his fair head rising above the rest, was the king. "Does he not treat you kindly?"

"Yes." She nodded vehemently, tears spilling over her inky lashes and trailing down her cheeks. "Yes, he is wonderful—he gives me all respect—"

"Respect," Lancelot repeated, beginning to glimpse the outline of her unhappiness.

"Yes, always. And courtesy, as well. He is—is all that is good—"

"Has he taken a mistress? Is that it?"

"No—or, at least, I do not think so. But you know how it is, no one would tell *me*. And I'm glad of that. I don't think I could bear it. If—when—he does, I can only hope he will be discreet. But I—I believe he will be. He would never do anything to shame me before the court."

"No," Lancelot said slowly, "he would not."

"So I have nothing to complain of, do I? I should be on my knees right now, thanking the Blessed Lady for my good fortune. 'Tis only . . . if I could just give him a son," she added in a whisper, "I swear by all that's holy I would never ask for more."

"You will," Lancelot said. "Given time—"

"Of course." She smiled tightly. "I am just being silly. After all, I am a queen, and all of Britain loves me."

All save one. He heard the echo of her thought as though she'd shouted it aloud.

"Why should he *not* love you?" Lancelot said, hardly realizing he'd spoken aloud until Guinevere answered.

"Oh, love!" She smoothed straggling tendrils back from her face. "What is love, really, but a foolish fancy dreamt up by minstrels? Come, tell me, Lance, do you *love* your Elaine?"

He could not give her the answer she so plainly wanted, but he would not lie. When the silence had gone on just a bit too long, Guinevere gave an unconvincing laugh. "Ah. Well. She is one of the lucky ones, then, isn't she?"

"Not so lucky, I think," Lancelot answered wryly. "I fear I'm not much of a bargain."

"Don't be silly, you're quite the catch. Everyone says so."

"Mmm. But they don't know me, do they?"

Guinevere laughed again, this time more naturally. "True. You'd best marry her quickly."

"God grant that I will."

"I never thought to hear *you* speak so piously! You have been spending too much time with Sir Bors!" She sighed, her fingers plucking restlessly at the brooch at her breast. "I know I should like Bors better . . . *He* is just the sort who will be granted a miracle, but *I* am not so good that I can count upon such favor. So far as I know, there is but one way to get a child, and to greet my lord with swollen eyes and splotched skin would run counter to my purpose. So run along, Lance, there's a dear, and let me mend the damage I have done."

What she said made perfect sense—yet he could scarce believe that she had said it. Surely this was not Guinevere, so proud and wild! Had she really been reduced to this, a woman who must plot and scheme to bring her husband to her bed?

"Why do you stare at me so strangely?" she demanded. "What are you thinking?"

"Nothing," he said at once, but it was no good. She could always read his thoughts. "Guinevere, don't cry, I didn't mean to make you cry. I'll go now, and you shall make yourself beautiful—"

"Not beautiful enough," she whispered, and then she laid her cheek upon his shoulder and wept as though her heart would break.

Lancelot patted her back, wishing he could find the words to ease her sorrow, knowing they did not exist. For she was right. Much as he enjoyed seeing Elaine robed richly and hung with jewels, such trappings had naught to do with love. That was in her scent, her smile, the way his heart lifted when their eyes met. It mattered not if she was garbed in velvet or clad in a muddy shift with her hair straggling damply down her back. He wanted her. He could not help but want her—not just her body in his bed, but she, herself—no more than he could choose to want another in her place. It was as simple—as inexplicable—as that.

His attention was caught by a sound, muffled by the distance, coming from the courtyard below. Looking down, he saw that the small crowd had dispersed, all save one who lingered. Sir Agravaine stood looking upward, his small eyes stretched wide and his mouth agape, one hand extended toward the open casement.

It was then Lancelot saw the second man, halted by

Agravaine's cry on the edge of the courtyard. He turned back, his gaze following Agravaine's pointing finger, his eyes meeting Lancelot's over Guinevere's bent head. Before Lancelot could move or even think, the king turned away abruptly and strode off toward the mews, the falcon baiting furiously upon his wrist and Agravaine hurrying in his wake.

Chapter 37

• • •

"IT was nothing," Lancelot said.

He knelt before Elaine, her hands in his. He knew he was holding her too tightly. Her wrists were so slender, the bones too fragile to bear his fevered clasp. But the moment he eased his grip, she tried to pull away.

"The queen was upset—distraught," he went on quickly, "I comforted her. Whatever you may have heard, it was no more than that, Elaine, I swear it."

"Why was she upset?" Elaine asked. "Was it because I lured you to my bed with love potions and pretended to be her so you would lie with me?"

"What?"

"Oh, come, Lancelot, don't tell me you haven't heard! Everyone else has, after all! How I tricked you and lied to you and—"

Lancelot sank back on his heels. "No," he whispered hoarsely.

"—how distraught the queen was to hear of your infidelity. But they say she forgave you when she learned how basely you had been deceived."

He could only gaze up at her blankly. The sunlight falling through the window behind her made a halo of her hair, so bright it almost hurt to look on it; her face was shadowy and indistinct. "It isn't true," he said at last.

"I *know* it isn't true," Elaine said, and each word was a sliver of ice that sliced into his skull. "I was there, remember? But how did such a story come to be?"

"I do not know," Lancelot said, bewildered. He blinked hard and put a hand to his brow, rubbing the throbbing space between his eyes.

"Are you sure *you* did not start it?"

He flinched as though she had struck him. "You do not think that of me; you cannot!"

She pulled her hands from his. "Why was the queen so distraught?" she demanded.

Lancelot shook his head blindly. "I cannot say. But Elaine, it had naught to do with you. Or me. She is . . . unhappy."

"*That* much I've already gathered." She stood abruptly. "I have had my fill of Camelot. I'm going home."

"Elaine, I love you," he said desperately, "there is no other."

The look she turned on him was chillingly familiar. Just so had Arthur looked at him that day in the queen's chamber so long ago and again, today, from the courtyard below Guinevere's window. *Liar,* that look said. *Oath-breaker.*

But he was innocent! He had done nothing wrong, betrayed no vow. Yet Arthur believed he had. Arthur had been hurt, and he, Lancelot, was responsible. Was that not in itself betrayal? He did not know, he did not understand how this had come about or what it meant. He only knew he could not bear that Elaine should look at him like that. He seized her wrists and rested his throbbing brow against her hands. "Elaine," he whispered, "please. Please take me with you."

The stone was hard against his knees, her hands cold and stiff in his. How could he bear it if she, too, rejected him? How could he survive all the endless, empty years alone?

"Very well," she said at last. "If you are certain . . ."

The relief was so shattering that he could barely speak. "Yes," he managed, "yes, I've never been more sure of anything. We can go today, as soon as the king gives me leave."

"Somehow I don't think *that* will be a problem."

"I will go to him now," he said, staggering a little as he rose to his feet.

"Are you all right?" she asked. "You are so pale . . ."

"It's just my head—it aches sometimes, but it will pass—" He turned toward the door and nearly lost his footing, catching himself upon the bedpost.

"Lie down," she ordered, "you aren't well."

"No, I must see Arthur."

"I will come with you."

"Yes." He grasped her hand. "We must tell him . . . tell him . . ."

"That you wish to retire from court," Elaine finished. "But you cannot tell him anything in this state. Come, rest for a bit—"

"No, we must go now."

Elaine's anger began to fade when he straightened, his face set as he walked with her to the doorway. The news of him and Guinevere, discovered by the king while locked in a passionate embrace, had not been long in finding her. Half a dozen ladies had hastened to her chamber with the tale, no doubt hoping to see her weep so they might have something new to embellish the story. She had not given them that satisfaction, though the past hour had been very hard to bear.

Now she wondered if the story had been quite accurate. Perhaps Lancelot was telling her the truth, and he had merely comforted the queen in her distress. As to why Guinevere had been distressed, that was another matter altogether. Elaine needed no court gossip to enlighten her to Guinevere's feelings about her own arrival—and Galahad's.

Wherever the truth lay, Lancelot would be better off away from Guinevere. They would speak of this when they reached Corbenic and Elaine would have the truth at last. Only then could they hope to regain the happiness they had shared.

A page led them through the corridor and up half a dozen steps to Arthur's chamber, a long, low apartment that overlooked the rose garden where Elaine had waited with Gawain. Arthur looked as though he had aged a decade since they'd sat together at supper. He greeted them coolly, and when Lancelot haltingly requested permission to leave court, he merely nodded.

"Thank you, my lord," Lancelot said, perfectly correct, but just as Elaine breathed a sigh of relief, he added, "Arthur, I am sorry—"

"Lady Elaine," the king cut in, "good fortune to you."

"And to you, sire," Elaine said. She tugged at Lancelot's arm, but he did not move.

"Arthur," he said again, his voice ragged. "Will you not wish me good fortune, too?"

"Don't," Elaine said under her breath, "not now."

"You don't—you can't believe—" Lancelot faltered. "Arthur, you know me—"

"I thought I did," the king said. "You have asked my leave to retire, and it is given. There is nothing more to say."

"Nothing—?" Lancelot was deadly pale; his voice shook as he threw off Elaine's restraining hand and started forward. "But you cannot do this, just order me away without even—"

"It is you who asked to go," Arthur began reasonably enough, then his composure snapped, and he half rose in his seat. "Now go! Get out! Save your excuses and your lies; I don't want to hear them!"

"I never lied to you."

Arthur made a low sound of disgust and dropped back into his chair.

"Lancelot, we must go," Elaine said pleadingly. "The king has dismissed us, we must—"

"I never lied to you," Lancelot said again, his voice shaking. "I have been true to my oath."

Arthur looked at him for a long moment; then at last the cold fury in his expression dissolved. "Lance—"

The door flew open, and the queen strode into the chamber. "Arthur, I—" She halted, one hand going to her throat. "Why, Lance, what do you here—and Lady Elaine—"

"Sir Lancelot and his lady are leaving us, Guinevere," the king said. "They are retiring to Corbenic. Wish them well, my lady, as I do."

"Leaving?" Guinevere stared, bewildered, from Arthur to Lancelot. "No, that isn't—Lance, you're not really leaving, are you?"

"Yes, madam," he said, and though a moment before Elaine could not drag him from the room, now he seemed quite eager to begone. "If you will excuse us . . ."

"But you cannot go!"

Elaine wished herself anywhere but where she was. What would the king say? What *could* he say? She prayed that Arthur would silence his wife before she could humiliate them further.

But Arthur did not silence her. He merely sat back, fixed her with that penetrating gaze, and asked in a voice all the more commanding for its softness, "Why not?"

"Why—?" The queen, as though realizing she had said

too much, flushed brilliantly. "Why, because tomorrow King Bagdemagus is coming with his dreadful son. I was counting on Lance to joust against him! You promised, Lance, don't you remember?"

"Did I?" Lancelot rubbed the space above his brows, his pallor deepening. "Madam, I beg to be excused. Sir Gawain can take my place."

"I don't *want* Gawain to take your place," Guinevere said, sounding so like a spoiled child that Elaine longed to slap her. "I want *you* to do it. You gave me your word."

"That is enough," Arthur said. "Sir Lancelot, you are dismissed."

"You have no right to do that!" Guinevere cried. "He is mine to command, my champion, and I order him to stay and do his duty."

"What duty is that, Guinevere?" Arthur asked, his mild eyes kindling with anger. "The duty I observed him performing earlier, through the window of your chamber?"

Guinevere lifted her chin and flashed Arthur a scornful glance. "Lance is my friend. He listens to me—he cares if I am unhappy—"

"What cause have you to be unhappy?" Arthur demanded.

"Do you think I do not know what people say? What you are thinking? A barren queen is no good to anyone."

Arthur's knuckles whitened on the arms of his chair. "Have I ever—*ever*—reproached you?"

"Not in words, but . . ." Tears trembled on Guinevere's lashes, but they did not fall. Something about the set of her mouth, the tilt of her head, reminded Elaine suddenly of someone else, though the impression fled before she could quite catch it.

"I know what I am, my lord," the queen said, "a royal broodmare who has failed in her duty to the realm. But would you grudge me even the comfort of a friend?"

"That would depend," Arthur said, "upon the form this comfort takes. 'Tis true I have hoped for an heir, but the last thing Britain needs is a prince whose paternity is open to question. Judging by what I witnessed earlier, this salient fact seems to have escaped you, but—"

"How dare you?" Guinevere cried. "That is a filthy thing to say!"

"And if you think I am the first to say it, you are a fool as well as—"

"Stop."

Lancelot, who had been staring at the floor, raised his head. "Arthur—Guinevere." He looked from one to the other, his expression pleading. "I—I do not know what you want of me. What am I to do?"

"Go," the king ordered.

"Stay," the queen commanded.

Once Lancelot began to laugh, he could not stop. He had been here before. They all had. Time had twisted back upon itself, the past become the present. Whey did they stare at him so strangely? Did they not see the jest?

His head was pounding, but he steeled himself against the pain, for he must find the words to make things right. Arthur was so angry, and Guinevere—damn her, why did she not *speak*? But it was wrong to blame her when the fault was King Ban's, poor mad King Ban who had betrayed his closest friend . . . Hadn't Arthur once said something about the sins of the father being visited upon the son?

"Come with me," Elaine said gently, taking his arm.

Lancelot shook his head. He could not go with her; he had promised to fight disguised in the king's tournament, but how could he when Sir Torre had taken back his shield?

Or no, he thought, wincing as fresh pain stabbed his temples, surely that had happened long ago, in the days when the Lady of the Lake had cast him from her service.

Now he was her creature once again. But that was as it should be, for only thus could he serve King Arthur as the Lady had intended. Arthur needed him exactly as he was, and he would not betray his liege lord and friend. So long as he was true to Arthur, all would be well.

Why was everyone so quiet? he wondered suddenly. The king and queen stared at him, unmoving, frozen like figures in a tapestry. Perhaps that's all they were, three characters in a song sung in Avalon by the Lady's harper . . . what had been his name? If only he could remember . . .

"Thomas," he said aloud. "The harper's name was Thomas!"

"Come," a voice said at his side, "Lancelot, come away; you need to rest."

It was Elaine, his own Elaine, looking up at him with those astonishingly blue eyes. What was she doing here? Why did she look so frightened as she clutched his arm? Something was wrong, but he could not remember what it was. If only this pain in his head would stop so he could *think* . . .

Something was wrong, so wrong that Elaine could not think what she should do. She could only stare in terror at Lancelot's ashen face, his feverish-bright eyes, the echo of his wild laughter still ringing in her ears.

"Come with me," she said again, her voice only a whisper.

"My love, I am so sorry," he said. "I should have sent you away, but I could not bring myself to do it. I have sworn oaths—so many oaths, they choke me so I cannot breathe. The Lady said—" He laid his palm flat upon his brow. "Forsworn—I cannot bear it, not again. My lord, please, will you not help me?"

"What is it, Lance?" Arthur said uneasily. "Are you in pain?"

" 'Tis just this space; here, between my eyes, where once my soul dwelt. Did you know, Arthur? Did you ever guess I'd lost it? I've often thought you must and kept silent out of pity."

"Send for your woman, the healer," Arthur said to Elaine, but she could not force herself to move. Turning to Lancelot, he added gently, "No, I never guessed."

"It had to be," Lancelot assured him, nodding. "It is my destiny, the Lady said so in the barn. We couldn't bring the hay in—though it wasn't I who killed the spider, whatever Will Reeve might think. But it's all right, Arthur, you mustn't mind about me—I don't, not anymore, save just before a battle. To watch them all ride out, never knowing what will happen—have you any idea, my lord, how brave your knights are?"

"Yes," Arthur murmured as he took Lancelot's free arm, "my knights are brave men all. Sit down, Lance."

"Take Sir Gawain," Lancelot went on as though the king had not spoken, "a goodly knight, but not, alas, impervious to theft." He drew himself up haughtily. "What, you doubt my word? I assure you, sire, I speak as one who knows."

Elaine and Arthur exchanged frightened glances. This was not fever; Lancelot's skin was cool and dry, though when he looked at Elaine, he did not seem to see her.

"Lancelot," she said, putting her hands to his cheeks. "Look at me, my love, do you not know me?"

His eyes sharpened, and he seized her wrists so hard that she cried out in surprise. "Elaine, what do you here? Why are you not in Corbenic? Get you gone, it is not safe to be near me."

"I am not afraid," Elaine said.

"You should be. Oh, love, if you only knew where I have been! The stars sing terrible songs too beautiful to bear, and the stones walk in the moonlight. But it is not for you, can you not see that?"

Guinevere's eyes were wide. "He is mad," she whispered. "Sweet Jesu, he is mad, like our—like King Ban—"

"Lancelot," Elaine began helplessly.

He threw her hands from him and backed clumsily away. "Do not touch me! I am not human anymore, not in any way that matters."

"You are not well," the king said firmly. "Lie down while I send for—"

"No!" Lancelot looked from the king to Elaine and then out across the rose garden. "Galahad," he said clearly. "Galahad."

Before anyone could stop him, he flung himself headlong from the window.

The fall was not a great one, and it ended in the rosebushes planted at the garden's edge. Elaine, leaning far over the windowsill, watched Lancelot scramble to his feet, blood streaming down his face from a dozen scratches.

"Lancelot!" she called, and though the king joined his voice to hers, Lancelot did not look back. He ran through the garden, vaulted the wall, and vanished into the forest.

Chapter 38

· · ·

ARTHUR strode from the chamber, shouting for his knights, the slam of the door cutting off his voice.

"They will find him," Guinevere said. "They will bring him back."

"And then what?" Elaine cried. "You have the king—he is a good man, an honorable man. Why could you not leave Lancelot alone?"

Guinevere looked at her, as ashen-faced as Lancelot had been before, the same shocked bewilderment clouding her eyes. Tears spilled over her lashes and trailed down her cheeks. Even weeping, she was lovely.

"I never meant to hurt him," Guinevere said, holding out her hands. "Not Lance."

"But you did. You have broken him. Good day, madam," Elaine said coldly. "I shall return to Corbenic alone, it seems."

"But stay . . . he may regain his senses and come home," Guinevere said faintly.

"That is my only hope. And if he does, I will be there waiting for him with his son."

Alone, Guinevere went to the window and watched the knights leaving Camelot, riding off in search of Lancelot. The horses' hooves made puffs of dust upon the road before they, too, disappeared beneath the trees. The sound of horns winding in the distance was carried back faintly on the evening breeze.

• • •

DUSK gathered in the hollows, then spread to drain the color from field and tree and flower. The knights were mere shadows when they returned. When the last gold faded from the treetops, the door opened behind Guinevere.

"He is not found?" she asked without turning.

"No."

"I am sorry for it. My lord," she added swiftly, before he could reply, "I would have speech with you."

"Now?" Arthur laughed harshly. "What is there left to say?"

"Only this."

She turned, hands braced on the windowsill behind her. She was coward enough to be glad the chamber was too dim for him to see her face.

"Lancelot is not my lover."

"Indeed?"

She could imagine Arthur's expression, one brow lifted and his mouth curled upward at the corner.

"He is, as I have said, my friend, but there is another bond between us." For a moment, she feared she would be sick, but she steeled herself and finished. "King Ban was father to us both."

When the silence had spun out beyond bearing, she said, "Did you hear me? I said—"

"That King Ban was your father. Yes, I heard. Why would you say such a thing to me?"

"Because it is the truth, my lord." Quickly, her voice shaking, she explained how it had happened.

"Do you always greet your . . . brother . . . by flinging yourself into his arms as you did earlier?"

"This fortnight past," Guinevere said, "I believed I was carrying your child. When I learned it was not so I was . . . upset. It was not the first time, you see. Twice before I hoped . . . There was no one I could tell," she went on, twisting her long sleeves between her fingers. "My women gossip so, and there is none I would confide in. Save Lance, of course. I could always—" Her throat tightened. "I could always tell him anything."

"Did it not occur to you to come to me?"

"Oh, no, my lord. I saw no reason to disturb you."

The moon was rising above the trees. It gave enough light for her to discern Arthur's outline, but not enough to read his expression.

"Was it for the same reason you kept silent about your birth when first we met in Cameliard? So I might not be *disturbed*?"

"I did not know until you sued for my hand. Then Leodegrance told me all."

"I would rather he'd told me," Arthur said. "But I suppose he wanted to have you on the throne. Was that it, Guinevere? Did he force you to keep silent?"

Guinevere closed her eyes briefly. "No. 'Twas I who begged *him* not to speak."

"You wanted to be queen that much?"

"I wanted to wed *you*. Do you remember the day you rode into Cameliard? I stood on the battlements—"

"Yes, I remember." Arthur's voice was brusque. "So you took a greensick fancy for your king?"

"To the man who smiled at me that day, a man whose name I did not know. I was young, my lord. I'd spent all my life shut away in a convent. I believed," she added very low, "in true love."

"And that it would flourish when rooted in a lie?"

"Yes," she said steadily. "I thought it wouldn't matter much. No one knew, save Leodegrance—and Lancelot, of course. Leodegrance told him, as well, when Lance came to Cameliard to bring me to my wedding. It was so strange—Lance and I met when we were grown, yet it seemed I'd always known him."

Arthur sighed. "I see. It must have come as a shock to learn he was such close kin to you."

"No, not a shock, more of a surprise. And such a happy one! I'd always longed for a brother, and Lance had no family of his own. He guessed at once how I felt about—about our marriage—but I didn't mind him knowing, because he was so fond of you himself. We only quarreled once, when I said you weren't to know about my mother and King Ban. Lance always said you would not mind if I told you, but you would be angry if you found out for yourself."

"He knows me well," Arthur said.

"I saw later that he was right, but by then it was too late. He hated me not telling you—it made him so unhappy. I did mean to. I planned to confess everything after the birth of our son. But as we both know that will never come to pass, I thought it best to tell you now."

"And what," Arthur said, "am I meant to do with this information?"

"Use it. Our marriage has failed, there is no point pretending anymore. I know some on your council have already suggested that you put me aside and seek a younger bride; it will hardly come as a surprise if you decide to do so. Tell them what you like; I shall pack at once and go wherever you see fit to send me. You can wed again, my lord; you are still a young man with time to beget a dozen heirs."

There, she had said it. It was over. She sank back against the windowsill, arms wrapped about herself to still her trembling.

"Upon my new queen," Arthur said thoughtfully, "I see." She heard the creak of a chair as he sat. "You will be relieved to go, won't you? I daresay our marriage has not been all your girlish dreams led you to expect."

Guinevere was grateful for the darkness that hid her tears. Careful to keep them from her voice, she answered, "No, my lord."

Arthur gave a grunt of laughter. "At least you don't deny it."

"How could I? I think we both know we are . . . ill suited."

"In bed, you mean."

She could not answer for a moment for the pain in her throat. At last she managed to whisper, "Yes. The fault is mine. My fa—King Leodegrance—told me it would be so, but I did not believe him."

"He told you that you would not enjoy bedding with me?"

"No. Not that. He said—my mother, he said, was a—a sinful woman who could not control her lust. He said he saw the same taint in me. I thought he spoke from bitterness, but I have always known, since the first night . . . Well, 'tis no matter now, my lord, only that I'm sure you will do better next time. And now, if you will excuse me—"

"No, stay a moment. I am curious, Guinevere. What did you learn that first night? That you were nothing like your mother, after all?"

"No, my lord," she said, feeling her face flame in the darkness. "I learned that I was very like her."

Arthur gave a short, mirthless laugh. "When? Where? I've seen no sign of it."

"I have always endeavored to perform my duties as befits a queen," she answered stiffly.

"And how does a queen perform her royal duty in the bedchamber?" he asked, his voice mocking. "With brave endurance?"

"With dignity."

"Dignity?" Arthur laughed again. *"Dignity?"*

All at once he stood before her, his hand upon her neck. "Why do you lie to me now?" he demanded harshly. "What can you hope to gain?"

She felt the pulse in her throat fluttering against his palm. "Nothing."

"Then admit the truth. You cannot bear for me to touch you." His hand traveled downward. "See, even now you shrink away."

"No," she whispered. " 'Tis but—but that I am weak and sinful." She caught his hand and drew it to her breast. "When you do this, I—"

He bent over her, his breath warm against her lips. "You what?"

"I do not want you to stop."

"A very great sin," he said, gravely mocking. "But 'tis best that you confess it. What else would you have me do to you?"

"I—I would—" She put her hand on his neck and drew him down. He hesitated but a moment, then his mouth closed over hers in a kiss unlike any she had known. This was no courteous touch of mouth to mouth, but a fierce assault upon her senses. A small moan escaped her when his tongue met hers, and she turned her head, deepening the kiss, abandoning herself to the dizzying sensations sweeping through her like a flame. She twined her hands in his fine, soft hair as she'd always longed to do, reveling in the iron strength of the arm around her waist, running her hands over the hard muscles of his back and shoulders that she had traced so often with her eyes when he lay sleeping.

At last he drew away. She could not see his face, but his voice was ragged as he said, "And have you slaked your sinful desires upon other men? You may as well tell me; there is nothing left to lose. If not Lancelot, then—"

"I never wanted any other," she said simply. "Only you."

He released her so suddenly that she stumbled, catching herself upon the windowsill. "Oh, very good, Guinevere! That was quite well acted, so well that you'll forgive me if I don't believe it was as unrehearsed as you would have me think."

"I do not take your meaning," Guinevere said, straightening her gown with shaking fingers. "I have told you nothing but the truth tonight—"

"But what of all the other nights? Do you think I could live with you so long and know you so little?"

"Yes. For I have lived with you equally as long, and I would have sworn you were incapable of such cruelty. I have admitted all to you, I have said that I will go wherever you will send me. What need had you to—to—"

She pushed past him and stumbled to the doorway. The torchlight from the corridor fell across the chamber, showing her Arthur standing by the window, his hair falling loose about his face. It seemed impossible that she could still desire him, and yet she did, with a force that brought hot tears to her eyes and left her nearly breathless.

"Farewell, my lord," she said, and despite her efforts, her

voice wavered. She lifted her chin and finished steadily, "I trust there will be no need for us to meet again."

Without waiting for the answer she could not bear to hear, she closed the door behind her and ran blindly to her chamber.

Chapter 39

• • •

"BRISEN," Elaine called, closing the door of her chamber carefully behind her. "Brisen, are you here?"

"Aye, m'lady. What's ado?"

"Pack everything; we are leaving. Where is Galahad—ah, here you are, my sweet," she said, taking him from his nurse's arms and holding him tightly. "We must go at once."

Brisen folded her arms and regarded Elaine curiously. "Where?"

"Home."

"We cannot leave tonight, lady," Brisen said reasonably.

"We must."

"But we'd hardly make it to the village before we'd have to stop. We'll go first thing to—"

"Now, Brisen," Elaine said tightly. "We must go now."

"Lotte, take Galahad inside," Brisen said. "Now, lady, why don't you sit down and I'll make you—"

"I do not want a posset." Elaine looked about the chamber, scattered with their belongings. Lancelot's blue cloak was tossed over a stool; his sword, bright Arondight, still hung upon the peg. "I will go tonight. You can follow in the morning. Get Torre to help you with the arrangements."

"But—"

"Don't argue with me! Just do as I say."

"What's happened to you, lady? Where is Sir Lan—"

"Don't speak of him!" Elaine seized her cloak from its hook and threw it over her shoulders. "I have no time, 'tis late already—"

"You cannot go riding alone at such an hour!" Brisen said, moving to block her path. "You've had a shock, haven't you? Tell me what has happened."

Elaine shook her head. She could not tell Brisen. She could not tell anyone. If she spoke the words, it would be real. Lancelot's mind would be broken, his reason fled—

"I cannot tarry," she cried. "Stop bothering me with questions! I haven't time—"

She stiffened at the sound of a step outside her door. It was Lancelot, he was back—oh, what a fool she'd been to worry! She threw open the door, then drew back with a cry of disappointment when she saw that it was only Torre. He stepped into the room and shut the door behind him.

"Is it true?" he asked.

Elaine pulled her cloak more tightly around her. "Is what true?"

"That Sir Lancelot is mad," Torre said bluntly.

"No!" Elaine cried. "No, it is a lie!"

"They say he leapt from a window and fled into the forest," Torre said. "They say that you were there. Were you?"

"I—I—"

He took her by the shoulders and shook her. "Elaine, tell me!"

"He isn't mad," she said desperately. "He was . . . upset. Unwell. But he'll be all right, Torre, won't he? Won't he?"

"Oh, Christ." Torre wrapped his arms around her, saying roughly, "Poor bastard, who would have guessed his wits were weak? Mayhap he was knocked on the head over in Gaul."

"Lady," Brisen said, "I will make you that posset now, and you will drink it. There's no good in rushing off tonight when for all you know, Sir Lancelot will be back before dawn. Tomorrow is time enough to decide what's to be done."

What's to be *done*? Elaine thought. There was nothing to be done. Lancelot was gone. She wanted to scream, to rage, to lean against her brother and dissolve into a flood of tears. But if she once began to weep, she feared she'd never stop.

Lancelot was gone. He was beyond her help. One day he might return, and if he did, she would be waiting. She must think of that and not fall into despair. Galahad had already lost his father; if Elaine were to give way now, he would have no one.

"Yes," she said, drawing back from Torre. "You're right, Brisen. Best to wait and see."

She drank the posset without protest, then lay in the bed she had shared with Lancelot. His scent still lingered among the sheets, and the pillow bore the impression of his head. She pulled it close and held it against her, staring dry-eyed into the darkness until the gray light slipped through the window.

She rose and dressed with leaden hands. Silently she followed Brisen from the chamber to the stables. The light was growing now, and the first red rays of sunlight fell upon Torre and Lavaine, already mounted, with Lotte and Galahad upon a sturdy little jennet beside them. Elaine's horse stood a bit apart, a knight holding its bridle.

Elaine nodded to Sir Bors, too moved to speak when she saw the tears standing in his eyes. Lionel walked from the darkness of the stable, leading his own horse and his brother's. When he saw Elaine, he dropped the reins and ran forward to catch her in a hard embrace. At last he stepped away and drew a hand across his eyes, turning to give a low whistle. Another knight emerged from the stable—Sir Ector De Maris, Lancelot's kinsman whom she had met the day before—and bowed deeply over her hand before helping her to mount.

The three knights made no move to join her. They stood by their horses' heads, and just as Elaine had almost made up her mind to speak, she heard the slow clop of hooves approaching from within the stable. A moment later, the king appeared, leading his own stallion. He, too, bowed to Elaine without speaking. Once mounted, Arthur pulled his horse beside hers, the knights falling in beside them as they rode slowly out of Camelot.

Chapter 40

• • •

*R*UN.
 The command was urgent, inescapable.
Run.

As blindly panicked as a stag who hears the hunter's horn, he ran until he dropped and lay where he had fallen until he had the strength to run again. Sometimes he slept, lying among the ferns, starting up at the least sound to flee. If he dreamed, he did not know it, no more than he knew his name or where he'd come from or even that he was a man. He simply was. He had always been here in the forest, always running, running until each breath he drew was white-hot pain.

He ate what he could find: berries, which for a time were abundant, fruit, roots he dug from the earth with bleeding hands. Later, when the leaves began to fall, there were nuts, and then there was nothing. Hunger drove him toward the dangerous places, where woodsmoke filled the air. Stealthy, cunning, he slipped into coops and barns and even cottages, seizing what was edible and bearing it back into the forest. When it rained, he took what shelter he could find, crouched beneath a bank or in the hollow of a tree.

Once, bending over a pool to drink, he scrambled back with a hoarse cry, terrified by the bearded skeleton leering back at him. He crept back again on hands and knees and flung a stone into the water, staring transfixed as the thing in the pool shattered into a thousand shimmering pieces, then slowly formed itself into a man, first wavering, then still and whole. He groped for another stone, and then another and another, and every time the miracle was repeated. At last he sat back on his heels, watching the face in the pool work as he tried to form a word that danced just out of reach . . . and when it was almost near enough to grasp, he leapt to his feet and fled.

He woke one morning to find the world transformed. A glittering coverlet of white lay over leaf and bush, and the forest was wrapped in silence. When he tried to stand, shaking off his coverlet of leaves, he could not feel his feet. He knew that he was close to death; only that could have driven him to approach the tiny cottage he had passed the night before. Now he followed the smell of smoke and hid behind the pile of cut wood beside the door.

The thought of knocking on the door did not cross his mind, no more than it would have done any other forest creature. Even if he had imagined such a thing, he had no words with which to ask for help and no memory of ever having known them. He only knew that inside was warmth and food, and if he did not have them, he would die. He groped among the logs, found one that fit his hand, and settled down to wait.

The sun stood straight above the trees before the door opened. Slowly he stood and raised the log, but no one emerged. Instead, something flew through the air and landed on the woodpile. He started back, but his frozen feet would not carry him. He stumbled and fell, the log falling from his hand. When he tried to lift himself, he found that he could not.

He heard a voice, very soft and pleasant, like the wind among the topmost branches of the trees in springtime. It lifted a little at the end, then stopped, seeming to wait for something. After a little time it went on again, now accompanied by the smell of food.

He raised himself to his knees and peered over the woodpile, his hand touching the thing that had been thrown. It was the fur of some animal, cured to softness and very thick. There on the doorstep stood a man, garbed in a brown woolen robe. The man—

(*monk*)

—gestured toward a pot from which steam was rising, then turned and went inside again.

The fur was long enough to drape over his shoulders and still trail behind him through the snow. He clutched it one-handed and cautiously, with many a false start, approached the pot still steaming on the doorstep, snatched it up, and retreated a few steps.

He kept one eye on the door while he ate. It was hot enough to burn fingers and mouth, but he did not care. He devoured it all before it had a chance to cool, and retreated behind the woodpile, wrapping his feet and huddling inside the fur. When darkness began to fall, the door opened again, the voice spoke, and another gift of food was placed outside, this time with a pair of slippers.

Each morning and each evening was the same. The door opened, the brown man spoke, left an offering, and went away. In time, he realized that the sounds were speech. Slowly the meaning of the words emerged.

He stayed until the first flowers bloomed beside the

cottage, poking through the drift of snow that still remained. One evening when the door opened, he stepped out and faced the man who had saved his life.

"Ah, so here you are." The monk smiled. "I always hoped to meet you."

"Thou hast rendered me a service which can never be repaid. God's blessing on thee, Brother." He stopped, frozen into immobility. He hadn't expected to speak, had no idea that he could. The words had simply come without conscious thought or plan.

The monk blinked. "You are quite welcome. May I know whom I have the pleasure of addressing? Your name, friend. Will you tell it to me?"

"My name? My . . ." He began to back away, shaking his head. A name. His name. He'd had one once—or no, that had been someone else, not him. Not him.

Run, the voice screamed in his mind.

And he obeyed.

Chapter 41

. . .

"SIR Lancelot is dead, Mother." Agravaine scowled, shifting his bulk in the saddle. "Why can't you let it go?"

Morgause cast her eyes to the canopy of red-gold leaves above her head. Why, why could it not be Gawain who rode with her today? Handsome, clever Gawain, who never needed to have anything explained to him. Agravaine—well, one only had to look at him to take his measure. He was good-looking—all her children had inherited some measure of her beauty—but his indulgences were catching up with him. And though he was loyal in his own plodding way, not even the fondest mother could call him clever. Gaheris and Gareth were Arthur's men; she'd dismissed them from her heart and counsels long ago. Mordred, though promising, was still a child.

Gawain was the best of her brood, and she had always meant for him to wear Arthur's crown. His defection still rankled sorely.

"Sir Lancelot was seen, dearest," she said through gritted teeth. "That monk—"

"Oh, blast the monk. He said himself he'd never met Sir Lancelot before."

"*And* the lady in the pavilion," Morgause continued, stifling a sigh. "Her knight said only Sir Lancelot could have dealt him such a blow."

Agravaine grunted and reached behind him, awkwardly because of his bulk, and fumbled for the wineskin. "But that was weeks ago."

There had been other sightings, some patently false, a few that might be true. But all the signs pointed in one direction: if Sir Lancelot indeed lived, he was heading for Corbenic.

"Even if it *was* him," Agravaine said sulkily, "he's surely dead by now."

"Perhaps."

It rankled, too, that Morgause could not be certain. How many hours had she wasted, hunched over her scrying bowl, searching for a glimpse of Arthur's most troublesome knight? And he must be found. She could not afford for Lancelot to resurface. He'd caused enough damage when he'd left. But Arthur had not set Guinevere aside as everyone expected he would. Indeed, with Sir Lancelot gone, they seemed to have found a new happiness together, though there were many who still believed Arthur would rid himself of her and seek a fertile queen.

They did not know him, not as Morgause did. Arthur was incurably sentimental, particularly when it came to women. So long as no new scandal arose, Arthur would keep his barren wife, and Gawain remain his heir. Should Gawain continue to prove himself disloyal to his clan, there was always Mordred. One way or another, Morgause reflected, her son would wear the crown of Britain . . . and she would rule.

It was only a matter of time. Time, and Arthur's death, which he could not avoid much longer. He'd been lucky twice already—poison was a clumsy tool, and Arthur was too good a horseman to be thrown, even by a stallion half crazed with pain. But there would be other opportunities, and even Gawain could not be at his king's side every moment of the day.

But she must move cautiously. Gawain was already suspicious. He'd looked at her very oddly once or twice during her last visit to Camelot. Gawain could well become a problem, but he was a problem Morgause felt confident that she could deal with.

Unlike Sir Lancelot.

Her hands clenched on the reins when she thought of him as first she'd seen him lying beneath a hedgerow, one arm folded beneath his head and the other outstretched, fingers curled loosely over his palm. There had been four of them that day, four queens riding nowhere in particular with nothing to look forward to but a meal taken out of doors.

Until they spied the sleeping knight.

His cheeks had been flushed, Morgause remembered, his red lips slightly parted. Sun and shadow flickered across his face as a light wind blew through the branches. The breeze stirred his raven hair and fluttered the sleeves of the thin shirt that clung to his chest and belly like a second skin. Morgause had looked on him and wanted him, and had she been alone, she would have had him. But she had not been alone. Fool that she had been, she agreed to the suggested wager, never once doubting the outcome.

Yet Lancelot had refused her. He, who was barely come to manhood, was impervious to both her words and touch . . . and to her magic. That made Lancelot a dangerous man, all the more so because he was unaware of his power. Damn the Lady of the Lake and her infernal meddling! Why did she not stay in Avalon and leave the affairs of Britain to those who understood them best? Arthur was already difficult enough to kill; should the Lady's champion return to Camelot, the king would once again be beyond Morgause's reach. No, Lancelot must die or remain forever mad.

She turned to Agravaine and smiled. "He may well be dead. But it does no harm to be certain."

"No harm?" Agravaine slapped a palm to his neck. "I'm being eaten alive in this fen!"

"We'll soon be there. I can see the tower now above the trees. Have that trumpeter ride ahead to announce us."

• • •

THE first shock came when Morgause was seated in the dreary little hall, pretending to sip the revolting ale Elaine had given her.

"I'm so sorry I didn't warn you," Morgause said, "but when Agravaine mentioned how closely we'd be passing, it seemed too bad to go by without paying you a visit. Are you certain this is not an inconvenience?"

"Of course not, madam," Elaine said. "But I fear you may find us a bit . . . rustic."

"Oh, no! Corbenic is quite charming!" Morgause said, repressing a little shudder as she set down the ale.

"Well, we have done rather well lately," Elaine said, picking up her spindle. "The harvest last year was the best we've had, and this year we hope to do even better."

Elaine chatted on, her spindle dipping up and down. She hardly seemed to have aged since Morgause saw her last. She was still slender as a birch, and her golden hair, braided in a plait that fell neatly, if unimaginatively over one shoulder, was as plentiful as ever. She did have a certain grace,

Morgause admitted grudgingly, with those slim hands and that extraordinary neck. Yet she was so cool, so completely self-contained that it was impossible to imagine her in the grip of any strong emotion. That she could engender the sort of devotion that would drive Sir Lancelot to seek her in his madness was nearly unbelievable.

Still, he did seem to be seeking her, and love had been known to work miracles before. Strange as it seemed, Elaine was a potential threat. Therefore, Elaine must be removed.

"I have thought of you so often, my dear, since . . ." Morgause lowered her voice. "Since poor Sir Lancelot . . ."

Elaine went on smiling. Only the smallest flicker of her eyelids betrayed that the name meant anything to her at all.

"How kind of you to remember me," she murmured.

"And young Galahad, of course. How does he fare?"

For the first time, a bit of animation lit Elaine's face, and Morgause realized that once she must have been very beautiful indeed. "Very well, madam. Here he is now."

Morgause turned, the smile freezing on her lips when she recognized the dark-haired woman who accompanied young Galahad into the hall. "Why, Mistress Brisen," she said blankly. "I had thought you with my sister Morgana. Did you not tell me you planned to return to her service?"

Morgause did not like surprises, particularly unpleasant ones. Morgana had always claimed that Brisen had more talent than any novice she had known. Of course Brisen had not completed her training, but still, it would be foolish to discount her.

"I had thought of it, madam," Brisen said, "but Lady Elaine asked me to return with her instead. Lady," she added to Elaine, "where is Sir Agravaine to sleep?"

"Let him have Sir Torre's chamber," Elaine said, "and he can share with Father."

"Sir Torre?" Morgause asked.

"My elder brother," Elaine said.

"Oh, yes, the crippled one," Morgause said dismissively.

Brisen's dark eyes narrowed. "Pray excuse me," she said coldly, "while I see to your chamber."

"Oh, dear," Morgause said when she was gone, "did I say something wrong?"

Elaine frowned slightly, looking after her maid. "Brisen healed my brother after he took the wound to his leg."

"Ah, I see. A matter of professional pride, is it? But as I remember, he was very lame."

"He is much improved, we think," Elaine said, holding out her hand to Galahad, a sturdy child and as golden fair as one of Morgause's own.

"He's nothing like Sir Lancelot, is he?" she said.

"Sometimes I think I see something of him around the eyes, and in the jaw . . . but that may just be my hope."

Elaine was right; Galahad's eyes, though different in color, were as deep-set as Lancelot's, with the same dark lashes and upward tilt at the corners. But their expression was quite different. Where Lancelot's gaze was always a bit wary, this boy looked her directly in the eye with an intensity that was a bit unsettling in one so young.

"Good day, Galahad," she said. "I am Queen Morgause of Orkney. We have met before, but I don't expect that you'll remember. You were just a baby at the time, and now you're such great boy!"

Galahad turned and buried his face in his mother's lap. Elaine picked him up and set him on her knee. "Come, Galahad, where are your manners? Say good day to Queen Morgause."

Galahad's face screwed up, and he clutched his mother around the neck.

Morgause stared at him, nonplussed. Children liked her.

She prided herself on being good with them, having brought up five lusty sons of her own and overseen half a dozen of Lot's brats into the bargain.

"He's tired," Elaine said apologetically. "Let me take him to his nurse."

She stood and bore Galahad away. He regarded Morgause over his mother's shoulder with that same unwavering intensity. *What a strange child,* she thought, oddly disconcerted. Perhaps he had inherited more than his father's eyes. Yes, that must be it, his wits were obviously not all they should be.

"Agravaine," she said.

He looked up, startled from his ale.

"Tonight you must find some way to distract Mistress Brisen."

Agravaine's face lightened. "My pleasure," he said, swiping the back of his hand across his lips.

"I think not," Morgause said. "Best to feign an illness. About an hour after supper—and you must keep her with you until the moon has risen."

Agravaine stifled a belch. "Whatever you say, Mother."

Chapter 42

• • •

"SHE is a bitch," Brisen said, her dark eyes snapping as she dropped the coverlet on the bed. "I can't imagine what she's doing here."

"She was passing by," Elaine said, straightening the coverlet, "and thought to stop."

"Why? That one never does anything for kindness. Where is she now?"

"Walking with Sir Agravaine in the garden. Stop punching that pillow, Brisen, you'll have feathers everywhere."

"Better the pillow than—" Brisen threw it down and whirled, hands fisted on her hips. "Oh, I would just love to tell her what I think of her!"

Elaine merely shook her head and swept a stack of her father's parchments into a neat pile.

"Wait here," Brisen said suddenly. "I'll be right back."

Elaine had nearly finished by the time Brisen returned, holding a few roses in a small clay pot. "Here," she said, "these will look well by the bed."

As Elaine turned to set the flowers down, she felt a spray of water hit her back. She looked over her shoulder to find Brisen with a dripping branch of rowan in her hands. "What *are* you doing?" she asked, half laughing as Brisen muttered beneath her breath and shook it again, spattering her face.

"A charm."

"I thought you'd given up that nonsense," Elaine said, gesturing toward the rowan.

"Nonsense, is it? I'll wager that Morgause wouldn't agree. I don't like her," Brisen said, moving her shoulders in a half shrug. "And I don't trust her, either."

"Queen Morgause *was* very rude," Elaine said, making an effort to be fair, "but we both know that what she said about Torre isn't true."

"Did it not bother you to hear your brother spoken of like that?"

Elaine shrugged. "She will be gone soon enough. It isn't worth being upset about."

Brisen began to speak, then checked herself. "Aye. You're right," she said after a moment. "But there was a time when you would have cared."

"Don't," Elaine said, very low.

"Well, someone has to! You can't go on like this, it isn't right!"

"What would you have me do, Brisen?"

"Cry—rage—hit someone! Here—" she offered Elaine a crystal vial belonging to Morgause. "Smash this."

"I don't see how destroying Morgause's scent will help anyone," Elaine answered, taking the bottle and setting it on the shelf.

"You never know until you try."

"I'm well enough, Brisen. Just leave me as I am."

And what am I? Elaine wondered as she left the chamber,

her arms piled high with linen. Sometimes it seemed that she had died the day Lancelot had gone, and all that was left was the shell that had once housed a woman called Elaine. But that was as it was, and for Galahad's sake she must go on as best she could.

* * *

SUPPER passed uneventfully. The only break in the dullness was Morgause's expression when Torre came into the hall, ruddy from the hunt and limping only slightly. Well, they said Morgause had an eye for young men, and Torre had shed years since their return from Camelot. Brisen noticed, too, of course. She paled and left the hall when Morgause smiled at Torre and beckoned him to her side, purring that he must tell her all about his hunt.

Poor Brisen, Elaine thought; *much as I would miss her, it might be better if she did go.* For all she'd claimed that she was over Torre, it was clear he still had the power to wound her.

Elaine finished her meal and stood, murmuring an excuse that no one heard, and went quickly to the nursery. Galahad had seemed to be sickening for something earlier. It was unlike him to fuss at bedtime, yet tonight he'd clung to her, screaming, until she pulled his arms from round her neck and left him to his nurse. He had not been fevered then, nor was he now, she noted with relief. She bent to kiss his curls, and he stirred with a plaintive little cry before settling back to sleep.

"You will watch him?" Elaine said to his nurse.

"Aye, lady," she said, "don't you fear. I reckon it's his teeth that are a-paining him."

By the time Elaine returned to the hall, the trestle tables had been taken down, and the piper she'd sent for from the vill was blowing out a merry tune. Brisen and Sir Agravaine were gone, Torre was playing at tables with Lord Pelleas, and Queen Morgause sat watching them.

"Oh, good," she said when Elaine returned. "I'm afraid I overindulged—the meal was so fine. Will you walk with me?"

"Of course," Elaine said dutifully.

"I was hoping you might show me yonder tower," Morgause said when they had walked through the garden. "It looks quite old. Did I understand Sir Torre aright when he said it is rumored to be haunted?"

"So the story goes. There are some chambers that have not been opened for years, and you know how servants are. It's a bit tumbledown, I'm afraid, but if you don't mind . . ."

"Not at all!" Morgause hooked her arm through Elaine's, laughing. "I take it you do not believe in ghosts?"

"No. My chamber is in the tower, you see, and I've never seen anything unusual or heard a sound that could not be put down to wind or creaking beams."

"How very sensible you are, my dear! But I should like nothing better than to meet a spirit! Particularly that of a young and handsome knight!"

Morgause was not so bad, Elaine thought as they walked together toward the tower. Indeed, she was that most pitiable of beings, a beautiful woman who could not accept the fact that she was growing old. Mayhap if King Lot had lived, it would be different. He'd been something of a scoundrel by all accounts, but Brisen had once said that Morgause always spoke of him with great affection. How sad that they could not have grown old together, she thought, and to her surprise, she felt tears start to her eyes as she led Morgause up the narrow, winding stairway.

I should have brought a torch, she thought. "Can you see, madam?"

"Oh, yes." Morgause, behind her, sounded slightly

breathless. "I see very well in the dark. Like a cat," she added with a little laugh that echoed strangely in the narrow stairway. "Let us begin with the highest chamber. Isn't that where the ghost is said to dwell?"

"Yes." Elaine, who had never felt the least uneasiness in this place, felt a strange reluctance to open the door. It had been barred from the outside some years before when a serving lad ran screaming from the tower, swearing he had seen a man in armor floating several feet above the floor. Nonsense, of course, and yet . . .

"Are you sure . . ." she began uncertainly, but Morgause had already reached past her and lifted the bar.

"Quite sure," she said, and there was something in her voice that raised the hairs on Elaine's neck. "Quite, quite sure," she added, and just as Elaine decided that something was very wrong, Morgause flung open the door and pushed her so sharply between the shoulder blades that she stumbled, falling painfully to her hands and knees.

"What—" she began, but she never had the chance to complete her question.

"Farewell, my dear!" Morgause's voice was harsh, her laughter like a shriek. "Alas, we shall not meet again!"

Elaine was on her feet in an instant, but the door had already slammed shut. Even as she put out her hand, a wall of flame rose before her, reaching to the ceiling.

"What—?" she said again, falling back before the blistering heat. "Morgause! Fire! Help me!"

No answer came. She tried reaching through the flames to seize the latch, but her groping hand met only searing air. She drew it back, frantically slapping at her burning sleeve as she flew to the one narrow window. Before she could scream for help, the fire had spread there, as well.

There was no way out. No hope of rescue, either, for no one save Morgause knew where she had gone. By the time

someone spotted the flames, it would be too late. There
was no smoke, she noted with the small corner of her mind
that was not swamped in panic. The flames were all around
her now, but there was no smoke at all.

She returned to the door, steeling herself against the
pain, but though she tried again and again to break through
the burning wall, there seemed to be no end to it.

She fell back to the center of the floor and went down on
her knees. *"Pater noster qui es in caelis,"* she began, but
could not remember what came next. Sweat poured down
her face and stung her eyes. *I don't want to die,* she
thought, *not now, not yet.*

"Help me!" she screamed with all her strength, though
she could scarce hear her own voice over the fire's roar.
She clasped her blistered hands and prayed that if help did
not arrive, she would not lose her courage. But even that
prayer was denied.

Just before the end, her cries changed. It was no longer
help she asked for, or courage, or even a quick death.
"Lancelot!" she screamed. "Lancelot!" Again and again
she called his name until darkness closed around her.

Chapter 43

• • •

MORGAUSE strolled through the garden, stopping now and then to sniff a blossom. When the moon had risen, she pulled her gown over one white shoulder and carefully untucked a small braid from the intricate arrangement on her brow, draping it so it fell artfully into the bodice of her gown. After a moment, she sighed and dipped her finger in the earth, then drew it across her cheek.

When she reached the garden's edge, she ran, arriving breathless in the hall. "Fire!" she cried. "Fire—in the tower—"

A handful of servants looked up, their mouths agape. Lord Pelleas leapt from his seat at the high table. "Fire?" he repeated, his voice quavering. "What—where—"

"Hurry!" Morgause cried. "Lady Elaine is—"

"What's ado?" Sir Torre called from the doorway. He was already half undressed, his unbound hair loose about his face. Morgause's eyes drifted over his broad shoulders and muscled chest, bared to the firelight, before recalling herself sharply to the present.

"Fire—in the tower—" she gasped. "Lady Elaine—the torch fell and caught—she would not come away, I begged her—oh, hurry, hurry!"

Torre was already gone, Pelleas following behind him. Morgause arranged herself on the settee, one arm draped across the back, hoping that Sir Torre might return and be moved to comfort her in her distress. She sighed, imagining the form that comfort might take, and closed her eyes. A moment later they flew open and she sputtered a shocked cry. Brisen stood over her, a dripping pitcher in her hand.

"Where is Lady Elaine?"

Morgause sat up, her eyes narrowing. "Why, you—" Remembering herself, she answered faintly, "In the tower— the torch dropped—"

"What were you doing there?"

"She—she was showing me the haunted chamber."

"Oh, was she?" Brisen leaned close. "If any harm comes to her—"

"I shall be utterly bereft. But she was the one who insisted on going there in the first place. Then she stumbled, the torch dropped and caught a pile of old linen. I told her to come away, I begged her, but she insisted on plunging in. The flames spread and—" Morgause laid a hand on her brow. "I tried to reach her, but . . ."

Before Morgause could finish, Brisen turned and ran from the hall.

Morgause stood and went to her chamber, calling for her maid. "Pack everything," she ordered curtly. "We leave first thing tomorrow. And bring me wine. I've had a fearsome shock."

She was lying in bed, sipping her wine and regretting that she would not have the opportunity to test Sir Torre's mettle on this visit, when the door opened and Brisen burst into the room.

"Why was the door barred from without?"

"Barred?" Morgause widened her eyes. "Oh, no, I left it open—it must have been a draught—" She paused a moment, then said, "Did you reach her in time?"

"We didn't reach her at all. The bar won't shift. But she's alive."

"How can you be certain?" Morgause asked uneasily.

Brisen's eyes were sharp upon her face. "Lady Elaine was under *my* protection. She is alive. Now tell me what you did so I can undo it."

"I?" Morgause drew herself up against the bolster. "What *can* you mean? I have told you already what happened."

"You lied." Brisen sat down on the edge of the bed. "A clumsy lie, Morgause. Have you forgotten that the blood of the Old Ones runs in my veins, as well?"

"You speak of what you do not understand," Morgause retorted coldly. "The fate of kingdoms . . ."

"The fate of kingdoms?" Brisen repeated with a derisive laugh. "Oh, is that what this is about? I would have said you care only for yourself and your ambition—had I an opinion on such matters, which I do not. I am but a simple country lass these days; no longer do I meddle in the destinies of kings. But Elaine is different. She is dear to me, Morgause. I thought I made that clear at Camelot."

Morgause straightened, her eyes flashing. The air crackled around them as she gathered power around her like a shimmering cloak. One lift of her hand, and Brisen's head snapped back, striking the bedpost with a crack. Morgause relaxed against the bolster and had just reached for her wine when Brisen's eyes fluttered open, and she dragged herself upright. The maid's face was ashen, her hands shaking as she pushed the hair back from her face. The dark strands now held a streak of white, starting at the center of her brow and running like a silver ribbon through the loose plait hanging past her hips.

A small price to pay, Morgause thought, reaching for her wine, *to learn respect for her superiors.*

Brisen drew an unsteady breath and leaned forward, one hand braced upon the wall beside the queen's head, dark eyes inches from Morgause's. Silly girl, had she not learned her lesson yet? Apparently stronger measures would be needed.

Morgause made to lift her hand again and found that she could not. Nor could she look away. *The girl is better than I thought,* she reflected with amusement, and reached for the power that always lay in wait.

Only to find it far beyond her grasp.

"What did you do?" Brisen asked distinctly.

"Called fire into the tower," Morgause answered, cursing herself but unable to hold back her reply.

"And what do you mean by the greatest knight in the world?"

"I have no idea what you are talking about."

"The placard," Brisen said impatiently. " 'Tis plain enough what it says, but—"

"What placard?"

"The one at the foot of the tower, the plinth with silver letters. Tell me what it means!"

"I cannot. It has naught to do with me."

Brisen leaned forward, her gaze so compelling that Morgause drew a hissing breath of pain. "You don't, do you?" Brisen said at last. She straightened and put her hands on her hips, then laughed. "You fool, calling on forces beyond your ken—I would think at your age you would know better. Lady Elaine lives, and one day she will be free."

"And when might that be?" Morgause asked.

"When the greatest knight in all the world releases her."

"When that happy day arrives, I shall be the first to drink the lady's health," Morgause replied, lifting her hand to cover a yawn. "But in the meantime, I would like to get some sleep."

Brisen laughed again, the sound pounding against Morgause's throbbing temples. "You won't sleep, not tonight or any other night until she's free. Nonetheless, you will be out of here at dawn."

Chapter 44

. . .

SIR Dinadan picked up his wooden mazer and sniffed, his nose wrinkling with fastidious distaste. "I say, Gawain, I wouldn't drink this if I were you. It smells of horse piss." He turned to a passing serving boy. "You! Take this away and bring us wine. Cold meat, as well, cheese—and bread if you have any fresh. I suppose it is too much to hope for fruit."

"Aye, sir—that is, no, sir—" the boy stammered, accepting the mazer Dinadan thrust toward him and reaching for the second. Gawain's hand closed over his wrist.

"Leave it. Just bring the wine. We haven't time to eat."

"Oh, Gawain, I am famished—" Dinadan began, but Gawain had already waved the boy away.

"You can eat up at the hall."

"Must we go back there?" Dinadan asked piteously.

"We said we would." Gawain sipped the ale, grimaced, and set it down. The knight looked weary and disheveled, his golden hair singed around the edges and a streak of

soot upon his brow. He turned a small vial—empty now of
the holy water it had contained—in his long fingers, and
his eyes moved over the village square where they sat at a
rickety table outside the tiny alehouse.

Corbenic was a wretched place, Dinadan thought; no
proper tavern, no shops to speak of, only a few dusty trees
drooping in the heat and a handful of depressed-looking
peasants wandering aimlessly about. A group of boys—
who should surely have been working at this hour—were
gathered by the smithy, obviously up to no good.

The wine, when it arrived, was so thin and sour that Dinadan was tempted to throw it in the serving boy's face.
But after his ordeal in that damned scorching tower, he was
too parched even to complain. He forced it down while
Gawain stared glumly up the hillside, where the tower
crouched above the village like some beast of prey just
waiting for the chance to spring.

"It isn't your fault," Dinadan said at last. "No one could
possibly have shifted that bar."

Gawain's eyes fixed suddenly on Dinadan's face, their
expression so bleak that Dinadan felt compelled to try
again. "The thing is obviously impossible. All that rubbish
about only the best knight succeeding—you *are* the best,
Gawain, no one disputes that . . . now."

Gawain's lips twisted in a smile. "Now that Sir Lancelot
is gone."

"Well, yes. And even when he was . . . himself, I doubt
he could have broken whatever enchantment has been laid
upon the lady. Oh, Lancelot was exceptional in his way, but
there was always something a bit off about him, I thought
so from the first. He was damned impertinent to *you* on
more than one occasion, and then all that business with the
queen . . ."

Dinadan trailed to a stop, suddenly remembering that

Gawain had never credited that tale and had sometimes been quite fierce with those who did. "What I mean to say," he went on quickly, "is that he treated Lady Elaine quite shabbily when he was in his senses, so there's no earthly reason to imagine he'd do her any good now that he is mad. Besides, a madman can hardly be considered the best knight in the world. It doesn't stand to reason."

"Nothing about this business stands to reason." Gawain tossed back the rest of his ale. "Come on, let's see Lord Pelleas."

"Oh, very well," Dinadan grumbled, heaving himself to his feet and trailing drearily toward the livery stable. "Though I hardly see the point. He must know by now we failed—not that anyone ever expected anything from *me*. Stand aside," he added impatiently to the peasants cluttering his path.

They were gathered on the roadway beside the smithy, a group comprised mostly of young men, laughing and jeering and wielding bits of rotting vegetable and offal. Dinadan stepped hastily aside as a turnip whistled past his ear.

"Move, churls," he cried. "We are knights of Camelot! What *is* that you're gaping at?" he added, peering over the shoulder of the nearest boy at an iron cage containing what appeared to be a naked man. "Is it a criminal?"

"It's the wild man," the churl said, laughing. "They caught him yestere'en. We're trying to wake him up."

"Yes, I see. Look, Gawain, a wild man. Fascinating, I'm sure, but we've no time to stop—"

"He's been lurking in the forest for weeks," the boy went on, "no one could catch more than a glimpse of him. But then, yesterday, Sir Torre was a-hunting stag—"

"'Twas a boar, you oaf," another lad cried, "and it gored Sir Torre's horse. And there was Sir Torre on the ground all topsy-turvy, having lost his spear when he fell, and the boar all set to charge him—"

"And out of the forest comes the wild man," a third interrupted, "and what does he do but pick up the spear and run the boar through? Killed it dead with one stroke—"

"'Twas a mighty blow," the second lad continued. "Sir Torre said he'd never seen the like. And so they tried to catch the wild man, but he was terrible strong—knocked down three of the serving men and was going after Sir Torre himself—"

"And then me da felled him with his cudgel," the third boy finished proudly. "So now we have him, but all he does is lie there. We want to stir him up a bit."

"Of course you do," Dinadan said, "and good luck to you. Now, we have business with your lord, so if you'd be so kind as to let us pass . . ."

The boys moved aside, and Dinadan realized that Gawain was not beside him. The knight was standing just before the cage, staring through the bars as though transfixed.

"Gawain," he called, "let us go."

"No, wait." Gawain gestured him over. "Dinadan, *look*."

Dinadan trotted over and gazed obediently into the cage. Though he'd never actually seen a wild man before, he supposed this one to be a fairly common specimen: filthy, emaciated, his face obscured by a tangled growth of beard and a great deal of matted hair.

"Mmm . . . yes. Quite." As there seemed no further comment to be made, he took a step away.

Gawain did not follow. His expression was a curious mixture of astonishment and horror as he regarded the iron cage. Puzzled, Dinadan looked more carefully, then shrugged. The wild man was not the least bit wild, just repulsive and rather tedious.

"Lord Pelleas is expecting us," he said at last. " 'Tis unkind to keep him waiting."

Gawain's peculiar trance broke. "Yes," he said, "yes, he is." They had traveled scarce half a dozen paces when Gawain halted and looked back. "Dinadan—"

"Oh, for God's sake, come *on*," Dinadan said, taking Gawain's arm and turning him toward the stable.

He hoped Gawain was not about to have a pious fit and insist on doing something about the wretched creature. Not that Gawain was prone to sentimentality, save in one respect, and that hardly fit the case. The knight, so fierce in battle, could not bear to pass a stray mongrel without throwing it a bit of food, and had once returned to Camelot with a bag full of kittens he'd fished out of a millpond. It was one of those oddities of human nature that Dinadan usually found amusing, but a wild man was not something one could keep in one's chamber and feed on orts.

"You leave him be, Gawain," he said sternly. "He's no concern of ours."

Gawain looked at him for a long moment, his gray eyes strangely clouded. Then his features hardened in the determined expression Dinadan knew too well. "You're wrong," he said.

He strode back across the square, shouting for someone to come unlock the cage. Dinadan followed, sighing. There was no point in arguing once Gawain made up his mind. Certainly a handful of churls could not stay his course. After only the feeblest of protests, the blacksmith unbolted the cage. Gawain knelt, slipped an arm beneath the wild man's neck to lift him, and brushed the matted hair back from his brow, speaking to him so quietly that Dinadan could not make out his words over the excited babble of the crowd.

Dinadan pushed his way through the throng. "Gawain,

do have a care there, they say he's vicious—not to mention the lice and . . ."

Fleas. That was what he meant to say, but the word remained unspoken. The wild man's eyes were open, and he was staring into Gawain's face. Those eyes—and the line of brow and nose—surely it was—but no, it couldn't be.

And yet it was.

"Come, Sir Lancelot," Gawain said, his voice very gentle, "allow me help you to my horse." And taking the cloak from his own shoulders, Gawain laid it over the wasted form of the knight before lifting him bodily and bearing him through the stunned and silent crowd.

Chapter 45

• • •

LANCELOT was halfway out of bed before he was properly awake. His legs were caught, and only after he had struggled to free himself did he realize they were not bound, only tangled in a heavy coverlet. He was indoors, lying in a bed. His heart racing, he repressed the urge to run and forced himself to lie back and consider his surroundings. The chamber was not one he knew, yet it did not seem to be a prison. The shutters were open, and a bar of sunlight fell across the rush-strewn floor. Sounds drifted through the window, and slowly he was able to put names to them: the musical clanging of a blacksmith's hammer, the creak of a windlass as someone raised a bucket from a well. All at once, he realized he was ravenous.

At that moment the door opened, and a dark-haired woman walked inside, carrying a tray. She took one look at him, shrinking back against the wall, and halted in the doorway. Her words were as soothing as water over stone and equally as meaningless.

After a time she left the tray and went away. He consumed every crumb and was asleep before his head hit the cushion.

When he woke again, it was to a blinding rush of images. The cage. The jeering faces. Sir Gawain—but no, surely that had been a dream. Elaine. Cold sweat broke out over his body when he finally realized who he had been searching for and why he had not rested for so long. It was Elaine—how could he not have known her face? Elaine in danger, calling out his name. Where was she? Where was he? How long had he been wandering?

"How long?" he rasped when the door opened again. The dark-haired woman—Brisen, he thought, Mistress Brisen was her name—started so the dishes on the tray clattered together.

"You left Camelot two years ago," she answered.

"Two *years*?" He ran a hand across his face, his fingers tangling in his matted beard. "Is this Corbenic?"

"Yes." She smiled and handed him the tray. "Eat."

Corbenic. Then where was Elaine? Something was wrong, he could see it in Brisen's face, in the way she moved about the chamber so she might avoid his gaze.

"Is she dead?" he asked.

"No. Now eat, Sir Lancelot."

And with that she went away.

Not dead, he thought, his hand shaking so that milk slopped over the cup. If she had been in some sort of danger, it had been months ago. Unless that had been another dream.

But why was it Brisen who tended him and not her mistress? He remembered their parting, going over and over it again, sparing himself no detail of his deluded ravings. He could see her face so clearly now, the horror in her eyes. It was no wonder she did not come to him.

When Brisen returned with a few strong lads, bearing a cask and water, he asked no further questions, nor did they trouble him with speech. Once bathed, he submitted without protest as Brisen shaved him and attempted to comb out his hair. In the end, she cut it off, leaving his head oddly cool and weightless.

Just as she was leaving, Lancelot said, "Galahad?"

Brisen smiled. "Well and strong. Good night."

He nodded and closed his eyes, willing himself to unconsciousness.

● ● ●

THE next morning when he woke, his mind was clear, and he knew what he must do. He found a trunk at the foot of his bed; his own trunk, which he had left behind in Camelot. He dressed in a robe that had once fit him well, though now his hands swam in the sleeves, and it hung in sagging folds from his shoulders. He sat down on the edge of the bed, hands clenched tightly on his knees as he waited for the knock upon the door. It was not long in coming, and Sir Gawain walked into the chamber. One quick glance showed him that Gawain dreaded this meeting as much as he did himself.

"Sir Gawain," he said. "I owe you my thanks."

"Think nothing of it, Sir Lancelot," Gawain replied. "It is my duty to aid a brother knight in need."

Lancelot forced himself to raise his head. Gawain stood just before the window, his expression gravely courteous, a beam of sunlight brightening the deep gold of his hair. He looked, Lancelot thought, as if he should be standing on a plinth . . .

"With Honor carved in foot-high letters at the base."

"I'm sorry, did you say something?"

Lancelot dropped his gaze, embarrassed to realize that he had spoken aloud. "No. Or yes. What I meant to say is that I know that only duty could have driven you to do what you did for me. But you were kind—I remember it, a little, now—far kinder than I deserved. I hope—" he had to stop a moment before he could trust his voice. "I hope you will accept my gratitude."

The words had sounded well when he tried them over this morning, but now they seemed all wrong. Gawain did not answer but merely turned to gaze out the window. Lancelot's head began to ache, and the gray cloud of despair clamped down on him.

"I am sorry," he ventured. "I've said too much. I only meant—"

"I know what you meant." Gawain's shoulders were rigid. "But you are mistaken."

"Oh. Forgive me, my memory is not quite . . . Still, you did all that was right—"

"Not that, either, I'm afraid." Gawain's voice was like ice.

"I did not mean to offend," Lancelot said wearily. "I am . . . unused to conversation. Please forgive me if I—"

Gawain turned sharply. "Stop asking me to forgive you. You've done nothing wrong. It is I who should be asking your forgiveness."

"For what?" Lancelot asked, astonished. "You acted with honor—as you always do. I know you would have done the same no matter what—or who—"

"Do you really believe that?"

"What?" Lancelot put a hand to his head. "That you . . . I'm sorry, I don't understand."

"When I saw you, lying in that cage—" He drew a sharp breath. "My first thought was to leave you there. I knew you at once—Dinadan had no idea, he kept urging me to go—and I did just that, I walked away—"

Lancelot remembered nothing before Gawain had been there in the cage. Why had he turned back? Had he himself recognized Gawain? Called out to him? Sweat sprang out on his brow as he imagined himself begging.

"I cannot recall," he said hoarsely. "Whatever I might have said or done, I am sorry, but—"

For the first time in his memory, Gawain cut in upon his speech. "Are ye no listening, man?" he demanded roughly, his accent thickening as it always did when he was distressed. "I stole away—crept off like some slinking, cowardly beastie and left ye in your sleep. You, a brother knight in dire need."

"But you came back."

"Aye, I did. But I tell ye, Sir Lancelot, 'twas a near thing."

Lancelot almost smiled. Even now, after all that had befallen him, Gawain still called him sir. So had he addressed him in the cage, and it was that, more than anything, that had pulled Lancelot from the dark dreams in which he'd dwelt. There were no words to express what he felt, but he made the effort.

"Sir Gawain," he said carefully, "I quite understand why you would have been tempted to leave me to my fate. I would not have blamed you if you had. From the first, I've been nothing but unkind to you—and unjust, as well, as Lady Elaine was always at great pains to point out. I'm sorry for it now, and I know I have no right to ask for your help . . ."

"What would ye ask of me?"

Lancelot's grip tightened on his knees. "I understand that El—that Lady Elaine does not wish to have speech with me, but I hoped to see Galahad before I left. Just once—it needn't be for long—and I won't—she needn't worry that I'll be a nuisance. Would you mind asking her if that could be arranged?"

Gawain was looking at him so strangely that Lancelot knew he had said something very wrong. "I'm sorry," he added swiftly, "if you would rather not—"

"Lancelot." Now Gawain was the one to look away. That, and the familiar address he'd never used before, sent a thrill of fear down Lancelot's spine.

"What?" he demanded. "Is Elaine—she isn't—"

"She's not dead."

"What is it, then? Is she ill? Married? Gone away?"

Gawain laid a hand on his shoulder. "Nay, none of those. Here," he said, pouring wine into a cup and handing it to Lancelot, "drink that. Ye will need it."

Chapter 46

· · ·

IT was midmorning before Gawain had finished his
story, and by noon they stood together inside the entrance to the tower. Though the day was chill at Lancelot's
back, the air before him was hot as a blacksmith's forge,
molten heat pouring down the steps. Sweat gathered on his
brow and stung his eyes.

"I'll come with you, if you like," Gawain offered.

"No. I must do this alone."

Lancelot climbed the narrow, twisting stairway, the heat
increasing with every step. By the time he reached the top,
he was breathing in choked gasps, and his hands were so
slick they sizzled on the iron bar across the door before he
quickly drew them back.

"Elaine!" he called, and waited twenty rapid heartbeats
without drawing breath. "Elaine! Answer me!"

And then he heard it, Elaine's own voice, though it
sounded as though it came from a thousand leagues away.

"Lancelot? Thank God! Hurry, please hurry, I cannot—"
Her words ended in a cry that filled him with dread.

He had heard that cry before, had followed it for days
and weeks and months through fen and forest. It was the
sound of his own madness—but no, he was not mad now,
not anymore—this was all real, the red-hot bar, the steam
curling from the edges of the door. All real. He was not
mad, he would not be mad while Elaine had need of him.
Hands shaking, he drew on thick leather gloves and over
them his gauntlets, then seized the bar. It did not yield to
his attempts, not by so much as an inch.

No one could shift this—save one. *But I am not a perfect knight,* he thought, *I never was. All there ever was to
me was the Lady's magic, and now I have lost even that. I
am only a mortal knight—and if any mortal knight could
do this, it would have been Gawain.*

But Gawain had not succeeded. And Elaine was still
trapped behind these doors. "Elaine!" he shouted, "Can
you hear me?"

Silence was his only answer, a deep, impenetrable silence more terrifying than her plea for help. With an effort
that seemed to tear his heart in two, he wrested the bar free
and threw it to one side.

The door yielded to his shoulder, and he burst into the
midst of hell. Flames licked his face; the stench of burning
hair clogged his nostrils. Each breath was pain, movement
almost impossible. "Elaine! Where are you?" he shouted,
and gathering his courage, he leapt into the flame and came
out the other side. "Elaine!"

Then he saw her, lying in the center of the floor in a space
perhaps three paces from end to end. Her eyes were closed,
her cheeks as pale as marble. Swiftly he knelt and called
her name, but she did not stir. Tearing off his gauntlets, he

chafed her icy hands between his own and lightly slapped her cheeks. "Wake," he begged her, "Elaine, look at me."

This was not death. The almost imperceptible rise and fall of her breast told him she yet lived. But it was more than sleep, deeper than a swoon. She was bound by some enchantment that he knew not how to break.

He must bear her back through the fire, there was no other way, and it must be done with no mistake or hesitation. Standing, he turned slowly round. Sweat ran down his face and into his eyes, narrowed against the heat and near unbearable brightness as he tried vainly to peer through the walls of flame. One leap must take them to the door or they were lost.

Be calm, he told himself. *Go slowly.* He dragged his heel across the floor, leaving a small mark to serve as a guide. And then he gathered himself into a crouch and leapt into the flame. It met him like a wall of stone, jarring every bone. He reeled back and fell, catching himself upon one hand and knee. When he regained his breath, he made a second mark and tried again.

And again. And again, until he was bruised and bloodied and the marks on the floor stretched round the circle where Elaine still lay unmoving.

He gathered her into his arms, holding her against his chest and rocking her like a child. "It is all right, love," he whispered, "do not fear, I am here now, all will be well."

Liar, a voice said in his mind, *you've failed her yet again.*

"I'm sorry," he said, "Elaine, I am so sorry." Bending, he kissed her brow, her cheeks, and then, at last, her mouth. No sooner had his lips touched hers than the floor gave way beneath them, and they fell together into swirling darkness.

• • •

IT was a sound that woke Lancelot, the sound of his childhood, the rushing whisper of small waves breaking rhythmically against a stony shore. He opened his eyes and found himself staring at an impossibly blue sky, dotted with plump white clouds. The grass beneath him was soft and thick and brilliantly green, the air as sweet as incense and intoxicating as rich wine.

He turned his head and found himself gazing at a woman seated cross-legged in the grass beside him, rich brown hair falling loose over her shoulders and a chaplet of daisies round her high white brow.

"Welcome home, King's Son."

"Lady? Where is—" He sat up quickly and saw that Elaine slept beside him, her face peaceful and relaxed. "How—?"

The Lady laughed. "You are here by my will, of course, as is your lady. She is dear to you, I know. As you are dear to me."

"*Dear?*" Lancelot repeated with a bitter laugh.

"Now, let us not dispute over what is past and done." The Lady frowned, plucking moodily at a few long blades of grass. "The destinies of men are not easily altered. In their world, even my plans can go awry."

Her head bent, she began to weave the blades together. "I do not say this lightly, child, nor was it a knowledge I found easy to accept. But it is finished now. I am done with meddling in the affairs of men."

She tossed her web into the air, where it stretched and grew into a glittering net. A wave of her hand sent it floating above the water, where a tiny incandescent being caught it and carried it away. She looked at Lancelot, her expression grave. "My Knight had the right of it; I kept you here too long. You are as unfit to live in that world as on the moon. I have watched you suffer—oh, I have been with you often during your wandering, though you saw me not—and it is enough. Now it is time for you to rest, here in your true home."

"Here? Forever?"

"Not forever, no; you are still a mortal man. But long life and health, rest and ease from care shall all be yours. And your lady, too, of course." The Lady's laughter was as sweet as silver bells. "Oh, these mortals, what nonsense they get up to! 'Tis fortunate I had her in my care. For your sake, I kept her safe and made certain only you could set her free. I knew you would not rest content without your lady love! Wake her—she will wake now, no enchantment made by mortals can endure within my realm."

"Elaine. Elaine, wake up."

Elaine turned her head, sighing, and looked into Lancelot's eyes. She knew this dream. Every night she prayed it would come to her again, though waking was so bitter that she sometimes feared it might destroy her. *But it will not,* she promised herself, *I will bear it . . . only let it go on a little longer.*

She smiled drowsily as his lips touched hers. *Yes,* she thought, *just a little longer . . .* But as she put her arms around his neck, he drew away. "Elaine," he said again, his voice breaking. "Do you know me?"

"*Know* you?" Her smile faded as she looked at him more closely. He was Lancelot, yet strangely altered, the bones in his face standing out sharply, and his lovely curling hair cropped short. She clutched his hand and it was solid, no dream but flesh and blood.

"Lancelot!" She sat up and touched his face. "Lancelot, is it—in truth, is it you?"

"Yes, my love, 'tis I." He turned his head and kissed her hand. "Elaine, I have so much to tell you, I hardly know where to begin. What is the last thing you remember?"

She frowned. "Queen Morgause came to visit. She wanted to see the tower, and—there was a fire, wasn't there? Yes, that's right, I called you and—and I must have fainted. Oh,

Lancelot, you did come for me! I knew you would! But . . ."

For the first time she noticed that she was not in her bed at all, nor in the tower, but lying in a muddy field beside a swamp. "Where are we?"

"Avalon," he said, and laughed. "You never did believe me, did you, but now you can see it for yourself." He waved a hand to encompass the barren field.

"Avalon?"

"There is the lake. I told you of it, do you remember?"

She remembered well his description of crystal lake of Avalon. Now she looked from the fetid swamp into his glowing eyes and felt her heart break anew.

"My love," she said carefully, "we must go home now, to Corbenic, where I can look after you."

He turned and gestured toward a patch of muddy reeds, flattened as though they had been trampled. "Lady," he said, bowing his head, "may I present Elaine of Corbenic? Elaine, this is my foster mother, the Lady of the Lake."

When Elaine merely stared, he tugged her hand, shooting her a puzzled look before he glanced away.

"Oh, no." Lancelot addressed the patch of reeds. "Of course she can." He turned to Elaine. "Why do you not greet the Lady? You—you do see her, don't you?"

Wordlessly, Elaine shook her head.

"But you must!" Lancelot insisted. "Look, just there!"

"Oh, Lancelot," Elaine began, her voice breaking. "Please, take me home."

"What is the matter?" Lancelot demanded of the Lady. "Why can she not see?"

"Her will is very strong," the Lady answered. "She cannot allow herself to see what she does not believe exists."

"Then make her see!"

"I cannot."

"Elaine," Lancelot said, "we are in Avalon. The Lady of the Lake sits just here, before you. You can see her if you want to. You have to try, Elaine."

His voice was so pleading that despite her own misgivings, Elaine screwed up her eyes and stared hard in the direction he was pointing. "There is nothing there, Lancelot, only the swamp and broken reeds. My love, it is all right. When we are home again you will be better."

"Lady," said Lancelot, "I thank you for your gift, but I cannot accept it."

"Child," the Lady answered, "you misunderstand me. This gift is not one you can refuse."

She spoke with such finality that Lancelot knew any argument was pointless. In Avalon, the Lady's will was absolute.

"Then send Elaine back," he said.

The Lady's arched brows drew together in the slightest of frowns. "I have said I will no longer meddle in the world of men. I can return her to her tower if you like, but without you to bring her forth, she will remain there until her years have run their course. I only thought to please you," she added reproachfully. "I could not know that she would be so . . . stubborn." She rose gracefully to her feet. "In time, she will accept her fate."

"No—wait, you cannot go—" Lancelot cried, but the Lady had already vanished.

"Let us go now," Elaine pleaded, taking Lancelot's hand and seeking to draw him to his feet. "Galahad will be missing me. You remember Galahad, do you not? He will be awake now, wondering where I am."

Lancelot stood and took both her hands in his. "Galahad is well, I saw him just this morning. He was sitting with your father, practicing his letters."

"His letters? But—"

Lancelot touched a finger to her lips. "Love, you must listen to me. You lay in the tower for a twelvemonth—no, listen, Elaine, it is the truth. Morgause put an enchantment on you—"

"No! Morgause set a fire in the tower last night. I panicked and swooned. You must have reached me soon after and brought me to this place before I woke. *That* is the truth, and you will remember it in time. But now—now I must get home to Galahad." She pulled her hands free. "I will go home. I must!"

Lancelot bowed his head. "Yes. You must. Very well, Elaine, I'll take you home. I know a way—I found it long ago. But you must promise to ask no questions and do everything I say, no matter how strange it may seem. Can you promise that?"

"Yes, anything, only take me from this place!"

Chapter 47

• • •

LANCELOT skirted the lake, Elaine's hand held fast in his, pausing now and then to listen. Water lapped against the shore. Moisture dripped from the branches overhead, falling with little plinks upon the rocks. A cuckoo trilled in the forest, its cry echoing across the water.

They had been walking for nearly an hour when he heard the sound he'd dreaded.

Clink. Clank.

"Hurry," he whispered. "And not a word."

Elaine obeyed, though her eyes were wide with fear and doubt as he dragged her closer to the lake, where a fine mist rose from the water.

"Where are you, boy?"

The voice boomed out, startling a heron three paces from Lancelot and Elaine. It rose with a clap of wings and an angry cry, a silver-white flash soon swallowed by the rising mist.

"You know you cannot hide from me!"

"Run," Lancelot said, pulling Elaine forward.

He glanced back over his shoulder and stumbled, sinking knee-deep in icy water, mud grasping at his foot as a living cloud buzzed around his face. Iridescent wings fanned his heated cheeks; tiny faces grinned, revealing pointed teeth.

"What do you here, King's Son?" the faeries shrieked. "Whither dost thou wander?"

"Ugh!" Elaine cried, beating at the air. "Flies!"

Sharp pain stung Lancelot's thumb, and he instinctively flung out his hand, sending a tiny creature spiraling into the mist.

"Ill done! Ill done!" they chorused in shrill discord as they swarmed him. He beat them off, cursing as tiny teeth drew blood, then froze as the Knight's voice rang out again.

"Where are you, boy?"

The faeries drew off at the sound, hovered for a moment, then darted off in a cloud of buzzing laughter. "Here, lord, he is here! This way, follow us—"

"Do you see that hawthorn bush in bloom?" Lancelot demanded, pointing.

"Yes," she said, too tired to argue.

"Elaine, tell me the truth."

"There is only a dead tree."

"Is there a branch—look closely now—about three feet from the bottom that falls like an archway to the earth?"

"Yes."

"Run, Elaine, and go under that bough. Not around, go under. Do you understand?"

"Yes, Lancelot, under the bough," she repeated wearily. "Come, you can show me."

"No, you must go ahead." He reached into the purse at his belt and brought forth a small pouch, which he emptied into his palm. With dull astonishment, she recognized the diamond he had won in the tournament so long ago. "I always meant to have it set for you," he said with a twisted smile. He returned it to the pouch and hung it round her neck.

"But what—"

He kissed her brow. "That is for Galahad." His mouth closed over hers. "And that for you." His hands were on her cheeks, framing her face, his eyes burning into hers. "If you ever loved me, Elaine, listen to me now and do exactly as I say. When you get through the archway, you'll see a chapel on the hill. Go there and ask for the priest."

"But—"

"Farewell, my love. Don't stop for anything and *don't look back.*"

And he was gone. Half blinded by tears, she saw him run into the field beside the swamp. His sword, bright Arondight, glinted through the rising mist as he drew it from its scabbard. He waved it as though in battle, thrusting it first into the air, then lifting it as though parrying a blow.

She stumbled toward the tree, brushing at the enormous flies that buzzed around her face, the stink of the swamp mud acrid in her nostrils. Twisted roots seemed to rise from the water to grasp her ankles. When at last she reached the tree, she ducked to pass beneath the bough as she had promised.

"Go," he had commanded. "Don't stop for anything."

Madness, surely . . . and yet his eyes had been so clear, his voice so steady. Even as she raised her foot to step through, she was seized by the unreasoning certainty that if she left Lancelot now, he would be lost again, this time forever.

"Don't look back," he had said, and she had promised to obey.

"No," she said aloud. "No, I will not leave him. Whatever demons he must face, I will stand with him."

She turned and halted, one hand clamped across her lips to still her cry.

The swamp was gone. In its place was impossibly blue water that rippled to the horizon. The field was hidden by an impenetrable mist, but even as Elaine started forward, it began to disperse, blown into ragged tatters by a sweet breeze off the lake, revealing a sweeping meadow starred with wildflowers.

Now she could glimpse Lancelot. And he was not alone. He was locked in deadly combat with a knight, clad in armor that covered him from neck to heels, emerald green without a dent or blemish. Shreds of mist twisted around shining green greaves that gripped his massive calves. A helm sat upon impossibly broad shoulders, the slit at eye level revealing naught but inky shadow. A green sword was clutched in one mailed hand; the other gripped a verdant shield.

"The Green Knight," she whispered, icy terror pooling in her belly. "The Green Knight."

She started forward, letting out a small cry of disgust when a cloud of winged creatures surrounded her. Her cry changed to one of astonished wonder when she saw that they were not flies but tiny beings in human form with wings that shone like rainbows in the sunlight. "Go," she pleaded, making gentle brushing motions as she ran, careful not to injure them. "Go!" she repeated more firmly, her wonder turning to annoyance as they continued to dart before her eyes.

She stumbled to her knees as something grasped her ankle. Stark terror seized her when she realized it was no root that held her, but a hand, tinged green and webbed between the fingers. She pulled and fought, but she was no match for the creature she could glimpse beneath the waves. It dragged her forward with inexorable strength, the tinny laughter of the fairies ringing in her ears. Her fingers scrabbled vainly at the earth, and then icy water closed around her.

The creature drew her closer, one hand closing round the pouch about her neck. She beat it off and broke free, rising to the surface long enough to take one gasping breath before it pulled her under. Twisting, struggling, they went down together into the waterweeds. The creature reached again for the pouch; Elaine eluded it again, but now black dots danced before her eyes. She crouched upon the bottom, then straightened her legs, fumbling at the pouch as she hurtled upward. She broke the surface once again, and now she held the diamond in her palm. When the creature's head emerged, she glimpsed its flat green features and huge black eyes before she flung the jewel with all her strength.

With a flash of scales, the creature turned and dove. Elaine struggled to the shore, dragged herself up upon the bank, and gasped like a landed fish. When the dancing spots subsided, she staggered to her feet.

The meadow lay before her now, each detail sharp and clear. Lancelot and the knight fought on, their blades ringing with each slash and parry. Around them rose banks of cushioned benches, filled with what Elaine first took to be people. Looking more closely, she realized her mistake. Some of the creatures watching were hideous, others were almost too beautiful to bear.

But none of them were human.

In a pavilion hung with rosy silk sat the most beautiful of all, and Elaine knew that at last she looked upon the Lady of the Lake. The Lady looked back at her, her lovely face rigid with cold fury.

"Bah, is this the best you can do?" the Green Knight taunted. "Have you forgotten everything I taught you?"

"Not quite," Lancelot replied, lunging forward with fluid grace. The Green Knight fell back a step, his blade barely catching Arondight's edge. Lancelot pressed his advantage, his sword weaving a pattern so intricate that

Elaine could not begin to follow it. The Green Knight
stumbled and went down upon one knee, awkwardly flinging up his sword to deflect a blow that would have severed
his neck had it landed squarely. As it was, Lancelot's blade
sliced through the green armor at the shoulder, though the
Knight gave no sign of having felt it as he leapt to his feet
and retreated out of reach.

"You are slow, old one," Lancelot cried, laughing.

"And you are but a foolish mortal."

"Give thanks for that! And for the magic that protects
you!" Lancelot leaned upon his sword, breathing hard. For
the first time Elaine saw that he was bleeding; a long
scratch ran across his brow and blood dripped from a gash
in his shoulder, falling like tiny garnets on the grass.

Yet his smile flashed out, the merry, reckless smile that
had always left her breathless. "Mortal I may be, but I will
live on in your memory—and that of the gentle company
gathered here today!" He laughed aloud, bowing to the
stands. "Forever is a long time, old one. A very long time
to remember that in a *true* test of arms, you were no match
for Lancelot du Lac!"

The Knight charged with a roar. Metal clashed on metal
when Lancelot caught the green blade upon his own. The
Knight turned and came in from below; the tip of the his
sword caught Lancelot's sleeve, tearing it from wrist to
shoulder, and Elaine clamped her hands across her mouth
when his blood began to flow.

The Green Knight hurtled forward as Lancelot retreated,
switching Arondight to his left hand long enough to wipe his
bloody palm upon his jerkin. As the Knight reached him,
Lancelot seized Arondight two-handed and swung it with
such speed that the Green Knight barely caught it on his
shield. The force of the blow rocked him back upon his heels
before he leapt forward with a cry. Again they engaged and

again retreated, back and forth upon the grass, while the eerie cries of the inhuman spectators urged them on.

At last they stood toe-to-toe, blades locked, for what seemed an eternity. Elaine could see every muscle of Lancelot's arms, corded beneath the bloodstained remnants of his shirt, and the tendons in his neck standing out sharply with the effort of holding the Green Knight's sword at bay.

Yet he could not last forever. He was a man, and the Knight was something more. Elaine watched in horror as slowly, inexorably, Lancelot was forced down to his knees. For a time, he managed to keep Arondight aloft, but at last the Green Knight struck the sword from his hand.

"Now we see who is the better," the Knight howled in an ecstasy of triumph, his blade pressed to Lancelot's bare throat. "Beg for mercy, mortal."

Lancelot's laughter rang out. "Men do not beg." He gazed up at the Knight, defiant to the last, a scornful smile on his lips.

"Stop this!" Elaine screamed to the pavilion. The Lady did not take her gaze from the field, but only shook her head.

Lancelot glanced over at her, his smile fading. "Elaine," he cried, "oh, love, what do you here? Run, go now—"

The Green Knight laughed. "Too late. Die, du Lac, die knowing you have failed, and when your blood is let, your lady will be mine."

Lancelot twisted and threw himself backward, the green blade missing him by inches as he scooped Arondight from the grass and surged up to his knees. With a hoarse cry, he thrust the blade hilt deep into the Green Knight's breast.

A trumpet sounded, its clear peal lost in the cheering from the stands. The Green Knight stood a moment, gazing at the sword protruding from his breast, then sheathed his own sword and drew Arondight from his body. He knelt and offered Lancelot the blade, hilt first, across his arm. The moment Lancelot had taken it, the Knight vanished, as did the stands, the pavilion, and the Lady. Lancelot knelt alone in the center of the meadow.

Elaine ran to him, her sodden skirt clinging to her legs. She stumbled the last steps, and Lancelot caught her in his arms, his sword dropping from his hand. It fell with a clanging thud upon the floor of the tower where they stood embraced with flames dancing all around them.

"Here again!" Lancelot laughed, and then Elaine was laughing, too, as he lifted her and spun her round.

"Am I mad?" she demanded, breathless.

"You ask *me* that?" Still laughing, he bent and slipped a hand beneath her knees, sweeping her up into his arms. "Which way, my lady, to the door?"

She pointed. "There."

The flames died as he stepped into them, and he grinned down at her, leaning forward to gaze out the window. "Your sense of direction leaves something to be desired." He shifted her in his arms. "Look."

"Is it a feast day?" she asked, gazing through the narrow slit. "Why is no one at work? There is Torre—and Lavaine! When did he arrive? And look, 'tis Sir Gawain! And Sir Dinadan, and see, Lancelot, there are Bors and Lionel and Ector. But where—oh, there he is, do you see Galahad? How big he looks!" She looked up at Lancelot, her eyes wide. "It was true?" she whispered. "I have been in here a twelvemonth?" She touched his face with shaking fingers. "I am sorry; I should have believed you—"

"Why? The last time we met, I was a madman."

"But not now."

"No, not now," Lancelot said as he bore her down the stairway. "Through God's grace, I heard you call and found myself in time to come to you."

Elaine leaned her head against his shoulder. "What of the Lady?" she asked. "She was so angry with me. Why did she let us go?"

"Avalon has its own laws. I do not understand them, but I know when they are at work. Nothing less would have brought the Green Knight to his knees to *me*!"

"But do you think—will she come for you again?"

"No. The Lady has spoken. She is finished with the world of men." He grinned, his dark eyes alight with happiness. "At least for now. In a hundred years or so she may change her mind, but she is done with me for good, and I am but a man."

"How very fortunate." Elaine looked up at him through her lashes, wondering that she still remembered how. "A man is precisely what I want."

"I should think a winsome lass like you could have any man she chose."

"There is only one I have ever wanted." She clasped him tightly round the neck. "And that is you."

"I think you *must* be a little mad, but you'll get no argument from me. For I am yours, Elaine, as I have always been and always will be."

With that he kicked open the door and stepped out into the sunlight and the cheering of the crowd.

Chapter 48

• • •

THE feast lasted far into the night. Elaine and Lancelot slipped away soon after it began, and Brisen smiled as she watched them go, then retired to her own chamber off the kitchens. She found a small scrap of parchment sitting in her empty trunk and read it, a frown creasing her brow, before packing her belongings and shutting the lid firmly.

She lay down upon her narrow pallet and stared at the ceiling for a time, then rose and took the parchment from the table. She glanced at it again as she went out the door and after only the briefest hesitation, crumpled it and tossed it in the fire. She went through the hall, stopping now and then to exchange a greeting, and finally reached the door.

The night was cool as she walked quickly through the garden, past the tower where a candle glowed in Elaine's window, and into the forest. Her steps led her to a small clearing where she lingered for a time, bidding a silent farewell to the place that had been both refuge and temple.

From there she wandered restlessly down the path to the river and sat upon the dock, watching the full moon ripple in the water until a sudden gust of icy wind drove her to her feet. She stood a moment, looking from the path to the boathouse, then walked the few steps to the door and opened it. Blinking in the dim light of a rushlight, she found Torre seated at the table.

"I thought you would not come," he said.

"I had things to do," she answered shortly.

"Now that you are here, come in and sit. If you would like, that is," he added gruffly.

A cup and pitcher stood before him, but when he poured, she saw it was only water that he drank. Following her eyes, he said, "I'm not drunk, Brisen, if that's what you are thinking."

"I did wonder," she admitted. "Everyone else is, after all."

"Everyone else doesn't have to be up at dawn." He kicked a stool from under the table. "Are you going to sit down or not?"

She sat, wondering why she bothered. All they had to say to one another had been said long since. In the past twelvemonth, she doubted they had exchanged a dozen words, and those but empty pleasantries.

She had not seen him so closely for many months. Looking at him now, she saw again the young knight who had caught her heart in the surgeon's tent so long ago. Since their return from Camelot, he had turned his energies to the management of Corbenic with the same single-minded zeal he had once given to debauchery. Both he and the manor had flourished.

It is finished, she thought. *He is truly well at last.* As he continued to sit silent, she glanced at the doorway. She, too, must be up at dawn, and the night was drawing on.

"Elaine told me you are leaving," he said abruptly. "Is it true?"

"Yes. Sir Gawain mentioned that Lady Morgana is at Camelot. He kindly offered to let me ride with him."

"But you can't abandon Elaine! She needs you."

Brisen smiled, tracing a pattern on the splintered table. "She and Sir Lancelot will be going to his home at Joyous Gard. It is a new life for her. I doubt that she will miss me."

"Others might."

"I can't think of anyone who would."

Torre scowled, then gave a short, unwilling laugh. "There was a time," he said, "when I thought you were a fiend. 'Try again,' you always said. And again and again and again. Even when I was half-dead with pain, you never would let up." His eyes, always so changeable, shone leaf green in the rushlight. "I hated you."

"I know."

"Why did you do it? I used to think you enjoyed watching me suffer."

"No." The table blurred before her eyes. "I never enjoyed it. But it had to be done." She frowned, blinking hard. "I can't abide waste."

He said no more, and at last, with a little sigh, she stood. "Good night, Sir Torre."

"Don't you mean farewell?"

All at once he was on his feet. In two steps he stood before her. Brisen had never realized quite how tall he was. She was used to seeing him slouched, not standing straight as he was now. She had to tip her head back to look into his eyes. "You told me once what you thought of me," he said, "and you were right. But I hope—I believe I have done better since."

"You are . . . somewhat improved." She tried to meet his

gaze with cool composure, but it wasn't easy when he looked at her that way, as though he wasn't sure whether to laugh or . . . or . . .

His kiss was all she had imagined it would be. She pulled the tie from his hair and buried her fingers in his curls, her lips parting beneath his. "Until the new year," he said huskily. "If you wish to leave then, I will not stop you."

She stepped back quickly. "I'll not be your leman, Torre."

"I never thought you would."

She waited for him to say more, but he did not. "Very well," she said, speaking firmly to cover her confusion. "I will stay until the new year."

His smile flashed out, and he drew her close, resting his cheek against her hair. "You won't be sorry." And slowly, with a gentleness she would not have imagined in him, he took her face between his hands and kissed her once again.

• • •

WHEN the chilly predawn light slipped through the shutters, Brisen tied off her braid and sighed. Then she walked to the pallet and bent to run a hand across Torre's curls, spiked in wild disarray upon the cushion, strands of cinnamon and nutmeg, gold and bronze and chestnut shimmering in the feeble rushlight. He smiled without opening his eyes and reached for her.

"I should have known you'd make a liar of me," she said ruefully, slipping into his embrace.

"Not for long. I won't wait for the new year to be wed."

"You never asked me," she pointed out.

He opened one eye. "Must I?"

She seized the coverlet and pulled it off him. "Out. Go! You have work to do, and dawn is almost here."

He stood reluctantly, blinking like a sleepy owl in the

dim light. "You said," he reminded her, "that you loved me. You said that you had loved me since—"

"Yes, well, I'm sure I spouted all manner of nonsense," she interrupted hastily.

He grinned. "It wasn't nonsense. It was the truth."

She threw his tunic at his head. "A moment of weakness. But I suppose now I'll never hear the end of it."

"Never." He traced a finger across her lips until they softened in a smile. "Never in this life. You have my word on it."

Chapter 49

. . .

"NOT another one!" Lancelot groaned, dropping his head into his hands. "Tell him I am not at home."

Elaine laughed and fell back against the feather pillows piled high upon the bed. "Oh, go on. Poor man, he's probably traveled days to meet you."

"I hate jousting," Lancelot said, his voice muffled.

"Then you shouldn't have begun."

"That," Lancelot said, raising his head to glare at her, "was your fault."

She met his gaze with a smile. "And you are all the better for it. The great du Lac," she added with satisfaction, "has nothing on you!"

He slid over the enormous expanse of coverlet to lie beside her. "And what if this one knocks me down?"

"I'll pick you up."

He rolled atop her, arms braced beside her head. "I'll do it for a kiss."

"Very well." When he bent to her, she tugged a lock of

his hair, which had grown to curl around the collar of his robe. "You may have it after. No, stop, Lancelot, we cannot, the man is waiting—"

"He isn't even across the moat yet."

"But . . . well, I suppose . . . if we hurry . . ."

"Oh, we will," he promised solemnly, wicked laughter in his eyes as his hand slid beneath her skirt.

When Elaine opened her eyes again, sunlight fell across the foot of the great bed. "Oh, dear," she said, turning her head on the pillow. "What is the time?"

"Who cares?" Lancelot murmured against her breast.

"We have a guest," she reminded him. "And Lancelot," she added, "will you ask this one to stay for supper?"

"No." He stood, stretching like a cat in the sunlight. "I will fight him if I must, but that is the end of it."

"We cannot live in solitary splendor all our days," Elaine said, "it isn't right."

"We are hardly solitary. We see Torre and Brisen nearly every week, and Lavaine spent a month with us last spring. Galahad all but lives at Corbenic, Elaine; he has plenty of company there."

Elaine lay back and watched him dress, lifting her face for his kiss before he went. At first, she, too, had wanted nothing but to be alone with him and Galahad while she set Joyous Gard to rights. When a year had passed, she suggested that Lancelot invite his kinsmen to celebrate the harvest, but he refused, saying he had no desire for any company but hers. She let the matter rest, for she was spending much time at Corbenic preparing for Brisen's lying-in. It was only when her nephew had been born and she returned home that she was struck by their isolation. Again she had suggested that they hold a feast, and again Lancelot refused her.

• • •

DURING the next year she watched him carefully, yet he seemed content. He spent hours in the practice yard each morning and in the afternoons rode out, sometimes with Galahad but more often on his own, for Galahad was often at Corbenic with his grandsire, listening rapt to Pelleas's tales. Sunset invariably found Lancelot atop the battlements, gazing down the road that ran to Camelot.

The first time she found him there, Elaine felt an echo of the old pain she'd thought forgotten. She turned away without speaking, but he called her over and put his arm around her, drawing her head down to his shoulder.

"You miss her, don't you?" Elaine asked, careful to speak calmly, determined to have only truth between them now.

"Her?"

"Guinevere."

He was silent for a time as they gazed together toward the horizon. "I worry for her sometimes," he said at last. "She was so terribly unhappy."

"I don't see what she had to be unhappy about," Elaine retorted. "The king is a kind man."

"Guinevere said the same to me once," Lancelot said quietly. "She said he always treated her with far more kindness than she deserved."

"Well, then—"

"In fact," he added, turning to gaze down at Elaine, "she was saying just that on the day the king saw us together. She was telling me how very fortunate she was to be wed to a man who always treated her with such unfailing courtesy."

Elaine frowned, wondering what Lancelot was getting at. He had said the queen was distraught that day, yet she could find no cause for complaint in anything he'd told her.

"The queen was right," she said. "She is fortunate."

"And well she knew it. She said," he went on pensively, "that when Arthur took a mistress—as she fully expected he would do—that she was certain she could rely upon his discretion. She was . . . grateful she would likely never know precisely when it happened, though she was sure it would."

"And that is why," Elaine said slowly, "she was distraught?"

"That, and other reasons—her bitter disappointment in failing to give her lord an heir, her fear that he would cast her off and seek a younger bride—"

"It is the king she loves?" Elaine interrupted. "Not you?"

"Not me, no, though she is fond of me—as I am of her. Even when I wanted to wring her neck—which was fairly often . . ." He gazed at her intently as he went on, speaking very slowly as though he chose each word with care. "Do you remember how it was when Torre was so unhappy? He did many things that angered you, and yet . . ."

"I never stopped loving him," she finished, her eyes widening with startled comprehension. "Lancelot, are you saying—"

"Only that fond as I am of Guinevere, we were never lovers. Even had we both been free, neither of us would have considered such a thing."

"Is that because—"

He touched a finger to her lips. "More I cannot say." He stroked her cheek and smiled down at her. "But know you this, Elaine: I never loved a woman until the day I came to Corbenic. Why, I never even kissed one until I first kissed you. And having once kissed you," he said, pinching her cheek, "there was no other for me, nor ever will be. You do believe that, don't you?"

Laughing, she clasped him round the neck, lifting herself to kiss him lightly on the mouth. "I do now."

She remembered his expression when first she'd seen him gazing toward Camelot, and now, at last, she understood his sorrow. "Lancelot, why do you not send a message to the king and tell him where you are?"

He shook his head, his eyes darkening with pain. "The king sent me from his side, Elaine. If he wants me, he will find me."

• • •

AT the end of the second year, Elaine announced that she was to hold a tournament at Joyous Gard and expected Lancelot to compete. This resulted in their first quarrel, which ended with Lancelot saying, "Very well, but I'll not fight under my own name. You can call me—" He stood a moment, shoulders stiff, then said, "Call me the Chevalier Mal Fet."

She had hoped that his success would cheer him, for he defeated every challenger. But when the time came for the feast, he was nowhere to be found, leaving Elaine alone to greet their guests. That had been the cause of their second quarrel, and they had not spoken for two days.

Now another year had passed, and they had both become accustomed to the knights who appeared from time to time to challenge the mysterious Chevalier Mal Fet. For all his grumbling, Elaine suspected Lancelot secretly enjoyed the chance to test his skill.

One day, she thought, rising and calling for her maid, *he will cast off his helm and invite one of his visitors to stay.* Much as she longed for that day, she dreaded it as well, for this time apart had held its own enchantment.

Once dressed, she went to watch the competition, stopping at Galahad's chamber to ask if he would join her. He begged to be excused, pleading a lesson not yet finished. Elaine left him with a kiss, sighing a little as she went down the winding stairway. Galahad resembled Lancelot even less as he grew older, both in looks and nature. Indeed, he was the image of his grandsire, Pelleas. And though he was always perfectly polite to his father, Galahad had little interest in arms and none at all in watching Lancelot win yet another joust. She hoped Lancelot would not be too hurt, yet she lacked the heart to force the child.

Still pondering the mysteries of sons and fathers, Elaine went through the hall and toward the corridor leading to the tourney field. When she reached the end, she looked into the small chamber where Lancelot's armor hung.

She stood, one hand braced against the doorway, as the breath left her body in a rush. Lancelot knelt before the bench, his dark head bent. Before him sat the king. Arthur looked up and smiled.

"Lady Elaine."

"Sire. Welcome to Joyous Gard."

"Thank you."

Lancelot had not lifted his head. Elaine smiled tremulously at Arthur. "I will leave you now."

"Until later, lady," he said, and through her tears she saw both understanding and pity in his eyes.

• • •

WHEN they were alone, Arthur said, "Sit beside me, Lance."

Lancelot obeyed, feeling as awkward as the boy who had once been scolded by his king for fighting. Arthur seemed in no better case. Twice he began to speak, only to check himself, then stare down at his hands.

"You are well, sire?" Lancelot ventured.

"Yes. Or, rather—" Arthur looked up suddenly. "I should have come sooner. I wanted to, but . . . well, the truth is I knew not how to face you."

"How to . . . ?" Lancelot repeated blankly.

"After you left us, I went to Cameliard. Leodegrance and I had quite a talk. Not a pleasant one, but . . . illuminating."

"Guinevere is still queen," Lancelot said, the words not quite a question.

"And always will be." He laid his hand on Lancelot's shoulder. "I should never have doubted you, Lance. Can you forgive me?"

Lancelot grasped his hand. "Need you even ask?"

"Yes. I must. When I remember the things I said to you that day—and to Guinevere—" He looked away. "I wronged you both most grievously."

"Sire, you take too much upon yourself. You had good cause to suspect we were not honest with you."

"That was Guinevere's doing, and I understand her reasons now." Arthur shook his head and sighed. "The fault was mine. She was so young, so beautiful, and I . . . well, I'm afraid I was all too ready to believe she would look elsewhere. I know very little about women—" He laughed softly. "But I am learning."

"I am happy for you both."

Arthur's smile vanished. "Yet that is no excuse for my behavior toward you. You were blameless."

Lancelot shook his head. "No, sire. Not blameless. I kept my own secrets."

"Will you not call me Arthur? You always did before."

"But that was when . . ." Lancelot made a helpless gesture. "Everything was different. *I* was different."

"In what way? Come, Lance, there was a time we could say anything to one another. I wish you'd trust me as you used to."

Arthur spoke so sadly that at last Lancelot was able to tell him everything, beginning with his first memories of

Avalon. He recounted his joust with Gawain and what he had learned then, and how he dared not confess that Britain's First Knight was no hero, but something more than human and so much less than the man Arthur believed him.

He told Arthur all he could remember of his madness, described his last adventure in Avalon and how he had parted from the Lady of the Lake. When at last he finished, Arthur was silent for a time.

"Yes, you are different," he said at last. "You have grown up." He slumped in his seat and smiled. "Oh, Lance, do you think you're the only boy who rode invincible into the world? We all dreamed that dream, even if we did not all have your reasons to believe it. But soon or late, every one of us must face the knowledge that we are not perfect, but only human, and that we may not achieve the glorious destiny we believed our right."

"If it were only that," Lancelot said, "I would not mind. It is not the glory I miss—I've never been so happy as these past few years. It is you I mind for, Arthur."

"Don't. Do you think I want some mindless knight with no choice but to serve me? I would rather have you as you are and a service freely offered. I do not ask for perfection."

He shook his head, a smile quirking his lips. "You and Gawain! Where the two of you got such a notion is beyond me, but I assure you it is false. We are all flawed, Lance, every one of us, all capable of cowardice and pride and pettiness and spite, all doomed to fail—not once, but many times—and to fall short of our ideals. That is what it means to be a man. And the true measure of a man lies in what he learns from his mistakes."

"But you are not like that," Lancelot protested. "You have never failed."

"I have failed many times, in many ways. Some small,

some great, and one . . ." He broke off and looked away.
"Oh, I have sinned, Lance. Never stood a man more in
need of God's mercy than your king."

"Then I will pray God grants it to you, Arthur."

"Now I *know* that you have changed! Lancelot du Lac at
prayer?"

Lancelot smiled. "As you say, I have grown up."

Silence fell between them, so comfortable and familiar
that it seemed no time had passed since they'd last met.
Arthur broke it with a sigh.

"I fear 'tis more than friendship that brings me here today. I have need of you, Lance."

"What's ado?"

"Trouble with the Saxons. What else? They've seized
Dumbarton." He pulled a map from his belt and unfolded
it. "I had thought to engage them here," he said, pointing.

"Why not here?" Lancelot asked, marking a spot a bit to
the north of the king's. He knelt on the floor and sketched
in the sand. "There is a rise—do you remember it—just beyond the Celidon Wood. If you gather your knights there
and come down upon them—"

Arthur nodded, frowning. "Yes, you may be right."

"We must use the horsemen to our best advantage. How
many can we count upon?"

Arthur looked at him, brows raised. "We?"

"Of course. I had a thought the other day about a new
formation—what? Why are you laughing?"

"Here I came, prepared with a dozen arguments to per-
suade you, but Guinevere said all along you were only
waiting to be asked. The troops are already mustering at
Camelot, and I need you to take charge of the horsemen.
Can you come with me tomorrow? You can tell me all your
thoughts upon the way. And your lady, too, of course.
Guinevere asked me particularly to beg Lady Elaine to

come to court with you while we make ready, and Galahad, if you will bring him."

"I will come." Lancelot drew his hand across the sand, blotting out his map. "As for Elaine . . . that will be for her to say."

• • •

HE found Elaine on the battlements in the place he'd made his own, gazing out toward Camelot. She did not turn at his approach.

"When do you leave?"

"Tomorrow. First for Camelot to prepare for battle and then the king rides north."

She nodded. "I see."

Of course she did. Elaine had always known him better than he knew himself. And he knew her, enough to be certain she would not wish to leave her home and friends and family to go to Camelot. How many times had she sworn never to set foot in the wretched place again?

Looking at her now, silhouetted against the setting sun, he realized this was only the first of many partings. No longer could he stay buried in the country while Arthur's great work went on without him; the time had come to take up his oath and serve his king again. Elaine would want nothing to do with that part of his life, nor could he blame her; he knew too well how unhappy she had been at court.

'Twas a common enough arrangement, he told himself. Knights often went months—sometimes years—without so much as a glimpse of their ladies. Most laughed about it, saying it kept their marriages from growing stale.

But none of them were married to Elaine.

Lancelot could never grow weary of her company, no more than he could grow weary of the air he breathed. Upon hearing any news—whether it concerned alliances in

distant kingdoms or a bit of village gossip—his first
thought was invariably, "I must tell Elaine of this." He often amused himself during his solitary rides in wondering
what she might make of this tale or that. That she would
have something interesting to say he did not doubt, and
even if he did not agree with every one of her opinions, he
never tired of hearing them.

Nor did he ever tire of the times they spent together in
the great bed. Their lovemaking had changed over the
years, grown less fevered but far sweeter. For all they had
learned of pleasuring one another, there were many mysteries yet to be explored. No man had ever been so blessed.
Even when they quarreled, Lancelot never ceased to give
God thanks for Elaine's presence in his life.

Yet tomorrow he would leave her. He must. Oh, he
would return as often as possible, but it would not be the
same. She would not be interested in the tales he had to
tell, for they would be concerned with Camelot and its inhabitants. Their love would not die—that, he knew to be
impossible—but something precious would have been lost.
And still he must go. It was a pain such as he had never
known, as though his very heart were being torn in two.

Elaine turned, the wind catching at the edges of her
hair, her expression unreadable against the sunset. "I suppose there will be a feast before you all ride north. Shall I
bring my blue gown or the silver?"

He stared at her in silence, hardly daring to believe he'd
heard aright. When he did believe, he could only shake his
head in wonder. How did she do it? Every time he thought
he understood her, she found some new way to take his
breath away.

Which was precisely how she had planned it. Now he
could make out the grin tugging at the corners of her

mouth; she was enjoying this, the minx, just as she always enjoyed surprising him.

A slow smile spread across his face. "The silver."

"Do you think so?" she asked doubtfully. "True, the cloth is lovely, but I am always afraid I will . . . well, tumble out. I cannot imagine what that seamstress was thinking to cut it so low."

Lancelot's hands fastened on her girdle, and he drew her forward. "I bribed her."

The faint, sweet sound of laughter reached Arthur in the gardens. He glanced up to see two figures on the battlements, silhouetted against the sunset blazing over Joyous Gard. As he stood, a smile touching his lips, they moved and merged until the space between them disappeared, and they were one.

Gwen Rowley's

Knights of the Round Table

series continues with...

Geraint
Coming in March 2007

~and~

Gawain
Coming in September 2007

King Arthur's knights were strong and powerful warriors of nobility
and honor. Brothers in arms, they were touched by magic.
But for these knights supreme, true love may be
the most perilous quest of all.

These are their stories—and those of the women they loved.

THE LEGENDS THAT WILL NEVER DIE.

penguin.com

FROM USA TODAY *BESTSELLING AUTHORS*

Lynn Kurland, Patricia Potter, Deborah Simmons, and Glynnis Campbell

A KNIGHT'S VOW

0-515-13151-2

Fantasies are made of knights in shining armor—and now they can be found in four breathtaking medieval tales by today's most acclaimed writers of historical romances...

Featuring:
"The Traveller"
Lynn Kurland

"The Minstrel"
Patricia Potter

"The Bachelor Knight"
Deborah Simmons

"The Siege"
Glynnis Campbell

Available wherever books are sold or at penguin.com

B094

NOW IN PAPERBACK

Dreams of Stardust

by
Lynn Kurland

From *USA Today* bestselling author
Lynn Kurland—"one of romance's finest writers"*—
comes a magical love story about a modern man who's
swept back into medieval England and the beautiful
woman he yearns to possess.

"[Kurland] consistently delivers the kind
of stories readers dream about."
—*Oakland Press*

"A vivid writer…She crafts an engrossing story."
—*All About Romance*

0-515-13948-3

Available wherever books are sold or at
penguin.com

b922

DISCOVER ROMANCE

berkleyjoveauthors.com

See what's coming up next from your favorite authors and explore all the latest fabulous Berkley and Jove selections.

berkleyjoveauthors.com

- See what's new
- Find author appearances
- Win fantastic prizes
- Get reading recommendations
- Chat with authors and other fans
- Read interviews with authors you love

Fall in love.

berkleyjoveauthors.com

Penguin Group (USA) Online

What will you be reading tomorrow?

Tom Clancy, Patricia Cornwell, W.E.B. Griffin,
Nora Roberts, William Gibson, Robin Cook,
Brian Jacques, Catherine Coulter, Stephen King,
Dean Koontz, Ken Follett, Clive Cussler,
Eric Jerome Dickey, John Sandford,
Terry McMillan, Sue Monk Kidd, Amy Tan,
John Berendt...

You'll find them all at
penguin.com

*Read excerpts and newsletters,
find tour schedules and reading group guides,
and enter contests.*

Subscribe to Penguin Group (USA) newsletters
and get an exclusive inside look
at exciting new titles and the authors you love
long before everyone else does.

PENGUIN GROUP (USA)
us.penguingroup.com